THE LAND ACROSS

BY GENE WOLFE
FROM TOM DOHERTY ASSOCIATES

THE WIZARD KNIGHT
The Knight
The Wizard

THE BOOK OF THE SHORT SUN
On Blue's Waters
In Green's Jungles
Return to the Whorl

THE BOOK OF THE NEW SUN
Shadow & Claw
  (comprising *The Shadow of the
  Torturer* and *The Claw of the
  Conciliator*)
Sword & Citadel
  (comprising *The Sword of the
  Lictor* and *The Citadel of the
  Autarch*)

THE BOOK OF THE LONG SUN
Litany of the Long Sun
  (comprising *Nightside of the Long
  Sun* and *Lake of the Long Sun*)
Epiphany of the Long Sun
  (comprising *Caldé of the Long Sun*
  and *Exodus from the Long Sun*)

NOVELS
The Fifth Head of Cerberus
The Devil in a Forest
Peace
Free Live Free

The Urth of the New Sun
Latro in the Mist
  (comprising *Soldier of the Mist*
  and *Soldier of Arete*)
Soldier of Sidon
There Are Doors
Castleview
Pandora by Holly Hollander
Pirate Freedom
An Evil Guest
The Sorcerer's House
Home Fires

NOVELLAS
The Death of Doctor Island
Seven American Nights

COLLECTIONS
Endangered Species
Storeys from the Old Hotel
Castle of Days
*The Island of Doctor Death and
  Other Stories and Other Stories*
Strange Travelers
Innocents Aboard
Starwater Strains

THE LAND ACROSS

GENE WOLFE

TOR®

A TOM DOHERTY ASSOCIATES BOOK

NEW YORK

This is a work of fiction. All of the characters, organizations, and events portrayed in this novel are either products of the author's imagination or are used fictitiously.

THE LAND ACROSS

A Tor Book
Published by Tom Doherty Associates, LLC
175 Fifth Avenue
New York, NY 10010

www.tor-forge.com

Tor® is a registered trademark of Tom Doherty Associates, LLC.

Library of Congress Cataloging-in-Publication Data

Wolfe, Gene.
     The land across / Gene Wolfe.—First Edition.
         p. cm.
     "A Tom Doherty Associates Book."
     ISBN 978-0-7653-3595-1 (hardcover)
     ISBN 978-1-4668-2635-9 (e-book)
     1. Travel writers—Fiction.   2. Corruption—Fiction.   3. Fantasy fiction.
     I. Title.
     PS3573.O52L36 2013
     813'.54—dc23

                                                        2013022126

Tor books may be purchased for educational, business, or promotional use. For information on bulk purchases, please contact Macmillan Corporate and Premium Sales Department at 1-800-221-7945, extension 5442, or write specialmarkets@macmillan.com.

First Edition: November 2013

Printed in the United States of America

0 9 8 7 6 5 4 3 2 1

This book is respectfully dedicated to
Michael Andre-Driussi by its grateful author.

THE LAND ACROSS

1

THE LAND ACROSS

Like most countries it is accessible by road or railroad, air or sea. Even though all those are possible, they are all tough. Visitors who try to drive get into a tangle of unmarked mountain roads, roads with zits and potholes and lots of landslides. Most drivers who make it through (I talked about it with two of them in New York and another one in London) get turned back at the border. There is something wrong with their passports, or their cars, or their luggage. They have not got visas, which everybody told them they would not need. Some are arrested and their cars impounded. A few of the ones who are arrested never get out. Or anyhow, that is how it seems.

It just made me more determined than ever. There are no travel books about the land across the mountains. NONE! Not in any language I could find. I was going to be the first, and maybe I still will be. Only this book you are holding comes before my travel book. You would not believe how long I have been writing and rewriting this one in my head, especially when I was a prisoner of the Legion of the Light and when I was in prison, sitting around in a cell with Russ Rathaus. I was lucky, I cannot even tell you how lucky, that I was never taken prisoner by the Unholy Way. Thank God for that!

At first I tried to get in by air. Lufthansa has service, but there are only two flights a week. I booked twice and had both canceled. The third did not land at the capital, saying bad weather. It went straight on to Ankara.

I decided to go by train and flew to Vienna, a real knockout city where there are lots of first-rate clubs. (See my first book, *Dreaming on the Danube*.) After some swell evenings dancing in the clubs and okay nights at the good old Hotel Sacher, I caught the Orient Express headed for Slovakia. For the rest of the day our train wound its way through hills and woods.

A lot of Americans think all of Europe is like Rouen or Cologne, crawling with people. It is not really like that. There is a whole lot more wilderness in Europe than foreigners like us imagine, and there is more and more as you go east. I hardly ever saw a house among the hills I saw from the Orient Express. Where there were a few, they were half-timbered and had those high sharp roofs you get where there is lots of snow.

A porter who would not talk to me made the bed in my compartment. When he had gone, I stripped and washed the way I generally do on trains, with a washcloth I dunked in a hand basin of water. Now it seems to me that I must have been asleep a long time before I got into bed.

I woke up during the night, and I will never forget it. We had stopped where they had fields of some kind of grain that grew a lot taller than a man. Silent men walked up and down the train, men I could just barely make out by starlight. They looked small, but I think they were really big men. They carried what I figured were dark lanterns, boxy black gadgets that shed floods of light you did not expect when they were opened. I had read about those but I had never seen any before. The train jolted and jolted again. I think it was probably the first of those jolts that woke me up.

One of the men stopped at my window to look up at me. I stared out at him through the dirty glass. He held up his lantern, which scared hell out of me. I do not know why. Anyway, I ducked down and backed away as far as I could without leaving my little compartment.

I was naked, and I decided right then that when I got back home I was going to buy pajamas as soon as I could. If I only had pajamas or a robe, both would have been better; I could have gone into the corridor outside where I might have found the porter and gotten him to talk to me. Traveling the way he did from Calais to Cairo and from Cairo back to Calais, he would have a lot of interesting stuff to tell if I could get him to tell it.

As it was, I stayed flat against the steel door of my compartment until the train got moving again, rattling and swaying along tracks that went up and down while they were turning left and right.

Everybody interested enough to read this book knows about the High Tatras and the Transylvanian Alps. Let me just say that the mountains I saw next morning were not particularly high, but rugged and dotted here and there with fir trees the wind had tortured. It was early spring, and the water spilling down their cliffs made me think of a certain type of girl, the tall cold blondes that knock your eyes out. Later I met Rosalee Rathaus, and she was a blond knockout even if she hardly came up to my chin in heels. I bet she would not weigh eighty pounds soaking wet. She was a good dancer, too. She promised me but I never collected. We will get into that in one of the later chapters.

After breakfast in the dining car, I went back to my compartment. I read until I got bored, then I had a look at the observation car. It was the double-decked kind, which I have always liked. I climbed the little stair to the upper deck and sat in one of the very cool swiveling red-leather seats there and watched the scenery whiz past until I fell asleep.

When I woke up, the train was going faster than ever, rattling and swaying as it crossed a big wasteland scarred with gullies.

Three border guards in uniforms were standing around me, and the biggest of the three was shaking my shoulder. Then the boss border guard, a skinny guy a lot shorter than me, started yelling questions in a language I did not know. The car was empty except for the four of us.

I got my passport out of my jacket and showed it to him. He passed it to the third border guard without looking at it. After that, they made me stand up, patted me down, took my iPhone, and tied my hands behind me. I guess I was scared, but mostly I was stunned.

The boss border guard marched along the upper deck of the observation car, motioning for me to follow. I did, noticing that the railing (which I knew darn well had been there when I had climbed to the upper deck) had been taken down. Steep little steps led from the upper deck to the main floor. The boss border guard trotted down them and I did my best to follow him. I was about halfway down when somebody pushed me. I fell, bumping into the boss border guard. I believe he must have landed on the lower steps. I rolled over him all the way to the bottom. He got up cursing and kicking. I could not understand his curses, but I knew what they were all right. I had never been kicked before and had not really known how bad it is. I think I must have blacked out.

The next thing I remember is being taken off the train, trying to walk and stumbling a lot while someone with strong hands held my arm.

The train had not slowed down but was roaring along beside a narrow black conveyer belt that was going even faster than it was, so that the shiny steel bands the sections were joined with looked like they were crawling slowly past us. We were waiting for the other two, or that was what it seemed like. When they joined us, the big guy who held me stepped from the train onto the belt, dragging me with him. Like I said, the belt went faster than the train had. It ran smoother, too. Beside it grass, brush, and dust pointed the way, blown by a howling wind. For us on the belt, it seemed like there was no wind at all. I noticed then that the train's diesel engine was gone, and there was a big steam engine up front. It was twice as big but looked old. It seemed to be trying to outrun its own smoke, but it could not do it.

If I had thought at all, I would have thought that we would be thrown off the end of the belt and die. It was not like that. Another, wider belt appeared to our right. This new belt was white, and moving slower than the black one. I fell when I tried to step onto it.

The boss border guard helped me up. His dark gray uniform cap had been mashed, and his scarlet-trimmed tunic was more than half-unbuttoned. (I think it was because three or four of the buttons had torn off.) Still he murmured, *"Auanactain! Profasis!"* like he was sorry I had been hurt. A minute later he helped me onto a red belt. I never did figure him out, only back then I thought maybe I could. My dad used to say foreigners' values were not the same as ours. Then he would dope them out anyway.

The red belt slowed down, I could feel the wind, and the biggest of the three helped me get off, lifting me like he would have picked up a little kid.

There was a car and a driver waiting for us. The biggest border guard, the boss, and I got into the backseat, with me pinned between them.

The third border guard took the front seat beside the driver. This third border guard was older than the other two. He had a black mustache, and in a lot of ways he looked like my father. Sometimes it seemed to me that the other two did not know he was there the same way I did. He never did talk, and nobody ever talked to him, except me. I did one time.

I asked whether we were going to the capital, at first in English, and then (when I was pretty sure neither of them understood it) in German. "No," the boss border guard told me in German. "We go to Puraustays."

I tried to remember a map I had seen. "Puraustays is a long way from the capital."

"No. It is near."

"Two hundred kilometers?"

The boss border guard just shrugged, reached into the pocket sewn onto the back of the seat in front of him, and took out a map. He opened it for me.

It was small and looked like it had been drawn for kids, with little pictures scattered here and there. I remember a miner and a wild ox. Looking up from it, I said, "This says three hundred and twenty kilometers."

The boss border guard chuckled. "All maps are wrong. If the Turks come, they will be lost."

We crossed a river that may have been the same river my train had roared across the day before. The little map called it the Taxus. Factories lined its bank, ugly gray buildings with tall chimneys of yellow brick. I asked what they made in there. The boss border guard shrugged, but the biggest of the three told me, "Fertilizer."

The city on the other side of the river was laid out in a way I have never seen anywhere else and had not known they used anywhere. Whether it was a big one or a little one, every building stood on its own block, with narrow streets on all four sides. A lot of these narrow, crooked streets could be called alleys. Some were not even paved. I am going to call them all streets because they use the same word for all of them. The size of the blocks varied depending on the size of the buildings. Large or small, they were mostly square or rectangular. There was always a strip of grass, trees, and shrubs around each building. That seemed to be the law, and it must have been the law there for a long time.

The variations in size meant that our car (and the wagons and so forth) could not go fast, turning left or right almost at the end of each block. Left turns were followed by rights, and the other way. When we had made half a dozen turns or so, it hit me that all the turns must make it hard to follow a particular street. After that, I watched for street signs, but there were not any. Pretty soon I asked the big man the name of the street we were on. He just shrugged and the boss border guard told me, "Our streets do not have names."

Then I stuck my neck out, saying that no street names must make it hard to find somebody's house. The boss border guard asked me, "Why do you want to find somebody's house in Puraustays?"

For a while we threaded our way among old buildings of three, four, or five stories, all of some dark stone. They said the biggest one, with gargoyles and lots of balconies, was the seat of the city's government. The trees around it were so tall I could not see a thing below a story that could have been the fourth or the third. This story, like the ones above it, was impressive and pretty interesting. I remember plants that looked an awful lot like jellyfish, and people who looked a lot like flowers.

Beyond that was a long yellow brick building with three stories. It was the first building I had seen that looked busy, and it seemed a whole lot busier than just about any building in America, with people hurrying in and out all the time. I asked what it was, and the big guy who had lifted me said, "The Mounted Guard."

I know I must have looked dumb. There were a lot of big doors, but I had seen no horses and no soldiers. The boss border guard told me, "They are on duty in the East."

After a while we got into a suburb or something like that. The streets there were more like those in American towns. The houses were all pretty much the same size, and that meant the blocks were pretty much the same size, too. So the streets were nearly straight except when they bent around.

Finally we stopped in front of a house that was not quite as big as the others, a little square house of dirty white concrete blocks. Our driver got out and trotted around to open the door for the third border guard. The sky was overcast, there was not a lot of time, and I could not be sure. But it seemed to me that the driver looked like the porter who had made my bed on the train. They could not have been the same guy. Still, they looked a lot alike.

There was no walk to the front door, only a little path among trees. Except for the driver, we trooped along it, the boss border guard, then the biggest and the third border guard. I limped along behind them, thinking I ought to run away but knowing I would be a darned fool to get separated from my passport. The boss border guard knocked with the barrel of his pistol.

A short, stocky man maybe thirty or so answered it, opening the door a crack then closing it again to unfasten a security chain before opening it wide. He had on a clean gray undershirt and gray wool pants that looked too big.

We crowded in and he talked. I think he was trying to get the boss border guard to sit down in the biggest chair. The boss border guard would not do it and lectured him. After a lot of that, the boss border guard asked me, "In Amerika, you build prisons for your prisoners, yes?" His German was not even as good as mine, but I understood him and nodded.

"Here we save." The boss border guard chuckled. "You are this man's prisoner."

I said I had not done anything.

"You come without visa, with no passport. These things are sufficient."

"You took my passport," I reminded him. "Give it back, please."

"It has been sent to the capital. I cannot give back. Until it is sent back, you have none. You must stay here. You see this man?" The boss border guard indicated the short man in the undershirt. "Do you like him?"

"I don't know him."

"So you like him. When you know him better, you do not like him so much, I think." The boss border guard shut one eye and pointed his pistol at the short man's head. "When you escape, him we shoot."

The short man gave me a sad glance.

"You see how nice to you we are. You do not like the food, you say it is rotten, you will go. He give better so you stay. Other things, too."

I said nothing. I was watching a girl who had peeked around the corner.

"You are to sleep here." Holstering his pistol, the boss border guard took a folded paper and a pen from a pocket of his uniform jacket and shoved them into the short man's hand. *"Grafote!"*

The short man signed, and the border guards trooped out.

I apologized to the short man in English, and then in German. He could not understand that either.

The girl who had peeped in before smiled. She was a cute girl, with lots of curves and bouncy amber curls. "I must help." She talked to the short man. It seemed to me she was translating what I said, so I thanked her.

"It is nothing. I am most happy to be of use. I am Martya. My husband is Kleon. They do not like us."

Her husband spoke.

"He too says they do not like us. They will kill him if you escape. He says we could tie you up and keep you a prisoner in that way, which many would do. He says please do you not escape, or take us with you if you do."

I told her I would not escape.

"Kleon does not understand, but learns from our faces. Has mine told you what I think?"

I said it had not.

"See that you do as I."

I nodded.

"What you just did he understands. For us it might be most fortunate if you were to remember this. Try also to make long answers to my short questions, long, long answers to my long questions. In this way he will know only what I tell him. It is good for you and me, I think."

"I have a great many questions to ask you," I said, "questions about your country, this city, this house, your husband, and yourself, lovely lady. Where can I telephone the American embassy and a bunch of other stuff. What I'm trying to tell you is that I'll have long questions as well as long answers."

"Here no one has the telephones you seek. In the capital, perhaps." She talked to her husband for two or three minutes. He shook his head, said a few words, and spat into the fireplace.

"He will answer none of your questions." She smiled. "He thinks you are a JAKA spy. He did not say this, but he thinks it."

I said he was wrong, and explained that I had come to collect material for a book.

"I believe you because I see your clothing. It is foreign and most well, lamb's wool and fine cottons. The silk shirt also. The shoes. You are fortunate the border guards did not take them."

"They would not rob a spy, would they?"

"They rob everyone. Who will arrest them? No, you are foreign, from a weak nation far away."

I told her she was right.

"If you escape you will return there. Could you bring with you another, perhaps?"

"Yes," I said. "That's never easy but it might be possible." It seemed to me it was the smart thing to say.

She smiled. "This is too short an answer, you see? You must answer me much more long, and who does not know *ja*? Now for you a new question.

These kind border guards who did not take your clothing, did they not take also your money, and did you before they came change some into our money? Is there other wealth of you that might be drawn upon, and do you still have it? Do not look at this money, this wealth you have, before you make the answer."

"I won't," I promised. "As to the currencies about which you asked me, I have dollars from my own country and euros. What I mean by this is that I have some of each. Don't you use euros—"

Somebody pounded on the door. Kleon looked frightened and the girl spat like a cat. "It is Aldos, the swine-dog. You must answer our door. It will confuse him."

The big man who had pounded it looked confused for less than a second. After that he shouted in my face, but I could see fear in his eyes. I talked to him in German, saying I could not understand him, but that I would try if only he would talk slower and keep his voice down.

He did not. When I backed away, he came at me. When I came at him, he backed away.

The short man, Kleon, came to stand beside me. From his tone, I believe he must have cursed the big man. His voice was low and bitter.

At last the big man stammered and stopped, jamming his clenched fists into the pockets of what looked like a pair of old golf pants. He was wearing an undershirt too, but his was dirty. Part of it was covered by an old wool vest.

Behind me the girl said, "He says our chickens get into his garden. We do not have chickens."

Her husband nodded almost imperceptibly to that. He spoke in his cursing tone to the big man, advancing toward him, making wild gestures that almost brushed the big man's nose. I advanced, too.

For a minute the big man rallied, shouting louder than ever. Then he turned and stamped away.

"I suppose somebody's chickens must get into his garden," I said to the girl.

"Ours did once or twice," she acknowledged. "Kleon had chickens before we were married."

Kleon spoke bitterly before retreating into his house and slamming the door behind him.

"He says he was rich once, that one may be rich or wed but not both."

I said, "I'm sure that isn't true."

"For him, yes." The girl smiled, making me feel like I was a lot younger than she was. (Really it was only two or three years.) "He has locked us out."

I stared.

"You do not believe? Try the door."

I did. It would not open.

"You see? I have hear the bar drop into place. We are cast out!" She grinned at me. "Are you afraid?" She had a great grin.

"A little bit," I admitted. "Is there an American Consulate? If there is one, I'd like to go there."

"Soon he thinks better." It was like she had not heard me. "Martya is with him, he will think. She will tell him he need only go to the police. He will say 'I am his prisoner! He lock me out!' Then the police will come and shoot him. He is right about this, but we will not go to them right away. Do you like these trees? The bushes?"

"They're really nice," I said.

"This bush here . . ." She caressed it. "It will bloom for us before the moon is old. For a week it is the most pretty one in Puraustays. Our trees give nuts. I do not know the German name, but the wood burns well. A hot fire and slow. A little stick burns for a long, long time."

"I see."

"Some have fruit trees. This is nice because of the fruit. Apples, pears, cherries are all good. These burn well, too. I think you have these in your land."

I said we did.

"But you, yourself? You have such trees?"

I tried to explain that I did not have a house, I lived in an apartment because I was on the road so much.

"If you had a house, you would have fruit trees. You are a fruit tree man. This I see." She had begun to walk, and I followed her. "My father had fruit trees but he is dead."

"My father is dead, too," I said. "He was with the State Department, so I grew up all over the world."

"Here?"

"No, not here. Mostly Germany, France, and Japan."

"Here there are three kinds of men. A fruit tree man like you, he is strong." She held up her clenched fist. "Strong, or perhaps he has the good friends." She drew an imaginary pistol. "You are such a one, I think."

I said I had a lot of friends in America.

"If a man who is not strong plants fruit trees, his neighbors take the fruit." She raised her chin, a proud daughter. "No one took my father's fruit!"

"That must have been nice."

"Yes, yes! Once Kleon had fruit trees. They took his fruit and he could not stop them. Now we have nut trees, so we eat the nuts." She pointed. "Do you see those?"

We had reached the edge of her husband's block, and she was pointing at the next one. The trees there were oaks. I said they looked fine.

"No, no! He is weak. No one takes acorns."

"I see."

"When a man dies his neighbors cut his trees to burn. My father is dead half a year before anyone is so brave." The girl sighed. "I take you now to a man who has fruit trees. If there is for you a consul, he will know."

2

THE STORY

They were cherry trees mostly, Martya said. Whatever they were, they were beautiful, tall trees in wedding gowns. The smell made me think about God and heaven, and the bees that swarmed over them about hell because I got stung twice before we got to the door. "Volitain will put wet tobacco on those," she told me. "It will take your pain."

He was pale and starvation thin, with straight black hair, as courtly and polite as Kleon had been abrupt and hostile. "Enter!" He bowed from the hips. "Enter and welcome! Any friend of dear little Martya's, a brother is to me." The look that passed between them told me Martya had tried to make him.

"He is bee-bitten." Her tone was flat, and her face held no expression. "Put tobacco on them."

"I see . . ." Volitain stalked over to a table in his parlor, which looked as big as Kleon's entire house. In the table drawer he found a magnifying glass.

"That will not help!"

Volitain bent over the sting on my cheek. "Sit here, please. Now incline the head, eh? I must have light from the window."

I did what he said.

"The sting is here. It must be drawn. The hand we see next, eh?" He moved my hand to bring it nearer the light. "Here, also. Wait a moment. Drink good wine."

He left us, slipping into some interior room through a door that was not quite open.

I asked, "Does he always do that? Not open the door?"

"He has no wife. The room where he go will be soiled, I think. He does not wish you to see it."

"Or you," I said.

Martya shrugged. "There is wine here. He desires us to drink. A woman brews tea, a man has wine." She went to a sideboard. "Is Tokay, I think. We drink it much here. You will drink?"

I nodded and she poured. It was pungent and a little too sweet.

Volitain returned with tweezers and iodine. "The bee that stings, dies," he murmured. "One would suppose that evolutionary processes would soon end such deaths. Is the hive stronger without him?"

I said, "Ouch!"

"First the face, because it must pain most. The hand next, where the pain is not so much."

I managed to keep quiet.

"You are hungry? I have little cakes. Martya?"

I looked at my watch. It was one p.m.

Martya said, "I will make for us the sandwiches if you allow it."

"There is little," Volitain said. "We go to a café." He had finished with the iodine and was taping on moist tobacco.

Martya looked at me, shrugging. "Volitain has much money, but he does not spend. Never for me, this money. Never for you, also, I think. You will pay?"

"Sure," I said. "I'll be glad to."

Volitain shook his head. "You will not. You must not listen to our sour chit. I say the café and I pay."

Martya giggled at that. She had drained her glass, so I thought it had probably been the wine.

"Now we will go out," Volitain was saying. "The bees sting you if you think of them, so not. Think of pleasant things alone and you shall be safe."

It sounded silly but I tried it, thinking what kind of food a café here might have. Sandwiches, sure. Soups and salads . . . I tried to concentrate on those, but I could not keep my eyes off Martya's hips. They were to die for, and she was leading the way.

"You see?" Volitain said. "You were not stung. Of what do you think?"

"Strabo's commentary on the Euxine," I told him. One of my professors used to talk about it.

"Ah! It is interesting, no doubt. I must read it."

"I'm a lot more interested in finding out why Martya's pestering you with me."

"She does not tell?"

I shook my head. There were no sidewalks, so we had to walk in the street. A man on a bicycle zoomed past us, staring at Volitain and pedaling faster and faster. "He's scared of you," I told him.

"He hates me." Volitain sighed. "Hating me, he supposes I hate him. Supposing I hate him, he expects some hurt. Expecting hurt, he fears me. His fear make him hate me all the more. Is that not a sad circle?"

I said yes.

"As you say, but I am not in it. God may make him a king or give him a knife. All is one to me."

I was watching for the long building I had seen when I first got to the city, the yellow brick building where the Mounted Guards stabled their horses in peacetime, but I did not see it. Here the streets were wider, and a lot of the buildings had shops on the ground floor.

We went into one of the biggest, following a path of well-worn cobbles and passing shoppers who carried their new stuff in string bags. Inside was a big atrium roofed with colored glass. There were balconies up the sides, and they were lined with shops like the floor we were on.

"The cafés here are." Volitain indicated the level where we stood. "Those who eat in them grow fat, then the steps are not convenient."

"Also," Martya added, "they are drunk and fall down them."

"We have logic in my country, you see. The most valuable things are sold highest, so we say their prices are high. Suppose a robber comes. He must descend many steps while those he robbed shout that he be stopped."

"And throw chamber pots." Martya was scanning the cafés. "You will pay, Grafton, so you are to choose."

I was tired of walking, so I said, "The closest." Do not come to this country unless you are ready to walk one hell of a lot. If you bring your bike, you will have to double-lock it every time you park it. You had better be ready to fight for it, too.

"This one is not good," Volitain told me. "Too many come, and we have things to speak of. That one over there. You will like it."

"It is a place for feeling," Martya said as we trudged across the atrium. "Most quick I feel Volitain's hand on my leg, and he my scissors."

I could not follow what Volitain said to the hostess, but his gestures made it clear that he wanted the booth in the corner. After a little argument he got it. The high backs of the seats in all the booths went up until they just about touched the ceiling, and our booth had a green cloth curtain to close the end that was open to the table area.

Martya translated the menu and we ordered. "Is there an American Consulate here?" I asked Volitain. "Martya said you would know."

Volitain shook his head. "I do know, and there is none. In other cities, perhaps, but not in this Puraustays of ours. There is the Amerikan ambassador at the capital. It may be there is a consulate also. That I do not know."

"She also told me you were well connected and you'd help me."

"I am not." Seeing Volitain smile was like watching a skull grin. "Even so, I help you—if I can. You have the troubles with our secret police, the JAKA?"

"With your border patrol. How did you know?"

"You are foreign. Many foreigners are arrested. Also dear little Martya brought you to me. Those are enough."

"What can you do?"

A glance passed between Martya and Volitain, and he said, "Not so much, it may be. First I must know your trouble. Tell me."

I told him all about my arrest, pretty much like I have told you here.

"You have done nothing." Volitain sighed and leaned back.

"Damn straight! So why was I arrested?"

"They needed someone. That is all." His voice had sunk to a sleepy whisper. "They must show their superiors they are active, alert. Arrest someone. They wish also to punish dear little Martya's husband. Arrest someone. You sleep in a place no one watches."

I nodded.

"So you are chosen. They can say whatever they wish."

"They took my passport."

"Of a surety. They always do."

The waiter arrived with our food. When he had gone and Volitain had drawn the curtain, I said, "How can I get my passport back? Would it help if I were to notify the American embassy?"

"I will not deceive you," Volitain said. "I do not deceive."

Martya sniffed.

"They may return it to you when you do nothing. That happens some-times."

"What if it doesn't?"

Volitain spread his hands. "You must discover the correct official, then you must win his friendship. It is most often done with money. Martya thinks you have money, and that is good, but you do not have enough for that. Not here. In Amerika?"

"Maybe." I thought about it. "I have some there and I might raise some more. How can I get it here?"

"Someone will have to bring it for you. Diamonds are best." Volitain hesitated. "They will have to be well concealed. He must pass the cus-toms, you understand. Not only ours, but other nations'."

"Unless he flies in."

"Let him attempt it." Volitain's sleepy whisper had nearly faded away. He straightened up and considered the meat rolls steaming on his plate. "I wish him well."

I remembered the canceled flights and the flight that had gone on to Ankara without landing here. "It seems just about hopeless."

"Fortunately"—Volitain pointed his fork at me—"there is the third way. You might grow rich here. If you wish to return to Amerika there is no difficulty. Our officials fear the rich. It is the same with you, eh?"

I said it was.

"Now let us turn the page. You may choose to remain with us. Much is here for the man of wealth. I offer a plan."

I probably looked like I did not believe him. That was the way I felt.

"I will not deceive you, for I do not deceive. My plan will make me rich, too, if it succeeds. It may be it fails. Failure is at least as likely as success. Will you close your ears to me?"

I shook my head.

"That is well. You are Kleon's prisoner. It is not a handicap, and may favor us."

"We together." Martya squeezed my hand.

"Exactly. There is a treasure, or there may be. The explanation will take some time."

I chewed and swallowed a mouthful of *fadennudeln*. "Then get going. I want to hear it."

"It require you to pay some money. Not much."

"Yeah, I figured. And?"

Volitain cut a meat roll and studied it. "You think I take your money. I do not. I say first that if we find this treasure, together or separately, it is to be shared equally between us three. It is understood? If Martya finds it alone, she must share with us. If I find it, and nothing you know of my finding, I will share with you and Martya. If you find it, you must share with both of us."

I said, "Okay," and the three of us clasped hands.

"Now we are partners," Martya said. "Tell him of the judge."

"Hear me. The year is eighteen sixty. A young man called Eion Demarates leaves home after a quarrel with his father. Twenty years pass, and he return a rich man. His father is dead. His mother likewise. There are brothers, sisters. All want his gold, but Eion Demarates give them nothing. There are old quarrels."

I nodded again to show I understood.

"He builds a fine house for himself. He has servants, a carriage with four horses, and many other things. We go forward. The year is eighteen eighty-eight, eh? Hear me, for this you must understand. In eighteen eighty-eight, our money was not rubbish." Volitain got out his wallet and scattered bills over his meat rolls. "Rotting garbage, this is. My *dolmades* are not so bad as this. In the year of which I speak, it was not so. Our money is silver and gold."

"Ours, too," I said.

"You were robbed in that case, just as we were."

Martya said, "If you don't want those, I'd like one."

Volitain said, "You are my guest," and she speared a bill and a meat roll with a single thrust of her fork. He stared for a moment, then laughed.

Grinning, Martya licked a little grease from her punctured loot.

"An ancestor of mine was the judge here at that time." Volitain was wiping the rest of his bills with his napkin. "We have half a dozen judges in Puraustays now. In that year, the city was smaller and there was little crime. We had only one, the ancestor of whom I speak. Demarates went to bed, eh? His valet helps him to undress, warms the bed, builds up the fire, does all those things. When his master is in bed the valet wishes him a good rest, puts the little cap on the candle, and goes out. Death finds his master asleep and does not wake him. A physician is brought, an inquest is held, all that. Nothing bad is found."

I said, "And then?"

"No gold either." Volitain smiled and licked his thin lips. "There are banks, but Eion Demarates? No accounts he has. His servants stole it, so my ancestor believes. They are questioned under torture. This one has taken a silver cup, that one the razor with which he shaves his master. A maid takes clothing for her son, fine stockings and other such things. Trivialities. The gold of Eion Demarates none ever finds."

Martya muttered, "Or your ancestor does not think it."

"Correct. He searches the house, with police to help. They find nothing. There is no will. The brothers, the sisters, loudly say many times everything belongs to them. My ancestor says no, taxes are owed upon the estate. He sells the horses and carriage and other things, and holds the money against these taxes. He does not wish to sell the house because he believe the hidden money will soon be found. It is under a floor, eh? Or in a wall. He will wreck the house and find it.

"Brothers and a sister journey to the capital. This judge will wreck our house, they say. You must stop him. The Prince Judicial issues an order: the house is not to be demolished."

"It's still standing?" I asked.

"It is. Some of the furniture has been sold. Some remains. It belongs to the state, that was decided when the taxes went unpaid. It has been rented more than once, long ago. People died there. No one will rent it."

Martya said, "You will rent it for us. You can get it most cheap."

"Legally," I told her, "I'm your husband's prisoner. I don't want to go to jail."

Volitain nodded. "You must sleep in Kleon's house, but you will rent the house I have told you of that you may repair it, rendering it a fit residence. Soon, you say to those who ask, the court will see that you are an innocent traveler. Then you will be released, and you must have this place to live until your passport is returned. It will be rented to you, and you and Martya will search, reporting to me what you have done."

My food was gone, but I sipped my wine. "Is a court looking into my case?"

Volitain shook his head. "At present? No."

"Then I should get a lawyer. I don't want to stay here forever."

"I will represent you." At long last, Volitain forked a piece of his remaining meat roll into his mouth.

"You're a lawyer?"

"He is many things." Martya looked sour and serious. "That is why I brought you to him."

"An attorney, as other things," Volitain told me. "I practice law for, oh, not quite three years. It bored me, and I did not require the money. I still represent a few friends and take cases of interest. Soon you ask why I do not search the Willows myself."

That sounded interesting. "The Willows?"

"It is the name of the house Eion Demarates built. At the tax office, you must know it. Tell them you hear the Willows is without a tenant. You will rent, if it is cheap enough. Can you bargain?"

I nodded. "Sure."

"Good. They will ask too much. Officials always do."

Martya said, "You are an official yourself, Volitain."

He wiped his lips to hide his smile. "A minor one, you understand. You need not be afraid of me."

"Can you get my passport back?"

"No. Certainly not. If we win our case, then I might do something. Until then, it is hopeless. Do you think I intend to charge you?"

I nodded again. "Lawyers do."

"I will not, provided you find the treasure and share it with me."

A waiter brought our check, parting the green curtain to push it through. Volitain laid it on the table, laid a bill on it, and weighted both with the salt shaker. "You see? I do not deceive."

"Thanks for lunch. Why don't you search the Willows yourself?"

He laughed. "That you would ask, I knew. First, because I must do many other things. Second, because already I have. For two months I searched whenever I had an hour to spare, but found nothing. A new searcher, one of foreign temperament, employing foreign methods, may succeed where I failed. Or so I hope."

3

THE WILLOWS

Martya and I went to an office on the second floor of the long yellow brick building called the Mounted Guard, where a sweating fat man in shirt-sleeves sat writing letters. "To those who are behind on their rent," he explained.

We had not asked, but we nodded. Anyway, I did.

"The police will come. If they are kind, they will permit the tenants to move out their personal belongings. If they are not, they will not. Then those who are too poor to pay will be poorer still."

Martya translated and added, "They have no money."

"They must get some." The fat man pointed his pen at her. "Let me tell you, young woman, it is one thing to be without money, quite another to be without the means of getting money. The state finds employment for everyone who applies."

I said, "Then why don't they apply?"

He turned his attention to me. "You are German?"

"American."

"Ah. You are most ignorant. I have heard this. They do not apply because they do not want to work. What is the purpose of the state?"

Neither of us spoke.

"I ask seriously, sir. What is it?" He laid aside his pen and fanned himself with a painted fan of thin wood.

"To defend the country," I said. I was trying to recall the Constitution. "To secure the property of its citizens."

He shook his head. "You have not been to school. For those things and more the nation is responsible. It is on the state that we rely to make all work, and to reward good work should there be any. This I explain in these letters you see, with certain other things. What is it you wish?"

"I want to rent a house," I said.

"You are German. Why would you rent a house here?"

"I will stay here in Puraustays for some time. It should be cheaper to rent a house here than to live in a hotel. Do you rent houses here? In this office?"

"I do. The houses I rent belong to the state, sir. When taxes are not paid, the state takes the house. Also for certain criminal offenses. If a serious offense is committed by the owner in his house, the house is forfeit." Grunting, the fat man lifted a heavy book onto his desk.

Martya said, "He wants to rent the Willows."

The fat man ignored her. "These houses I have, sir. All good houses, though some are in need of minor repairs." He flipped pages. "Here is one of the sequestered kind I just described. The owner lured women to his house, raped them, strangled them, and raped them again. He was put to death and his house confiscated. Seven rooms, full bath. Full of interest, too, for a visitor. It is said that one of the dead women walks up the cellar stairs by night." He smacked his lips. "I would advise keeping the cellar door shut and bolted by night, and not going down there save in a case of dire necessity. Which is not likely to arise."

He waited for my comment. When I did not talk he said, "Think of the tales you will tell when you return to Germany. Why, a man might dine out for a year on it!"

"He doesn't want that one," Martya said.

I explained that I had already selected a house, the Willows, and asked him to rent it to me.

He pursed his lips. "You are bold, sir. Indeed you are bold. I myself . . . Well, no matter. You have seen it, sir?"

"The exterior, yes. We looked at that and peeped in through the windows. We couldn't get in."

"It is kept locked. I see to it that all the vacant houses are locked." The fat man paused to fan his sweating face and became business-like. "Normally, sir, we require a security deposit equal to three months' rent. It is to be refunded when the tenant vacates. I inspect the house. If it is in good condition, your deposit is refunded."

I said, "I understand."

"In this case . . ." He was paging through his book. "For the house you have selected, sir, we will not. The house is not in good condition."

Martya said, "We know that."

I promised I would make any necessary repairs.

He cleared his throat. "You may post the bills to me. Should I approve them, they will be settled by the state. Should I decline them, you must pay them yourself. . . . Ah, here it is. The rent will be twenty euros per month, sir."

I said it seemed quite cheap.

"It is." He cleared his throat again. "We take into consideration the poor condition of the house and its long vacancy. Let me see. . . ." He bent over the page. "One Volitain Aeneaos rented it years ago. He remained for two months. It has remained vacant ever since. Are you sure you want it, sir? At twenty euros per month?"

"Yes," I said. "Certain. I'll give you the first month's rent in advance, if I may."

"You must give me two months' rent in advance," he told me. "Forty euros. That is the law, sir. I cannot make exceptions."

I gave him the money, and he filled out a printed receipt, signed it, and handed it to me. "Crucifixes are said to be effectual, sir. There is a little store in the cathedral. You might get holy water there, too. My own grandmother swore by cold iron. Large nails, by choice. She was a woman of wide experience. Should you have need of the assistance of the state, you might speak to me. I will direct you to the proper persons."

I thanked him and told him I appreciated his help.

He nodded, frowning as he handed me two rusty iron keys. "The trees, sir. The willows. You must have seen them when you looked at the house."

I had.

"I would cut them. You will cut them, if you take my advice. Root out the stumps. Plant grass and clover, and leave it so until the soil recovers. You have been stung by bees?"

"He will plant fruit trees," Martya declared.

"They will not do well until the soil recovers. Plow in manure, sir, before you plant your clover. When it has sprouted, beware of bees. Clover attracts them."

I said, "Good advice. Thanks a lot."

When we had left his office and stepped into the hall, I heard him say, "Would you eat their fruit, young woman?"

Martya was silent until we had left the Mounted Guard, then she said, "He thought I was a cousin."

"My cousin, you mean?"

"Not a real cousin." She laughed. "When foreigners come, girls attach themselves. Did I say that well? The girl shows her friend the city and interprets for him. He buys her gifts and she sleeps with him. Sometimes he gives her money. They are called cousins because it is what she says: 'He is my cousin.'"

I said I would be happy to buy her a gift.

"Would you really? A hat? Would you buy me a winter hat?"

"It's spring," I said. "Why would you want a winter hat?"

She laughed. "How little you understand! You are married, yes?"

I shook my head.

"No wonder! Because it is spring, the winter things are most cheap. Besides, the hat I wore all last winter is old. Most ragged! It is a hat to laugh at, an old wool hat that was not good when it was new." She tugged at my arm. "Come! There is a shop near. I show you."

It was not near, but she did. The hat I eventually bought for her was a perky round cap of what looked to me like fox fur. She was thrilled with it, posing a dozen times in front of the mirror in the store before we left.

When we were out on the street again, I said, "How will you explain your new hat to Kleon?"

"He does not see it until autumn."

"Yes, but he'll see it then. What'll you tell him?"

Her chin went up and her shoulders back. "The truth! I will tell him you bought it for me."

"He'll be jealous."

"Good! Let him be most jealous. He needs much more jealous, that Kleon."

We were walking, of course. The police have their patrol cars, and there are limousines for high officials. In a day, you might see three or four trucks and a dozen wagons. But private cars? Buses and cabs? All that shit? Forget it! Ordinary people walk everywhere.

The way to the Willows was not hard, but it seemed to me like it went on forever. We walked in the street like everybody else. The crazy plan of the streets, which zig to the right or zag to the left every few blocks, wears out a walker.

"Your streets should have names," I told Martya.

"If this street had a name and I called to it, would it come to me?" Seeing I had no answer, she laughed.

After a while I said, "You give names to your houses."

"To cats and dogs also. If you call a dog, it will come to you sometimes. Cats will not come. So our houses are cats."

I asked the name of Kleon's house.

"I do not wish to tell. It is ill luck for me."

"Then I'll ask Kleon. We're going back tonight, aren't we?"

"We must. If he does not let us in, we go to the police and they shoot him."

"You'll be a wealthy widow," I said.

Martya sniffed. "He has nothing."

"He has his house."

She shrugged. "We must turn here, why do you walk straight ahead?"

"Here" was the little path through the dark, crowding trees to the door of the Willows. We had walked so far that I had nearly forgotten that eventually we would get there.

When we had gone to the Willows earlier, the sun had been high overhead, and lonely sunbeams had penetrated the crowding leaves. Now the sun was low, and a cloudy sky promised a dark night. Martya's hand found mine and we walked together, not quite side by side, down a path I could not see that was barely wide enough for one person.

"You do not have a light?"

"No," I said. "Do you have matches?"

"No. We should have bought a . . . I do not know this word. To hold in the hand and give light."

"*Taschenlampe.*"

"Yes, a flashlight, where there were shops. Someone would have them."

"We'll get one tomorrow," I told her.

"Tomorrow will be too late."

After that I stumbled, she swore for me, and we walked on silently while the trees made fun of us. Their silence was a lot bigger and a lot older than ours. As I tried the most likely looking key in the front door lock, Martya asked, "Are you going to start searching now?"

"Yeah. I want to look the whole place over and make plans. What to do first, what tools I'll need, and so on."

"It is haunted. This you must know."

"I know you said it was." The likely key squeaked and balked in the lock. "People always say these old houses are haunted. If nobody's living there, it'll be a haunted house in a year." I wrestled with the key. "This lock needs a squirt of WD40, or if we can't get that a squirt of oil."

"We will see no ghosts because the sun is still in the sky." It seemed like Martya was talking to herself instead of me. "One cannot see ghosts by daylight. Who does not know this?"

The key turned at last. "Then we won't see them," I told her.

"We will not see them, but they will be there."

"So what? So will we. Maybe they'll tell us where the treasure is."

I opened the door and went in. It was dim, but not as dark as I had expected, maybe because the ceilings were so high. The windows, pointed at the top like the ones in a church, rose high above my head.

"He would not have had willows." Martya's voice, hushed and kind of querulous, sounded behind me. "Not the one who builds thus. Fruit trees for him."

I agreed without giving her much attention. The foyer we stood in was pretty clearly a preliminary room. Benches stuck out from two walls and there were hooks for hanging coats. Even so, it was big and imposing, with great big fireplaces at both ends. Looking back at Martya, I said, "They didn't have central heating when this was built, I guess."

She stopped, looking frightened. "What is it you talk of? I do not know."

"A furnace to heat the whole building."

"Oh, that. Public buildings have these. We do not. Can we go out?"

"I haven't even started." The door to the next room stood open, and I walked into it.

It was nearly empty but really interesting just the same. A few pieces of furniture were covered with dirty white drop cloths. A dozen or so more, the ones with no upholstery, had none and were thick with dust. You could tell that pictures and tapestries had hung on the walls back when the room was new, but they were gone now. Over the big fireplace at the other end, crooked swords and a little round shield of dark iron and peeling leather had been left behind. I pointed and said, "I wonder why they didn't take those."

"Who would want things from such a house?"

"We do," I told her. "We want the treasure, and we'd like to find it. Your friend Volitain does, too."

"Perhaps they are fastened to the wall."

That made sense. I stepped up onto the hearth, which was a good foot above the floor. The swords and the little shield were higher than that, too high for me to do more than touch them. I got out my pen and my little notebook.

"What are you writing?"

"That I've got to get a stepladder."

"So that you can take those things? Let us go. I do not like this place."

"I do," I said. "Or anyhow I like it so far. And I don't want the swords or the shield. I want to look in back of them. There could be a hole in the stonework in back. We ought to look."

"Volitain will have thought of it."

"You're right. He may have looked there. When you think of a place nobody who searched this place will have thought of, you let me know straight off." Having finished my note, I snapped my notebook shut.

"There are mirrors in here," Martya muttered.

I stepped down. "I'd think they'd have been taken."

She shook her head. "Not all of them."

"Come on! We need to look at some more rooms." I led the way without looking back to see if she was following me. "Is this something Volitain told you?"

"They call to me." She sounded like she had not moved an inch.

"Magic mirrors?" It made me think about this book, which I had already been planning. "I'll have to find out about them."

Martya said, "Do you not know mirrors call out to women?"

I had thought the foyer was pretty big. The next room was three times its size, a lot bigger than Kleon's whole house. A lot of furniture remained, dark and heavy tables, chairs, and cabinets. The floorboards had been torn up in places.

The cabinets, I decided, were way too obvious to be worth searching. They would have been searched a long time ago. I opened one to see. It had originally been locked, but somebody had pried it open, busting the lock.

There were a few dusty odds and ends left, like a long, bent screw and an empty ink bottle. In the angle between a shelf and the back . . .

My fingernail pried it out: a chewed-up pencil.

Martya was pulling a dustcover from the picture above the near-est mantel. The dustcover gone, it turned out to be no picture at all, but a big mirror. "Here is one," she told me. "There is a dead woman buried behind it."

I did not believe her. "How do you know that?"

She shrugged.

"How? Did Volitain tell you?"

"I saw her." Martya paused, groping, probably because she was looking for the right German. "I look at it. It does not show me, but she."

"A dead woman."

"Yes."

I went to the mirror and, just as I expected, saw my own reflection. The mirror was in a heavy brass frame, and the frame fastened with big screws to the black wood over the mantel. "If I had tools, I'd take this down so you could see there's no dead woman hiding back there."

"You would do that for me?"

I shook my head. "We're treasure hunting. This looks as if it hasn't been disturbed in quite a while, so it's at least possible the treasure's back there, in a hole behind the mirror."

"Someone might have looked and put it back."

It seemed to me that a searcher would have had no reason to put back the mirror, which looked pretty heavy. But I was checking out the heads of the big brass screws and kept my yap shut. The slots would have showed bright scratches if the screws had been turned lately with a steel screw-driver. None did, but there was one missing.

I picked up the cloth dustcover and covered the mirror.

"Make many notes," Martya told me. "We must have tools and a light."

I did.

"Are we to go now?"

"Soon," I told her. "I want to look around a little more."

"Soon it will be night. I make the suggestion. We go through the house." Martya gestured. "When we have reach the end there will be a door. This must be so. We go out this door of which I speak and so back to make Kleon let us in and give us supper."

I said I wanted to look things over a little more thoroughly.

"If I wish to go, how do you prevent me?"

"I wouldn't stop you at all, except for arguing that it would be better if you were to stay."

"This we are doing. I will go. Will you find Kleon's house again? It is not far."

I thought about it.

"Answer! You could not."

"I could ask directions."

"They will tell you nothing. This you will most soon find, and know I am right. So! You will not find it. The police will shoot Kleon. For me this is good. I will have the house and sell him, and I go to the capital. You go to prison. For you it is most bad."

"All right," I told her, "we'll go through the house like you want. But first we ought to lock the front door. I'm sure we can lock it from inside."

"No one will wish to enter into such a place as this. You and Volitain solely."

"Let me lock it. It will only take a minute."

The large keyhole on the inside of the door was pretty obvious, but the lock seemed stiffer and rustier than ever. I got out my notebook again, and made a note about spray lubricant, underlining it. It worked magic. Just making the note seemed to fix the lock, which let my key turn almost easily. I shook the door.

"It is locked! Let us go."

I nodded as I pocketed the key and followed her out of the reception hall. In the next room the tall windows had changed to smaller ones, square or round, some broken. The fireplaces were gone, and there was a big Dutch stove instead.

"We do not need your swears," Martya told me. "They are most vile. This your voice says. I do not understand them. This house either. We have come through the wrong door. It is no more than that."

"Yeah, you're right. How about this? You go back to the reception hall and find the right door. I'll keep on going toward the back from here. We'll meet at the back and see who gets there first."

"You would leave me! Kleon will be shot, and you will go to prison. This I have said."

I shook my head. "You said nobody will give me directions. If you're telling the truth—which I don't believe, by the way—I'll pay somebody to guide me."

"I will be at Kleon's before you!"

"When I get there I'll tell you how smart you are."

"You think me afraid!"

"Only you're not? You can prove it pretty easily." I gestured toward the door through which we had come into the room.

"I am afraid—most afraid for you. You are like a foolish child. You think himself wise. I must protect you."

Since I did not really want us to be separated, I smiled at that, calling her Mother Martya. She laughed, and we crossed the room together, exiting through the door at the farther end.

Here I would like to stop to tell you that I had never really sensed the sinister atmosphere of the Willows until Martya laughed. There was something in there that hated laughter, and her laugh woke it up. Woke it only in my own mind, you will say. But I had not been afraid before and was scared then. There is no arguing against that.

The setting sun may have had something to do with it, too. I did not see it, but I may have sensed it in the changed quality of the light. In Australia I watched Ayers Rock change color at sunset. Of course the space-traveling stone does not really change. It just makes the change in the sunlight show up better. Did the Willows really change some way? I would rather write no, but I think maybe it did.

Either the next room was windowless or its windows had been boarded up. It would have been as dark as the heart of an alderman if we had not left the door open. As it was, we walked slowly and carefully because I remembered the torn-up floorboards in the other room.

We were halfway through when Martya yelled, "A thing run on my foot!"

"Just a rat," I said. "There's bound to be rats in an old house like this."

"What is it they eat here? What is it their food?"

I said I had no idea.

"I will tell. They gnaw the bodies of the dead! We—" Martya paused. "That you heard. That you must hear. Tell me you hear."

"Hear what?"

"Somebody laugh when I say that. Not you, I have hear you laugh at me too often. I could not mistake. You hear? Say you hear it, too."

"No. No, I didn't."

"There is another here with us!"

"It was probably the wind."

"What wind? I do not feel him."

"The next time we do this—," I began.

I was interrupted. "We do not next time. No! You do it, with none."

I would have closed her mouth with my hand, but she moved away. I had heard something, and hoped—scared half to death—to hear it again. As it was, all I could do was urge Martya, in whispers, to be quiet and listen.

Somebody was walking around upstairs. The noises were faint, but I felt sure I knew exactly what they were. He would walk toward the back of the house, and then toward the front again.

A door slammed, and after that everything got quiet.

"We must get out," Martya was whispering.

I nodded, hoping she could see it, turned, and steered her toward what I thought was the door we had come through.

It showed us into another room, smaller than the one we had left and five or six sided, but a room with windows.

Martya went to a broken one, felt along the bottom of the frame for broken glass, found some, and by what seemed like a real miracle got the window to open, swinging like the door of a cabinet in a rusty frame that creaked and squeaked.

"I cannot climb over. You are strong. You must lift me over and drop me."

"I'm not strong," I told her, "and you're perfectly capable of climbing out by yourself. That can't be more than a couple of feet high."

"I must have care for my hat." She displayed the little cardboard hat-box. "Besides, lifting is more romantic." Outside, a gust of wind brought in spattering rain.

I climbed out. It was maybe three feet from the bottom of the window to the muddy ground underneath. The willows that had been so silent when we came to the house were muttering now, like a crowd getting set to riot.

Martya leaned out the window. My hands nearly circled her waist as I lifted her out. She threw her arms around my neck, hatbox and all, and kissed me before I put her down.

After that, there is nothing much to tell. We ran through the dripping willows all the way to the windswept street, running blindly and getting there mostly by good luck. As Martya had said, it was not far from the Willows to Kleon's house—not far, anyhow, the way they figured in Puraustays.

Pounding on the door brought Kleon from his bed, naked and mad as hell. He announced loudly (Martya interpreting for me) that he had no intention of making supper. Martya apparently told him to go back to bed, and told me that we would have soup.

It was on the kitchen stove already, kept warm by a banked fire. She stirred up the fire, added fresh coal, cut thick slices of dark bread, and put on water for tea.

I told her I was too tired to eat.

She said I had to take off my wet clothes and hang them in the kitchen to dry. I did, except for my shorts.

She took off her soaked dress and hung it up. "We will put these near the stove when we have go."

I suppose I nodded. I was listening to spring rain rattle against the window.

"You have the bad day, I think. Did they beat you?"

I said that they had not, only pushed me down a flight of stairs.

"That is not so much, but you must eat my soup and sleep. It is morning, I see you again."

I agreed and said I hoped her new hat had not been ruined.

"No, no! The box is for burn but the hat is fur. It will be most fine." She laid aside the long spoon she had been stirring the soup with, tore open the wet box, and put on the hat. "You see? It is little water, but most soon will it be dry. Is pretty, no?"

She posed, moving from one pose to the next like a dancer, in a fox-fur hat and a worn, wet cotton bra and panties. "It suits me?"

"Yes," I said. "It looks great on you."

"You are straighten up. That is good. I must get butter."

When she pulled a ring in the floor, a trapdoor almost at my feet swung up, showing rough steps that led down into darkness. She lit a candle from the stove and went down them, still wearing the fox-fur hat.

I closed my eyes to rest them. When I opened them a minute later, there was butter on the kitchen table, and a bowl of steaming soup in front of me.

"This is good. I think I must wake you. Eat! Dip first in the bread. Soup is most hot."

I did. The bread was the kind kids hate, but solid and nourishing. The soup was foreign and delicious. I asked what kind it was.

"All kind." Martya laughed. "What is good for soup, I put in. We have meat, there is here no dog. My soup get the bones."

I was eating soup and too busy to smart off.

4

THE MAN FROM THE MINISTRY

I have no idea what time it was when I went to bed. After dark, of course. But we had walked quite a ways, trying to hurry while pushed around by rain and wind. There had been a squabble with Kleon, and so forth. Worst of all, I had nodded off when Martya went down into the cellar to get butter. How long had I slept then? Half an hour might be a pretty good guess.

Certainly Martya woke me early the next morning. Gray light filled the sky, but the sun had not shown any part of his royal roundness. I can say all this because she shook my shoulder and made me look out the window.

"He is Kleon. You see? He goes to his work."

I said, "I do now. I hadn't noticed him before."

"You are rest, yes?"

I said that I was still tired and wanted to stay in bed for another hour or so.

"I, too." She had been wrapped in a blanket that I had at first taken for a robe. As she spoke she let it drop, slipping into bed beside me. She was buck naked.

"You do not wear nothing." Her right hand had gone exploring.

"I was soaked to the skin. I didn't want to get into a dry bed wearing wet shorts."

"For me the same. I think Kleon will tire me most terribly, but he is asleep." She giggled. "You must tire me now, or I don't make nice breakfast."

It was certainly a nice breakfast by the standards of her country. There were savory sausages, little fried cakes of what seemed to be a mixture of some kind of meat ground up and oatmeal, two kinds of cheese, and the bread and butter we had the previous night. All this was washed down with strong, unsweetened tea. I was hungry, ate everything she put on the table, and promised to buy her more groceries as soon as we had finished.

"You go market with me?"

I nodded. "I want to buy tools—stuff we'll need in that empty house. We can buy food, too."

"Twice we go. First for me, then for you. For me we bring here. We go back, buy for you the ladder and what else, and take these things to Willows. Is not so much to carry, or so far."

I said all right, and we set off as soon as she had washed the breakfast dishes. (I dried.) I asked if Kleon had eaten.

She shrugged. "Bread and cheese. Water to drink. I would cook for him if he makes me. For himself is better. But he must hurry away or no more work. Always he sleeps late and must go most quick after."

"I see."

"I stay in the bed until he is gone." She closed her eyes and pretended to sleep. "He does not bother me then. If he wishes to tire me, he must do it when I go to bed. At that time I do not fight him."

"You'll never have to fight me," I told her. "If you don't want to, just say so."

"Ah! You will find another."

"I won't," I told her, "but another might find me."

The market was larger than I had expected and carried foodstuffs from the surrounding farms. There were eggs and cheeses, plenty of both, live fowls, and a ton of dried fruit, mostly apples, plums, and cherries. Fish were for sale too, although not a lot. Many things Americans would never consider eating were for sale. There was a guy there who had lined up the heads of a couple of dozen freshly decapitated pigs on board shelves. He sold one while I was watching.

Martya bought a ham, eggs, brown flour so coarse it might almost be called meal, potatoes, and salt, all of which she haggled over and I paid for. I wanted to carry everything, to which she objected vociferously—the ladies of the neighborhood would see her carrying nothing and call her a lazy slut.

I gave her the ham, the flour, and the potatoes. She did not like that either, saying she would be carrying more than I did. Both of us wanted to carry the eggs, since it seemed obvious that the person who carried those could not carry much else for fear some would be broken. In the end, she carried the eggs and the salt, and I carried everything else. As we were leaving the market she saw some fresh, bright red cherries, which she said had come a long way on the train. I bought some, but only after she agreed to carry them.

After that we trudged back to Kleon's, Martya eating fresh cherries as she walked and spitting out the pits.

It was not yet noon when we reached the house, but I laid down the law, saying we had to get lunch before we went out to buy tools—I said it because I wanted to sit down and take off my shoes. Martya wanted me to buy our lunches at a café she would show me. "Is really most good food there and most true to old city. This you must write in your book." (I had explained that I was a travel writer and had come to collect materials.) After another argument like the one about carrying the groceries, we settled on a compromise. She would make tea for us both. I would get what was left of the cherries, with bread, butter, and cheese. When I had finished, we would walk to the café and I would buy our lunches. After that, we would shop for tools. Martya's arguments confirmed what I had already begun to suspect: everyone here eats everything he or she can hold at every meal but walks so much that most people do not get fat.

While I chewed dark bread and cheese and Martya drank tea, we talked about the Willows. I described the sort of ladder I wanted—an aluminum extension ladder light enough that Martya and I could carry it. She insisted that there were no such ladders here. I wanted a steel pry bar. She wanted two of them, so she could make a cross of them. And so on.

The café fronted on the river. The fertilizer plants (if that is what they really were) were only too visible across the water, but they could have been any kind of building—castles, incinerators, prisons, public housing. You name it. Martya and I sat outside like a dozen other people, under a faded old umbrella that might have been red when it was new. European waiters despise tourists, but I was not one and felt pretty sure I did not look like one. I knew I was right when the waiter asked whether I had come to buy pork for Germany.

I told him I had not, without explaining that I was an American and a prisoner. He thanked me and said exports were raising food prices beyond the reach of the poor.

The food in his café was pretty cheap by American standards. Martya had an apple dumpling doused with syrup. I had roast duckling stuffed with mushrooms, white raisins, and apricots. There was good, hot coffee laced with malt liqueur afterward, and the two meals cost only a little more than two Americans would pay for hamburgers and soft drinks at a fast-food franchise. As I said, this café is by the river. It is called the Skiadeion.

The big screwdriver, oilcan, and pry bars I wanted (one large and one small) gave us no problems. We must have tried half a dozen stores, though, before we found flashlights. We bought two (with spare batteries, string, and more tools) even though they were smaller than I would have liked. Martya suggested candles, so we bought some, with matches and a tin lantern to hold them.

The ladder just about stumped us. We could have a little stepladder or a four-meter wooden ladder that must have weighed a hundred pounds. Another man and I might have carried one as far as the Willows, if we did not have to carry anything else. For Martya and me—already loaded with candles, lantern, flashlights, batteries, and tools . . . well, forget it.

No, the long and dusty shop in which we had found the big ladder did not deliver. Very reluctantly, as though he was afraid I would scoff at his suggestion, the shopkeeper confided that porters could be hired at the Mounted Guard. He was willing to hold our purchases for us upon my promise to buy his four-meter ladder if I could find men to carry it. So off we marched to the Mounted Guard.

I had imagined a sort of hiring hall in which the porters could sit while they waited for somebody to hire them. There was nothing like that, only a small ground-floor office with a window looking out onto the street. Placement was by seniority, so we got a couple of grandpas with gray mustaches. To tell the truth I was happy to get them. Some of the guys my age looked like they would cut your throat.

They followed us back to the ladder shop, inspected and approved the ladder we had decided on, and suggested we buy a stepladder, too. I said it would be all Martya and I could do to carry the tools, which were numerous and very heavy.

They insisted that we would not have to carry it. They would carry it themselves. After laying our ladder flat, they chose a stepladder for us and

laid it on the rungs of the big ladder. After that, they tied our other stuff
to the rails and picked the whole thing up, each resting a side rail on each
shoulder. With Martya leading the way, we went back to the Willows, she
and I carrying nothing at all and our porters a credit to the profession.

"Funny old place," said one.

I explained that I was renting it and meant to get it fixed up, adding
that Martya and I might live there.

The other porter spit. "A good house must got a good roof."

I nodded.

"You trim these trees, sir. Look up there. Every little wind will drag
those branches across your shingles."

I saw he was right and told him I was planning to have the willows cut
for firewood.

We got the ladders and tools inside, and I paid the porters, adding
a pretty good tip. Tipping here is about the same as in America. You give
a tip for good service, and keep your money for bad. Waitresses in greasy
spoons think anything over ten percent is pretty nice. Waiters expect
more but do not always get it from me. In the pricier places like Skiadeion,
the usual tip is twenty percent for small parties and fifteen for big ones.

I was trying to take down the big brass-framed mirror I mentioned in
Chapter 3 when there was a knock on the front door. Martya ran to get
it and came back to tell me that somebody from the Ministry of Internal
Order wanted to talk with us. I left the mirror hanging by two screws and
went into the reception room with her.

I had expected him to be fat and pompous, but he was a little man with
a little mustache, a bowler hat, and smart eyes. I invited him to sit down.

At that, Martya jumped in with both feet. "We cannot discuss important matters in such a place. There is a much nicer one not far from here,
outside, in a garden. It will be lovely today. Let us go there."

Naturally I said okay.

The small man asked my name, nodded, and said, "You and I have
much to speak of."

The café Martya led us to is the Haysuxia, a patio in what looks like a
private house. The three of us were put at a tiny table and told that the first
strawberries of the year had just arrived "from the south." Martya

consulted with the small man in their own language, asked whether I, too, would like coffee, berries, and cream (nodding as she said it), and ordered for the three of us.

"You are Amerikan," the little man said.

I said yes and asked how he knew, hoping he would say he had seen my passport.

He shrugged. "I have heard your name, and you speak German with the accent of an Amerikan. Those suffice. It is difficult to change your Amerikan dollars here. Give some to me and I will change them for you."

I have traveled enough to know when I am being asked for a bribe, but I was, not sure how big a bribe he wanted. I saw his eyes widen a trifle when I got out a hundred dollars. "Could you change this for me? These big bills are hard to change even in America."

"I will try," he said. He took it from me, held it up to the light, and put it into a tall, old-fashioned wallet with a catch.

Bowls of strawberries and cream arrived, together with cups and a carafe of good coffee.

After a cautious sip of his coffee, the small man made a steeple of his fingers. "To begin, let us dispose of the matters that brought you to my attention, sir. You have engaged the ruinous house in which I discovered you. You, or possibly another who used your name. Since I found you there, I am inclined to think it was you yourself."

I nodded. "It was me. The official at the Mounted Guard who rented it to me knew I was foreign but made no objection."

"That," said the small man, "is scarcely a matter of wonder, sir. There is no law against foreigners renting, leasing, or purchasing houses here. It is entirely within the law."

I thanked him for clarifying the point.

"There is, however, a person under citizen detention whose name is your own. Were you aware of that, sir?"

"Sure I am. I'm him." I stirred my coffee and sipped a little to straighten up my thoughts. "As a foreigner I'm pretty unfamiliar with your law. I guess you know that."

"I do, sir."

"My understanding is that I have to live in the house of the citizen who's looking after me, but that I can leave it to shop, go to clubs, see a movie or a play, or eat in cafés like we are now, as long as I go back to my host's house at night."

"You must sleep there, sir. That is correct."

Martya said, "He sleep there last night. To this I swear."

"I am inclined to believe you," the small man told her, "but you force me to inquire concerning your own status. Do you yourself sleep there?"

Martya nodded. "With my husband. Yes, always. My husband own the house, which he buy with money my father leave us when he die."

"I see. You were not sweeping its floors when first I saw you, but answering the door of the ruin this gentleman has engaged."

"He desire to rent this house. I come with him to help. He is my cousin from America."

The small man nodded. "I understand. How unfortunate that he should be arrested! Can you tell me why he engaged the house?"

"He say he wish a house near ours, but he does not pay much. It is such a house, and large. I do not decide. He decides."

"I see." The small man turned to me. "Can you tell me, sir, why you engaged this house?"

I put down my spoon. "Are you asking me why I wanted a house, or why I chose the one I did?"

"Both, I think."

"Okay. I came here—I mean, here to your country—to collect materials for a travel book. I'm good at them. If you want to check up on me, I'll give you the name and address of my publisher back in New York."

The small man waved my offer aside. "I doubt that it will be necessary. Why did you come without a passport?"

"I didn't, I had one. It was taken away from me by your border guards."

The small man nodded. "They thought it fraudulent, sir. That it was or might be. Such passports are sent to the capital for laboratory examination."

"I guess they're given back to their owners when they check out."

The small man nodded again, more slowly. "If their owners are still alive, yes. If they can be found. In many cases . . ." He shrugged. "They are not returned. Possibly I can help. You wished a house not far from the house in which this woman resides. I understand that. But you are living in that very house at present, provided I have understood you both correctly."

"I am. But I figure the charges against me will be dropped pretty soon. When they are, I'm going to move out of their house and into the house I've rented. I ought to have it fixed up by then."

"Your nation does not maintain a consulate here in Puraustays."

It was my turn to nod. "That's what everybody tells me."

"There is, however, an embassy in the capital."

I nodded. "I'll go there when I can travel again. You seem to know a lot about this stuff. When I've talked to somebody at the embassy, will I be sent back to America straight off?"

The small man shook his head. "It will be months, certainly. Years, possibly. Do you have influential friends in your own country?"

"A few," I told him.

"In that case, months, perhaps. Or a year or two."

I nodded again. "Okay, if that's the way it is, I'll tour your lovely country with my cousin as my interpreter, and collect materials for a new book. Take a bunch of pictures, if I can get my camera bag back."

"Ah! The police seized your luggage as well?"

"I don't think so. It got left behind on the train when I was taken off."

"I see. It may be that I can have it returned to you. I will try. You find the Willows attractive?"

"Yes," I said, "certainly. I'll have the trees cut and replaced with fruit trees and a nice lawn. When that's been done and the roof fixed, with a few other things, the house should be really nice."

"The state will not increase your rent?"

"Well, I hope not. To tell you the truth, I hadn't thought about it."

The small man sniffed. "You need fear no increase. I will see to it, sir."

"Thanks! I'll owe you for that."

"If you are alive, sir. The house is most attractive? You are drawn to it while you sleep? It may be that I have employed the wrong word. This German we speak is not my native tongue."

"It isn't mine either," I said.

"Does the house you have rented from us draw you in the way that a magnet draws iron filings?"

"Not so far."

"Your cousin is attractive. You agree, I hope? See her as she eats the strawberry. Does she not attract you?"

"Sure she does."

"But the house that you have rented from us, is it hideous?"

I thought quite a bit about that one. Finally I said, "It's like a woman a hundred years old. Just seeing her, you know she used to be beautiful. You'd fix her up if you could."

The small man chuckled. "Houses can be repaired."

"That's my point. Probably the house will attract me when it's been fixed up, but by that time I might be as free as anybody. My passport wasn't forged, and I've never committed a crime."

"You are in my country," the small man said slowly, "while I have never been in yours. Do you confuse ghosts with demons there? Or conflate either with fairies?"

That question made me a little dizzy. I ate a couple of strawberries while I thought about it. "No," I told him, "I don't believe we do. Ghosts are the souls of the dead, still hanging around. Demons are fallen angels, but fairies are nature spirits—or that's what they said in a class I took one time."

He nodded. "You have heard of Vlad the Impaler? A stake of some size was driven into the earth. Its top was sharpened to a point, and the condemned man was forced down on it and left there. In that manner he killed thousands. Some endured this agony for days before the merciful death freed them."

Martya shuddered. "We should not talk of him."

"His summer home was near here, on the lake. Someone or something is seen there, in summer particularly. A man, often large, with eyes of fire. Is this a demon, you would say? Or a ghost?"

"I've got no idea. What do you think?"

"No more have I. When my grandfather lay dying, he was visited by a small boy with golden hair, also wings like a flying flower. Roque was this boy's name. I could not see him. You understand this? My grandfather sees him and describes him to me."

I nodded. "Sure."

"For his sufferings, my grandfather's sins had been forgiven by God. Roque told him this. When he is no more, his soul will go to God in heaven where no sickness is, no filth. 'Always Roque is so happy,' my grandfather told me. 'He laughs and makes jokes. Listen, Peterke, and you may hear him laughing.'"

I nodded again. "Did you listen?"

"Yes. I hear the tinkle of a little bell. There is such a bell on the garden gate. It rings when callers come into the garden. It does not ring in wind, unless the wind blows storm. You understand this?"

Martya said, "Many peoples have such bells."

"I go to a window and look. Never have I seen the bell dance so, but I cannot hear it. The wind does not blow for the trees do not move. I open the window. There is no wind, and still I cannot hear the dancing bell. There is no one in the garden. Is Roque an angel, do you think? Or a fairy?"

I said, "I have no idea."

Martya shook her head. "I do. It is a fairy"—(*Fee*)—"your grandfather see."

"You are young and wise." The small man shrugged. "I am old and stupid. I do not know."

I ate another strawberry and asked him why he was telling us this.

"Because of the house you rent. There are many tales. What is it in your country that waits near a treasure to guard?"

"The cops."

The small man chuckled. "Here, not. They send it to the capital and it is not seen again. Here . . ." He paused for a wry grin. "Sometimes ghosts, sometimes demons, sometimes fairies. Most often, we do not know. I know a man who saw such a one, a black dog with eyes of fire."

"Like Vlad," I said.

He agreed. "But who shall say what it was? The angel drives Adam from paradise with a sword of fire, and fairies take such shapes to frighten us. Who shall say?"

Martya asked, "Where is it he see this dog?"

The small man ignored her. "I have said many things I shall do for you," he told me. "I will have your baggage returned to you, seek to have your charges dismissed and your passport in your hands once more, and arrange that the rent shall remain unchanged. One thing more I do. There is a priest I shall send to you."

5

A MAN IN BLACK

When Martya and I returned to the Willows, I took down the mirror.
I was on the top step of our stepladder, and it was all I could do to get
down the steps holding the mirror out in front of me. Martya screamed
and I nearly dropped it.

There had been, just like Martya had told me, a dead woman behind it.
She was scooched down in a hollow in the wall, looking like a mummy
nobody had wrapped up. She had long, pale hair.

"We must get her down." Martya was still gasping. "With one of these
sheets we will cover her. A Christian burial. She need that."

I said, "It might be better to leave her right where she is and call the
police."

"What is this! You wish to rot in Herrtay? Never do you get out, fool!
Someone they must blame. No!"

It was hard to get myself to touch the dead girl at first, but pretty soon
I was worrying about hurting her when I did it. She felt like I might break
off an arm or something trying to get her out. Her skin felt like rotten
leather and it seemed like she might fall apart any minute. I was about to
lay her on the floor when I saw Martya had pulled the dustcover off a narrow couch upholstered in peacock blue silk. As reverently as I could man-
age, I laid the dead girl's mummy on that while Martya made the sign of
the cross. When the old couch's dirty white dustcover was back in place,
you could not see the mummy anymore, but boy oh boy did we ever know
she was in there.

"She is dead already, do you think, when they are put her there? Or she
is lives, and—and . . ."

I comforted Martya as well as I could.

She must have cried for ten or fifteen minutes, maybe longer. Finally she said, "I will go home, and you must come too so I do not fear. Tomorrow we come back, perhaps. Or you alone. I do not know."

I said okay. It seemed like she got it together while we walked back to Kleon's place. If she ever smiled I did not see it, but she stopped crying and it seemed like she was not so scared. If we talked, I guess I have forgotten everything we said. Maybe we did not talk about anything. I know I was thinking about the dead-girl problem. What were we going to do about her and how should I handle it? Only I knew it would be way too fast to spring anything about it on Martya.

When we got to Kleon's and were sitting at the kitchen table sipping hot tea, I took a big chance. "According to what we heard that guy from the ministry say, there's a big lake near here. Is that right?"

Martya nodded. "The city crowd it, but it does not move. Formerly, the rich houses pressed upon it. These were blow up when the Russians came. Now there is a park and a beach. There are thieves, also wolves, so this park is most dangerous by night. There is the beach beyond and the wolves are sometimes not hungered, so people take their children there to swim."

"Wolves?" I had heard it but I could not believe it.

"Yes, for the thieves. They hunt by night, like them. They come into the city from the east. The streets they do not like, there is too much houses, too many people. In the park, they think, is better. The thieves hide there. They wait for someone to come, such women as me or old bent men. The wolves do not wait. They fall upon the thief and he is dead. They eat him. The police say we shoot them, but they shoot only two, I think, and there is trouble about those. So they let them live and the wolves do not attack them. If the sun is bright and you are more than one, you are safe."

I asked, "What about women like you, and the old people?"

"We do not go into the park alone because of the thieves, so we are safe. Do you wish to see the lake?"

Of course I said I did.

"Do you fish? Many fish there. I have fished, though I am not so skilled. My father took me when I was small." She giggled. "I promise him I bait the hook myself, but when we are in the boat he must do everything. There are many fish, some most big. What you catch, I will cook for us."

I said that a lot of fish were not good to eat.

"No, no! All our fish are good. This you will see. We have . . ." Martya

reeled off the names of a couple of dozen fish, but they were in her language. None of them meant a thing to me. "You fish," she finished. "You
row the boat, also. What you catch I clean and cook for us."

I said okay, only I told myself I would not row any boat if I could help it.

There were no motorboats, but for twice the price of a rowboat we could
rent a little sloop. It was about noon when we put out. I am no expert
sailor, but I know the rudiments. Besides, the rig of our little sloop was as
simple as a rig can be, and sailing the quiet blue waters of Lake Perilimna
was nothing like crossing the North Pacific from Dutch Harbor to Hok-
kaido. My dad and I did that one time.

Martya was in her glory, lounging on a beach towel spread on the roof
of our cabin and looking sexy as hell. She had brought a bottle of stinking
oil that was supposed to keep you from getting sunburned and greased
her skin with it whenever she thought somebody was paying attention.
Since she had nothing on but the faded bottom of what had probably
started out as a bikini, her skin took a lot of greasing. When the sail and
the tiller could handle things on their own, I kept busy rubbing stinky oil
on her back and drying my hands on my face and ears.

With the sloop the man had let us have a couple of long bamboo poles
and a few hooks. Our bait was pretty various. Martya had supplied balls
of flour and rancid fat. I had added a can of chopped fish and a big can of
slimy little animals I suppose must have been newts. I trolled, putting my
pole in a socket and changing bait from time to time. Each fish we caught
delighted Martya. As for me, I was happy there were not more.

Lake Perilimna is big, irregular, and cold. Really long, too. Martya
told me the capital was at the other end. There are bays and inlets all over,
and islands covered with trees scattered around. They probably have names,
but Martya did not know them and I never learned them. When we had
sailed along the coast quite a ways, and had begun to sail back toward the
yellow bricks and church spires of Puraustays, I broke down and asked
Martya where Vlad's summer home had been.

She shook her head until her amber curls danced. "I have never hear of
this place. It is a tale to frighten children, I think."

"That man from the ministry of whatever it was seemed pretty serious
about it. He was warning us, and trying to do it without putting down his
own country."

"Then ask him! I do not know."

"If there's anything like that here, it will probably fill a whole chapter in my book. I can't just pass over a thing like that."

We were nearing an island bigger than most of them, and it was like what I said had broken a spell, or maybe cast one. I caught sight of battlements above the tops of a bunch of hemlocks, and I pointed and shouted.

Martya would not look. "What is this? You are not nice all today."

"A castle! There's a castle on that island."

"You will go there." It was not a question.

"Damn straight!"

"Also you will wish me to go with you, into another terrible place like your house."

"Not unless you want to," I told her. "You can wait here on the boat."

"Then you do not come. . . ." Martya's voice was so low I could scarcely hear her. "I will think he has fallen. Somewhere he lie with the broken legs. Perhaps he scream, or lie quiet with the strike of the head. I must come to help. I come, and we are seen no more."

I said, "I don't think it will be like that."

"It will not. I will cut the rope and go fast away. You will see. No! You will not see, because I wait until you are out of sight."

"Can you sail?"

"Yes! I am the fine sailor. I do not speak of this because I wish to sun myself."

I dropped the sail. "In that case you'll have an easy time of it. Only if you just let her drift, you'll go anyplace the wind takes you, and you could spend tonight out here on the lake. If you try to sail but don't know how, you'll probably capsize and drown."

She did not say a thing to that.

"An American boat would have life vests stowed somewhere. This one doesn't. I looked."

"I will not worry for you, and you have not to worry for me."

"Good here," I told her, and put the tiller over. Ten minutes later I had our little boat moored to a tree.

The edge of the wood was choked with brush. I pushed through it. As the hemlocks got bigger and the sunlight faded, the brush turned to ferns and moss. The wall of the castle (which I got to pretty soon) was damp

gray stone so dark it looked black, big stones only roughly squared but fitted together so well that the placing of each, trying one stone then another, must have taken twenty or thirty men I do not know how many
years of patient work. There were no windows, and no doors I could find.
I walked along the wall, hoping to find some kind of gate.

A stretch of fallen wall fixed that. Whether it had been undermined by
besiegers or just fallen because it was old, I had no way of telling. Which-
ever it was, the big stones had been laid low, and I climbed over them feeling like I ought to have had a sword and worn a knight-shirt of chain mail.

I thought I was going to see a courtyard, but there was none. Instead
I saw empty rooms that had been open to the wind and weather for five or
six hundred years. I got into one of the biggest and from it went into a
bunch of others, each one darker than the last. In there, pretty well lost in
the dark, a stair with high narrow steps went up to the next floor.

I went up and found another stair, one you could see only as a darker
area on an uneven floor that was already plenty dark. This one went down,
hundreds of worn, broken steps that got slippery with water if you went
down far enough. That was enough for me.

"Martya was right," I said out loud. "She'd hate this place." Echoes
were the only answer I got.

I had thought there was nobody on the island but me, but when I left I
found a man in black sitting on one of the tumbled stones as if he were
waiting for me. I spoke to him in German until I saw he did not understand it. He got up. I am tall, but he was a quite a bit taller than I am,
NBA tall. When he talked it was in a language that was not like Martya's,
one I could not even recognize. Pretty soon he saw I did not understand,
and so we talked with signs.

He came here to think, or it seemed to me that was what he said.
Maybe he meant he was mourning. His black clothes would have been
just right for a funeral. He knew the ruined castle well. He had been in
every part of it and would show me around, although a lot was dangerous.
(He pretended he was falling.)

The shadows had gotten long, and I was anxious to get away. I tried to
say that I had to go, that somebody was waiting for me, but that I hoped
to come back later to take pictures.

He said he would rather I not take his, and I promised I would not. I would only photograph the castle. That was what we said by signs, or at least I think it was.

The boat was still tied up where I had left it, which to tell you the truth did not surprise me a whole lot. I thanked Martya for not sailing away.

She sat up. "I could not find the knife. I looked and looked but you have take him with you. It was a bad place you went?"

"An old place," I said, "and I doubt that it had running water."

"When it rain." She giggled. "What you think of me? I am red a lot?"

"You are, and if I were you, I'd go into the cabin and put on your clothes."

"We go back? Go home?" She smiled.

"Yes, I think we'd better. We have six fish, but they won't live long with a string through their gills."

"First we go in here, where you tire me."

I shook my head. "We'd have to lie on the floor. Try me tomorrow morning."

"You mean!" She stuck her lip out.

"It's all this German," I said. "It has that effect on Americans. Now get ready to get mad, because I want to sail around the island before we go."

"What is use of this? We must go into wind. Such a boat cannot do this."

"We'll never sail straight into it," I told her. "Stay down off that roof and you'll see. If I can buy a decent camera here without breaking the bank, I want to take pictures of Vlad's castle. One I'll certainly want will be a picture of the whole island taken from a boat, with the castle showing as plainly as I can get it through those damn trees."

We made our circuit, during which I found two good angles from which to shoot the castle, and sailed away.

There is a lot more I could tell here, but it is pretty ordinary so I am going to skip it. After that I lived at Kleon's for a couple of weeks. He did not like that or me. Martya did, maybe too much. Eight or ten times we waited until he was asleep and went out to the clubs to dance and drink and listen to lousy rock. There are only three clubs in Puraustays, and I never did decide which one was the worst. They were all cheap. They all watered the drinks, and all of them would push you around, or try to, if you complained. Days she showed me around the city or I searched the Willows, and three or four times we went to the beach.

Kleon kept getting worse if you know what I mean. I think a big part of it was that nobody came to see if I was still at his house. Then one evening Martya and I were talking and I was watching her peel vegetables for supper when someone began rattling the front door. I told her I would get it, and I did. I had just long enough to recognize Kleon and see he was drunk before he knocked me down.

For a moment or two I must have been dazed. When I realized what was going on he was kicking me, kicking as hard as he could but not always effectively. Somehow I managed to roll away from the kicks and get back on my feet.

For a few seconds we fought—or to cut the crap, I tried to fight Kleon while Kleon fought me. Then I was down again, and Martya was clinging to Kleon and begging. I could tell from her tone that it was begging, and I thought she was begging him not to kick me again. She may really have been begging him to forgive her and swearing I had forced her mornings, which was when we made love. That is a pretty good bet.

Whatever it was she said, it worked. They went off together to their bedroom. I limped out the open door and down the little path to the street with no ideas beyond putting as much distance as I could between Kleon and me.

6

NIGHT, AND NIGHT'S DENIZENS

The expression of the first woman I passed in the street told me I ought to get my bruised and bleeding face out of sight. At first I could think of no place where I could hide but the Willows. When it finally occurred to me that I could go to a hospital, I began asking where I could find one. Most of the people I stopped could speak no German—or anyhow pretended they could speak none. One lady gave me directions that left me completely lost.

At last a kind old man directed me sensibly, warning me at least three times that the distance was long and the hospital might not take me. I set off anyway, thinking a lot about how any distance these people thought was a long walk was likely to be way too long for me.

I walked until I felt terribly tired, and I believe I would have been tired even if I had not been all set to fall over before I started out. Then I saw the cherry trees, fragrant ghosts towering through the twilight and still in full bloom though the bees had gone home to their hives. Beyond those trees, I knew, stood Volitain's house. Was Volitain a doctor? I could not remember, but he had sure acted like one when he had treated my stings.

It was all I could do to walk to his door and bang his knocker twice. After that I just listened, and it seemed to me I heard, barely (only barely) heard, somebody crying inside. Soon the crying stopped.

The door was thrown wide. Until that moment I suppose I thought Volitain's death's-head face could never look surprised. If I did, I had been wrong. His eyes flew wide and his jaw dropped. Then he took me by the arm and pulled me into his parlor. "Were you set upon by thieves?"

"By Kleon," I said.

"Ah! I see." Volitain chuckled. "And now you'll stay away, and Kleon will be shot. He will be shot, at least, if you confess your escape to the police. Will you do it?"

"No," I said. "I don't want that."

"Ah! You are afraid of him."

"Sure I am, but that's not the reason. His wife was cheating with me. We were pretty open about it. He had a right to get mad."

"You let him beat you."

"I didn't. I fought him, and I would've beaten him every bit as bad as he beat me if I could." I thought back to our fight and remembered things Martya and I had done before the fight and told Volitain, "I'm not going to claim it would have been right, but it's the truth."

"I see."

"Can I sit down? I'm tired."

"Certainly! Certainly! Here. This chair."

I sat and leaned back. The upholstery felt as soft as a pillow.

Volitain tapped my chest here and there. "Have you been spitting blood?"

"Sure. From my tongue. I guess I bit it during the fight."

"That's not uncommon. Does it hurt you to talk?"

"Not much. No."

"Good." Volitain straightened up. "I'll stop asking you questions for the moment. Your face is bruised and cut. He kick you, eh? He does not seem to break the facial bones."

"I tried to protect it."

"Naturally. We always do. I will provide the local anesthetic and clean the worst. I see nothing here that needs stitches."

When he had finished patching me up, he said, "I take it you do not go back tonight?"

I shook my head.

"Where will you sleep?"

"Here, if you'll let me."

"I will not. I help if I can, but you cannot sleep here. My decision I will not defend with argument. This house is mine, and I decide. You must sleep elsewhere. Where will you go?"

"To a hotel in that case."

"By this you sign a death warrant for Martya's husband. His name . . . ? I hear you say it."

"Kleon."

"Kleon will be shot. A moment ago you do not want that."

I was silent, trying to think.

"A foreigner without luggage, with a bandaged face? They will ask for payment in advance, most polite. You will provide it. As soon as they show the room, they telephone the police."

"I was told there were no telephones here—no telephones in Puraustays."

"There are but few, yet the better hotels have them and the police. If the hotel does not have the telephone, a boy will run with a note. The police will pound on your door and soon after Kleon dies. Somewhere else?"

"The Willows then."

"More reasonable—if you have the courage to sleep."

"I do," I said. The honest truth was that I felt I could sleep anywhere.

"That is very well. You are hungry?"

I shook my head. "I'm too tired to be hungry."

"You ate last when?"

"Lunch, I think it was."

"Thus you tire, my friend. Wait here."

I fell asleep as soon as he left the room.

When Volitain woke me, he had lit every lamp. The windows were dark, though no darker than the coffee he had made for us—strong coffee with sugar but no cream, and a plate of rolls still hot from the oven.

"Eat and drink," he said. "For you are two blankets and a pillow. We must carry them. It is not far."

"Nothing is far," I said, and got ignored. "Nothing but the hospital."

The rolls were dark and heavy. I smeared them with Volitain's dark yellow butter and found them delicious. He had baked a dozen perhaps, or a baker's dozen. He ate one. When we left, three were left on the plate.

He had brought a tin lantern like the one Martya and I had bought earlier, and he carried the blankets—they were rolled up tight—slung on his right shoulder and tied beside his left hip. I carried the pillow, which was big and awkward but weighed less than a shoe. A blister on my foot had broken. I was vaguely aware of it, and the pain in my ankles and the throbbing of both legs. "Vaguely" is what I wrote because I do not know a better word. All three seemed like something happening to somebody else a long, long way away.

My key turned easily in the lock I had oiled. "If you are wise," Volitain said, "it is here you sleep. If you go farther into the house you may be lost."

I agreed because agreement was simpler.

"I am going to take my lamp. This you see. I wish to leave it with you, but I myself have need of it."

He took off the blankets. I pulled them free of the string with which he had tied them, and together we spread them on the floor. I lay down on them and he pulled the free side over me. I think I was asleep before he had gone out the door.

I woke shivering, I suppose three or four hours later. There was a fire-place near the place where I lay, and I remembered that there had been fireplaces in the big room beyond it—also that Martya and I had bought matches and flashlights after our early lunch. Feeling certain there would be deadwood between the willows, I got a flashlight and went out.

The moon had risen, but its pale light was helpless among the crowding trees. Even so, I was able to collect a good deal of fallen wood, some of it dry and some pretty wet. Back inside I laid a fire. I had hoped that broken twigs and splintered wood would do for kindling. I wasted a bunch of matches before I gave up on that, took off my shoes, and lay down again. All that I can remember about that second sleep is that I had scary, horror-movie dreams that seemed terribly real. Now they are gone, which is fine with me. Sometimes I wish I could forget things that happened in that house later.

When I woke up the second time, a fire filled the big room with flick-ering shadows.

I sat up. Had I gotten the wood to burn after all? Scooting to get away from the heat, I stood up and stared. Leaping flames hissed, crackled, and exploded in sparks. Only a few sticks of wood were left. A long look at my watch said it was half past two in the morning.

Sleepy and scared, I turned away from the fire. The ghostly shapes all around the room were nothing worse than crummy old furniture under dirty white dustcovers. Then I remembered the mummy. She waited under one of those filthy sheets. Our ladders and tools lay all around like they were waiting to trip me. I picked up the flashlight I had used when I col-lected the wood, searching that big, ruined room for the eyes that seemed to reach out and touch me.

It was not until I turned back to the fire that I saw the man in black. He was sitting motionless in a nook not far from it and looked like he was thinking hard.

"You must have lit the fire," I said in German. "Thank you! I thank you very much!"

He looked up at the sound of my voice. When I finally remembered he did not understand German, I tried to show him how I felt by gestures.

He smiled, and the flames shone in his dark eyes.

"I wonder how you knew I was in here," I said. "If Martya were with us, she could ask for me. Then she could tell me what you said."

A blazing stick popped so loud I jumped. "Kleon beat me," I told the man in black. "He kicked me and threw me out of his house. If the police hear about it, they'll kill him." The popping of the fire had sounded about like a pistol shot.

The man in black watched me, his smooth, handsome face holding no expression at all. I was no longer sure that he did not know German.

"It isn't right for me to spend the night here. Not if it means Kleon gets killed." I paused, and when the man in black stayed quiet I added, "Kleon works very hard." I knew how dopey it sounded, but I could not come up with anything better.

I found my shoes. "Believe me, I really appreciate your getting the fire going, but I'm going back now. I've got to. Martya will let me in if I pound on the door long enough. Or maybe Kleon will. I wouldn't be surprised if he was glad to see me."

Tying my shoes took about half a minute. Folding Volitain's blankets and topping them with his pillow took maybe five. Even so, the fire had died down a lot by the time we left. I locked the door behind me and led the way down the path through the willows, guided by my flashlight. I remember wishing the man in black were ahead instead of behind me, even though he had seemed friendly at the castle and had done me a favor by lighting the fire. He scared the hell out of me, and I am not too proud to admit it.

When we reached the street, I hesitated. "I don't suppose you know the way to Kleon's? Or Martya's? She's the girl who was with me on the boat."

I was surprised and happy when he nodded and motioned for me to follow him. We made tracks for ten or fifteen minutes, then turned into what seemed like a forest.

A forest—only gravel crunched underneath my feet. The trees looked smaller than the willows, and they were more separated, letting in patches of moonlight here and there. Probably I should have switched on my flashlight, but it was really not necessary and I felt somehow that it would piss off the man in black.

When he got into a spot of moonlight, I saw something black that looked like a big dog trotting at his heels. It was joined by another dog just like it before I had taken eight or ten steps.

"Those are wolves," I said to myself. Then I realized that I had said it in English, so I said the same thing in German, but although the wolves looked back at me the man in black did not. As soon as we left the moonlight, another wolf came in behind the first two.

Pretty soon I heard twigs rattling and snapping to our right. Something there was running away from us, and the ears of the wolves went up. Then the man in black held out his arm like a general on a battlefield and all three were off like arrows from a bow. I expected yells and barks and lots of commotion, but there was just one scream, and it was not loud.

Half a minute after that, I heard a few soft snarls. And pretty soon the man in black and I stepped out of the trees and into a street.

We had not gone far when a black car with a silver shield on the door rolled to a stop ahead us. Looking out the front window, the driver motioned for me to come over.

I did. He spoke in his own language, and I explained in German that I did not understand it.

"You are foreign."

It was not a question, but I nodded.

"Show your passport."

"It was taken away from me by the police."

"I am the police. Why are you out so late?"

"By the border guards. I thought they were police—a kind of police. I'm the prisoner of a man named Kleon. He has to feed me in his house and let me sleep there."

I waited until the cop nodded.

"He beat me tonight." I handed the cop my flashlight. "Look at my face."

He did. "You have seen a doctor."

I nodded. "I left Kleon's house to find a doctor, and it took a long time. Most doctors will not see patients so late."

"That is so."

"I got lost. At last I found a doctor who bandaged my face. I got lost again, and by that time there was nobody in the street to direct me. Do you know the way to Kleon's house?"

The cop shook his head. It was about then, I believe, that I recognized the silent man who sat beside him as the third of the border guards who had arrested me, the one who looked like my father. I wanted to tell the cop he had my passport, but I knew that was going to make trouble, so I said, "Well, I have to get back to Kleon's house and sleep there. Otherwise you'll kill him—that's what I've been told."

"That is correct. You must sleep there. Who was the doctor who treated you?"

"What difference does that make?"

"I ask, you answer. What is his name?"

For half a second I went nuts trying to remember Volitain's last name. "Dr. Aeneaos."

The police car glided away.

"They didn't question you at all," I said to the man in black.

He gave me a smile, white teeth flashing under his black mustache.

We had not gone far when the police car came back. The cop waved me over the same as before, handed me my flashlight, and drove away again without saying a word.

The man in black had already set off. I hurried after him and asked whether we were near Kleon's. He pointed in reply.

I recognized nothing and felt sure we were a long way from it, but the man in black left the street when we had passed two or three more of the little blocks that held private houses and started up a narrow path.

After we detoured around a ruined chicken coop, we reached a door in a wall that looked white. The man in black stood aside and signed that I was to knock. I did, knocking softly at first, then harder. Pretty soon it was opened by Martya.

She stared. "Where have you been?"

"Let me in." I pushed past her and stepped into her kitchen.

"You . . ."

I grabbed the door to keep her from shutting it, and opened it wide. The man in black had gone.

"What it is?"

I switched on my flashlight and looked about for him. "There was a guy with me. I was going to ask him in."

"It is not your house!"

"Then I'll go away," I told her. "I can sleep in the park."

Her mouth opened and closed. With no lipstick it was not as pretty as I remembered.

"In the morning—and it's got to be almost morning—I'll go to the police. I'll tell them the truth, that your husband beat me and threw me out. Is that what you want?"

She hesitated before she shook her head.

"Then you'd better be really, really careful about what you say."

"You are hungry. You men are always angry when you are hungry. I will make you something. We have sausage, eggs, many good things."

"That I bought." I did not dare to sit down for fear I would never stand up. "I'm not hungry or angry. I'm too tired to think or talk. I'm going to bed."

There was no bar for my bedroom door, but I shut it, tried to move the dresser to block it, and hid my wallet, hanging my clothes on the chair in a special way I felt sure I would remember in the morning.

If I dreamed I cannot remember the dreams, only waking up and seeing sunlight at the window, getting up and using the chamber pot, and lying down again feeling absolutely sure that I would never get away from this crazy country, that I would die right here and be buried right here, too. In my imagination, or maybe in a dream, I remember seeing the little gray stone that would mark my grave, a stone cut with my name and after that a "d" and the date of my death.

Was it a real prophesy? I think maybe it was.

7

THE LEGION OF THE LIGHT

Martya shook me awake. "It is nearly noon! Get up!"

I blinked, called her a bitch under my breath, and sat up.

"Do not take my arm."

I had not tried to.

"You will wish to tire me."

"No." I shook my head.

"You must not. The beach yesterday? I am burn by the sun. It hurt me very much."

"I got kicked, mostly in the face. I guess that's painless compared to sunburn."

My irony went right over her head. "That is most good. This morning Kleon tire me very much. My back is most pain. I scream, I twist. He thinks he is big, big man because of this." She giggled.

"You won't have to let me screw you to laugh at me." I found my watch and put it on. It was eleven fifteen. Either my clothes had not been searched, or the searcher had been smart enough to replace all my things just as I had left them.

"There are"—she groped for a word—"boxes outside the front door. Three boxes such as are for travel with clothes. They were not there when Kleon go to his work, I think. He will move them, I think, if they are there. They are not mine or Kleon's."

I had never dressed faster. Both of my suitcases and my wonderful old camera bag were on the stoop. "This is great!" I told Martya. "I can take pictures of that ruined castle. Pictures of the Willows, too, and I'll have clean jeans, shirts, everything."

"You must not take my picture. I am too much red."

"I don't *want* to take your picture."

"You are mean." She pouted. "For this I do not make the breakfast for you."

"That's okay, I'll find a café when I'm hungry." The truth was that I was hungry already, but I was not about to admit it.

"You will take me with you?"

"Sure," I said, "if you want to come."

"But you do not like me."

"I like breakfast a lot," I told her. "Lunch for you, I guess." I had slung my camera bag on my shoulder and was picking up my suitcases. "If I put these in my room, will Kleon take them?"

"I do not think but I do not know."

After I had changed clothes, I put them under the bed, pushed far back. "If he does, there'll be more trouble."

She giggled. "He have win the first trouble, I think."

"So do I," I told her. "We'll have to see who wins the last one. That's the one that matters."

It was a new café, closer and maybe a little cheaper than the ones we had been to before. The coffee was not up to Vienna standards but not at all bad.

"You will take pictures of the Willows?"

I nodded. "Film and electronic. The first to use if I can, the second for backup."

"It will not be good, you show everything."

"I won't show everything in the book. What I decide to show will depend on the text, the stuff I'm going to write." Honesty made me add, "And my editor. Editors are pure hell."

"Many things are from hell," said a small man in black at the next table. A cartoonist I know would have made him a mouse. He had the bright eyes and the scared daredevil look, so a mouse with black clothes and a backward collar. "I've come to help you deal with them."

I just stared.

He stood up, picking up his plate and coffee cup. "I am Papa Zenon." He put his stuff on our table and pulled up a chair. "You were not at the Willows."

"You're right. I overslept."

"Many times. I was told I would find you there. It is a bad place? You have need of me, it seem."

"We have find someone," Martya told him. "We do not wish to be troubled."

His smile was almost a grin. "By those who dwell in hell or the authorities?"

"We do not wish to be troubled at all. She have show herself to me in a mirror and is dead. You know? Who wish trouble by those others you name? No one, I think."

The priest talked to me. "How long since . . . ?" He drew a finger across his throat.

"Years," I told him. "I don't know what killed her."

"Bones only?"

I shook my head. "Pretty much the whole body. The arms and legs and so on."

"If I lay her to rest," the priest said, "it must be in consecrated ground." Martya said, "This is what we wish, so she be at peace."

"We must have a coffin, also." The priest looked troubled. "She is large?"

"Small," I said. "A small woman, very thin."

"Yes. Speak more."

"I was just thinking that it may not be possible to straighten the body out without tearing it up. We haven't tried."

Martya said, "She is like so," and demonstrated, pulling her feet onto the seat of her chair and clasping her knees. "Only more than this. I cannot because I am . . ."

"More womanly," the priest suggested.

"Yes, yes! Like that, Papa."

"It will be a strange coffin. I do not know that I could obtain such a thing."

"I know!" Martya looked at me triumphantly. "We must use one of your clothes boxes." She turned back to the priest. "They are large, most strong. They do not let the water in, I think."

"They'd leak in wet dirt," I told her, "and I wouldn't give you one even if it didn't. Couldn't we buy a suitcase here?"

The priest nodded. "Of course. As for the rest, you must find a roll of waterproof plastic, and tape. We will wrap your luggage many times in this and seal him with the tape. I will bury her aboveground so she may remain more dry."

I must have looked dumb, because he smiled and said, "You shall see. Tonight?"

"Yes. Martya and I will buy a suitcase as soon as we leave here."

"Let us meet at the Willows tonight."

I nodded. "What time?"

"An hour after sunset. Do you fear the wolves?"

I shook my head.

"You are a brave man." He grinned. "I, also!" He rose and blessed us, and was out the door before I could thank him.

"He didn't pay," I told Martya. "I can pick up his bill, I suppose."

"You are a fool. He is a spy of the JAKA."

For a moment or two I tried to collect myself, sipping coffee and looking around at the shabby, cheerful room in which we sat—the mismatched chairs and the worn carpet, the yellowed hunting prints on the walls and the flowery cracked saucer that had held my cup. They told me (quietly and sadly, like old ladies who know they may never get up from mama's old chaise longue, never get out of the warm, friendly bed) that there had been aristocrats here once, with Strauss waltzes at the castle and commoners who pulled off their caps to the countess—commoners who had been happier and richer and one hell of a lot freer than their great-grandkids were here in the Democratic Republic. When I thought all that I never imagined that people would make a religion out of it, but I was about to find out.

"You did not know this?" Martya asked. "That he spy for the JAKA?"

I shook my head.

"The little man who come from the ministry send him. So he is a spy. He thinks you will know. I think the same. You gave him money."

I nodded. "A hundred dollars."

"So he must tell those who sit at desks that you are watched and all will be well. But you will know you are watched."

"And be *umsichtig*."

"I do not know that word, but yes."

"It was nice of him."

"For us, yes. For him better. And now?"

"Finish eating."

"We are almost finish. And then?"

"Buy a suitcase, the biggest we can find, and take pictures of the Willows."

That went well enough at first. Martya went with me and helped put the body in the suitcase we bought. I could have locked it—there was a little flat key that any kid could have replaced with a paperclip—but I left it unlocked, figuring that Papa Zenon might want to sprinkle the body with holy water or something.

After that I took pictures of Martya, mostly to show the scale of things. She was pretty small and made the rooms look humongous. There were five or six of her coming down the big staircase, and we even built a new fire in the fireplace where my fire had been the night before. Martya got it going with one of the candles we had bought for our lantern, something I wanted to kick myself for not thinking of. After I got the fireplace shots she said she was tired and went home. I stuck around, taking a few pictures here and a few more there. Most of them were in rooms I haven't talked about in this, and some were up on the second floor. There was a third floor, too, but I did not go up there.

The most interesting room I found was on the ground floor, anyway. It was the master bedroom. You could tell right off that it was the master bedroom even if it was not very big. For one thing, there was a great big bed right in the middle of it, a really high bed with a tester and a little two-step ladder so you could climb into it. For another thing, the ceiling was all one big picture painted right on the plaster, naked girls having a picnic in the woods. There were trees and wildflowers and all that, and a guy with horns like a goat's peeking out of the bushes to look at them. Some of the paint was gone and some of the plaster had fallen but I liked it anyway and when it was new it must really have been something, even if the girls were kind of fat.

There was a chest of drawers and a fireplace and some other stuff, but the big thing for me was that picture. I must have taken twenty shots of it, trying to get it right. It was hard to get all of it in, or even most of it, and it was hard to light even with the strobes. I had just gotten the best shot of all when I heard somebody tapping on the front door.

This is something I remember so well it hurts. I had been lying on the floor taking pictures, and I sat up and put my camera back in my camera bag, and shut it (turning the little catches), and got up and went to the door.

There were three guys standing around on the porch, one wearing a raincoat, one a big sweater, and one a long black wool vest over a T-shirt. Raincoat said, "Can we come in?"

It did not hit me right off that he had said it in German, and how did he know I did not understand much of the language here but I spoke German? I just said, "What do you want?"

"We want to talk to you. It would be more friendly, perhaps, if all of us could sit down. So we hope that you will ask us in."

I shook my head. There was something about them that made me edgy. "We can talk right here," I said.

"Then let us go to a café. A café will not be as private, but perhaps we can get a good table, yes? You will be our guest, to be sure."

I shook my head again. "What's this about?"

Wool vest edged past Raincoat. I thought he was going to explain something, but he just grabbed the front of my shirt and jerked me out of the house. It was probably Sweater who pulled the bag over my head.

Here is where I feel like I need to explain something. You may not give a shit, but I feel like it is important and I ought to put it in. This was where I learned how to hit people.

Maybe you think you know already, and maybe you do. Only I thought I knew before when I did not. I had fights in elementary school like we all do, and two or three in middle school and even one in high school. None after that until I tangled with Kleon. Some I won and some I lost, like with Kleon. Only I did not know what I was doing, I just thought I did.

When they pulled the bag over my head I started fighting for real. I had not been hitting anybody really hard up until then, not hitting them like I would drive a nail. Something about the bag made me do it. Sometimes I could hear somebody grunt when I hit him, and sometimes feel him stagger, only I did not pay any attention to it then, only after. Once I got the bag off my head for a minute. That was great, and it was when I learned not to hit the face. Faces are too hard and will hurt your hands. The body is good anywhere. The neck is best of all, and I do not think there was one of those three guys that I did not down at least once. I am not bragging. I really think I could say twice.

If there had been two of them, I think I might have beaten them. There were three, and three was too many. I was fighting like hell when I lost track of everything.

When I woke up my head ached so much I wished I had not. I was lying on my face, the floor rocked, my hands were behind me so I could not touch my head, and my feet were fastened together some way. In my whole life I had never felt so rotten as I did just then.

And afterward, for hours. I learned that my hands were not tied—they were in metal handcuffs. I felt them all over, but there was no way to get them off. When I turned over and sat up, I saw my feet were tied with rope. It was not just my head that made the floor rock, it was really doing it. Now and then I could hear footsteps, and once in a while voices. Only nobody came.

Finally somebody did. It was Raincoat, with the beady little eyes and big sharp nose, only he was not wearing the raincoat anymore, just baggy black pants and an old white shirt. There was a gun, not very big, in a black flap holster on his belt. He said, "Would you like some soup?"

I said, "I've got to piss."

He laughed. "A good excuse to get my handcuffs off it is."

"No, I've really got to go."

"Do you now?" There was a narrow bench fastened to the cabin's wall. He sat down on it.

I said, "I can hold it awhile, but not forever. It will come out and soak my pants and I'll stink. You won't like it."

"So we shoot you and throw you over the side."

That was a bluff and somehow I knew it. I shrugged. "I can't hold it forever. Nobody can."

"So I am to pull down your pants and hold your whistle for you."

I shook my head. "Take the handcuffs off and I'll do it myself."

"No." He turned away and yelled, "Croton!"

Croton was Sweater, I was pretty sure, only he had taken it off. There was a gun, a pretty big one, stuck in his pants. He went off and came back

with an old tin can. When we were done, he took it out. I suppose he
emptied it over the side.

"That was a lot." Raincoat was grinning.

"I told you."

"You would like the handcuffs gone. Your legs free also."

"Sure," I said.

"By your good conduct you may earn those things. Do you like this
country?"

Here was the prof's big question on the final exam, and I knew it. If
I could guess what he wanted to hear, I was in. If I fumbled it, I flunked.
Was he secret police or communist reactionary? Or just plain crook? I
could not decide, and in the end I decided the best way was just to be honest. That way I would not have a bunch of lies to keep straight.

So I told him, "I really like your country a lot, only not the clubs in
Puraustays and not your cops. They nabbed me as soon as I got here when
I hadn't done anything wrong, and they took my passport. If they would
give it back, I'd like them a whole lot better."

He nodded like he understood. "Are we well governed, you would say?"

I shrugged. "It's pretty bad in America, which is where I'm from, and—"

"It is because you are Amerikan that we have taken you."

"No shit?"

"Of this we may speak later. Are we well governed?"

I shook my head. "It's so bad in America that I want to say it's got to be
better everyplace else, only I've been around enough to know that's not
true. Every place I've been to, the people are generally pretty nice but the
government stinks. The clubs in France and Germany are pretty good,
and there's some terrific clubs in Austria, but the government stinks in all
of them, especially France."

Raincoat nodded hard. "They have not the Light of Stability."

"Yeah," I said, "that's it exactly."

"You are hungry, perhaps?"

"I'm not starved, but I could eat. I'd like some water, too."

"You shall have better. Soon I return."

Off he went, and I sat there feeling the rock of the boat and the tilt of
the deck and wondering. I knew I had been handed something when he
said the Light of Stability, only I did not know what it was or how to use

it. I thought that if I could find out what it meant I would figure out how to use it. That is the way I was thinking then, when my head hurt so much it was hard to think.

Finally he came back, carrying a tray. "You have not the seasickness. That is well."

"I've been seasick twice in my life," I told him, "only not very much."

He put down his tray in front of me and went around behind me. "If I unlock your hands you must do as you are told. This you understand, I hope."

I said, "Sure."

"Then I unlock so that you may eat. We have only the most small stove on this boat. One burner. But we do the better we can."

I said I would behave and I did, just feeling the big soft lump on my head before I pitched into the food. It was fried fish and fried potatoes mixed with onions, none of it too bad. There was wine, too, I think Tokay. I would rather have had Pepsi or even water, but I drank every drop.

"Our government does not believe in God," Raincoat said.

I nodded. "That's too bad."

"The churches believe, but all they teach is wrong. Would you be enlightened?"

I said, "Sure."

"God exists and is real, but he did not create us. We create him."

I told him I had not known that, and it sure was interesting.

"It is, and is true." Raincoat stood up. "There is another, higher universe above this one we inhabit. Call it the Universe of the Ideal. There God dwells. He grants our prayers at times because he must. The more of us who pray for something, the more he must grant whatever it is so many pray for."

"Like if everybody prays for peace?"

Raincoat had not heard me. "Thus all must pray for the Light of Stability. In change there is no progress. What is progress?"

I waited and he said, "Speak! You must tell me."

"When things get better."

"That is change. No! One prays for long hot summers so that she may lounge upon the beach, her sister for long cold winters so she may ski. Crops fail and fail again. The people starve."

"That's bad," I said.

"That is the progress for which you have wished." Raincoat turned away from me and stood looking out the porthole.

I drank a little sweet wine and waited.

"I have taken away from you my handcuffs."

"That's nice. I really appreciate it."

"You will seize my pistol. Shoot me in the back. Escape."

I had been thinking the same thing, only my legs were still tied. So I said he had been nice to me and the Light of Stability said it would be better to let him live.

"Exactly so. What is, is right. The enlightened will preserve it. The unenlightened destroy it, promising to bring into being something better, but to bring into being is more difficult than to destroy, and the somethings they bring better are always worse. Thus it is that we do not seek to overthrow the government, though the government seeks to overthrow us."

"If you don't want to overthrow the government," I said, "why would the government want to overthrow you? It would seem to me that it would just pat you on the head and tell you to go ahead and have some fun."

He turned to face me. "Ah! You do not understand governments."

"That's the flipping truth," I said. I said *flipping* because I had the feeling he was not the type that would overlook *fucking*.

"A government is not so many men behind desks," he told me. "A government is an idea. Without the idea . . ." He shrugged.

"Only you've got a different idea?"

"Exactly so."

"But you ought to preserve the government, right? I mean from what you said a minute ago."

"Which we seek to do. A government is an idea; if that idea is mistaken, it is a building built upon the water. Such a building may float for a time. You come to see him and are told, 'This is our foundation, a foundation so solid it can never fail. Islands wash away. Continents rise but sink again into the sea. But there has always been water and there will always be water. Here we stand!' The next day they are gone."

I said, "I got it."

"There was in the cellar a door that must not be opened, you see. Someone opened—the water rushed in. The communists sink while I watch. It was very quick. Very quiet, too."

"So you want to change government's idea."

Raincoat nodded. "We are the Legion of the Light. We will tow it to shore, you see, and because you are Amerikan you will help us."

"That's right," I said. It was not a lie the way I meant it.

From then on I was loose on the boat. Yes, I could have grabbed somebody's gun and maybe I could have killed all three of them, but what were the odds? I figured I had about one chance in fifty. And maybe I would not even be wounded. And maybe, just maybe, I could handle that big boat all by myself. But the sails generally took two men and during the thunder storms (we hit a couple of bad ones before we tied up at the capital) they took at least three. We had four because I pitched in, figuring that if we sunk I would drown, too.

8

THE CAPITAL

What they wanted was for me to make radio broadcasts. I told them it would not help and nobody in America would even listen, but they said it did not matter. What did was that the government would hear them and think it mattered. The government would tune in and have everything I said translated and study it, and in that way the idea of the Light of Stability would sink in.

When Raincoat told me that, I pointed out that he had a gun.

"It is a tool," he said. "To do good work, one must have tools."

That is the way it was with those people. On the one hand they did not like to destroy anything. On the other hand they were willing to destroy everything. The Light of Stability was really important to them, but winning was a lot more important. That was one way to put it.

I had taped two or three broadcasts for them when it hit me. None of them spoke English, but if the government had me translated like they said it would, the government had somebody who did. I was broadcasting from an old factory down by the river, and by that time I knew what had been made there. So in the middle of my next I said, "We here where so many women once sewed shirts are sewing the shroud that will wrap all those who oppose the Light of Stability. For them to perish is change, but having perished they will change no more. You in America who hear my words must think on this. Listen again."

After that I waited, wondering how long it would be and telling myself it might be an hour or even a couple of hours. It took me a long time to go to sleep that night, only when I woke up nothing had changed.

They had given me a book in English to read. It was called the *Code of Unchanging* and nothing in it made a whole lot of sense, but I had learned early on that the way to do it was to pick up phrases from it and drop them into my broadcasts. So I got them to give me a notebook and a ballpoint and wrote down some things I thought I might use. It would be interesting to know who had translated that book for them, but from the way it read I thought it had to be machine translation.

Like I said, it did not make much sense, but looking for good phrases gave me something to do, and having the pen and notebook I started making notes for this book.

One thing I came on straight off was the staircase. I had gone up it to take some pictures of the upstairs rooms, and Martya had climbed it so I could take pictures of her coming down. Only it had always seemed colder than the rest of the house—colder than it was outside, too.

Also it was too long. The first-floor rooms had really high ceilings. I think I have written about that before, and it is true. But that stairway seemed like it had too many steps. I wanted to get back to the Willows and count them, but I could not.

The next night I never got to sleep. They had given me a bed that had ARMY written all over it, a steel-frame bed with flat wire springs and a thin mattress. It was not as good as my bed at Kleon's had been, but a ton better than sleeping on deck, which I had done out on the lake. I undressed and washed up as well as I could, then put on my clothes—the jeans and cool shirt I had been so happy to take out of my suitcase—and lay down and pulled the thin cotton blanket they had given me over me. I was thinking of the big dining room at the Hotel Sacher and how nice it would be to eat there again when I heard shots.

I jumped up and ran to the door of my room. It was locked and there was wire over the windows, which would not open anyway. The door was old and I had always thought it probably was not as strong as it looked. I kicked it a couple of times, knowing that would bring Vest in if he was still out there. Nobody came, so I hit it three or four times with my shoulder and it flew open.

The first thing I saw was a cop with a gun. He fired, and right then I thought he had missed me. Later I found out he had not.

I turned and ran, only not back into the room where they had kept me locked up. I got out into a big, dark place where they must have had a couple of hundred sewing machines in the old days. It would have been a good place to hide in, only getting shot at like that had put a real scare into me and I just wanted to get away.

Which I did. The cops had the place surrounded, or thought they did, but I guess they had not seen the door I found. It opened on a stack of old steel drums like you might ship diesel in, with just room enough for me to wiggle between the drums and the wall. When I got out of there, I saw a couple of police cars with searchlights aimed at the building, and soldiers, too, holding the kind of rifles soldiers have.

You can guess what I did next. I got out of there as fast as I could, you know it! I had not gone far when I saw a poster. It was half torn off and somebody had spray painted a short word I could not read on what was left. But it was a picture of the third border guard wearing a suit. Part of the face was gone and there was some spray paint on the rest, but it was him. After that I saw at least two others, not painted and not torn. They did not seem important; still I wondered about them. You would have, too.

The city was mostly dark, but I got lucky and found the district where the bars and clubs and so forth were. They call it the Mousukos. (I found that out later.) There were a lot of places I would have liked to see, only I did not have any money.

Also I was bleeding just above my belt. It was not all that bad until my side started to stiffen up. The bullet had almost missed me clean, just not quite. After I found out I had been hit, looking around the Mousukos was not as much fun as it had been, and it had not been a whole lot of fun then. Pretty soon I was just looking for any workable place where I could hole up. There were streets that were no better than alleys, but they stunk and there were rats in them. If I had been in New York or even New Orleans—in LA or Chicago or someplace like that—I might have been able to find a car somebody had forgotten to lock. Then I would have crawled into the back and gone to sleep there, and anybody who found me would just think I had gone over my limit and chase me out. Only this was not New York or New Orleans either, or even Chicago or LA. Those people in the bars and clubs had walked to get there, or maybe ridden in one of the wagons with long benches that would take you downtown for a little change.

I kept looking, but after a while the crowd thinned out and it started to get light. So I went up to a guy who looked pretty decent and asked the way to the park. His German was not as good as mine, but it was better than a lot of people's and he told me.

There would be bushes in the park is what I thought, and I could hide in them and get some sleep. After I had rested up, I might be able to find something to eat. And after that I would start looking for the American embassy.

It seemed to me like a good plan, only I never even got started on it. A cop spotted the bloodstain on my shirt. When he found out I did not speak his language, he put cuffs on me, steel ones like Raincoat's, and marched me off to a police station. By then I was so tired I could not walk fast for more than three or four steps. Pretty soon I would start lagging and he would hit me with his club. Cops here in the U.S. call that a baton, only it is really a club and not anything anybody would conduct an orchestra with.

In a way it was good that we had to walk, because it gave me time to think. I decided the way to handle things was to pretend I did not understand German. Or French, either, although my French is really pretty good.

So when we got to the station, I would talk nothing but English. They tried German on me, and a couple of languages I could not identify, maybe Polish and Russian, or Romanian and Hungarian. They were all Greek to me, and Greek might be a pretty good guess, too. How about Greek and Turkish?

Then a guy came in and looked at my wound. He could have been a doctor, but my guess is he was an ambulance attendant or something. He gave me shots and probed it a little, then he sewed up both holes.

When he had finished they shoved me in a cell. There were two other guys there already and no bunks, but one guy was asleep anyway, just lying on the floor. Which is what I did. The other guy was sitting in a corner and looking deep blue. He did not try to talk to me, and I did not try to talk to him, not even English.

I went to sleep, and pretty fast.

When I woke up it was afternoon, I think. My wound hurt again because the shots had worn off, and I had to pee. A slop jar took care of the peeing, but nothing stopped my wound from hurting. It just kept on and after a while I sort of got used to it.

Then they marched me out and put me in a car and drove me to a big gray building that might have been a couple of miles outside the city. Pretty soon I was sitting in a real honest-to-God waiting room with beat-up chairs, and old magazines I could not read, and a cop to make sure I did not run. He put cuffs on me, too, but with my hands in front instead of in back. That was really nice of him, and I tried to show him I appreciated it.

After about an hour I was taken to a little meeting room, and there was a red-headed guy in there who smiled at me and said, "How about a cigarette? Want one?" He was maybe two years older than I was, and he said it in English.

I said no thanks and asked if he was American.

"Nope. I did my growing up in Saint Louis, though. Went to high school there and all that crap." He offered his hand. "Demetrios Bobokis— Butch Bobokis. How about some coffee?"

I shook and said I would love some, and something to eat if he could arrange for it. So he went to the door and talked to somebody out there, then came back and sat down. "It will be a while. Where you from?"

I said I had lived all over, which was the truth.

"Here?"

"No, that's why I came here. I'd never been here before and I wanted to see it. Listen, I'm not a spy or anything like that."

"You're a revolutionary." He grinned at me. "You were broadcasting for them, that crazy religion."

"They made me, and that's the absolute truth. I was under arrest in Puraustays. I was supposed to live with a guy there, and they were going to shoot him if I didn't. Only I could go out in the daytime and take pictures for the travel book I'm going to write about your country. I found this very big, run-down old house, the Willows. I wanted to take a lot of pictures there. There were painted ceilings and lots of other neat stuff, and it's supposed to be haunted."

"You get any pictures of ghosts?"

"No." After I said that I pulled up short to think. "You know, I really don't know. Sometimes ghosts will show up in a picture even if you didn't see them when you took it. I read a thing about that once, and I never had a chance to look at mine. Three guys knocked on the door, I opened it up to see what they wanted, and they grabbed me."

He nodded to that.

"They put me in a boat and took me across the lake—"

"Up the lake."

"Okay, up the lake to here. After that they held me in an old factory where they used to make shirts or dresses or something."

He nodded again. "Go on."

"They gave me a copy of their holy book that had been translated on somebody's computer. And they—"

"Wait a minute. Is English the only language you know?"

"Huh-uh. I know German and French pretty well. A little Japanese, too, only not very much."

"The report I got on you said that you only spoke English."

"Yeah." My mind was working so fast it damned near flew apart. "That's what I pretended, okay? Put yourself in my shoes. I'm from America and I'm in big trouble. Do I want to talk to somebody who knows German or somebody who knows English?"

He nodded, slowly this time. "I've got it. Was this with the Legion of the Light, too?"

"No. They knew I spoke German, because that's how I talked to them when I answered the door."

He got out a little notebook and made a note in it. "Okay, I want you to think about this and think hard. Did you ever hear any of them speak English? Just one word, maybe?"

I shook my head. "Absolutely not. Believe me, I'd have jumped all over him if anybody had."

"What they gave you was a computer translation? Did they say so?"

"No, it just read like one. What's so big about this?"

"It's my job to ask the questions. Your job is to answer them."

"All right, I'll take a stab at it. It seems like hardly anybody has computers here."

I waited for him, but he did not say a word.

"It's not like that in America. Suppose you were in America and somebody told you to go find a guy who owned a computer, it would take you about five minutes. Only not here. I've met quite a few of you, none of you seemed like you had a computer." As soon as I had said that, I got the feeling it was not quite true. I could have named one guy who might have had one, and I wanted to kick myself for not having braced him on it.

"Go on."

"So you can go looking for somebody who's got one and software to translate your language into English."

"Or German into English. We know they've got a German translation already, and we know who did that one."

"Want to tell me?"

"Hell, no. Or anyway, not yet. You were forced to broadcast for the Legion?"

"Right."

"Would you call them friends of yours?"

"No way!" I shook my head.

"Would you consider working for us? Coming over to our side?"

I did not say anything for a minute or two.

"Well? A straight answer."

"Okay. The straight answer is that I'd have to think about it. For one thing I came over to your side already. I wrote all the things I said in my broadcasts. Did you know that? I wrote my own scripts."

"I assumed it."

"They gave me the book, like I said, and they lectured me a lot about the Light of Stability. After that I wrote myself a script. I'd found out we were in an old factory, and there was a room there with a million kinds of buttons in wooden boxes, so they'd been making clothes. Probably a lot of different kinds. I put that in a broadcast and you guys came like I knew you would."

"We rescued you."

I raised my shoulders and let them drop. "I've been in jail, and I've seen enough of this building to tell it's a prison. If you want more, one of the cops I tipped off shot me. Want to see the place?"

He waved that one away. "I'll get our doctor to take a look at it. What else can I do for you?"

"You can let me talk to somebody at the American embassy."

"If I can." He sounded tired. "I can let them know you're here, and I will. They probably won't come."

"Why not?"

"Ask them. I don't know. If you'll work with us, you won't be in prison. That's a promise."

"What if I quit?"

"Get real! What do you think?"

There was more, but I do not want to write it and you would not want to read it. We talked about America and the European Union, and he did not know as much as I wanted him to, and I did not know as much as he wanted me to. So after a while a guard—not the cop I had before—came and took me to a cell.

It was not as bad as I expected, which was something Butch had promised over Danish and coffee, a nice cell. There were two bunks in it, but no other prisoner. Right away I figured there would be somebody shoved in with me pretty soon, and he would be a plant.

Do you want more? There was a little window with wire over it, low enough for me to look through. That was bad in winter until they put a cover over it, but when I got there the nights were pretty warm and it was not bad at all. There was a toilet and a washbowl, too. There was no hot water, but I used my hands and my shirttail for a washrag and cleaned up as well as I could, telling myself that if I ever saw Butch Bobokis again I would ask him for soap.

The bunk was better than the one in the old factory, and the blanket was wool. I was more than ready for both of them.

I slept all night and half the morning. Probably they had called the prisoners for breakfast, but I slept right through it. When I sat up, there was a big guy in my cell sitting on the other bunk and looking at me. So I told him, "Good morning," in German.

He said, "I don't suppose you understand English?" It was in English, and you could tell he had about given up hope by the sound of his voice.

I said, "Sure I do. Where you from?"

"Cincinnati. We call it the Queen City." He sighed. "And I wish to God I was back there."

We talked some more, and I found out that his name was Russ Rathaus and he was sixty-three. He looked quite a bit younger than that to me, maybe fifty or fifty-five tops.

"I had a neat little novelty business," he said. "We made voodoo dolls and sold them all over the country. I don't mean we dealt with customers direct. We wholesaled them to novelty shops, the kind of stores where they sell souvenirs and plates with the presidents on them. All that junk. My partner invented the process, and I bankrolled him, running the business out of my garage at first. You looked at me funny when I said voodoo dolls. I guess anybody would."

I said I thought you had to make those yourself.

"Hey, it doesn't work, so who cares? The thing was the faces, see? Suppose you've got it in for the mayor. You ask around for a doll with the mayor's face, only nobody's got one because they'd have to have a contract with him and pay a royalty, and all that crap. Then you hear about our Imprinting Dolls. That was what we called them, Imprinting Dolls. You look at the dolls and the clerk explains how everything works. So you buy the complete kit. That will run you thirty-two ninety-nine to about forty-four ninety-five, depending on where you buy it. For your money you get one doll—male or female, your choice—an imprinting lens, about a hundred of our special pins, and our special book of spells and instructions. That's everything you need except a picture of the mayor and a strong light source. The doll works sort of like film used to. You remember film cameras?"

I told him I did, and I even owned a few.

"Then you'll understand a lot better than most people. Well, the book shows you how you set up your Imprinting Doll and the imprinting lens, and the guy's picture and the light. You set 'em up and leave them like that for six or seven hours. How long depends on how good the picture is and how strong your light is—how many lumens. When the time's up you've got a voodoo doll with the mayor's face, see? If he's got fat cheeks, the cheeks swell. And the eyes are his eyes, just like in the picture you used. It was neat and people loved it."

I said he must have sold a bunch of them.

"You bet we did. We were selling to shops all over the country, and getting orders from overseas. Suppose you had it in for somebody else, too. Let's say there was this lousy actor and you hated him and everything he'd ever been in, see? So you decided to get another doll. Well, this time you didn't have to buy a whole kit. You already had the lens and the book, and a bunch of pins. All you needed was another doll and you were set. The same place that sold you your kit would sell you a new doll for nineteen ninety-nine, if you were lucky. Twenty-nine ninety-five in most outlets. Actors will sell anybody a nice big glossy for ten or fifteen bucks—get one and you're set. Only if you're smart, you'll cut a picture out of a magazine."

"I've got it," I told him. "You must have made quite a bit of money."

"We did." For a minute he smiled. "We made quite a pile, and the big doll manufacturers were all after us to sell out. Finally we did. I handled the negotiations, and got us quite a bit more than the company was worth. Pete actually ended up with more than I did, because he'd held on to fifty-five percent of the patent. But I got quite a bit, and we get royalties, too. Two bucks on every doll they make doesn't sound like much, but it adds up."

"They must make thousands of them," I said.

"Hundreds of thousands, and a hundred thousand dolls is two hundred thousand bucks. So I get my cut of that, and I got half the money from our company. Only I don't have it here."

"Yeah. I know how that is."

"Damn these bastards anyway!"

I waited.

"Rosalee and I had decided we'd tour Europe, see? We started in Germany because my folks were German way back. We bought a nice Mercedes there. I figured we'd drive it around Europe for a couple of years, sell it, and go home. We went to Austria next, then east and south."

"They don't get a lot of tourists here," I said.

"We didn't think we were tourists." Russ looked a little mad and a lot sad. "Tourists go around and look at certain things, old churches and all that junk, and never see the country. We called ourselves travelers, and that's what we felt like." He took a big breath and let it out.

"So you came here."

"No. Not really. Rosalee'd had an aunt, her aunt Lilly. Aunt Lilly'd married some guy from Europe, but he got hurt on the job and had to quit work. He was disabled, see, and couldn't work. But he got disability benefits. He'd get those for the rest of his life."

"Sure," I said.

"He'd get them anywhere he lived. The government would mail him a check or just stick the money in his account if that was what he wanted. So he told Aunt Lilly that this was a nice place and they could live here cheap. With the money he'd be getting they'd be rich here, okay?"

"Right."

"So off they went, only the family never heard a thing after that. Lilly didn't write letters or anything, or if she did, they didn't get through. So Rosalee wanted to find out what had happened to her. We'd come here and look in phone books and like that, and ask around a little. I thought sure somebody at our embassy would know about her."

I said, "You could have written to them from the States."

"We did. Or Rosalee did, anyhow. Only she never heard back. We figured the mail here was lousy and maybe somebody at the embassy had written, except we never got it."

"Diplomatic mail goes special," I told him.

"No shit? Well maybe nobody ever got Rosalee's letter." Russ's voice, which had been pretty loud, went soft. "Rosalee's not the sharpest knife in the drawer, anyway. Know what I mean?"

"Sure. I've dated a couple of those."

"That's your private life." Russ had been sitting on his bunk. He stood up when he said it and went over to the window. "I don't want to stick my nose into that. That's not my way."

I said I had nothing to hide, which was the truth.

He turned around to look at me. "Damned nice of you, but everybody's got something to hide."

"Not me. I'll level with you, and here's a question. Will you level with me?"

"About everything? Hell, no. But you probably won't ask about that stuff. It was a long time ago, see? So you can ask me anything you want to. If I have to lie, I'll lie. But I won't get my back up."

"Swell, I will. Do you speak any languages besides English?"

"A little German I picked up in Germany and Austria."

"Anything else?"

He shook his head.

After that I asked him two or three questions in German, but he did not understand any of them, or said he did not. It was a long time before I found out how good his German really was.

I switched back to English. "Who'd you talk to before they put you in here with me?"

"All the names?"

"If you can, sure."

"Mostly they don't give you their last names, and I'm not sure I remember them right. They probably didn't give me their real names anyway."

"Okay," I said, "but try."

"The first one was a young guy who kept playing with his gun. At first I thought he was just a jerk, later I could see he was trying to make me nervous. Hell, I was nervous as a cat already. They'd separated us. Did I tell you that? About Rosalee?"

He had not and I said so.

"Well, they arrested her, too. They didn't say what for. They just marched her away. That was the last time I saw her, and I keep thinking I may never see her anymore. Will I? What do you think?"

"You want a guess?"

He nodded. "An honest guess. Sure I do."

"Okay. I think they've released her already and she's gone back to Austria or Germany, and she's trying to find out what happened to you. She doesn't know whether they've still got you, or what. If you get out of here, you'll see her again, but if you don't you won't."

"I hope it's really that good," Russ said.

"I was just guessing," I told him, "but that's what I think. They're probably not as tough on women as they are on men. Do they think you're a spy or something?"

"Maybe. I don't know."

"Same here," I said.

And he said, "Well, are you?"

So that was Russ Rathaus, my cellmate. We got to be pretty good friends. I had never been in a prison before, but here is the way I figured it. You are going to have to spend a lot of time with the guy you are locked up with, and if you are not friends that is going to be pure hell. He was a lot older than I am and got a little patronizing sometimes. But I put up with it and I have to say I learned a good deal about business just listening to him. It was something I had never known a lot about or cared much about, either. Only after I had heard him talk a couple of times I realized that it was something I ought to know more about. Every time you buy a hamburger or a car you are dealing with somebody's business, and business is not like government. It is more like poker.

Another thing I learned from Russ was the language. He had been locked up for over a year and had learned a lot more of it than I had. He coached me as well as he could and sometimes he got other prisoners to coach me a little, too.

I have already told you most of the important things about Russ, but there are others. One was the spells. He got to talking about the spells in his voodoo book, and being a writer myself I asked him who wrote them. That shut him up hard and right away, and he would not even say why he did not want to talk about it.

Another thing was that when they pulled me out of our cell to talk to me, they always asked about him. He said he had been questioned by five different guys at one time or another, but then they had had him a hell of a lot longer. For me it was just two. Butch was the good cop and Aegis was the bad cop. You probably know what I mean.

Butch would offer his cigarettes and give me coffee and see that I got little stuff I wanted, like soap. Aegis would knock me around and yell. I tried to fight him a couple times, but he was bigger and stronger than I am, and a better fighter, too. I suppose he could have yelled for help if he had needed it, but he never did. Both of them always asked me about Russ, and after a while I noticed that.

Reading over all the stuff about him that I have just written, I see that I have never mentioned anything about Russ's smoking. That is mostly because he did not have any cigarettes when I first met him. He would bitch about it now and then, but I never paid a lot of attention to that. After we had been in that prison for almost a year, I asked him whether Butch did not offer him a cigarette sometimes and if he took it. And he said yeah he did, but he could not keep it. He had to smoke it right there.

That gave me an idea. The next time Butch offered me a cigarette I took it and explained that it was not for me, I was going to take it back and give it to Russ. Russ was always wanting to smoke, I said, which was pretty much the truth.

"You'll need matches," Butch told me. "I can give you some, but if you set fire to your mattress or any dumb shit like that, I'll get in trouble."

I said I would not do anything like that, and I would light Russ's cigarette for him and not let him touch the matches.

"Oh, that's okay. Russ will behave. How about a drink?"

I said I would love one but could I have the matches first?

He gave me a folder of matches after that. It was pretty beat up and did
not advertise anything. It just had the name of the match company on it,
and a price. I had bought big wooden matches back in Puraustays and
they had been the same way. I have probably told you about them. There
were only three matches left in the folder I got from Butch.

When a screw took me back to my cell, I gave the cigarette and the
matches to Russ. His eyes sort of lit up, you probably know what I mean,
and he thanked me. I asked if he was not going to smoke it, and he said
no, he was going to save it awhile, a few hours at least, and get used to the
idea that he had it and could smoke it anytime he wanted to.

After that I went to bed. I am not sure what time I woke up, but midnight would probably be about right. It was the smell of smoke that woke
me. It was sort of like the smell of cigarette smoke, but there was other
stuff, a lot rougher stuff, in there, too. I opened my eyes and turned my
head, and there was Russ sitting cross-legged on the floor with a tiny little
fire in front of him.

He was not looking at me, and he was not looking at his fire either. He
was looking up at the window. I watched him for a while and listened to
him murmuring to himself in some language that was not English, French,
or German, or even Japanese. It was not the way they talked where we
were, either. Something else.

Then his fire went out. He blew on it and got it to burning again for a
couple of minutes, but he quit praying or whatever it was he had been doing.

The fire went out again and he blew some more, but this time he could
not bring it back to life. So he cleaned it up and got into bed, and I was
about ready to go back to sleep when somebody came into our cell without
opening the door. Here I want to say that I knew him right off, and I should
have. But it would be a lie. I did not, and he was standing in the corner with
his pale face really plain and his black clothes just about invisible before I
recognized him. Russ's little fire had gone out and its ashes had been dropped
into our slop jar, and the big stone fireplace at the Willows was miles and
miles away, but fire from somewhere was still reflected in his eyes.

9

FREE ALMOST

When I woke up next it was still really early, but the man in black had gone. Or anyhow, that was how it looked. I sat up and put on my shoes and more clothes, and went to the window to look out. The sky was gray, but the sun was not up. You probably know that time. I knew I would be able to see it out of that window when it rose, and it was not there.

Then it came to me that he was like the sun. He was still there, I just could not see him. I tried to remember whether he had said anything to me and whether I had said anything to him. We had not talked at all. I had looked at him and sort of smiled, meaning I am glad to see you. He had not smiled. (His eyes never did smile, even when his mouth did.) But he had nodded just the tiniest bit, meaning I am glad to see you, too. You know how you do.

Of course I remembered pretty soon that the next time I was questioned they would ask about Russ, but that was an easy one. I had been asleep and had not seen a thing. I had given him the cigarette and the matches, and I was pretty sure he must have smoked the cigarette by this time.

So that was a piece of cake. The big question was whether Russ had seen the man in black, too. I did not know and did not want to ask because I would not have trusted the answer either way. If he had, there was a good strong chance he would say he had not. If he had not, there was an even stronger chance that he would say he had so as to try to find out what the heck I was talking about.

Okay, that was the big question and there was no way I was going to learn anything by quizzing Russ. If I kept my eyes and ears open I might find out something. Or not.

The little question was whether what Russ had done with his fire and the cigarette, plus whatever it was he had been saying, had fetched the man in black. It seemed pretty clear that the answer was yes, and after that I got to wondering about those voodoo dolls. Had they worked? Any of them? Most people probably had not tried the spells, and most of those who had, had not done them right. But were the spells any good? There was no way of telling.

I was still thinking about all that, about the dolls especially, when the screw came up the corridor unlocking cells so the guys could go to breakfast. Russ was still in his bunk, so I said, "Hey, breakfast!" He did not move, so I let him sleep. When I got back from breakfast, his bunk was empty. I figured somebody had decided he was on a hunger strike or something and he was getting slapped around.

Later on a screw and a cop came for me. The cop made me put my hands behind me the way they do and snapped cuffs on me. Then they marched me down to Butch and Aegis in one of the interrogation rooms in the basement. It was the first time I had seen the two of them together.

(So much for my idea that they were the same guy with different clothes and so forth. I had never really been serious about that one anyhow.)

Butch looked worried, something I had never seen before, and Aegis looked mad, something I had seen a lot of. Aegis said, "Do we make him stand or let him sit?"

"We let him sit," Butch said, "if he has something to tell us. If he doesn't, he stands."

"That is good. It hurts more when they fall down."

They were talking in their own language, but by that time I had picked up enough of it to have a pretty good idea of what they were saying.

Butch switched to English. "Where is your cellmate?"

"I don't know," I told him. "He was asleep in his bunk when I went down to breakfast. When I came back he was gone."

Butch told Aegis what I had said, although I was not sure he had to. From now on I will not mention that much.

In German, Aegis said, "He was not asleep in his bed at breakfast."

I sort of shrugged and said he was a lot smarter than I was.

"You don't know where he is now?" That was Butch.

I said I did not, which was the truth.

"You saw Rathaus lying in his bunk this morning?"

I said sure.

"You didn't. If you don't believe that, I think I can prove it to you."

"Of course I believe you. Not to change the subject, but I notice I'm still not sitting down."

Aegis laughed.

Butch said, "You don't believe us because you feel certain you saw Rathaus."

I said, "No, I believe you. I made a mistake, that's all."

"Let me show you what you saw," Butch said. He left, but he was only gone for a minute or two. When he came back he was dragging something that looked so much like Russ that for a second I thought it must be Russ's body. He held it up, then sat it down on the floor with its back propped by a table leg.

That was when the truth jumped up and smacked me in the face like a rake handle. It was a big doll—just a big doll!

Pretty soon I was sitting down and telling them all about Russ's business in the States. Butch bought my story, but Aegis did not. He wanted to send a letter by courier to the U.S. embassy, asking them if there were such dolls and requesting a dozen or so.

Butch said, "In a year we get them—or perhaps we don't. Listen to me. If an artist make this there is something inside in which he has cut the face. Rubber it might be, or synthetic. If it is as he says, this is something else. Let us open it and see."

Aegis agreed, and they slit the side of the doll's face with a pocketknife. Granules poured out, little multicolored spheres no bigger than coarse sand. As they did, Russ's face vanished. All that was left was a doll with a blank face.

They sent me away after that, and I suppose they must have reported what they had learned from me to somebody higher up.

Three days, or maybe four, went by without anything happening. One day I did factory work, which Russ and I had been doing off and on all year. Mostly I just sat in my cell staring at the wall. When the door was unlocked for meals, I went out and ate with the other prisoners. There was supposed to be no talking, but we whispered. Once they let us go outside for exercise, and I went out into the yard and met a couple of other Americans. Both of them had been in longer than I had, and neither of them had known I was in, too. Once I was taken down to the shower. The screw was surprised that I had soap but did not take it away from me.

Then a couple of screws came for me. One told me to take anything I wanted to keep, because he did not think I was coming back. So I got my soap and a few other things Butch had given me.

I had thought we would be going someplace in the prison, but we did not. It was outside and into a big green car that looked like it was at least ten years old but seemed to be in good shape. Probably I should explain that we were handcuffed together, me to a screw on each side. I knew which one had the keys and which pocket he had put them in. I had been careful to notice all that, but it did not do me a bit of good.

We drove into the city, which was a lot bigger than Puraustays. I have probably said that already somewhere in here, but it will stand saying again. When we had driven through as much city as Puraustays, we were not past the suburbs yet.

Every once in a while our driver said something. He was not talking to me or to the screws on each side of me. They were talking about what they were going to do tonight, because by the time I got out they would be off work and have the next two days off. One was going to get drunk and the other one was going to play some game. I think it was probably billiards, but I could not be sure. Whatever it was, he said he was going to play it tonight and tomorrow night and maybe Sunday night, too, and win a lot of money.

After I had listened awhile I got the idea that our driver was talking to somebody sitting next to him who was too short for his head to show over the back of the seat. Either that, or he was invisible. Or most likely of all, our driver was nuts and there was really nobody there.

But thinking "Nuts!" reminded me that there were those nut trees all around Martya's house. They had nut trees because the neighbors were not scared enough of Kleon to let his fruit alone, but they did not bother with the nuts. Or at least not much. But Martya and I had made out, and that was kind of nice to think about. Four times for sure were all I could remember, which did not seem like enough. It ought to have been five or six. There ought to have been one time on the boat, or else on the island where the ruined castle was. And maybe one time in the Willows. I kept telling myself that someday I would go back and make both those come true.

Then the green car stopped and we got out and went into a building that looked like an old warehouse—old but not abandoned. An old warehouse that somebody was still using. Our driver stayed with his car, and the two screws and I got out (which was clumsy because we were cuffed together) and went up to the door. There was a phone there in a steel box. I think it was the first phone I had seen since coming to the country. One of the screws picked it up and talked, keeping his voice too low for me to hear what he was saying.

What I could hear was the door unlocking. The other screw pushed it open and we went in. It was dark inside and not like a warehouse. There was a long passage with only two or three doors along it. Those doors had mirrors in them instead of glass. At the end of it was a steel booth with a machine gun poking out of it. When we got close to that, the gunner said, "Keep going."

We turned left and went down another hall to the biggest, fanciest elevator I have ever seen. It was maybe twelve feet square, and there were screens and keyboards in it, with nice chairs in front of them and a padded bench in the middle. None of us sat down, and I noticed that the elevator was pretty slow and clanked.

We got out on what was probably the top floor of the old building. The hall there was a lot nicer. Scarier, too, for me. That hall had thick carpets, and good tables and really nice leather-upholstered armchairs off to the sides. Everything said: *The people up here have real power, the no-shit kind that pays no attention to the law or anything else. If they say you die, you die.* There were no pictures on the walls that I could see, just framed seashells and bones. One was the front of a skull.

One of the doors opened and a woman came out. I got to know her really well, so I might as well describe her here for you. She was not bad looking if you did not mind a hard face, and her hair always looked dark under lights. When I saw her out in the sunlight it was really a tawny red. In there you might have thought it was black. She was quite a bit older than I was but I was never sure how much. Her eyes were hazel and her name was Naala.

She stopped the screws and told them to take the cuffs off me. They did not like that but they did it. "You do not speak this tongue?" she asked me.

"Not well," I said. "Just a little bit."

"That is good." She gave me a hard smile. "They fear you will run. Will you?"

I shook my head. "They'd catch me while I was waiting for the elevator."

It made her laugh. "You are wise, too. We shall get on well, I know. Come with me."

I followed her into a big room with a lot of windows. It was a relief to look out of them after what I had seen of that building already, even if they did not show much except a lot of roofs and chimneys, and the night sky.

There was a table in the middle, a table not nearly as big as the room. It had six chairs, but there were only two men sitting at it, both middle-aged, well dressed, and tough looking. The bald one was at the end of the table. Naala motioned to a chair and we sat down.

Hair said, "What do you think of him?"

Naala opened her purse and got out a gold pen. There was a tablet at her place already. "We could not ask for better."

"You rush to judgment."

"As you asked."

Hair grinned. "Tell me why."

"For many reasons. One, he thinks of himself." She was writing as she talked. "Two, he is of Amerika, like this Rathaus. Three, he know him. They are in the same cell. Four, Rathaus know this man. He may trust him more than us. Is that enough? I have more."

Baldy said, "That is enough. Will he escape, too? You cannot know, Naala, but what do you think and why do you think it?"

"I can know, as you do not say. He will not, and that is number five. He may try. Is it that which you intend? It will depend on his treatment and his hopes."

She turned to me. "You wish to return to Amerika?"

I said, "First I'd like to get my passport back."

She nodded.

"Second, I'd like to collect enough information and take enough pictures for a book about your beautiful country. When I have those—they're what I came here for—I'll want to go back, yes."

Baldy grunted. It did not tell me whether he had liked my answer.

Hair said, "We were given to understand that you did not speak as we do."

"I don't," I said, "or not very well."

Naala gave me the hard smile. "You learn in prison?"

"In prison and in Puraustays, and while I broadcast for the Legion of the Light. Was it the Legion who got Russ out? Is that what you think?"

Hair said, "Would not they have taken you and left him? So I think."

I said, "You're right."

"Thus you will not escape," Naala told me. "Rathaus has friends here, you see? He believe they get him back to Amerika and they may try. I do not know. You, having no friends, might slip away from us and wander the streets." She pointed to the door. "Do you wish it? Go! Not one here will shoot you."

"In prison clothes," I said.

"You will get others. You will steal them. Or you will steal money and so buy them."

I shook my head, and she turned to Baldy.

"You see? He helps us, and we let him go free. Let him write this book as he wishes. He is a sensible young man."

Hair grumbled, "He speaks like a child."

"Like a little child he speaks a foreign tongue he has learned by listening. Soon he speaks better."

"I do not mean a foreign—," Hair began.

Baldy moved his hand a quarter of an inch or so, and that was enough.

"If he runs, it looks bad for me," Naala told him. "It must be thus. I want him even so."

There was more after that, but I have given you the main things and tried to quote all four of us as accurately as I could. Maybe this is the place to explain. I had taken notes, and I find that even when something happens to them later having written them down fixes them in my mind. So it is good to take notes, and when they get lost I have not lost the information, usually. Maybe you will doubt me when I say that, but there was one time when my notes were lost for a while then found again. There was not one thing in them that I had not remembered.

All right, Naala and I left together and walked maybe a mile to her apartment building. The shops and offices were all closed or looked like they were, and that was not where the bars and clubs were, so it was pretty quiet. I saw a couple of posters like the ones I described when I told about getting clear of the Legion of the Light, but I do not think I asked Naala about them.

In general, we did not talk much on that walk. I remember I said that we were likely to get busted because of my prison clothes.

She said, "Do not be concerned. They will not take you while you are with me. Tomorrow we get new clothing for you. I know a shop and I have good taste."

I said, "I do, too. Or anyway, I think I have."

"Men never do. Women sometimes, but not much."

There was no elevator in her building, but that did not matter because she had a first-floor apartment. "You will like it," she promised me. "It is nice, no?"

Of course I said it was. It was just three rooms and a bath, but all the rooms were big. The biggest room was a corner room with a lot of windows, maybe four feet above the ground. The kitchen was in one corner—a stove, a sink, and a little fridge. There was a desk in an alcove, too, with a telephone on the desk. I saw the telephone and thought, wow! But I did not say anything then. It was a spinning dial phone, something I had read about somewhere but never seen.

My bedroom was not as big as Naala's, but it was still pretty big—a lot bigger than the cell I had shared with Russ Rathaus. There was a bed big enough to sleep two, a dresser, two bureaus, and two chairs. You could tell Naala was proud of everything. She pointed out all the pieces and told me all the drawers were empty, which I found out later was not quite true.

"It is better you keep the blind down, at night most particularly. If the window is light, people in the street see through the trees."

I had already figured that out.

"They see through, or it may be they come to spy. When the sun come up, the blind may rise also. Then you have the light. You are hungry?"

"I'm too tired to be hungry," I told her. "I'd just like a shower. Then I'll go to bed, if that's all right."

"With me, you think." She laughed.

I said no.

"For me you will be clean and smell sweet. This I appreciate, but you must sleep here."

I said I would.

"If you come for me in the night, you will be hurt." She had turned serious. "You may be killed, though I hope not. Do not tell others you were never warned."

I said I would stay in my room unless I had to use the toilet.

"Still you wish a bath?"

I said I did.

"You may have one, but this you must do for me. Leave the uniform of correction on the floor beside my bathtub. You may take your shoes. Your stockings also."

I said that was fine.

And that was what I did, wrapping a towel around me to make a kilt when I went back to my bedroom. I could hear Naala talking on the phone in the big room, but I could not tell what she said. She listened more than she talked, or that is how it seemed to me.

My new bed was a lot bigger than my bunk in the prison had been, and a lot cleaner, too. I got in bed and covered up, and for a little while I thought about the man in black and Russ Rathaus. Like, suppose we found Russ. Would the man in black be mad at us? And did I really want to help Naala find him? Stuff like that.

She thought I was just a kid. I knew that, and maybe she was right in certain ways. But I knew she was with the secret police, the JAKA. That warehouse the screws had taken me to was probably JAKA headquarters here in the capital, and Baldy and Hair had been pretty far up in the organization, especially Baldy.

So thinking about that I could see they were not as interested in Russ Rathaus as they thought they were. What they were really interested in was the people they thought had helped Russ escape.

Well, would the man in black be mad at me? I kept coming back to that as I got sleepier and sleepier. Why had he helped Russ, and where was Russ now? Would he be seriously pissed at me . . . ?

About then I fell asleep and had a dream that has stayed with me better than a lot of things that really happened. Maybe I should not tell it but maybe telling it, writing it down for you to read, will help me get away from it a little bit.

In my dream I was back at the ruined castle, although it was in better shape in my dream than it really was. I was tied or chained to a wall or something. I could not move. The man in black was in front of me, driving a stake into the ground by hitting it with the back of an axe. At first he tapped it to get it started. When it was started he took his axe in both hands and really slammed it, driving it deep in. Then he turned his axe around so as to hit it with the sharp edge of the blade. Just two or three strokes, and he had cut a point on it. I remember thinking I could not have done that, and I know that is right. I could not have. If I practiced a lot I could learn to do it, probably. But it would take a lot of practice.

He went away then, and I waited, watching the stake and wondering what he was going to do. The sky was very blue, I remember that clearly, the blueness of it and the black of the castle wall. There were just a few little white clouds in that sky, and some black birds that flew but hardly ever moved their wings. They were pretty big, and I wondered what they were.

Then the man in black came back. The axe was gone, and he was carrying something. I could not see the face, but I knew somehow that I would recognize it if I could see it. He was tied like I was on the boat, his hands behind him and his feet tied together with rope. The man in black carried him like he did not weigh anything, like you might carry a dummy stuffed with straw.

He took him over to the stake he had pounded in and sharpened and lifted him, and turned him over so he was looking up at the blue sky and the black birds.

For what felt like a long time he held him like that, then he slammed him down on the point of the stake. I saw the wooden point come up out of him all smeared with blood. Maybe the man in black went away then, because I do not remember him anymore. It was just me and the man with the stake through him, only it was not really a man, it was the doll with Russ's face. It wiggled around, trying to get off it, but wiggling only made the point go in deeper. I wanted to tell it how it could get off the stake, but I did not know what to say. It seemed to me there was no way it ever could.

Then I woke up.

10

NAALA

For a long time after that I lay awake, remembering where I was and thinking about the dream. Finally I got up and went to the bathroom. When I flushed the toilet it made so much noise I felt sure it would wake up Naala, but it did not. I washed my hands and went out into the big room, naked. There was milk and butter in Naala's little refrigerator, and bread in her breadbox. I ate some and drank a glass of milk, washed up, and went back to bed to think some more.

It seemed to me that this country I was in was the stake. I was stuck on it just like Russ and trying to get off, but I never would. I would die here, like the doll on the stake in my dream. It might be better to resign myself to that, I thought. To accept it. I decided I would try, but there was always a little piece of me that was looking for a way off the stake, a way home.

In the morning Naala asked me to fix our breakfasts. I am not really much of a cook, but I can boil water if you know what I mean. I can do simple things and fix good, simple food. We had poached eggs on toast and one sausage apiece, with hot tea because there was no coffee. (I would have cooked more if there had been more to cook.) Naala did not compliment me on the food, but she did not complain either. She just said to stay the way I was, with shoes and socks and a towel tied around me for a kilt, until she got back. Then she went out.

That was my chance to snoop around the whole apartment and I took it. If I had found anything really sensational, I would tell you here, but I did not. What impressed me most was what I did not find. I did not find any pictures of Naala. None at all. I thought maybe there would be one of her with some guy. Or a school picture with two or three other girls. Something like that. There were not any.

The big handicap I had was that even though I could speak the language a little I could not read it. I found an address book, and I could see that some of the numbers had something to do with location and some were probably phone numbers. But I could not read the names. Nothing like that. There were a few books. One with pictures seemed to be about stage magicians, not how the tricks worked but how they looked on stage. There were pictures of their posters and photographs. I looked at all the faces without recognizing a single one.

Most of the books did not have pictures, so I could not even guess what they were about. There were maybe a dozen books altogether, plus the address book.

I found a douche bag and three condoms, and some pills and so forth that I could not be sure of. I also found a cleaning kit for a handgun. (I could tell it was for a handgun because the cleaning rod was only about a foot long.) There was a good deal of other stuff, of course, pots and pans, cosmetics, a sewing basket, and so forth. But nothing else that really told me anything about her.

There was a radio, too, but no TV. I turned on the radio wondering who was broadcasting for the Legion now, and it was me.

They had gotten me because I was an American. I am sure I said that. The idea was to make the government think they were getting their ideas over to the U.S. and getting new members here and so on. They wanted to look bigger than they were because they were not really very big at all. So they had been broadcasting in German and they had wanted to add English to it.

Maybe they had found out that making the government think they were big made the government want to cut them down to size. I hoped they had and were being more careful, and I was surprised at myself when I found out I hoped that. Pretty soon I got tired of listening to a bad recording of one of my old broadcasts and found some music. Some of it was pretty good, but I figured it was probably Austrian or German.

When Naala came home she had two shopping bags full of clothes for me. They were not as cool as the clothes I would have bought for myself back home, and everything was ready-made. But they were better than most people had where I was.

She said, "You like them. I will not ask."

I turned off the radio. "Yeah, I do."

"I see you smile. They have take all you have? In the prison?"

I tried to explain that the Legion of the Light had not brought any-thing but me and the clothes I was wearing.

"Possessions come and go." She sat down. "We have them until we lose them or they wear out. Money the same. Perhaps we lose it. Perhaps we spend it. These are the same."

I said, "Sure. Lose it where I'll find it, please."

She laughed. "Now you have again the nice clothes. For these you owe me very much and must tell me something. Rathaus is now free. Where will he go?"

"That's easy. He'll go to the American embassy."

"It is watched. If he go, we have him. Another place."

"Maybe he got past your watchers. Why don't you let me check it out?"

"No. He is not there. Where else?"

I thought.

"While you think, we must eat. There is a café I like. You can sit in the trousers that cost me so much?"

I said, "Sure."

She stood up. "Then come with me. You must not spill food. Or coffee, or any such thing."

The café we went to is the Tetrasemnos. It was eight or ten streets away, which made me glad she had not bought me new shoes. Maybe I can ex-plain here that the Legion of the Light had taken my money and my watch and so forth but had left me my clothes and my shoes. The prison had taken the clothes but left me my shoes. It got me to thinking that if I ever got my hands on something really fancy I would put it in my shoes. Right then the only things I had in my shoes were my feet and my socks. I had not gone through her bags enough to know whether Naala had bought me new socks, but I hoped she had.

The café was up three flights of stairs and was sort of refined and quiet. You got the feeling that not many people went there, and the ones that did went because it was a place where you could sit for a long time and not get hassled. There was a sad guy with a thin mustache who played the vio-lin. That was the only music there. He was good, too, I had to admit. He would play for a while up on a little stage they had there. Then he would start going around to tables. He would stand by your table and play something beautiful. If you gave him money, he would go away, but if you did not he would play something else beautiful. And so on, until you gave him money or you left. I would have given him money if I had any. I did not, and I was glad when Naala gave him something.

So that was the kind of place it was. A man and a really pretty girl were sitting at a table not very far from ours. The girl had a red fountain pen and was writing something on lined paper. She had small neat writing from what I could see of it, with none of the fancy flourishes some girls use. I could see she was not drawing little hearts for dots or anything like that.

The man just watched her. He had coffee and a little stem glass of brandy, and he would sip his coffee without looking at it, always watching her. He looked like he meant to eat her. Every so often a waiter would come by and pour more coffee in his cup, and he would pour a little brandy from his glass into the coffee. He never took his eyes off her to do it, though. When the violinist came around the pretty girl looked up at him and smiled, and the man took a bill from the side pocket of his jacket and gave it to him, but he never looked at him.

Only at the girl. That was after we had been there quite a while.

We sat down, and a waiter brought menus and wandered away. I said, "What's good here?"

"Are you hungry?" Naala was grinning.

"Hell, yes."

"Then everything is good. You have thought?"

"Yeah," I said, "I've thought a lot."

"That is well." She had a mean grin. "Those who work may eat. You understand this? So it is and so it must be. Those who do not work shall not eat. That is so, also."

"Is thinking work?" I asked her.

"*Some* thinking is work. Yes? What is it you think? Rathaus does not go to your embassy. Where is it he goes instead? If you wish to eat, you must tell me."

"You know about the dolls?"

She nodded in a way that told me absolutely nothing. Maybe she knew more than I did. Maybe she did not know a thing. Most likely it was some-where between those two, but where was that? The nod did not tell.

"He and his partner made those dolls and sold them, in America at first but later all over the world. His partner was in change of production and R&D. Russ was in charge of sales and advertising. All that stuff. I don't know if he sold any here."

"I do not know also," Naala said.

"My guess is he did. He didn't tell me that, but I think so anyhow. He didn't talk like this was some weird foreign country at the edge of the earth. You know what I mean? He talked like it was someplace most people know about. That's not true, not in America anyway. But that was how Russ Rathaus thought."

"So you think—?"

I nodded. "If he sold them here, he had connections here. Probably people he had never met face to face. But there's lots of ways for business-people to get together on the Net. They see each other's faces in their screens, or whatever the other guy wants to show them, a graph or a spread-sheet. Whatever. For Russ it would have had to be somebody who speaks English and is in the novelty business here. There can't be a lot of guys like that."

"None, perhaps. That could be."

"He knew somebody here," I insisted. "Somebody he'd done business with, somebody who might help him now, when he's in a bind."

Naala was quiet for a minute or two. Then she said, "You have thought, so you eat. What is it you like?"

I shrugged and said I would have whatever she was having. She ordered something I had never heard of that turned out to be a thick stew with lots of meat topped with sour cream. When it finally came, we ate it with fresh bread and butter and slices of raw onion. So nothing fancy, but the bowls were big, the stew was wonderful, the butter was soft enough to spread, and the bread was still warm from the oven.

As well as I can remember there had not been even one single time when I had left the table in the prison feeling like I had eaten a good meal, so I tore into this. Maybe I stopped once or twice to wonder whether the meat was beef or lamb. I know that before I was finished I asked the waiter and he said it was both, with some pork, too. Naala grinned and said it was good horse meat and she would never take me to a place where they served mule meat, but she was kidding.

I had about finished when a priest came over to our table. He smiled at us, and I knew right away who he was, but I could not remember his name. He must have known it from my face, because the first thing he said was, "Papa Zenon."

Whatever it was I said then was meant to be polite. Probably I asked him to sit down, because he sat. "You speak our language now."

"A little," I told him. "I know I'm not very good."

"We are none of us very good, as God knows. You have a new cousin?"

Naala said, "We are friends, that is all. I try to help him. He tries to help me. You will approve of this?"

"Oh, surely—I am sure you do well. You are fine people." He looked back to me. "The funeral went well. You were concerned, I know. Everything was as you would have wished."

I knew what he meant and said I would have liked to have been there.

"Another time, perhaps. You help this lady, whose name I do not know. . . ."

Naala introduced herself.

"While she helps you. I will help you both, if I can. What is it you do?"

Naala said, "He is from Amerika. You must know this."

Papa Zenon nodded.

"Our police do not like foreigners. Many are spies, and our police fear them. He is not a spy, but they put him in prison, a foolish charge so they are safe from him. I have arranged his release. For this he is grateful, I hope."

"Very grateful," I said.

"Now I buy the lunch. He has no money, no passport. He owes to the church for this funeral you speak of? He cannot pay, not now. Soon he will have money again, sent from Amerika where he has much. Then you will be paid."

Papa Zenon smiled. "We do not charge for funerals. The dead repay us with their prayers. Should the living wish to make an offering in gratitude, their offering is accepted in the spirit in which it was given."

"I'll make an offering when I can," I said. "I'll be glad to, if I can find you."

"I will not be difficult to find, my son. My church is that of Saint

Barachisios in Puraustays. I travel, indeed, but only rarely and only when I must. A shepherd forced from his flock. One worries. One cannot do otherwise." He licked his lips. "Tell me, do you know where your cousin is staying? Does she assist you?"

I said I thought she was back in Puraustays. I knew Naala would not want me to talk about what we were doing, and I had no idea what story she might cook up, so I asked what had brought him to the capital.

"Would you like lunch, Papa?" she put in. "I have said I pay for his, as I do. I will pay for yours, also."

"You are kindness itself, but I have eaten. I came to your table only to say that the funeral went well, and the burial. I did not intend to intrude."

"You do not intrude, Papa." Naala looked at me as if to say *what's going on here?*

I said, "Did you know I was here in the capital?"

"Oh, no! No one knows where you are, and certainly I did not." He paused for a second to let me chew on that. "I came because His Excellency the Archbishop wishes to speak with me."

I wanted to ask him about Kleon and Martya then, but I did not dare to.

Naala rescued me for the time being. "This is most interesting, and I hope to persuade you to tell us about it. I have seen His Excellency in the cathedral a score of times, it might be. Still I have never spoken to him. My Amerikan friend has never spoken to him either, of that I feel most sure. You must drink more coffee now—and eat something, too, if you wish it—and tell us of this. What is he like in private? What is it he says to you? There is trouble at your church in Puraustays?"

"No, none at all." Papa Zenon looked deadly serious for a change. "I have written a book. It is a great mistake, I find, to write a book, because everyone looks upon you as an expert."

Still sweating bullets I said, "I know what you mean."

"As for His Excellency, it is far beyond my modest skill to capture his personality in mere words. He is a venerable priest, enfeebled in body though not in mind, a man of great kindness and great penetration." Papa Zenon sighed. "A man who guards his tongue, and has a tongue to be feared. I am happy to say that I have escaped it thus far. But only thus far."

"I am not one who pries." Naala held her hand to her chest and did her best to look innocent. "If I pry now, you will tell me, I hope. Yet thousands must know. What is it, this book you have written? I might like to read. Has the library copies?"

Papa Zenon nodded. "I believe it does. I must look. There is a store below the cathedral. You will know it, I am sure. Crucifixes and icons, also religious books. We priests may write books, you understand."

She nodded. "With the approval of the State, yes."

"Of course. The archbishop must approve as well. This means he reads all the books we write while he sits on the throne. Mine, for example. May I for a moment boast? He congratulated me upon it."

Naala signaled to the waiter that he was to bring Papa Zenon something.

"Its title is *A Manual of Exorcism for Those in Holy Orders.* May I explain?"

I said, "Yeah, I wish you would."

"You must know that although small parishes have only a single priest, the pastor, larger ones have a pastor and an assistant, or several assistants. In your country it is different, perhaps. But in ours every pastor must appoint an exorcist. A pastor who has several assistants, as I do, appoints one of them in most cases. He may hold the office himself, however, if he chooses."

The waiter brought more coffee, with a clean cup for Papa Zenon and a little plate of *kolacky*.

"I had been appointed exorcist while I was an assistant and had performed exorcisms, some successful, others less so. When I myself became a pastor, I quizzed my assistants on the subject. None knew anything beyond what is taught at the seminary. What seminarians learn concerning exorcism is quite perfunctory, I am sorry to say, and these scarcely knew that." He sipped.

"In any event, I decided to retain the post myself. Since that time I have gained a certain fame, at least in Puraustays. Other exorcists visit me for advice and so on. As I have indicated, I decided to write a book. It was the labor of four years, but I am vain enough to believe that it contains much of value and some things of value that are not to be found elsewhere."

"This is a large city," Naala remarked.

"It is, and there must be many possessions here, fifty or sixty a year, I would imagine. Possibly His Excellency wishes me to treat such a case." Papa Zenon picked up one of the little cakes, examined it, and returned it to the plate. "That is entirely possible, although he has not said so."

I asked, "What does he say?"

Papa Zenon shook his head. "You can scarcely expect me to make His Excellency's confidences a part of my table talk, my son."

When he had gone, Naala asked, "Why did he come to you, and why did he join us so readily?"

I quoted, "'I don't trust that conductor. Why is he so short?'"

"And you mean by that . . . ?"

"Nothing. It's from a cartoon I watched one time, that's all. Papa Zenon's pretty short, and it popped into my head."

"Those cakes." Naala pointed to them. "Why did the waiter bring them?"

"Beats me. Maybe he was just being hospitable."

"No. This priest of yours enters this café and does not look at the menu. He orders. It is not much, because he talks little to the waiter. Soon he sees you, and at once comes to our table. The waiter sees him there when I point to him. He brings more coffee and the little cakes, because the priest has ordered them."

I said, "Maybe."

"Not it may be. It is. Those things are so. The priest picks up a little cake, but his stomach is now tight. He does not eat. I, too, know this tightness of the stomach. When I see it in others, I know what it is I see."

"Maybe he's worried about me."

"He is worried by you. Possibly me, also, but mostly by you. So it appeared. He talks to you without result. Then he is more worried. He leaves, fearing we may see his concern. He makes the funeral for you? He blesses the burial? So he said."

I nodded.

"Who is buried? A relative? A friend?"

"Just a body." I told her about the Willows. "We didn't want to put it back behind that mirror, and Martya thought it would be less likely to bother us if a priest buried it."

Naala looked thoughtful. "You did not see her in the mirror, you say. It is this girl."

"Yes, it was. I never saw it until I took down the mirror."

"Then it is this Martya the priest should fear, no? She has the second sight. Is she here, in this city?"

I shook my head. "She's still back in Puraustays, as far as I know."

"She is your cousin? Says she is?"

I nodded. "Sometimes."

"In a bar you met her?"

"No, but we went to some clubs together afterward. We'd wait until Kleon—that's her husband—was asleep, then go to a club and dance for an hour or so." I stopped, thinking how weird it must have sounded to Naala. "I was his prisoner, or supposed to be."

She chuckled. "This they do in the provinces. With what were you charged?"

"I don't know. They never told me."

"The charges have been dropped? You have left this Kleon's house before you are taken?"

I tried to explain.

"If what you say is so, he has been shot. Your Martya is now become a widow lady." Naala laughed. "She is good for you between the sheets? You liked her?"

I shrugged. "She was okay."

"You think I do not understand your English word, but I do. It is as I say. Your Martya has come here to look for you. So it seems. The priest has seen her here. This I also believe. Should we let her find you?"

I said, "I don't know."

"No more do I. How old do you think me?"

I made the best guess I could, then knocked off ten years. "About twenty-seven."

She smiled. "Never again, and this you know. There are things I can show, and I will. Martya I cannot show. Not yet. But we will find her." She waved the waiter over and asked for more coffee.

When he had gone, I said, "Aren't we about finished here?"

"Where will we go if we leave as you wish?"

I shrugged. "Up to you."

"So. We leave, then stand in the street discussing where we go. To the art museum, I say. You say to the concert. A passerby stops to say the zoo. I shake my head, fearing the keepers there will never let you leave." Naala laughed. "Let us discuss here instead. They will not force us to go, I have not paid our bill. Let us rationally consider what it is we do. You knew Rathaus in Puraustays?"

I explained that I had never met any other Americans in Puraustays.

"In Amerika you know him."

"No. I never so much as saw him until they put him in my cell."

"The Legion has him, you think?"

"You said it didn't, that they would have taken me instead."

"What I think does not matter. What is it you think?"

I said, "I don't know what has taken him."

"But not the Legion of the Light?"

I shook my head.

"You think something you fear. That is what I think, because I see it in your eyes. What is it?"

I said, "I don't know what it is."

"I ask again, where is it we should go?"

"I've already answered that. We ought to find out whether he had business connections here and check them out."

"This still you think."

I nodded.

"I have the idea, too. First I make the telephone call. You must excuse me."

I thought she was going to the rest room, but she waltzed out of the café. I sat there awhile, mostly watching the pretty girl with the big red pen and the man who watched her, until the waiter came over. "You wish something more, sir?"

"No, I'm fine."

"The lady . . . ?"

"She'll be back," I said. I thought of telling him I had no money, which was the truth. But I did not say it.

"Perhaps she will want something more." The waiter rubbed his chin.

I told him I did not know.

"Some nice fruits, it might be. I will tell the kitchen."

The girl with the red pen looked up at me and smiled, and I smiled back. When Naala sat down with me again the girl was bent over her paper like before but I was still smiling.

"You are happy. You have think of something new."

I shook my head. "I was just thinking that now I'm out of that prison and sitting in this nice café drinking good coffee. Where did you find a phone?"

"There are painted boxes on poles. Them you must have seen. They are for the police and I have a key. What is it, this new thing you think of? You must tell me."

"I wasn't even thinking about our problem," I said. "How did your phone call go?"

"Well, of course. I have called the station nearest the palace. The archbishop must be at home for us at three o'clock. They will send a policeman to him. His secretary will protest, our policeman will insist that it must be so. He has a gun, the secretary none. Perhaps he fires at the floor. A better chance there is no need. The archbishop will be at home at three. He waits and more nervous grows. At four we come, I think. A little after four it may be. He tells us why he summons—"

"Hold on," I said. "I've got that, anyway. But the archbishop lives in a palace?"

Naala lifted a shoulder and let it drop. "In a big house. Always this is called a palace. For bishops also. It must be big because offices are needed, not just rooms for sleeping and eating. What is your new idea? Still you do not say?"

"Because it isn't much of an idea, really. Anybody would think of it."

"I, not." She touched her chest. "Tell me."

"Well, Russ has a wife. Her name is Rosalee, and she got arrested the same time he did."

"Ah! He will try to arrange the escape for her."

"If she's still in prison." I nodded. "She may have been released by this time. If she has, she's probably back in the States. That's the first thing he'll try to find out—whether she's safe back home. If she is, he might try to get her to help him. It'll depend on what he needs."

I stopped for a minute to think. Russ and I had been pretty good friends.

"He's not really a spy, you know. He isn't dangerous to your government at all."

"About him I do not care," Naala told me. "It is those who have freed him who concern me. You say he is not a spy, and it may be you are right. If you are, why it is they free him?"

I thought I knew, but I just shook my head.

"In time, we learn this. I think your new idea most good. This surprises you?"

"Yes. I'm surprised all right."

"It is good first because we can begin before we speak with His Excellency. The Harktay—the prison for women—is here in this city. We will go there and speak with them. Perhaps also to this wife."

11

NO TORTURE

As soon as we got there I saw I had been right when I told Russ they were easier on women. I had been expecting a big gray building, but it was not like that at all. There was a wire fence, maybe ten feet high, with barbed wire on top. Inside it were regular streets and buildings. Some were apartment buildings like the one Naala lived in, some had been stores once, and some had been houses. There were trees and grass around each building just like always, and you could see the women in there were proud of them and were taking care of them as good as they could. It looked to me like the trees were all fruit trees.

Here I have gotten ahead of myself again. I ought to have said first that the guards who let us in were women. They looked tough and they had uniforms and guns, but they were women. When they saw Naala's badge they got very polite, and one of them walked us inside and pretty close to the middle of the compound where the warden's office was. It had been an office supply store before, Naala said. We went in there, and a woman with no gun showed us into the warden's office.

She was probably fifty-five or sixty, a big raw-boned woman with gray hair. Seeing her, I figured she had most likely been around while the communists still had power, and I wondered what she had been doing back then. People here do not shake hands much, but she stood up and shook Naala's, and mine, too.

"Welcome!" She motioned toward a couple of swivel chairs. "You will get whatever it is you ask, if it is possible. We at the People's Detention for Women are always glad to cooperate."

Naala thanked her, and she clapped her hands and told the women who had showed us in to bring tea.

Naala said, "Eighteen months ago two Amerikan spies, husband and wife, were arrested at the border. The husband was taken to the Rural Reeducation Center. The wife was taken here."

"I see. He has been released?"

Naala shook her head. "He has escaped. That he will try to communicate with her we think certain. He may try to free her as well."

I said, "She could have been released."

"So you think. It would be a major error."

The warden asked the wife's name, Naala gave it, and the warden turned to her computer. "She sleeps in Building One Twenty-four."

"She is outside it now? Perhaps at work?"

"She should be, yes. Now it is the work-time. She will be . . ." More typing and tapping the screen. "Sewing. Building Seventeen. We make uniforms for the army."

Naala spoke to me. "We can have her brought to us, or we can go to her. You think which?"

"Go to her," I said.

"Why is this?"

"If we go to her, we can see what she's doing, what her surroundings are like, who she's working with, and so on. We can bring her here later if we want to, or take her someplace else."

The warden wanted to know if I was Russian, and Naala shook her head. "You need not take us to the place where she works. I know you must be busy. Tell us where it is, and we will find it."

"I could never be so discourteous," the warden said. "I will assign a guide."

"That will not be necessary. Where is it we must go?"

Stuff like this went on for a while, and I would not give it all here if I could. Pretty soon I could see that Naala wanted us to be free to snoop around, and the warden wanted to keep us from doing it.

Finally we got the guide, a short fat woman with a whistle around her neck. She lectured us about the prison the whole way. Most of the women were in for shoplifting, and they got reeducation to teach them that stealing from stores was wrong. I could tell it was strictly the company line and did not pay a lot of attention to it.

The factory had been a barn at one time, and not a very nice barn either, a long, low, whitewashed building that could have used a lot more windows. The floor was dirty and splintery, but the walls were covered with pictures—some torn out of newspapers and magazines, some photos, stuck up there with pins.

Right then is when I got a surprise. All the women prisoners had big numbers just like the ones we had worn in prison sewn on their uniforms, and I could see our guide was looking at those. She did not know what Rosalee Rathaus looked like. We passed on a bunch of women who were working at sewing machines and making quite a racket, and finally our guide asked one of the guards, women with uniforms but no guns who were lounging around here and there. The guard just pointed.

She was a blonde, pretty thin and not much older than I was. Of course she had no makeup and she looked tired, but right off I noticed the bones in her face and her blue eyes. Fix her hair and give her a good night's sleep and she would be a whole lot better than decent. Give her the right makeup, too, and the right clothes, and she might knock your eyes out. She was working a machine I had never seen before. You stacked cloth on it, then laid a pattern on top of the cloth and cut around it. It was sort of like a band saw but not exactly.

Naala said something to our guide, and she went over and pulled Rosalee away from her machine. After that we marched her outside where we could hear ourselves talk.

"You are Amerikan?" Naala asked. "The wife of Russell Rathaus?"

The blonde nodded. She looked a little angry and a little dazed, like she had just been smacked hard.

"Where is he?"

The blonde shrugged.

"He has communicated with you?"

She did not understand that, and you could see it. I said, "Maybe I'd better translate."

Naala turned to our guide. "You! Get out of here!"

The guide objected.

"You were to show us where this woman was. You have done so. Now go!"

The guide argued, pretty loudly.

Naala's voice dropped almost to a whisper. "Do you know who we are? We are the JAKA, you fool. Go, or you will wish you had never seen me."

It is funny, but when somebody with a bad complexion goes pale, you don't notice it. What you notice is that all the zits and things seemed to have jumped out at you.

I said, "We ought to go where she lives." I had a couple of reasons for saying that, but the main one was I wanted to sit down.

Naala agreed, so I told Rosalee we wanted to see her cell block or whatever it was they called them here. It was the first time she had heard me speak English, and her eyes got big. While we were walking along, she told me it was called a group house. For three or four steps she held my hand.

The group house was pretty big and there were beds everywhere, real beds and what were probably army cots, and others that were just places various women had rigged up to sleep on. All the beds were sort of straightened around, and all of them had quilts sewn together out of scraps of uniform cloth. Those were about the color of mustard. Rosalee showed us hers, meaning a pad of scrap cloth on the floor.

There was a real bed not far from it. I sat down on that and said, "How much younger are you?"

"I'm twenty-four. He's sixty-three." She had known what I meant right away.

"Has he been in touch with you?"

There was a little tiny pause before she shook her head. "Can that woman understand what we're saying?"

I did not think Naala really knew much English, but that did not matter. I knew what I had to say to get Rosalee to talk. "Hell no!" I made it definite.

"Then listen, please. Please, please listen because I mean every word. Get me out of here, and I'll do anything you want me to do. Everything! Just get me out. Can you get me back to America?"

I said, "Maybe. It won't be easy."

"Russ's rich, and there's a joint account. I'm not sure how much is in there, but at least fifty thousand. I'll give you the entire amount, every last dollar."

I nodded and turned to Naala, keeping my voice down and talking fast. "I don't know how much she's going to understand, but she'll have picked up a lot while she was in here. She probably knows more than she's willing to let on."

Naala nodded.

"I asked if Rathaus had been in touch. She said no, but she was lying. She wants out of here really bad. If we get her out but show her we can pop her back in anytime we're pissed off at her we'll get cooperation."

Naala nodded again. "Outside we can beat her, also."

I did not like that, but I think I covered it pretty good. I said, "Right. And if Rathaus finds out we've got her, he may want to bargain. Or try to get her away from us."

"Either is good. In the last he will not succeed. Do you wish to take her now?"

"This minute, no. But today?" I shrugged. "Probably yes, if we can do it."

I turned back to Rosalee. "How close were you to Rathaus's business?"

"I was his secretary."

"I see." Of course I was trying to figure out whether she had heard what I said to Naala, and how much she had understood. "Up until you two were married?"

"And afterward, too. He didn't want me sitting at home twiddling my thumbs, and I didn't want him getting another secretary. Then they sold the business—he and Mr. Debussy did. That was when we came here."

"Got it. Now listen up. I may be able to get you out, but I'm going to have to have some cooperation. Do you seriously want out—want it really bad—or are you just stringing me?"

"Oh, my God!" Rosalee looked like she was about to cry. "Please, please listen! I meant every word I said."

"Okay. You've got an aunt who married some guy from this country."

"Did Russ tell you that? Yes, I do."

"Maybe he talked to your uncle about doing some business over here?"

"They argued about it. Russ wanted to make the dolls in our factory, but Uncle Eneas kept saying he could make them just as good and much cheaper here. I think Russ was thinking about setting up a little factory here, and that was why he agreed to come."

"I thought he'd sold his company."

"You didn't know him."

It took me a minute to digest that, because I had known Russ really well. Pretty soon I decided she was right. I said, "He thought dolls might go over here?"

She nodded. "There were two or three places here that were buying them."

That was what I had been waiting to hear. "You say you want out. This is your chance to prove it. I can get you out, and if you can name all three I'll do it."

"Oh, Lord!" Rosalee backed over to another bed and sat down. "I can't. I really can't. The company names were, you know, so ordinary. If—if I had a keyboard, maybe. Two were stores and the other one was just a man's name, and it was terribly foreign. I remember that. I—do you have to have this?"

I shook my head. "We have other ways of finding out. Only if you can tell us now it will impress my partner, and that'll be good for you."

She tried and tried hard. I could see that. But in the end she came up empty.

Naala said, "Ask where Rathaus is now. This she may know."

So I did.

She thought about that one, too. Finally she said, "He's outdoors someplace. That's all I can tell you. Not in a building."

That one threw me. I asked why she felt like that.

"He was in prison, wasn't he? I think you said that."

"I don't think I did. I just asked if he'd been in touch."

"Oh. Well, they put me in prison, so I always thought they must have put Russ in prison somewhere, too. If he weren't in prison he would have been trying to get me out. That's what I thought."

I said, "Okay, let's say that he was in prison from the time you were arrested until last week. What then? Take it from there."

"He would want to get outdoors, that's all. He liked to get out. He hardly ever stayed in the office all day, unless the weather was just awful. The weather's been nice lately."

"You're holding something back," I told her. "What is it?"

"I—" She started to cry, so I put my arms around her. I figured that if Naala and I were going to do good cop/bad cop, I was going to be the good cop. So there was no harm in trying to calm her down.

Naala said, "We will take her. Then you will have more time. That will help, I think."

"Take her now?"

Naala shook her head. "No. We must speak with the archbishop. We leave her here and come back when we are finish. You may tell her this. She will fear we do not come and that will be good for her."

So we gave Rosalee Naala's handkerchief, which was a good big one, and when she had stopped crying I told her, "I'm going to get you out, I promise. Like we talked about, okay?"

She nodded.

"Only not right now. I can't. Soon. Are you going to cooperate when I do?"

She was not up to talking yet, but she nodded hard.

"That's good, because you're going to have to. If you don't, you'll go back here—or maybe to someplace worse. If you do, I may be able to get you back to America."

She just stared.

"You could go back home. Are your folks still alive?"

That got another nod.

"You could see them. Home cooking and hugs from your mother. All that stuff. I want you to keep it in mind."

We took her back to the sewing barn, checked in at the warden's office to tell her we were going, and left. I had an idea that the archbishop's palace was going to be a long way from the women's prison. I was dead right about that, but it turned out to work in my favor. It was so far that we went to a police station instead and got a car. I was happy enough to—well, you know.

It was a quiet ride. I knew it was too soon for me to start talking up Rosalee to Naala, and Naala did not want to say much of anything that would be overheard by the cop driving. So we kept pretty quiet. I looked at the city, mostly, trying to make mental notes about buildings that might make good landmarks.

One of those was the cathedral, which looked like it was about five hundred years old and had not been kept up too well for the past couple of centuries. Another, not quite so good, was the bishop's palace, a big stone house that had been the work of at least three architects. I thought the rococo part was definitely overdone, and I suspected that if the stones were to get sandblasted it would be even worse.

Naala looked at her watch. "Four forty it is. That is perfect."

I got out, went around to the other side, and held the door for her. The cop gave a little snort at that, which was as close to talking as he ever came.

A priest, young, thin, and hollow chested, opened the door for us. "We must see His Excellency at once," Naala snapped. "Show us in."

"I'll have to speak to His Excellency." The priest looked apologetic.

"We, too," Naala told him. We were right at his heels, and when we got to what turned out to be the archbishop's study we pushed past.

He stood up, smiling, as if our busting in on him was just what he had been expecting, which it probably was. "Welcome!" Old as he was, he still had one of those golden voices that are exactly right for public speaking. "You will always be welcome here, my children."

"Thank you," Naala said, and sat down. I took my cue from her and sat, too.

"I trust you had a pleasant walk?" The archbishop sat quite a bit more slowly.

"We did not walk. A police car. We have been at the women's prison, you see. Even with the car we are late, for which you must forgive us."

"As I do, and gladly." His smile had not lost a single kilowatt. I decided it would take a lot to ruffle him.

Naala turned to me. "What is the name of the priest from Puraustays?"

I told her Papa Zenon.

"He is here now in the capital. Summoned by you?"

The archbishop nodded.

"An important matter, since he has a parish there he must neglect while he is here."

"His parish is in excellent condition," the archbishop murmured, "and he leaves three assistants. I feel sure it will survive without its shepherd for a few weeks."

"That long?"

"I hope not, but . . ." His shoulders rose a quarter inch, and subsided one at a time.

"The police there speak well of him."

Well, well, well, I said to myself. *Those phones on the light poles are pretty useful.*

"I would expect them to." The archbishop smiled again.

Naala said, "May I ask why you have brought him here?"

"You may, of course. The question, I fear, is whether you will credit my answer. Papa Zenon is an experienced exorcist." He cleared his throat. "Every parish has an exorcist. I see you know it."

"I do," Naala told him.

"Most never perform an exorcism. Those who do . . ." The archbishop left it hanging.

I decided I had been quiet long enough, and asked, "Who's possessed?"

"You will not believe me, young man, when I say we do not know. You do not, yet it is the truth."

Naala leaned forward. "That someone is you know."

"I do not know it. I feel it." The archbishop picked a pen up from his desk, fiddled with it, and put it down again. "I may be mistaken, but I do not believe I am."

"You have no evidence?"

"You wish me to take something from a drawer of my desk and show it to you."

Naala said, "Which you cannot do. I understand."

"There are rumors. There are reports I have received from good, reliable priests. The tower of my cathedral is very tall."

Naala waited, and so did I.

"You will not credit that a man of my age climbs, every day, to the top of that tower."

"It seems unlikely," she said. "Do you?"

"I have climbed it every day for the past fifteen years, always early in the morning. Often before sunrise, in winter. There are three staircases. All are steep, and all are high. I pray as I climb, a prayer for every step, and a longer prayer at the landings. At the top, I stand among the bells and listen for the voice of God."

"What has He told you?"

"Many things, though He is often silent. When I can no longer climb to the top of my tower, I will retire. He has told me to do this, and I will not disobey."

"It may be that your successor will keep better to the point," Naala said. "We search for one Russell Rathaus, an escaped prisoner. Your exorcist has involved himself in our investigation. Why is this?"

The archbishop chuckled, which surprised the hell out of me. "We must find out. It may be that Papa Zenon would say you have involved yourselves in his. As I listen for the voice of God, I look out over this city. In winter the sky is dark, but there are many lights. It is summer and we know God's own clear sunlight, but the city is wrapped in darkness. I sense it and, almost, I see it."

"There are always evil men," Naala murmured.

The archbishop nodded. "Evil women as well. As for the rest, our entire race is corrupted by original sin. This is something more. This is Satanism, the worship of evil. I have learned that these Satanists call themselves the Unholy Way."

When Naala did not speak, the archbishop looked at me. "I once encountered an old woman who had been visited by an angel. You will not believe it."

"You're right, Your Excellency. I don't."

"I never saw it, for it had gone by the time I met her. This was when I was a young priest. But she talked of it and named it, and told me things it had told her that would unravel the tangles of certain theologians—if they could be persuaded to believe them." The archbishop opened a little box on his desk and took out a key. For a few seconds he looked at it.

He laid it down. "One thing she told me has remained with me to this day. She said that she was the only one who ever saw the angel. It was always in another room when visitors came. She would ask it where it had been, and it would explain that it had been in the attic, or in the spring house, or in the root cellar, or in the kitchen. Nevertheless, her visitors always commented favorably on her house. How bright and smiling all her rooms were, how clean everything was, how good the air smelled there."

It seemed like Naala was not going to say anything then, either. To fill in I said, "Why are you telling us this?"

"It is not so for my city—for our city. There is a darkness now that the sun cannot drive out, and its air is close and fetid. It is possessed."

I nodded to show I understood.

"I do not know how to exorcise a city. Neither does Papa Zenon. We must get closer. We must find the right room. Can you help us, young man?"

I said, "I will if I can."

"I will not," Naala told him. "I will not, because I do not believe you. We ask an explanation, and you give us a bogey tale."

The archbishop nodded as though he had expected it. "You want evidence, and I have no evidence. I have only this."

He picked up the key again and unlocked a drawer of his desk. For just a second I thought the thing he took out might be a dead tarantula. When he laid it on his desk, I saw it was somebody's hand, dried and shriveled up.

I heard Naala's breath, a hiss like a snake's.

"One of my priests brought this to me yesterday," the archbishop explained. "He told me the woman who had given it to him said she had found it. He did not say where. What do you think of it?"

Naala picked it up. "It—the purple color."

"Those are tattoos." The archbishop had taken a big magnifying glass from another drawer. "You will wish to read them, but you will find it difficult. They are old, and the ink has blurred. Some are blasphemous. I take it that will not trouble you."

Naala shook her head. I was surprised that she had even heard him.

I asked, "Did you say you just got this yesterday, Your Excellency?"

He nodded.

"You seem to have gone over it pretty thoroughly."

He nodded again. "I did, this morning. It interests me, and I was looking at it when my secretary informed me that you would be here at three. You have not looked at it."

"Not very much, Your Excellency. I'll have a look when Naala's through with it."

She glanced up. "Who told you about tattoos?"

"That the ink blurs? No one." The archbishop smiled. "I happen to know something about them. The blurring takes place only very slowly, you understand. Years must pass. Decades."

"These are terribly dim."

"Yes, they are. If you desire to read them, you will require my lens. Would you like it?" He held it up, and passed it to Naala when she reached for it.

I said, "That's a woman's hand."

"I agree, although we may both be wrong. There were traces of wax under the nails. Does that mean anything to you?"

I shook my head. The nails were long, and some of them were broken or split.

"Some superstitious people believe that the hand of a corpse can be made to reveal the location of treasure. There is a ceremony, dark invocations, and so on. Those vary with the magician. The key points are that the hand is laid on its back and candles of corpse fat are placed upon its fingers. Five candles. They are lit with more ceremony, of course. After that, the hand is said to point to the treasure. It's nonsense, but the wax suggests that someone tried it."

"It doesn't seem like corpse fat would make very good candles," I said.

"I agree, young man." The archbishop was smiling a little. "What I found was wax, as I told you."

Naala laid the magnifying glass on his desk. "I must take this." She seemed to hesitate. "I will require a bag for it. A bag or a box. Tell your secretary to bring me one."

There was a little bell on the desk. The archbishop picked it up and rang it. It was just a little glass bell, but for some reason I did not like the sound it made.

"The hand will be returned to you when we are through with it," Naala told him.

"You are most gracious." He looked quite happy.

"A priest, you said. A priest gave it to you. You did not give us his name. It was Zenon!"

The archbishop stopped smiling. "No, it was not."

"I must have the name, and it must be the correct one. We will investigate this, I think. It is with this priest that we begin. Give me his name."

"I will, if you wish it. You would seem to think the hand involved with your search."

Naala shrugged. "The black magicians you fear freed Rathaus. This I think. Why should your priest be given such a thing?"

"One of his parishioners brought it to him, I believe. May I ask why you believe the Satanists are involved in your case?"

I said, "I don't think they are. Naala does, probably because a big doll with a face like Russ Rathaus's was left in his bunk."

The archbishop's eyes went wide, and he leaned forward.

"I guess you know about the dolls. Only I don't think Satanists made that one. Russ made dolls and sold them, on the outside."

"I see." The archbishop leaned back, smiling. "I no longer wonder, madame, why the hand interests you. Or why the presence here of Papa Zenon does, for that matter. You wish the name of the priest who brought me the hand?"

Naala nodded. "I do. The hand itself I also wish."

"You will have it. The priest is Papa Iason. His parish is Saint Isidore's, near the canal. I trust that you will respect his person. He is a priest of God."

The secretary came in about then, and the archbishop asked him to find a stout box large enough to hold the hand. You could tell he was curious, but he did not ask any questions. He just hurried away.

"I have cooperated fully with you," the archbishop told Naala. "Will you concede that?"

She nodded again, still looking at the hand.

"That being the case, will you promise me that there will be no torture of Papa Iason?"

"I cannot bind my superiors," Naala told him.

"I ask only that you bind yourself and this young man."

"You have cooperated with me," Naala told him. "You say this, but I have no way of verifying it. You may be holding something back. I will now demonstrate my charity, which is very great. You have my word that if Papa Iason cooperates fully with me, I will not order him tortured. Papa Zenon is investigating for you? Investigating the bad magic?"

The archbishop hesitated before he nodded.

"I assumed, though you did not say it. My charity, the charity of the JAKA, is such that I give you, unasked, the same guarantee concerning him. If he cooperates, I will not order him tortured. You may rejoice."

The secretary came back with a wooden box big enough to hold the hand. There were pictures on it, carved and painted, that looked pretty old. As we left, I told Naala that Papa Zenon had been a good friend to me and I hoped she would really take it easy on him.

She laughed. "We of the JAKA do not torture, but for us it is useful that others think we do. Your Papa Zenon is quite safe."

"That's good," I said. "Where are we going now? To see this other priest?"

"Of course no. We go to fetch the woman from prison, the Rosalee."

That surprised me so much I did not say anything more for a long time. But when we were back in the police car and it was turning and turning through the crooked streets and scaring horses with its flashing light, Naala told me, "We never torture unless torture is absolutely necessary."

12

WORTH A THOUSAND WORDS

Naala did not want to take Rosalee in her prison uniform, so we stopped at a shop and bought a checkered cotton dress for her. Naala thought it would be too small and I thought it would be too big. As soon as each of us had said our piece, we both thought it would probably be about right. When Rosalee tried it on, it was a little loose. The way I figured I had won, but it would have been dumb for me to say so. Now when I think of Rosalee, it is always in that loose red-and-white dress.

"We are going to take you to see a priest," Naala told her. "This priest may know what happen to your husband. If he does, he may tell us. If not now, then later."

When I had interpreted that, Rosalee asked what we wanted her to do.

"I want him to see you," Naala told her. "That will be enough."

Just looking at Rosalee I knew she could not figure out what the game was. Neither could I, but I kept my mouth shut. Here I ought to get to Papa Iason and all that, but before I do I want to tell you how it was when we went out the gate.

Naala was not very tall, but when she walked it was always fast, striding along with her skirt whipping around her legs. Strolling was not in her makeup. Most of the time that was all right with me. I have long legs and it was not much of a strain for me to keep up. Rosalee was small, and she had been standing at that cutting machine since early in the morning. She just about had to run to keep up, and she was gasping before we had gone a hundred yards.

Then we got close to the gate, and I saw the fear hit her. She thought the guards were going to stop her, and probably punish her for not wearing prison clothes, that they were going to rip that little cotton dress right off of her, and beat her, too.

I told Naala to slow down, but she only snorted. "For why? Because they must see my papers? These they saw when we came."

She had the right idea. The guards just saluted her and did not say a thing about Rosalee. I figure the warden had sent somebody to tell them what was up as soon as we left her office.

When Rosalee stepped out of the gate, she could not believe it. Her eyes just shone, and you could see it in the way she held herself and everything else. Then Naala whistled and waved to our police car, which had not been parked in front because of the vegetable stands. We all piled into the backseat, Naala on one end and me on the other, with Rosalee in the middle. And I knew that she thought we were really taking her to JAKA headquarters or something like that. Naala told the driver about Saint Isidore's, but I do not think Rosalee understood.

Naala sent our police car away when we got to the church. You could have lost that church in a corner of the cathedral, but it looked pretty new, concrete block about as high as my waist and wood above that. The dull yellow paint was not all that new, but it had not started to flake off either.

We went in there, but there was nobody there except two old ladies praying. So we went to the priest's house, which looked older than his church, and a friendly lady about sixty told us he was in Demas's having a meeting.

We had gotten directions, so we found the canal and walked along it for about a mile. Demas's was what we would probably call a bar and grill in America, a place where you could buy drinks and sandwiches, roasted garlic, and raw vegetable sticks. All that kind of stuff.

It should not have taken me long to spot Papa Iason but it did, probably two minutes or a little more. There is a kind of man who goes straight from being a boy to being middle-aged. Generally he is heavy, and he starts losing his hair really early. That is what Papa Iason was like. His hair was about half gone and his face was red. I had been looking at the people who talked, and that was why it had taken me so long. He was a listener, just sitting there in his black suit sipping beer from a big mug and tapping his lips with a pencil. Later I was surprised how young he was.

Naala spotted him about the same time I did. She pulled up a chair and sat down in the group, then motioned for us to do the same. There was only one empty chair left, so I let Rosalee have it and sat on the floor up front.

They were talking about a sort of street fair they were going to put on.

People would bring things they wanted to get rid of. They would be sold at the fair and the money would go to the church. Some other people would bring cider and cookies and things like that. They could give them away to attract customers or they could sell them. If they sold them, that money would have to go to the church, too. Some people were afraid these people would keep the money—after all, it was their cookies and their cider. So maybe somebody else should sell those, and they talked about that quite a while. Papa Iason wanted to trust them. He did not say that but you could tell from his face when a lady who felt the same way talked.

Also, he kept looking at Naala out of the corner of his eye. I did not bother him and neither did Rosalee, but Naala did. Naala was holding the box on her lap, and he looked at that three or four times, too.

After about half an hour he closed the meeting and asked the lady who had been taking notes to read what had been decided. She did and there was some arguing, but you could tell that three or four of them were getting pretty nervous about us and wanted to get out of there.

When most of them had gone, Papa Iason said, "I believe it is to me you wish to speak."

Naala nodded.

"Perhaps you would like some beer. I will order it for you."

"For me, no." She turned to me. "Tell her she may have beer if she wishes it."

So I stood up and asked Rosalee, and she surprised me by saying yes. I told Naala that Rosalee and I would like some, and Papa Iason ordered.

"My beer is given to me without charge," he told Naala. "For your friends I will pay."

Naala said, "You know who I am."

"I believe I do. Yes."

"His Excellency sent someone with a message."

"Surely there can be no harm in that."

"In which case you know also why I have come."

"About the hand. It might be best not to speak of it loudly."

"I have not spoken of it all," Naala said. "What can you tell me?"

"You will wish to know whose hand it is. I do not know."

"What do you know? Let us talk of that. Who gave it to you?"

"A woman I do not know."

"How convenient!" Naala leaned forward. "You saw her? You spoke with her?"

"She came to the rectory. It was quite late—I had started to ready myself for bed. When she came in, she tried to give me something wrapped in a shawl. I thought it a foundling, so I told her she must sit down, that I would not take what she offered unless she did."

"You asked her name."

Papa Iason shook his head. "I did not. When someone brings a foundling, we never do."

I guess Naala thought he looked like he wanted to say something else, because she said, "Go on."

"If we were to ask names they would only lie, and the unhappy infants would be left on the doorstep in the cold. It is warmer now, but there are dogs. Strays."

"What did this woman look like?"

"You are trying to find her," Papa Iason said. "So am I. I will help you, and hope you help me."

"Before I decide, I must know more. Describe her."

"Quite young. Red hair, I think. She was wearing a black scarf over her head. What do women call those?"

Naala waved the question to one side.

"She had on that black scarf. At least, it looked black in our parlor. There was a lock of hair peeping out, and it seemed to be red. By electric light it is always hard to judge."

"Tall? Short?" Naala was getting irritated.

"The height of most women, I would say. Her face was rather pretty, but not striking."

Our beer came, and since there were a lot of empty chairs now, I took the one next to Rosalee. She had time for one sip of beer before Naala made her stand up.

"Look at this woman," Naala said. "Was the woman who brought the hand taller?"

Papa Iason asked, "Do you have it in that box?"

"Answer my question."

"A little taller, yes. Not much."

"Did you notice her shoes?"

Papa Iason shook his head.

"Her dress? What was she wearing?"

"A plain black dress."

"Black? Are you sure?"

Papa Iason shook his head again. "Some dark color. It could have been blue or green."

"Rings on her fingers?"

"I did not notice any."

"Was she beautiful?"

That took him by surprise. After a couple of seconds he said, "I am a priest."

"You are a priest and I am an operator. If you ask me a question while I kneel in the confessional, I will answer you honestly. You must answer me honestly when I do my duty."

Papa Iason seemed to be trying to find words.

"See this woman." Naala caught Rosalee's chin on the point of her finger and turned her head to show Papa Iason her profile. "Was she as good-looking as this?"

He shook his head.

"Do not be gallant. Was she?"

"She was pretty, I think, which I told you before. Perhaps very pretty if she had smiled. This woman you bring is beautiful. Who is she?"

"My prisoner, although I will free her if she assists me. You made the woman who carried something come inside. What did she say?"

"She told me she had a bad thing. I must take it, but I must be careful with it. I told her she ought to take it to the police. She said they would arrest her and it would do no good. She laid it on the hearth to unwrap." Papa Iason paused. "It was a warm night."

Naala nodded.

"We had no fire. People bring us wood, but hardly ever in summer."

"What did she say when she unwrapped it?"

"Nothing—or if she spoke, I paid no attention. I had tried to touch it but found I could not. Begging God for courage I struggled to lay my hand on it, but it only trembled. Soon I heard the door close and looked around. The woman was gone."

I said, "Didn't she tell you how to use it?"

Papa Iason shook his head. "She told me only what I have told you, nothing else. Next day I carried it to His Excellency. I told him I thought it should be burned, and I would see that it was if he wished. He thanked me, but told me he wished to examine it first."

I had been trying to decide whether he was lying and had about decided he was not.

Naala asked, "Did he speak to you about Papa Zenon?"

Papa Iason shook his head again.

"You do not ask me who he is."

"I know. He came to see me this morning. He told me that His Excellency believes that many in this city are worshipping demons, and he is looking into the abomination at His Excellency's request."

"He asked you about the hand?"

"He did, among other matters. I described the young woman to him as I have described her to you." Papa Iason hesitated. "He seemed to know her."

"That is most interesting!" Naala put the box on the floor between her feet. "What was it that makes you say so?"

"He asked her hair color, which I had not mentioned. I told him her hair was covered by a black cloth, but that one lock of hair had straggled from under it and that lock appeared red—I do not mean a bright red like fire. When I said this he looked pleased, and it seemed to me he knew who the young woman was."

"Describe this Papa Zenon to me."

Papa Iason did, and it was fairly good. Of course I knew that Naala had seen him, but I did not say anything.

"Do you know where he lives?"

"He is from the wrong end of the lake. So he told me. There is a house for visiting priests near His Excellency's palace. I assume he is staying there, but I did not ask him."

"He did not tell you to notify him if you saw the young woman again?"

Papa Iason shook his head.

"Or if you learned anything more?"

"No, but I would report it to His Excellency."

Rosalee had sat down again and was sipping her beer. I wondered how much of this she had understood. One thing for sure was that she was paying close attention, so it was not all going over her head.

"There is an escaped prisoner, an Amerikan. Possibly you have heard."

"No, nothing."

Naala reached down and picked up the box. "Does this move of itself?"

Papa Iason made a disrespectful noise. "I would have called that impossible."

"It seemed to me that it has moved since I set it down. No doubt I struck it with my foot." Naala opened the lid. "Would you like to see it again?"

"I would prefer not to."

She held out the box, but he did not look. I told Naala I would like to see it, and she passed it to me.

"I mentioned an escaped prisoner. You said you knew nothing of him."

"I did not even know that anyone had escaped."

"You do not ask me for a description?"

"He has my sympathy," Papa Iason said.

"This is intended to distract me." Naala smiled. "It is a trick we hear often. As a favor to me, will you stand up, Papa? I desire to see you standing."

He stood, and she told him he might sit again.

"May I see your identity card? I will show you my own first, if you desire to see it." She opened her purse.

"You are of the secret police."

"No, no!" She smiled. "We are not secret. It is only that we do not wear uniforms. We of the JAKA have these badges, and identity cards with our photographs on them. Look at this, Papa." It was like a wallet, but when she flipped it open I could see a gold badge and a picture inside.

"I am rarely asked to display my card," Papa Iason said. He was getting his own wallet out of a hip pocket.

"You should thank me," Naala told him. "You will no longer feel you are made to bear a useless card."

"Here it is." He had pulled it out.

Naala glanced at the card. "A new card. When you are ordained?"

"Yes, naturally. My card must show my vocation."

"I see. You are twenty-six. The Amerikan who has escaped is sixty-three. May I ask your father's name?"

"It was Zetes Soukis."

"Thank you. He is not more? You have my sympathy. He died when you were a child?"

"No," Papa Iason said. "Last year."

"That is most interesting." Naala picked up the box again and stood up. "You will have pictures of him and of your mother at the rectory. Let us look at them."

I got up and so did Rosalee, maybe because I did. Papa Iason did not. "My mother and father did nothing wrong."

"You need not be concerned," Naala told him. "I do not accuse them of any crime. We will go to the rectory, but you may remain here if you wish. Your housekeeper will let us in."

Papa Iason stood. "It will be better if I am with you."

The four of us went outside, Papa Iason and Naala leading the way and Rosalee and me walking behind. Naala said, "I have not shown you a picture of the man who has escaped. That is stupid of me. Though you may not find it interesting, I hope you will give it study. If you should see him, you will report it?"

Papa Iason said, "Certainly I will do my duty."

She gave me the box and got a photo out of her purse. "I have seen more interesting faces, yet his is a face that repays diligence."

Papa Iason, who was looking at the picture as he walked, said nothing. Naala glanced back at me. "Does he speak German? Do you know?"

I said I did not think so.

"I see. Good German? He is fluent?"

I said, "I don't think he speaks much German at all. We generally talked English, except out in the yard talking to the other guys."

Naala nodded to show that she understood and went back to Papa Iason. "What is your opinion of the picture?"

He stopped for a minute to look at it again, then he said, "I do not believe I have seen him, though perhaps I have. It seems a very ordinary face."

Naala began to walk again. She took long strides, her skirt snapping and flapping around her legs. "Perhaps you have seen someone who resembles him?"

"I do not believe I have." Papa Iason returned the picture.

"That is odd, because I have. You have seen the girl with us, I know. Only a short time ago you were looking at her. She is beautiful. You say this."

Papa Iason did not want to nod, but he nodded.

"She is the wife of the man whose picture you saw. She does not wear the wedding ring because prisoners are not permitted to keep such things."

Papa Iason said, "I understand. I wish I understood what you are talking about as well, my daughter."

"Ah, you grow impatient. You need not concern yourself. I will soon leave, and these others with me."

Pretty soon Naala glanced back. "She has not tried to slip away?"

I said she had not.

"You must watch her. If she escapes the JAKA will blame me, but I will blame you."

I said, "I don't think she'll even try."

"That is good. There are questions I wish to ask. Not now, but later. Now we must see more pictures."

Back at the house where the priest lived, we looked at pictures. Not just pictures of something special, but all the pictures he had. His father was dead, but his mother was still alive. There were a lot of pictures of them, and some of him, and some with his mother or his father or both of them or an uncle or an aunt.

"You have no brothers?" Naala asked him. "I would like to see pictures of them, and of your sisters also."

He shook his head.

"You had a lonely childhood, I think. My own was not so lonely. I have two brothers."

"I was sometimes unhappy as a child," Papa Iason told her, "and I do not believe I was ever as happy as I am now. When one answers God's call, one is rewarded."

I said, "I'm an only child, too. A lot of my friends had sisters and brothers, but after I got to know them I decided I didn't want any."

"Your father is kind to you?" Naala smiled at me. "That makes a great difference to a young man, I know."

"He was wonderful, only he's dead. We used to sail together, and fish, and talk about boats and books."

Papa Iason said, "My own father was sometimes kind but always re-mote." There was a dusty shotgun standing in the corner, and he stopped talking for a minute to look at it. "Sometimes I felt that he was only kind to me because it was his duty. Now there are times when I feel that I, too, am being kind in that fashion. I remind myself that Christ is in us all."

"I know He is also," Naala said, "but frequently I must forget."

She turned to me. "You are so kind as to hold the box for me. I must be kind, too. Does it tire you?"

"Not at all," I told her. "I could carry it all day."

"That I will not ask. Soon we return to my apartment, where you can put it down."

I said that was good because Rosalee was tired. She was sitting on the bed, and she certainly looked tired.

"She will be hungry also," Naala said. "Prisoners are always hungry. We will feed her, then we take her back."

If Rosalee had understood that, she gave no sign of it. It made me won-der just how good she was.

"I wish I could invite all three of you to have dinner here with me," Papa Iason told us. "I cannot. We have very little."

"Then you may eat with us, if you like," Naala told him. "You will not inconvenience me. The JAKA pays."

"No, no. Mrs. Vagaros will be preparing food for two. She will be ter-ribly upset if I do not eat."

"I understand. You are the only child of this lovely couple." Naala held up a picture. "Do you not have their wedding pictures? I have seen no wedding pictures."

"My mother has those," Papa Iason said. "We look at them sometimes when I visit her." When Naala said nothing, he said, "I visit her as often as I can, and she lives with her sister. She is not alone."

"It is nearby?"

"In Ogulinos. I ride wagons when I can."

Naala laughed. "We will not go there, I think. Thank you, Papa. I have enjoyed looking at your pictures, but I must be about the business of the state."

Rosalee and I followed her out. She led us down a couple of really ugly streets, where you saw chickens and sometimes ducks, but no coops for them. When I asked about that, she told me that people took them into their houses at night.

"They lose some, even so. There are dogs, as the priest informed us. People also." She laughed. "You someday it might be. Do you like chicken?"

I said I could take it or leave it.

"Beef you like, I think. You may order what you wish, provided you eat it afterward."

She took us to a place facing a market square. I liked it even more than the café that was up all those stairs because all kinds of people came there, farmers, porters like the ones I had hired in Puraustays, grandmas who had come to buy food and needed a place to sit down, cops who were there to break up fights and keep the people in the stalls from cheating customers—everybody.

"We do not get white tablecloths and crystal here," Naala told us, "but the food is good and the portions large. Also it is cheap, so that my superiors will not question me about it." She gave us her mean grin. "Noisy it is, too. You can hear me?"

I said I could.

"That is very good. We speak and are not overheard. What did you think of the priest?"

I could not see what she was getting at and tried to be careful. "He seemed like a good man."

"This he also thinks, so he is not. Did he tell us the truth?"

That one had me thinking. Finally I said, "I think what he told us was true, but I don't think he told us everything."

"We progress! As you think I also think. The box is in your lap?"

I nodded and held it up.

"Put it on the table so I may see. Truly, here is a wonderful question, one I am clever to think of and you are lucky to hear. Upon what topics did Papa not tell us all he knew? Name them."

"Well, about the girl bringing the hand."

"You are correct, because all answers are correct. On no topic on which he spoke did he tell everything. How was it this girl gets into his house?"

"He didn't say. I suppose he went to the door and let her in."

"That I do not believe. He was preparing for bed when she arrived. His housekeeper will know this, and know he will not go to the door half-dressed. In this way, the housekeeper sees the woman who brings the hand. He tells as much as the housekeeper will have seen. That much, so she does not give him the lie. Why tell so little?"

I thought. "I suppose it's because he doesn't want us to find her."

A waiter brought us menus. Naala did not look at hers. "There is someone else looking for her, perhaps. Let us say this is so. Who is this other searcher Papa Iason favors?"

I nodded. "It would have to be Papa Zenon."

"Now I am not so wise. I am only a fool who shoots at the water hoping to kill a fish. You have told me of your cousin, who sees a dead woman in a mirror."

"Martya," I said. "Her name is Martya."

"I have tell you Papa Zenon has seen her here. In this I was perhaps mistaken. He has not, I think. But he has heard her described. There was that which Papa Iason said. Papa Zenon hears it and there is light. He knows who is this woman, and knows he knows."

"What was it Papa Iason told him?" I asked.

"That I cannot say. It may have been anything. A brooch she wears, the shawl in which she wrapped the hand. Must I guess?"

"Not unless you want to."

"Then I guess for joy. She mentions you. She tells Papa Iason you would help her if you were here. Some such thing as that." Naala sat back, smiling.

I said, "I've been answering questions for you, or trying to. Now I'd like you to answer one for me. Why were you so interested in those old pictures?"

"You saw the priest, but do not understand. Wait. I show you his picture." She took a photo from her purse.

Looking at it I said, "You boosted one of his photos."

"Of himself he had a full score, and the state has need of it. Look at it. Does it tell you nothing?"

I felt dumb and did not answer.

"Another picture I have also. Here, I hold them side by side."

The second one was the prison photo of Russ Rathaus. Rosalee and I leaned forward to see them better. "All right," I confessed, "I'm dumb. Yeah, they look a lot alike except Russ's older. Does it mean anything?"

"This I think. The priest had also pictures of his father, and those I did not borrow. No, not even one! You saw them?"

I nodded. "A little guy with a big nose and a big mustache."

"The mustache we leave to one side. Does Rathaus have the big nose? Is he, too, small?"

"No," I said. "No to both."

"Papa Iason is taller than you, though you are tall. He is heavy, likewise. A hundred kilos or more. More, I think. His mother is a woman not tall, not heavy."

Remembering the pictures, I nodded.

"Let us sum up. Rathaus escapes. Martya, who is now here, brings the hand to a priest. From the wrong side of the blanket this priest comes. Also he resembles Rathaus. What is happening? This I want to know."

"What you're saying is that Russ thought his son, Papa Iason, could be trusted with the hand. Nobody was looking for Martya, so he got her to take it to him and tell him to keep it safe. Only he didn't do that. He brought it to the archbishop the next day."

Naala shook her head. "I do not say this. You say it. It may be that you are correct. It may be otherwise, also."

The waiter came back. I had not even peeked at my menu because I knew I would not be able to read it. I listened to what Naala ordered and said I would have the same. Rosalee asked me what I had ordered, and when I told her it was pork tenderloin with noodles she said that would be fine for her.

I was not as hungry as I had been the first time, but I cleaned up the pork and noodles anyway, and sweet cabbage and some other stuff. Naala went out and phoned for a new police car when she had finished. When it came there were two cops, so we sat in back like before, Rosalee in the middle and Naala and I on the ends. Driving in the capital was like walking in Puraustays—you had to turn after just about every block and the blocks were pretty small. It slowed us down a lot and that may have been why Rosalee saw what she did.

She yelped and pointed, and Naala told the driver to stop. I thought maybe Rosalee had seen Russ, but that was not it. She was pointing to a big building that had a row of shops in it.

"That one!" she said. "In the middle. That's one of our customers!"

13

LEFT-HAND MAGIC

"Wait a minute," I said in English when we stopped. "You can't hardly speak the language. How come you could read that shop window?"

"I can't," Rosalee told me. "It's the picture, the hand with the white rabbit. It was on their stationery."

I told Naala what she had said.

"We go there. This is better than the priest, I hope. Ask her the name."

I did and Rosalee said, "Left-Hand Magic Supplies."

"Did Russ tell you? I thought you couldn't read their letters."

"No! I could! I did! Only I couldn't remember the name of the company. The letters were in English, and Russ wrote back in English."

I nodded. "Makes sense." After I had told Naala all that she told the driver to turn around and go back to the magic shop. He looked at the guy sitting next to him for a minute, and that was when I realized he looked like the guy who had been sitting next to the cop who had stopped his car to talk to me in Puraustays. Also that he looked an awful lot like that guy I had been seeing on posters.

Maybe I should have asked Naala whether she wanted us to get out, too. But I did not. I just assumed she did and got out and helped Rosalee get out.

The shop was bigger than I had expected, narrow but it went a long way back. The old guy behind the counter had white hair. He was pretty bent over.

Naala smiled at him, very friendly. "I hope you can help us, sir. This Amerikan lady has become separated from her husband, and we are trying to bring them together once more. You must know many magicians."

The old guy nodded. "I know every magician in the city, and many in the provinces. I will be glad to help you if I can, officer."

So he had seen right away that Naala was some kind of cop. I wondered if he knew what kind.

"He is an Amerikan magician. Do you speak German?"

The old guy straightened up a little. "I do, officer. English likewise. He would not have to speak German with me."

"That is fortunate. I believe he speaks German, but perhaps not well. Amerikans speak no language well, not even the English. You have had no Amerikan magician come here?"

"Not in many years, officer."

"This is unfortunate, but perhaps he comes. You will tell him his wife seeks him?"

"Of a certainty, if you wish it."

"I do, you may be sure. We strive to assist her. Let me leave you my card. You will be able to tell him at once where she is to be found." Naala pulled a card out of her purse and handed it over.

"I will guard it with care. It may be that he comes." The old guy took the card and it disappeared before I could blink.

"You yourself do magic." Naala was still smiling, very friendly. "Show me more."

"I fear I am out of practice."

"I will make allowances. What you do with my card is most clever."

"Do you see many customers in my store?"

Naala made a little show of looking around. "No. None at all."

"I have not much money." The old guy looked awfully sad. I had the feeling it came easy to him.

"Nor I. Who does, in these bad times? Do you fear I will take your tricks away? I will not." Naala raised her hand. "You will tell me if you see the Amerikan magician?"

The old guy nodded hard. "I will, at once!"

"Then I take nothing of yours. You have my word. Show me another trick."

"This is one of the best. You will not take it? Or ask how it is done?"

Naala promised again, and he took a long yellow pencil from a pocket of his dusty old coat. When he passed his hand over it, it turned into two pencils. I guess I must have looked pretty surprised because he grinned, and there were three pencils. Rosalee clapped, and as soon as she started Naala clapped, too.

He handed a pencil to each of us. "You may keep these if you like," the old guy told Naala and me. Then he said the same thing to Rosalee in English. He had a pretty thick accent.

Naala said, "You did not wish us to keep your tricks," and handed her pencil back.

"That is not the trick," he told her. I had figured that out already.

"Another I show." He got down a narrow, wooden box and took a man-doll with no face out of a cardboard box. He let us look into the wooden box, but I was looking at the doll. When he put it in the box, its head and feet stuck out the ends. "I need a knife, a big one. Do you have such a knife, young man?"

I said, "I don't even have a little one."

"In the back there is a gas ring and a loaf of bread. You must excuse me."

He came back with a big bread knife. "Now I cut the box in two without damaging the doll. This you must watch carefully!" He flourished the bread knife so it really looked like it was slashing through the box, but the box was wood and the knife was for cutting bread so I knew it had not.

As soon as he had made the flourish, half the box fell off. He pulled the doll out of the other half and showed it to us. "When the magician uses a big sharp knife this is a very good trick," he said.

"I want that doll," Naala told him.

"Please! To me you swore, only a moment ago."

"I do not collect for evidence. I will pay." She opened her purse.

He relaxed quite a bit. "It belongs to another trick. I borrowed it for this."

"It is that other trick I buy from you."

"Let me get the things." He took down the cardboard box again and pulled out a plastic lens in a blue plastic stand. "In this way it must be arranged." He put the doll on the counter and set up the lens to show her. "We must have a picture. Wait. I will find one."

"I have one here," Naala told him. "This is the lady's husband, the Amerikan magician."

The old guy did a double take, and I do not believe he faked it. "That face I know. . . ."

"Tell us!" Naala leaned toward him.

"He was here," the old guy said. "Not this year. Some while ago."

"Twenty-five years ago, perhaps? Twenty-six? Such a number as that?"

"No. That is too long. Two years? Let me think."

I was thinking, too—thinking that Russ had talked like he had never been in this country before.

The old guy snapped his fingers. "Two years . . . No, three Christmases ago. He comes the day I reopen. He buys . . . the snake that foretells the future, and the vanishing cigarettes. In Germany I lived three years, and we talked about it."

I said, "I guess he showed you one of these dolls and how it worked."

The old guy shook his head. "That is another man, a man in Amerika. He writes and sends a sample."

"You said it had been many years since an Amerikan magician had been in your store. Now you say it is only three years. That's not so long."

"This man?" The old guy pointed to Russ's picture. "He is not Amerikan. He is German."

Back in the police car I wanted to know why Naala looked so pleased with herself. "Do you think Russ's been after the old guy for help? If he has, the old guy's the world's best actor."

"That I do not think," Naala said. "Rather I think we have done much and rub my hands. We have showed this woman to him, which was all I wished when we came. Now more. We have learned Rathaus is German, or if he is not German he is enough fluent to make others think. Also Rathaus was here not many years ago, when he uses another name. These three things in the past half-hour, and none of them are nothing. Do you wish for more?"

I nodded.

"We have eliminated one of the three customers. It may be as you think that he has come to one for help. You say it was not that one, with which I agree."

I was holding the box with the hand on my lap when she said that, and I felt the hand move. That was the first time. It may have moved before, but if it did I had not noticed. Not until I was sitting in the police car when we were taking Rosalee back. It just moved the once, and I told myself I was crazy, I must have tilted the box, and thought about other things.

Such as Rosalee, and what I would give to get her in the sack. She had promised me, and now she was going back. I leaned over toward her a little bit and whispered, and of course I talked English: "You're going back to jail, but I got you out once and I'll get you out again. Trust me."

She did not look happy, but she nodded.

So we let her out at the gate after Naala explained to the guards and told them we would be back to get her again tomorrow. They were mad because we did not have her prison clothes, but Naala was a JAKA operator so they did not say it.

When we were rolling again I said, "What if Russ comes to the prison to try to get her out?"

"This is what I seek to prevent. His son knows we have her. The old man who shows us tricks knows, too. Tomorrow we take her again, perhaps."

"Why don't we keep her in your apartment?"

"We must sleep and she would go away. Let us suppose Rathaus learns of us as we wish. He comes by night and all is lost. Be happy that you are no longer in prison. Now I must think."

So I shut up, but I was thinking, too. The JAKA had gotten me released to Naala's custody so she could use me to find Russ. Suppose she decided that Rosalee was better than me, which seemed to be where she was headed. I would be back behind bars, right?

Only if Rosalee escaped I would be more valuable than ever. So how could I work that?

Now let us get real. I could escape a lot better than Rosalee. I was not doing it because I had no money, no passport, and no friends.

Except Russ. And Russ was out. He would help me, if I would help him, maybe. How could I get in touch when all I had was a pencil? You will be way ahead of me on that, probably.

I did it while Naala was in the shower. She had told me to shower first, which I did. Then she said she wanted to wash her hair and fix it up in various ways, and if I slept she might wake me up with a kiss.

So fine. Only first I sharpened my pencil with a nice sharp kitchen knife I found, and second I tore a couple of flyleaves out of one of Naala's books.

Afterward, when we had both cleaned up a little, she told me she had done it a lot for the JAKA when she was younger.

I said, "No kidding? Well, you're sure good-looking enough, but I wouldn't have thought . . ." I just let it peter out, like I was thinking about it.

"We wish information. It is easy when one knows how. First I must get the man to buy us drinks. Two for each is better. There is no man anywhere who will not boast after two drinks."

"Sure," I said. "He'll brag, but will you get what you want?"

"Very likely I do not. Not then. I look impressed but—this is important—it is in such a way I look that he believe I am trying to hide my impress. I lie with him and it is oh, so good for me. Now he wish to impress more than ever. He tells me what he should not tell. When there is no more I caution him. He should not speak of these things to anyone, not even to me. I stop my ears. The least word, I say, might shake the world. Now he is very proud and tell me more." She laughed.

Women always say the guy goes to sleep first and too quick, and maybe I did. She wanted to be cuddled, but she was too proud to say it. So I cuddled her and pretty soon I thought she was asleep only maybe not. Then I went to sleep for sure, and when I woke up Naala was snoring.

I have known some guys who got very mad because some lady snored with them, but I have always thought that was really, really juvenile. I was not mad, but I had a big problem.

If I just lay there and listened to her, I was pretty sure I was never going to get back to sleep. I would be awake the rest of the night, and it was only a little bit past one, meaning I would be yawning all day. Not good.

If I poked her in the ribs she might not stop. And if it really woke her up she was going to be mad. She had a gun, and anytime she wanted to she could send me back to prison. So even worse.

Well, suppose I was to sneak out of her bed and go to bed in my room? If I made it and got back to sleep it would probably not be too bad and something I could smooth over. Great. But if she caught me while I was sneaking, she might think I was giving her the slip. From then on I'd spend my nights in the steel-bar Sheraton.

I had just about settled on trying to roll her over when something like a rat ran across my chest. I froze.

Next thing was that Naala's snore sounded more like gagging and then it went silent. She sat up fast, but not before her elbow had socked me in the face.

Maybe I should have known right off. Maybe I should have done something else even if I did not know, Heimlich maneuver or something.

Maybe a lot of things. What I really did was jump out of bed, run to the doorway, and switch on the light.

Something gray had Naala by the throat, and she was trying to pull it off. I had rats on the brain and figured it was a rat and would bite the hell out of me if I grabbed it. I grabbed it anyway, squeezing it as hard as I could, jerked it off and threw it against the wall, all in one motion. It landed on its back and for maybe a quarter of a second had trouble turning over. It looked to me like a big spider then, and I tried to stomp on it.

That was when Naala started yelling. I looked at her and looked back quick, but by the time I looked back it was gone.

So that was a mess. I tried to quiet Naala down, and it did not work. Then all of a sudden she shut up and went for her gun. I had not known where she kept it, but it was hanging from a hook in her closet behind some clothes.

"There was a woman who strangles me. Where is she?"

I said there was not, that at first I thought it was a rat, but it was really just a big spider or something like that.

"A woman! Her I see! Her I remember! Where she is?"

I wanted to say I thought she had crawled under the bed, but I did not. I got the broom instead and swung it back and forth underneath the bed without finding anything except dust bunnies. To put the broom back next to the stove, I had to walk across the living room. That was where I saw it. It was climbing back into its box, which was on a little end table there. Only when I saw it, it seemed like it saw me. It must have gone over the edge of the table on the far side. That is how I thought then and how I think now.

When I brought the empty box to Naala she wanted to know what I had done with it. I had seen that one coming a mile and should have had an answer all ready, but I had not been able to think of one. "It isn't really a cut-off hand, like we thought," I told her. "It's more like some kind of animal somebody has fixed up to look like a hand."

"Rotting garbage," she said. (It is one word in their language.) "It is a hand, and if you do not in this box have it the woman who chokes me has taken it."

So after that we searched the apartment, and I mean we searched it good. I did, particularly. That was because Naala was looking for a person, but I was looking for the hand, which could hide in a pretty small space. I did not find it and neither did Naala. Finally we had a couple of drinks and she went back to bed and made me lie down beside her. It must have been about two-thirty by then. Maybe three. This time she put her gun under her pillow.

Right here I probably ought to say something about that gun. It was pretty small, but not the smallest I have ever seen. It was also pretty light, but there are lighter ones. On the side of the slide it said, "CAL 9 BROWN-ING COURT," which I had never heard of. Naala told me not to touch it, and I said I would not. Later I got one pretty much like it.

She had some bad scratches on her neck, which I should have talked about before. She had put iodine on them and I had put little strips of some kind of surgical tape on a couple of the worst ones, and I figured they would keep her awake. Wrong. She went right to sleep, but I did not.

To tell the truth, I was too scared. First and mainly I was scared of the hand. I knew it had been just a hand and not a whole woman. It was not some kind of animal that looked like one, either. It was a hand, and somehow somebody had found out how to keep a hand alive after it had been cut off. It could probably jump using all five fingers and it would jump up on the bed, and this time it would go for me.

Or else it would grab the bedspread where it hung down and pull itself up. Then it would crawl really quietly, crawling up toward me until it could grab my neck.

Second, I was scared about the gun. I was not afraid Naala would panic and shoot me. I was pretty sure that was not going to happen. I was afraid I would sneak it out from under her pillow and shoot her.

Then I would be on the loose, with no way out, a gun, and no place to hide. I could see how that might start looking like a swell idea when I got sleepy. That was one thing. The other one was that I do not trust myself when I have had much of anything to drink. Generally two beers are my limit for the night, especially if I am going to have to drive, which I generally do. That night I had drunk two stiff shots of some dark stuff that was probably local whiskey. It tasted so bad it had been hard not to gag, and the first one just about knocked my head off. I felt like I was falling-down drunk and might do anything. Pretty soon I got up and puked in the bathroom.

The funny thing was it made me feel better. I was still drunk, but I knew I was and knew I was getting over it. Also I got some ice out of the refrigerator and made ice water. I must have done for five or six glasses of that, just sitting at the little table, staring at the door, and sipping water.

I was thinking about the hand. What I had told Naala was bullshit, and I knew it. It was a hand, and it was still alive. It did not matter how it was done, that was the fact. If it had gotten out of the apartment, how had it done it? If it had not, where was it? Those questions went round and round in my head, and I kept telling myself that if I thought of a way it could have gotten out, or a place where it could be hiding, I would go and look there.

Only I never had to stand up.

There was only one door, and it was bolted on the inside. Maybe the hand could have climbed up and unbolted it. Maybe it could have turned the doorknob somehow. But how the heck could it have bolted that door again after it went out?

And I had looked everywhere. In the fridge. In the stove. In every closet. In the bedclothes on both beds. Under both beds. I had even looked in the flush tanks of the toilets, and eventually I went back to bed.

Next morning Naala did not want to talk about it. That was fine with me, because I had a headache and knew I did not have anything useful to say. So instead of that we argued about what I was going to wear. She wanted me to put on the wool sport jacket, which I knew was going to be too warm. Eventually we went out for breakfast, and I said maybe it would be better to pick up Rosalee first so she could eat breakfast with us. Naala said no and it was her money, so we did not.

On the way to the prison I had another brainstorm. I said how about this? What we really need is to know who Russ's other customers here were. So we send somebody to America. He contacts the new owners and finds out. I am here, I am American, I know the case, and I knew Russ, so I would be the perfect person.

I saw that one go down the drain before I had even gotten through speaking. I will not tell you what she said.

After that I had another idea. I would go to the American embassy and talk them into finding that stuff out for us through the Department of Commerce. But I knew if I sprung that idea on Naala right after my last one, it would be a goner, too. So I did not.

At the prison, people were running around every which way yelling at each other. Nobody would talk to us, JAKA or no JAKA, except to tell us we would have to talk to the warden. She was not in her office, and nobody seemed to know where she was. Pretty soon I could see we were not going to get anything out of them and started keeping an eye out for a prisoner who looked familiar, one of the women I had seen working in that barn where Rosalee had been cutting cloth.

I did not see anybody, but I saw something I thought might be almost as good, Building 124. The number was painted on the side, and they use Arabic numbers just like we do. I touched Naala and pointed. She took a minute to think about it before she nodded, but she did.

Inside it looked a lot different, because it had been empty before but the women were in there now, each standing at the foot of her bed. I remembered where Rosalee's was and went to it. She was not there, and it seemed to be the only bed in the whole place that did not have a woman waiting at the foot. Naala buttonholed a little woman at the bed next to it and flashed her badge.

"I do not know, operator. I do not know anything about Madame Rathaus."

"Are you telling us you never spoke to her?"

"I could not, operator. She did not speak as we speak, operator. She was of Amerika."

"I have talked with her! You, also, have talked with her. Tell me!"

"Only a little, operator. We speak of the weather, of which guards are most cruel."

"We will return to that. The Rathaus woman slept here last night?"

"Last night yes, operator. This morning no."

"When you woke she was gone?"

"When we went outside, operator." The little woman was almost whispering. "We must stand in lines, each in our places, operator. Her place was empty, operator."

"But she was here when you woke up?"

"I am unsure, operator."

I was listening in, and I noticed a tall dark woman listening in, too. She looked like she wanted to talk, so I went over to her and asked if she had seen Rosalee this morning.

"I see she is missing, operator. So did that fool, but she will not say it out of fear. When Madame Rathaus goes, I do not know. She goes in the night while I slept."

Here you will think I had bathrooms on the brain, but I started looking around for theirs. Building 124 had been a private house once, so the bathroom was not hard to find. Most of the windows in the whole place were open, and the one in the bathroom was no different. Wide open, and plenty big enough for a slender girl like Rosalee to crawl out of. I could have gotten through it myself.

By the time I got back to Naala, she was finished with the little woman and was questioning another woman. I took her aside and said, "Hey, it was easy. These ladies have got to get up during the night sometimes just like other people. So Rosalee gets up and goes to the bathroom and out the window. I'll show you."

Naala shook her head. "You, I believe. Do they sleep in their clothes?"

I did not know, so we asked around. Most of them did. They had a few little personal things, like letters from outside or maybe their baby's picture in a locket, and they were afraid they would be stolen. Also some women whose prison grays did not fit so good might want to trade. That happened, too, they said.

"She did not have to dress to escape," Naala murmured. She looked thoughtful, so I kept quiet while we left the prison. Pretty soon she got on one of the police phones and had a long talk with JAKA headquarters.

14

FINDING ROSALEE

When she hung up, she smiled. "They blame me, as is only nature. I have show them nothing could be more useful for us."

I was thoughtful all the way back inside the prison and into the warden's office.

By that time she was sitting behind her desk again, writing something. Naala sat down without being asked, so I did, too. We did not talk, just waited until the warden stopped writing and looked around. "I do not recall that I wished to speak to you."

Naala said, "Clearly because you had nothing to tell us and nothing to ask us. With us it is otherwise. We have things to tell and ask. I have an office myself. It is in our Central Building. Perhaps you are aware of our Central Building?"

The warden just looked at her.

"With a few words I could have you brought to me there. When we were finished, perhaps you would return here. I cannot say."

The warden had no answer.

Naala gave her plenty of time before she said, "Let us first be clear. The Rathaus woman was in my custody all day yesterday. She does not escape. She is return to your custody in the evening. She escapes in the night. Now you compose a report about this? So I think. A press of the button will submit this report, but you may wish to revise it before you send."

"The question, operator, is whether there is reason to revise." The warden sounded scared.

"A question you must answer. For your assistance I tell you this. We of the JAKA are happy with what we have achieved."

"Achieved? I wish to laugh, though an escape is not a thing to laugh at."

"When I return the Rathaus woman to your custody, she is in a dress I buy for her, a dress of red and white. Why do you not require her to re-sume the gray uniform of those in your custody?"

"We did!" The warden jumped up. "Your dress we tear from her back! You have keep the uniform she wore! We are forced to supply another!"

"It fit her well, I hope." Naala was smiling. "This is in your report? The new uniform?"

"Yes!"

"That is good. Already two men and two women visit dress shops. Before the shops close they will have visited every shop in the city that sells such clothes. They ask about a man who come to buy for a slender woman, or a woman as it may be who buys clothes she does not try on, clothes too small. This may be fruitful. You have find how she passes over the wire?"

The warden shook her head.

"She has not. So it may be. She has gone out a gate. You have very many?"

"Only one, operator."

Naala jumped up. "You lie to me! For this alone—" She stopped and laughed, and I about fell off my chair. "You will pay, warden." Naala was finished laughing. "Never think you will not. How much you pay, I do not know."

"Please, operator . . ."

Naala sat again. "It is too late for 'please' and you are a fool. The gate in front is narrow and well guarded. Yesterday I go to the place where the Rathaus women work. They make uniforms, and there is a wagon and a truck, a wagon to bring more cloth, more thread. I see the boxes on it. Also the army truck. It will be to take away the uniforms, I think. These must come in here, and go out, too. So a wider gate there must be."

The warden hated doing it, but she nodded.

"How did the Rathaus woman escape? You do not know. No more do I, but I will guess. It is not single shifts that work making army clothes. No. Your prisoners tell me this. When the day workers stop the work, the night workers begin it. In this way the machines are keep busy. The Rathaus woman know boxes will be loaded on the army truck. Those who will load them are her friends. They will make a small space for her among the boxes. The truck must go slowly along the city streets. She move the boxes and jump off. This I cannot prove. Not yet."

Naala paused for another smile. "When her we catch, she will tell us."

After we got out of there I thought Naala would call for another police car, but we walked. "You will have the big questions for me," she said.

I told her she was dead on about that.

"We must think and think, you and I. We will find a café. There will be coffee for us. Rolls also if you wish them. You will have questions for me, and I a task for you. Are you to be trusted?"

Of course I said I was.

"I think yes and that is well. What do you think of Papa Iason? Is he, too, to be trusted?"

I said he had not told us everything.

"Not by us. No. By his father."

"You mean Russ. The other one's dead."

"Yes, by Rathaus, his true father. He can trust him, do you think?"

"I'll have to think that one over," I said.

Naala gave me the mean grin. "This you must do as we walk, Grafton. When we are seated, you must tell me. Not yes only, or no. Explain."

There were plenty of cafés as soon as we got into a better part of town. Naala liked the fifth one (I think it was) and we sat down at an outside table with a shiny pink umbrella. I asked if she wanted my answer.

She smiled. "You are sure of it?"

"Stone certain. First, Papa Iason is religious. Not just because he's a priest but because he never once griped about it. So religious, and the Bible says to honor your father and mother. So I say, yes, if he knows Russ is his real father, Russ could trust him."

"Does he know? What is it you think?"

"We haven't got any way to tell."

"Then we must guess. He looks at the picture of Rathaus and says it is an ordinary face. Possibly you recall this?"

"But it meant something to him. I could see that."

"Three years ago Rathaus comes here. This the shopman tells. Why?"

I said, "Beats me."

"You are familiar with our identity cards?"

"No. I've never had one."

"There is on each card the date of issuance. This is for my JAKA and the police. If a woman has held her card twenty years, her face will have changed in certain ways. A man the same. Information is like bread. If it is not eaten it grow stale. So we must know. Papa's card is of three years."

"O-o-o-kay." I was trying to think what it might mean.

"Does his son get a new card because he comes?"

"I don't see why he would."

"He does not. He get a new card because he is become a priest. He is ordained. For a priest, this is a great, great thing. His father learn of it, I think. How I do not know, but there may be many ways. Perhaps the mother tell him. Perhaps Papa Iason himself tell, or someone at the seminary. It does not matter. He learns, and comes to see his son ordained. He will shake his hand and give him some money it may be. He does not tell, the mother does not tell, Papa does not tell. He is a friend from the old years, they say. Or the son of the mother's aunt who is dead. Whatever. But they know. Rathaus knows, the mother knows, and Papa Iason knows. Those three are sure. If you do not agree, I do not care. I too am sure." Naala sipped her coffee, watching me over the rim of her cup.

I told her, "I'm not as sure as you are, but you're probably right."

"This I think. There is a cult, the Unholy Way. They make dark magic. Rumors have reach the JAKA long ago, and yesterday the archbishop tells us."

I nodded.

"Rathaus makes the magic dolls. They have taken him. You agree?"

I shook my head.

"This the JAKA think. You do not. Tell me why."

"Russ was a pretty good guy. He didn't always tell me the truth, but mostly he did. When he didn't, he didn't lie outright, generally. He talked like he had never been here until he and Rosalee came. But he didn't actually say that, he just let me think it. That's one thing."

Naala nodded. "Speak more."

"If the cult could just go in that prison and take people out, they would have taken a lot of them. That's how it seems to me. There were some really bad guys in there, so why not? Only they haven't, or it would have been all over in there. Everybody would talk about it, about all the escapes, and how somebody did and what it meant for the rest of us. It wasn't like that at all. When Russ went missing there was a lot of fuss and I got shopped to the JAKA."

Naala nodded. "We may be right. I think so. Here for you is another question. They have who that we know? Name this person."

"That's easy, and I've been thinking a lot about it. Martya. They had her, but she stole their hand and got away. She brought it to a priest because she thought he'd be the right guy to destroy it. By this time the cult may have killed her. I just hope they can't find her."

"In what you say now you are entirely wrong, I think. She serve them. What is it the hand try to do last night?"

"It tried to kill you, and it almost did. Only you said it was a whole woman. I know it wasn't, that it was really the hand, but I didn't think you knew that. What wised you up?"

"Reason." Naala chuckled. "Two great teachers we have, of which reason is one. We are both right. I see the long hair, the little face, you see only her hand. You would lie to me, I think, but not about such a thing as this. Also when we search, we find no woman. She cannot have slip away."

I nodded. "The door and all the windows were locked from inside."

"Just so. I am of the JAKA and am known to be so. You understand? This I hope. Also my apartment is on the lowest floor. This for me is nice, I do not have to climb the steps. Everyone want the lowest floor. But perhaps someone wish to slide the blade into my throat, so I have good locks. Alarms also. The locks are locked, the alarms silent. . . ." Naala fell silent herself.

"So you knew it was really just the hand."

She shook her head. "It is both. The hand is a hand. It is solid. I have pick it up. You also. The woman is a soul by God condemned, a bad ghost."

"I can't see that," I said.

"You have the eyes."

That one stopped me dead. I sipped my coffee, which was thick with honey, hot, and black. Finally I said, "The hand doesn't. That's what you mean. Only it seems like it sees."

"Also thinks, without a brain. It hide so well we do not find it. Could this young woman I see hide from us in my apartment? No, this is absurd to think. The hand is wise. It find a place we do not think of, we the so clever ones. Yesterday we see the old man work his magic. His hands are oh, so clever because his brain think for them. Who think for that hand?"

"I'm an American," I told her. "We don't believe in ghosts."

"You are not there." She gave me the mean grin. "You do not ask me big questions. This you promised."

I looked away, seeing the empty, dusty street and the shabby buildings, each in its cheerful rectangle of trees. I wanted it to be America, and all these wine bottles and bright umbrellas wanted it to be Paris. But it was about as far from America and Paris as you could get. I said, "Russ had that dummy that looked like him. Where'd he get it?"

"That is not a big question. He is helped in his escape. My friends at the JAKA think by the cult. You think by those who buy his dolls, and this may be correct. If we find him, we may learn. Ask another question."

"All right, here's a big one. Why is it important that Russ could trust Papa Iason?"

"If Rathaus can trust him, he have no reason to wish him no more. The hand snatch away life. It has try to snatch mine. A priest it would hate, I think, but your Martya bring it to a priest and leave it with him. Now you see?"

I shook my head.

"Does she wish him dead? This I do not credit. She is of Puraustays. It is not to be believed that she knows him. You have kiss her and share her bed. Does she have such a hand?"

"Absolutely not," I said.

"She serves, I think. It is her master who wish the priest dead. Ah, you say, Rathaus. But the priest is his son. Even a bad man loves his son. So it often is, even if not always. Also this son is to be trusted. Why kill him? Why in such a fashion? There is no reason."

"But whoever sent Martya must have had a reason."

Naala nodded. "I offer one where I might offer many. The priest is Rathaus's son and can be trusted by him. The first reason tell me, and the second I am told by you. This bad master think like me, so I think. He think around corners. You see? He cannot kill Rathaus, perhaps because he cannot find him. Very well, he will kill the son. In this fashion he rob Rathaus of an ally, also give him much sorrow. Both, he think, will be good."

I thought, too. "You're saying that Martya gave Papa the hand so it would kill him, but it didn't."

Naala nodded.

"Well, why didn't it? Why didn't it work?"

"We cannot know, only hope to find out. I will guess now, and quickly. But it is a guess merely. It try to choke me, yes?"

It was my turn to nod. "Right. It did."

"You grasp it with both hands and tear it away. The priest does the same. He is a man, young and large. He will be stronger than I, perhaps as strong as you. He catch it and lock it away, who know where? It could be many places. In the morning he take it to the archbishop, who keep it where?"

"In that box he gave us."

"No. In a drawer of his desk, a drawer he unlock with a key. He tell us Papa Iason offer to destroy it if he wish. The archbishop thank him but refuse. He will give it to us, to the JAKA. Perhaps he does not believe what Papa tell him. He does, I think, but knows we will not believe."

"You think the cult wants Russ dead. Why would they?"

Naala sighed. "This is not hard to guess. He make the dolls and sell them. They are magic, or so many think. With them is sold a book of spells. To them he is a rival. In prison he cannot do this, so let him rot there. Now he gets out, so he must die."

"You want me to work on it."

Naala sipped more coffee. "It is a test for you. If you are wise, if you are to be trusted and have courage, we make great use of you, here and in Amerika. This I will judge as time passes."

I told her, "I've lived all over, but I'm an American. I won't betray my country."

She smiled. "I do not ask for that. We do not seek the destruction of Amerika, which you yourselves have too much destroyed already. We can make use of you in many other ways, and this we will do."

You know what I was thinking. I would get back to the States and tell the JAKA to kiss off. Naturally I did not say that. Instead I asked what she wanted me to do.

"First, you have hear me tell of the operators who visit dress shops."

"Sure."

"I wish you, also, to visit those shops. You I give a different question.

Who comes and asks such questions but has not the JAKA badge? How does this one appear? What does he say and do?"

That one took me a little time. I watched Naala sip coffee and saw how her eyes sparkled, but it did not make me any smarter.

"You do not understand."

"You're right," I said. "What's going on here?"

"Who is it who gets credit for closing a case? I know but ask even so. Who is it?"

"Whoever solves it, I suppose. If it's not that, I don't know."

"Those who ask at the dress shops now are not me. To someone they make the reports, but he is not me." Here I got the mean grin again. "You are mine."

"O-o-okay."

"Let us look back. The Rathaus woman escape. It seem to me there are three ways. First, it may be that Rathaus help her."

I nodded.

"That is what I hope when we begin. In the prison for women I ask and ask, but I see no tracks of Rathaus. Now I hope you understand. Does she have help? What is it this help do? There is nothing."

"I've got it."

"Second, the cult who pull strings of Martya. They wish Rathaus dead, I think. If no, why send her with the hand to Papa Iason? I see no tracks of them, no more than Rathaus. All I learn, the Rathaus woman could have done alone. This I think she did."

I probably scratched my head.

"We take her out, buy for her the dress and good food. She have hope. We take her back and all hope is gone. You understand how she feel, I think."

"Then she's outside, but without friends or money. Hell, she's only a kid." Just thinking about it made me feel sick.

"She has no money, but friends she has. These are you and I. If Rathaus knows she has escaped, perhaps he seeks to find her. If those of the cult know also, they too will seek her, perhaps to kill, perhaps for bait. Let us find out who seeks if either does. For this I send you."

"If it can be found out, I'll find it," I told her.

Naala put down her cup. "Now a second task. Go to the priest. You are Martya's friend?"

"Yes," I said. "I want to help her. If the cult's got her I want to get her away from them."

"Good. Tell him the truth. When the truth will serve, it is better than a thousand lies. Find out from the priest what he did not tell us, all that she says to him when she brings the hand. Has he see her before or since that time? What of the housekeeper? What did your Martya tell her? Find the shawl she wrap the hand in. Examine it closely. Bring it to me if this is possible."

"All right," I said. "Where will you be?"

"In my apartment. If you knock and none answer . . ."

"I'll wait," I said. "Outside, under the trees."

Naala shook her head. "Go to the police. Tell them I am perhaps dead."

You can guess the questions I asked her after that. I am not going to give them here because she would not answer any of them. After four or five, she told me to start with the dress shops and get going.

I had said that about Rosalee having no money and no friends, and now that was me. Or at least that was how I felt then. I did not have a single euro. Naala had been my friend and pretty close to being my girl-friend, even if she was twice my age. Heck, I had scored with her. Now she had sent me off on what she figured was a really safe errand while she did the dangerous stuff.

I would have hidden and tried to follow her if I had thought I could get away with it. Only I knew I could not. She was an operator and had been one for ten or fifteen years minimum. She would have forgotten more about tailing somebody than I knew. On top of that, there was a good chance she would call a police car as soon as she finished her coffee. What was I supposed to do? Jump in a cab and say, "Follow that car?" There were not any cabs and I did not have any money.

So I went to dress shops instead. At first it was pretty tough for me to find them because I could not read the signs, but I looked in the windows and pretty soon I started recognizing certain words that were in the signs of a lot of the shops. My guess is that one meant "dresses" and one meant "women," but I still do not know what is which.

The first two were duds. Maybe they knew something, but if they did they were not telling me. By the third I had sort of put together my story, which was that my sister's bags had been stolen and my mom and dad were out trying to get clothes she would like, only I had bought her some so she could go out and choose her own. That got me some cooperation, especially when I said what a nice shop this was and I would bring her here. The truth is a great tool if you can use it, but I could not. If I went around saying the JAKA had sent me, which was the truth, they would want to see some ID. I did not have any, so they might call the cops.

Pretty soon somebody described a woman who had been in there, only she had not bought anything. She had only described a man and asked if he had been in. I would give the number of that one if I remembered it, but I had lost count by then. It could have been six or seven, or even eight. I got a pretty good description of the woman and said she sounded a lot like my mom, but she was too young. The lady said maybe it was my sister only she did not sound American, and I said if she talked pretty good it could not have been.

Finally I went into a shop and had that feeling. You know how it is? You go someplace you would swear you had never seen before, only there's something familiar about it. I was already talking to a lady when it snapped into place for me. It was the shop where Naala had bought the red-and-white-checked dress for Rosalee. Then the lady, who seemed pretty nervous, said she had to talk to another lady before she told me anything, and I had to stay up front while she did it.

You can bet the rent I did not. I let her get a couple of steps ahead of me and edged along behind her. The shop ended with a metal door and I figured there was an office or something back there, but I was dead wrong. She opened it, and I could see into an alley. Then she closed it, and I figured she had gone for the cops and I had better get out of there. I turned around and took a step, and one of the mannequins grabbed me by the shoulder. I about jumped out of my skin.

It was Rosalee, and when she saw how scared I was she grabbed me and kissed me. Then she said, "Remember me? You promised you'd get me out of that place."

I said, "Yeah." Then when I had my breath back, "It seems like you got yourself out."

"I had to. Somebody was going to kill me."

I wanted to hear a lot more about that, but I was afraid we did not have much time and said we had better get out of there.

"I can't go out where they'll see me. The police have already been here twice. I hid in a fitting room. Did you really think I was a dummy?"

I said, "I wasn't paying any attention to you. What if the lady calls the cops?"

"She won't. She was hiding me—I remind her of her daughter. She thought you were going to arrest her."

I told her, "Okay, what I have to do is come back with Naala. She's JAKA, so nobody's going to take you away from her."

"She'll put me back in the prison! There was a girl in there called Yelena who looked like me. A man came in during the night. My bed was on the floor, remember? I slept on the floor."

I nodded.

"He stabbed Yelena. I saw it! He stabbed her and walked out. He never made a sound. He was looking for me, and he thought he'd found me."

I said, "I was there today, and nobody said anything about any girl getting stabbed."

"Well, they wouldn't unless you went into our building!"

"We did. That's where we went." I shut my face and thought a lot.

"Don't tell Naala. Promise me you won't tell Naala?"

"Yeah," I said. "Not if you don't want me to. Sure."

"I'm not going out on the street til after dark, no matter what you say. It's too dangerous." Rosalee went quiet for a minute, too. "I'll go out with you then, if you promise not to take me to Naala. But I'm safe here for now—"

A lady had come in, and Rosalee froze, chin up, one hand bent back a little. You see that on mannequins more often than on real women.

I went to the front of the store to keep the lady from coming back where we were to talk to me. She said, "Where is Madame? You do not work here, do you?"

I shook my head and said I was looking for her, too, but it seemed like she had stepped out.

"You are foreign. You did not take her cash box, did you?"

"Hell, no!" I raised my hands to show I was not carrying anything. "I don't even know where it is."

"I do," the lady said.

I do not know where we would have gone with that, if the lady who ran the shop had not come back. I waved to her and said hello. She still looked scared, but she kept coming.

The other lady, the customer, said, "I do not know what he wants. He may have taken your cash box."

I shook my head hard, and the lady who ran the store went and looked at her cash box. It was all right, which got me off the hook.

The customer wanted to look at hats and the lady must have showed her a dozen of them. Plain hats, hats with ribbons, hats with feathers, and one with a toy bird on it. The customer did not like any of them, and finally she went out of the store.

I said, "I don't think she wanted a hat at all. She just had some time to kill." All the hats had reminded me of Martya, how I had bought the fox-fur hat for her, and how she had posed in it in front of the store's big mirror. I had not expected that to hurt, but it did.

The lady said, "She had time and nothing to do. I see many such. Later, it may be, they come back and buy."

I said I hoped she would.

"Mostly not," the lady told me. "You are foreign, so not police."

"I'm American," I explained. "I was talking to His Excellency the archbishop yesterday, and he asked me to ask a few questions for him."

"You were speaking to the archbishop? Speaking the way we speak now?"

"Not exactly like this," I told her. "We were both sitting down in his study."

"He gave you his blessing?"

I shook my head. "I should have asked for it, but I forgot. I'll ask when I come back with answers to his questions."

"In the cathedral you spoke?"

"In his palace," I said. "That's what they call it. It's really just a big house. He's got a study upstairs."

"You talk face-to-face? With His Excellency?"

I said I had and asked whether she knew he climbed the bell tower of the cathedral every morning.

"He is so old! God must give him the strength."

"Yeah, that's what I think, too. I'm supposed to ask you if there's been a man or a woman in here buying clothes for a woman that size." I pointed to Rosalee, and she stepped down off the little platform and said, "He's my friend, Petya. He's trying to help me, to keep me safe from those who want me back in prison." Part of that was English and part was not. A lot was pointing to herself and grabbing imaginary bars. I am going to skip all that stuff.

Petya shook her head. "No! No one! It is what the woman asks, also. I say no. I tell the truth, always!"

I said, "Wait a minute. What woman are you talking about?"

"The woman just now! The woman who tries so many hats!"

"And I missed it! Oh, my God. . . ." I felt like shit in the street.

Naturally Rosalee wanted to know who the hat woman had been, but I did not want to tell her much with Petya there. Petya was plenty scared already and that might have tipped her over the edge. So I got out as soon as I could.

As far as Rosalee was concerned, I felt like I could relax a little. The police had been in that shop twice and had not found her. The hat lady had been from JAKA and had not found her either. It did not seem likely that more cops would be around anytime soon.

As for Russ and the cult, they were not going to go to dress shops trying to get clothes for Rosalee until they had her, which they did not. What was more, she would not be in prison clothes even if they got her later, because Petya had given her nice street clothes from her shop. So snooping around dress shops was out, but where should I go now?

The way I saw it then, there were two pretty strong possibilities. First I could go see Papa Iason, which was what Naala had told me to do. That would be good if it worked because right now I was more worried about Martya than I was about Rosalee.

Also I felt a little dirty every time I thought about Rosalee. Sure, I had gotten it on with Martya when she was married to Kleon, knowing damned well it was a crooked sort of thing to do. But I had not liked Kleon anyway and he sure as hell did not like me.

"On the other hand there's warts," is something my dad used to say a lot. What he meant is there are just about always some negatives to get in the way of the positives. Or every silver lining has a cloud, which is something I have heard some other people say. The thing on the other hand here was that Russ had been my friend. He had liked me and I had liked him, and we had talked about what our lives had been like when we were out and all that stuff. Sure, Russ had never told me he had been in this country before, but he had not lied to me about it, either. And how the hell could I blame him for not telling me that he had knocked up a girl here and now his son was a priest? If that had gotten out his son would have been washed up, most likely. No way did I have a bitch coming because he had not told me about it, and now I was thinking about screwing his wife.

I was thinking about that a lot.

You will be way ahead of me on the other one. I could go back to Naala's apartment. If she was there, I could tell her what happened and explain that Rosalee was scared of her and why. But if she was not, I was supposed to tell the cops. It was early yet, and I thought the odds that she would not be there were pretty good. So I would have to tell the cops, probably make a fool of myself, and maybe get sent back to the prison.

A third thing was that I could have ditched the whole business and gone to the American embassy, if I could have found out where it was. I did not know and Rosalee did not know, but maybe Russ knew if I could find him.

Which got me nowhere, so I went off to see Papa Iason again—if I could find *him*.

15

REVISITING

Like I said in the last chapter, I was planning to go back and look up Papa Iason. What stopped me was looking to my right down one of those short, crazy streets and seeing the front gate of the women's prison. I was tired and hungry and my feet hurt, and it seemed to me that if I went there I could sit down and question a bunch of people—eight or ten, easy—and probably promote a sandwich and a cup of coffee or a beer. As far as anybody there knew, I was some kind of minor JAKA guy, and that ought to be plenty.

So I tried it. I went to the gate and said hello to the guards and told them I wanted to talk to the warden. They said it was too late. She had gone home, and the deputy warden was in charge. I said that was fine, I would talk to her, it was just routine anyway.

The deputy warden was a little skinny lady in a black dress with black hair that I would bet the rent was dyed and a face that had worn out three bodies. By the time I saw her, I had cooked up a story. I started by asking if she was familiar with Naala, a lady who was high up in JAKA, and the deputy warden said she had heard she had been here.

"I'm working for her," I explained, "and she sent me here to do a little follow-up. We found out there's a prisoner here who looks quite a bit like Rosalee Rathaus. This prisoner's name is Yelena, and I'm supposed to ask her a few questions."

I expected the deputy warden to say, "Yeah, no sweat," or words to that effect. But she did not. Instead she looked like she had just tasted something sour. "She is in the infirmary."

I said, "You're kidding."

"I do not jest. Ordinarily I do not know her. I would look up the name and so discover her full name and number. In this case I need not. She collapsed in the prisoners' dining hall and was carried to the infirmary. She is turn blue. This I am told when I come in, and I look her up then."

I said, "Are you sure this is the right Yelena? There must be plenty of them."

"A scant handful, yes. More it might be. The Yelena you seek is where to sleep? Do you know?"

"Building One Twenty-four."

"You must look here." She pointed to her screen and I went over and looked at it. There was a picture of a blond girl who might have been a little bit younger than Rosalee. She did not look exactly like her because she did not have the cute nose or the cheek bones, but except for those they were pretty much the same type. The deputy warden pointed to a number in one of the spaces on the screen. I could not read what that space was for, but I could guess pretty easily because the number was 124.

Naturally I said I would have to go to the infirmary and ask her some questions and after that I would probably want to go to Building 124 and talk to some of the women there. I got a guide, not the same one, to take me to the infirmary. This one was a trustee and did not want to talk, which would have been super with me except that I was still hoping for certain things. So when I was sitting next to Yelena's bed I pointed at her and said, "You! Go get me a sandwich and something to drink."

It was magic. She hurried off without a word, and I looked down at Yelena and asked, "How are you feeling?"

She just shook her head.

So I told her, "I'm not a doctor, just a friend of Rosalee's. You remember Rosalee?"

That got a nod.

"You look a lot like her. I bet people got the two of you mixed up sometimes."

Another nod.

"Now I've got a serious question. Maybe you hated Rosalee, and if you did you don't have to answer. Hell, you could just tell me to go off and have an intimate affair with a powdered-sugar doughnut. But if you like her, a little bit of cooperation might save her life. Do you know anybody, anybody at all, who would want to kill you?"

It brought back the head shake.

"Don't just leave it there. Husband, ex-boyfriend, anybody. You're really nice looking even when you're so sick, and nice-looking girls have to tell guys to take a hike pretty often. Was there some guy who kept hanging around when you didn't want him to? Maybe he followed you?"

That time she nodded and gave me a name, Ferenc. I asked, "Is that his first name or his last name?"

"Narkatsos." She took time off to breathe. "Ferenc Narkatsos. He is a good man. He would not."

"Nobody else?"

She shook her head.

"Somebody's trying to kill Rosalee," I told her. When I said that, I thought it was stretching things a little, but as soon as the words were out of my mouth I realized that I believed it and was probably right. "It looked to us like there was a chance he thought you were her, so I'm trying to check that out. I don't like to pester you, and you've already given me one name, Ferenc Narkatsos. All right, I appreciate that very much, but I'm going to have to keep after you and try to get another one. Like maybe your boyfriend dumped some other girl and went for you? Is there a girl like that who might hold a grudge?"

"Nurse," she said. It was more of a gasp. "Call the nurse."

I looked around for a button or something like we would have in one of our hospitals, but I did not see anything. Finally I just went out in the hall and yelled, *"Nurse!"*

When I went back in, Yelena said, "Sit up. Please. I want to sit up."

There was a crank on the bed for that. It was pretty obvious. I turned it until Yelena motioned for me to stop. Then I sat down again.

"Closer. I wish to die sitting up."

I told her she was not going to die, she was going to get well.

When I had finished with that, she said, "I would die standing, if I could. Take my hand."

I did.

"You are good man. I meet you so late. There are so few good men."

We were quiet for a while after that. Then she said, "My heart jumps about and falls silent."

And then she shook and threw her arms around and died. I heard her go and watched her eyes glaze over. I have hardly ever prayed in my whole life, but I did then. I was still praying when my guide brought my sandwich and a mug of something that was probably tea.

Here I am not going to write any more about it, okay? About leaving that place or tramping through the city asking directions or any of that shit. To tell you the truth, I hardly noticed it myself. I kept thinking about Yelena.

It was after dark before I found the rectory, but I figured that was good because a priest would probably be back home by that time. I knocked and the housekeeper opened the door and told me Papa had not come home yet. He was visiting the sick.

I said, "Maybe this is better. May I come in, please? I need to talk to you."

She shook her head. "It is not permitted."

"Please? I won't hurt anything. I have to talk to Papa, and I have to talk to you, too." I had my foot in the door, but she had not tried to shut it.

"Come closer, so the light is on your face." I did, and she said, "You have been crying."

"Yeah. I'm sorry."

"You wish to tell me of it?"

"No," I said. Only in a second or so I changed my mind. "Yes. Yes, I would. I need to tell somebody, and at the prison I didn't even try. Somebody died. A girl named Yelena. Do you pray?"

The housekeeper nodded. She was maybe sixty or so, with gray hair.

"I don't," I said. "Or hardly ever. Only when she died I tried to. I knew God wasn't going to bring her back, but I tried to talk to him anyway. I'm sorry! I'm s-o s-s-sorry!"

By that time I was backing away and starting to bawl all over again. I do not remember what the housekeeper said then, and maybe she did not say anything, just opened the door wide. Anyway I went in and followed her into the kitchen and sat down at the old table there while she made tea for us. Pretty soon I got myself back under control.

When she sat down at the table she said, "You loved Yelena but she died?"

I shook my head. "I didn't love her. I love Martya." I had not known that, either, until I said it. "But Yelena looked like such a nice girl and I was sitting right beside her bed. I'm an American."

The housekeeper nodded. "I have heard of that. Drink your tea."

I had not even known she had given me any. It was too hot to really drink, but I sipped a little. "I came to this country and I was staying with Martya and—and her family. We sort of hit it off, so we went to some clubs together to listen to music and dance. You know. Only then I had to come here."

"You said you were in prison." The housekeeper did not look like that worried her.

"I was for a while, yes. I'd been doing broadcasts in English, so they put me in prison for a while. They said I was going to get tried eventually, or maybe released. But it never really happened."

She nodded, looking sad.

"Then your JAKA wanted me to help them, so they got me out—"

"The JAKA should not bother Papa Iason. He is a good man."

I nodded, thinking of Ferenc Narkatsos. "I know he is, but sometimes they have to bother good people anyway. Sometimes they know something. You're a good person, for example, but I'm hoping you know something about Martya that will help me find her. We think she's probably in terrible trouble, and if she is I'm going to get her out if it kills me."

"I would like to help you." The housekeeper looked like she meant it. "Alas, I do not even know this person."

"You saw her and you must have talked to her, at least a little. She was the girl who brought the hand to Papa Iason. That's what we think, anyway."

The housekeeper's mouth got round and she sucked air, but she did not say anything.

"You let her in."

She nodded. "Because Papa was here then. When Papa is here I let people in."

"Something she said made you let her in. What was it?"

"It was nothing she said. It was the way she looked, like a dog that is kicked." The housekeeper shut up and took a couple of deep breaths.

I said, "Go on."

"Have you been kicked?"

"Yes," I said. "Twice."

"I also, but more than you. If I did not let in that girl, someone would beat her. I saw that, and that is why I let her in."

I nodded to show I understood. "You must have seen that she was carrying something."

"Yes. She has a basket."

"I thought it was wrapped in a shawl."

"She has a basket over her arm, a shopping basket."

"Did she say anything about it?"

The housekeeper shook her head.

"What did she say?"

"She said . . ."

I leaned closer. "What did she say?"

"I cannot remember. I try to remember the words."

"What was it about?"

"It was—wait! I find it now. She asks does Papa have a crucifix. She says he must have a crucifix. I say he does, and she nods and smiles."

"You brought her in to see him?"

"Not then. He is undressing for bed. I go to him and tell him a girl is come and he may wish to see her, then I leave him to dress again. I see the girl eats nothing, all day it might be. I try to give her a piece of ham, but she will not take it. She is a Jew?"

I said I did not think so.

"She will eat only a piece of bread with butter. She eats that and drinks a little milk, and Papa is ready so she goes in. I do not hear what they say."

I had some more questions, but they did not get me anywhere and then Papa Iason came home. He said he was very tired and I could see it was true. His face sagged. I think mine must have been sagging the same way. We went into the parlor. There was a little fire in there on the grate, and I remember what he had said about people not bringing wood in the summer. He took off his shoes, then apologized for it.

I said that was okay, it did not bother me. What did, a little, was the hole in one sock. I could see where the other one had been darned, too. So I said I wished I could give something to his church. I explained that I had no money at all, but I said I would get back on my feet pretty soon and then I would have money and would give something.

Then I told him what had happened to me, only with a lot more detail than I had told his housekeeper. I will not go over that again here, because you have already read it. I told him about Martya and Kleon and the Willows and all that.

"You're going to lay into me good for sleeping with Martya," I said. "She was cheating and I knew it, so I've got it coming. Only here's the thing. I really loved her and I still do. I didn't mean to escape but I was brought here at gunpoint, like I said, and I've never been back to Puraustays. Most of the time I was in jail, and for quite a while I was taping those broadcasts for the Legion, too. I hope I made all that clear."

He nodded, and it seemed like he felt worse than I did about it.

"So the cops have shot Kleon, and Martya's a widow—or I hope she is." I took a deep breath. "That girl who brought you the hand? That was Martya. Or we think it was. Somebody wants to kill you, and that somebody's got Martya and is making her follow orders. I mean to get her away from them."

He did not say anything, so after that I said, "That's what I want to do, and I'm going to do it or get myself killed trying. One or the other."

After that Papa Iason was quiet for what seemed like a long, long time. I remember how he rubbed his jaw, and how the little fire hissed and popped. Then he said, "She told me it was an evil thing. That I must destroy it."

I said, "You didn't tell us that when I was here with Naala."

He shrugged.

"Why not? I'd really like to know."

"Because I did not destroy it, or even try to. There was a fire on the grate. I said there was none, but there was. She wanted me to put it in there when she had gone. Also to sprinkle it with holy water. Other things, too. I did not follow any of her suggestions. She thought it very dangerous. I did not. I thought it a dead hand cut off, a thing to frighten the credulous."

"What did you do with it?"

"When she had gone? I have a leather case, strong and almost new, given me by my mother. It is a case for razors and the like. I put the hand in that case and put the case in my traveling bag, which I locked. You will ask why I did this."

"Yeah," I said. "I sure would."

"I did not want Mrs. Vagaros to find it. It would have frightened her badly." Papa Iason sighed. "After hearing this you will have more questions. Ask them."

"Did Martya tell you her name?"

He shook his head. "You are sure this woman is one you met in Puraustays. I am not."

I said, "You told the archbishop that the hand should be destroyed. That's what he told us."

Papa Iason nodded.

"You even offered to do it."

"Yes, I did. I would destroy it tonight if he were to return it to me and tell me I might do as I liked."

I said, "It's old and interesting, and there's all the tattoos."

"I warned him about it and told him to keep it safe. I told him he must lock it up." It seemed like Papa Iason had not even heard me. "I told you about my leather case. I keep my razor there when I travel, with my shaving mug and other things. When I opened my traveling bag after mass the next morning, the hand was no longer in that leather case."

I thought that one over. Then I said, "When Martya brought it here, did she really bring it wrapped up in a shawl?"

He nodded.

"I would have thought she'd have it locked up someway. In a box or something."

"It was in a shopping basket, such as every woman has. There is a lid, and a catch for the lid."

"I see. Let's get back to Martya. She told you to destroy it? No shit?"

"She did. She wanted me to grasp my crucifix in my right hand and with the left throw the hand she had brought into the fire. She appeared to think that might be enough, but if the hand was not entirely destroyed, I was to bathe it in holy water." Papa Iason stopped talking to remember.

Then he said, "If it were burned to ashes, I was to douse the ashes with holy water, and cast everything into a swift stream. Our peasants think swift water a sovereign cure for evil, I'm afraid." He tried to smile. "For this you must forgive us."

"Sure. Did Martya tell you where she was staying? Did she give you some way of getting in touch with her? Anything like that?"

Papa Iason shook his head.

"Do you think Papa Zenon will find her?"

That one caught him off guard. For a minute he just stared at me.

"Well, do you?"

"I don't know." I heard him swallow. "Who can say?"

"You, mostly. You told him something that tipped him off to who she was. Maybe it even told him where she was—I don't know. Now he seems to be gone." (I was stretching it, but not enough that my conscience hurt me much.) "He's supposed to be snooping around, right? That's what the archbishop brought him here for. I've been snooping around all day myself, and I've never come across his tracks. Not once."

"He is in the house for visiting priests, perhaps."

"I sure hope so, but His Excellency brought him here to look for some really bad people. I guess you know about that."

Papa Iason did not say anything to that, but he nodded.

"'He that hunts the devil need pack a long spear,'" I quoted. It is an old proverb I made up myself right there in Papa Iason's parlor that night, and I was proud of it. Heck, I still am.

"I would not want to see Papa Zenon come to harm," Papa Iason said.

When I heard that, I knew I had him. I said, "Papa Zenon did me a good turn back in Puraustays. Maybe I told you. I owe him a big, big favor. So if he's in the soup, I'll do my damnedest to pull him out."

Just about then, the housekeeper stuck her head in to ask if we would like some tea. Papa Iason said we would, so she brought tea and some kind of hard crispy bread with a pot of plum jam.

Maybe all that was good. It gave Papa Iason time to think and even worry a little. When she had gone and we both had tea and I had put a lot of their brown, grainy sugar in mine and stirred it up, he said, "You believe that I told Papa Zenon where the girl might be found."

I sipped my tea. It was still hot. "Yeah. I do. If you were just some ordinary guy, I'd tell Naala and she'd have a couple of friends pick you up and sweat you. Only I'd hate to do that to a priest."

"They would learn nothing, because there is nothing to learn. I described her to him as I have to you. If you want my description again, I will give it."

I shook my head.

"I told him what she had told me. That I have told you also. She said she had an evil thing, one that must be destroyed. She asked whether I had a crucifix. I said I did, and showed it to her. She opened her basket and took out the hand. It was wrapped in a shawl, which someone had sealed. She broke the seals, unwrapped it, and laid it on the table. I picked it up to look at."

I said for him to go on.

"I saw that it had been tattooed in life." He paused. "My father did that work when he could not find other work. He was a stonemason." Papa Iason stopped and I could see him remembering.

"Did you read them?" I asked.

"The tattoos on the hand? Some I read, yes. I have a lens, a good one an old woman gave me. She said I would find it hard to read my Bible as I grew older, and her lens would help me. I said she should keep it for her own use. This does not interest you, I see."

I nodded and said, "What about the things you read, Papa? What did it say?"

"They were prayers, for the most part. Prayers to entities whose names meant nothing to me. Perhaps they were angels, fallen or holy. I remember a few, but I will not repeat them. The names of demons may be prominent in them, and when one calls upon demons they sometimes come." He smiled. "Sending them home is less easy. So many find."

"What about the things that weren't curses? What were they?"

He thought that over. "There was only one. You are hungry."

I had eaten three or four pieces of the crunchy bread with jam on them. "Yes," I said. "This afternoon a lady brought me a sandwich, but I didn't eat it. Somebody had just died, and I didn't want it."

He nodded. "Death does that, though one is very hungry afterward."

"You don't want to tell me about the writing that was not a curse?"

"No. When you ask I thought, why does he not read the hand for himself? Then I recalled that it was Greek. Can you read Greek?"

I shook my head. "Not a word."

"It is a spell for finding treasure. It is on the palm, and very short. Would you like me to translate it for you?"

"No demons, huh?"

"You are right. There are no names in it at all." He licked his lips. "It is a rhyme in Greek. I will make it so if I can. 'All you ghosts tight-bound with chain, hear me well or here remain. Show me where your treasure's hid, and I shall serve you as you bid.'" He smiled. "It would be a danger-ous thing, or so I would think, to be bound to the service of a ghost, far more to the service of a senate of bound spirits."

"Do you think it would work?" I was remembering what the arch-bishop had told us about the hand's pointing out treasure.

Papa Iason shook his head. "Prayers by the righteous might free such spirits, or at least assist them in gaining their freedom. Bound spirits would not ask for those, however. Or so I think. The kinds of spirits who might ask such prayers would not remain bound for long. These are still at-tached to the things of this sad realm into which we are born. They would ask to be avenged upon men long dead, perhaps. More likely, they would not give up their gold for any vengeance."

I said, "If they were real ghosts, I'd think they could get all the revenge they wanted by haunting people. Do you think Martya read the hand? Did she say anything about it?"

"She did not. Could she read Greek?"

I did not know, but I shook my head.

"Someone else could have read it for her and told her what it said, I suppose. She was not curious about the tattoos, or so it appeared to me."

"Did she mention treasure at all?"

Papa Iason shook his head.

"What did she say the hand was for?"

"She did not propose any use for it. She said it was an evil thing—you will agree that it looks evil—and that it must be destroyed. I think she was too frightened to destroy it herself, although she did not say so."

"Let's move along to Papa Zenon. Maybe we'll come back to Martya later. Papa Zenon came to see you when?"

"Yesterday, before you came. About ten o'clock, perhaps. I had said my morning mass and eaten breakfast."

That reminded me of the archbishop and the bell tower. "Do you say mass every morning?"

"I try to. As priests we are required to say a mass every day and to read our breviary. On weekdays I try to say mine very early, so those who wish to hear mass may attend before going to their work. I had shaved and dressed, said mass, eaten breakfast, and looked through the newspaper when Papa Zenon knocked."

I nodded. "You let him in?"

"I did. I was in the parlor going over the parish accounts. Mrs. Varagos was in the kitchen, washing up."

"What did Papa Zenon say?"

"He introduced himself. His Excellency had called him away from his parish in Puraustays, and we talked a little about that. He asked about the hand, whether I had read the tattoos. I explained that I had read some of them, but not all of them. We talked for a time about their wording, whether they were prayers or curses. He feared they might be invocations addressed to demons. After that, he asked many questions about the young woman you call Martya. He even inquired about her shoes. I remember that."

I nodded. "What did you say about them?"

"That they were plain black shoes such as many women wear. She had told me she was a poor woman, but—what was it I said?"

I told him never mind, and to keep going.

"I was going to say that she could not have been as poor as many here, since her shoes looked new. Also the shawl in which she had wrapped the hand is of good quality. Have I mentioned the wax seals?"

I nodded.

"They are very plain, but I showed them to Papa Zenon and he seemed interested in them. The pieces are still attached to the shawl, you understand. She broke them but did not tear them away."

"You've still got them?"

"They are here." Papa Iason stood up. "I'll show you."

He took out the shawl. It was larger than I expected, with a pattern of ivy leaves and a long dark green fringe. There had been three seals, all of red wax. The stamp on all three was a plain cross.

Papa Iason pointed to it. "The same seal made all three impressions. I have compared them carefully, and it is so. There is no writing, not even a trace. Either the seal that imprinted them is very old or it was cut by someone who knew nothing of the making of seals. I think the latter."

"Yeah," I said. "He got a wooden dowel and cut this with a pen knife. Probably he drew the cross on first, then cut around it. He did a pretty good job, but he was no pro." I had already stopped looking at the seals and was looking at the shawl. It looked new, and it felt warm and rich.

What Papa Iason said next was exactly what I was thinking. "That is not the shawl of a poor woman."

I should not have said, "Hell, no!" but I believe I did.

"It is of silk and lamb's wool woven together. My cassock is wool and much rougher than this. But in a shop where such things are sold, I have seen cassocks of cloth like this. They were very costly."

I spread the shawl out and saw a little label sewn into one side. I could not read it, but I borrowed paper from Papa Iason and copied it down. When I was sure I had all the letters right, I asked him to translate it for me. Here it is in English:

BEST MILLINERY
LILY & CIVET, UPSTAIRS

I said I thought the streets here did not have names, and he said, "They do not. It is the lily and the civet that bother you?"

"Sure. If they're not street names, what are they?"

"There will be a sign. It will say 'Lily and Civet,' and there will be pictures on it. A lily is a flower." He shaped a trumpet with his hands. "A civet is a kind of cat. Its fur has stripes and dots."

"Got it. Do you know where this place is?"

He shook his head. "Look where costly things are sold."

So I was back to the dress shops and so forth. Maybe I had walked right under that sign already, but if I had I did not remember it. I wanted to take the shawl with me, but he did not want me to and got mad, so I let him keep it.

16

A LONG DAY'S END

Maybe you will say that I ought to have gone looking for Best Millinery, but I was tired and knew it was a long way back to Naala's building. What was worse was that the sun was about down, which meant the shops would be closing. The streets were not as crowded as they had been, and every so often you could hear somebody pulling down one of those rolling grills over a shop window.

The good part was that it was getting cooler. Just the little fire in Papa Iason's parlor had seemed like way too much to me, but a stiff wind off the lake played with dust and dirty papers in the street, the sun was as good as gone, and I felt like I would wish pretty soon that I had the wool sports jacket Naala had wanted me to wear.

I was thinking a lot about that when I heard my own voice. It is a funny sensation if it happens when you're not expecting it, and that time it stopped me dead. After a minute or two I realized that I was talking about the Legion, and that I was hearing a radio. Somebody had an apartment over the street-level shop in the building I was passing, and he had left his radio on and his window open a little. I listened for maybe a minute more before it hit me that it was not a good thing for me to be doing if a cop passed by.

So I got moving after that and told myself I was not even looking for a sign with a lily and striped cat on it, there would be plenty of time for that tomorrow morning. Only I *was* looking for it. I could not help it. All that I was really doing was telling myself I was not.

Then I saw it. Just when I was practically out of downtown and could feel a couple of blisters on my feet, I saw it. The cat had pushed aside the lily to look out at you. Under my breath I said, "Oh gosh, isn't that *cute!*" Meaning I would have liked to set it on fire.

There were doors to two shops, and a third door with a little sign I could not read. Both shop doors were locked, so I figured the third one would be, too. But I shook the handle like you do and the door opened right up and showed me a flight of stairs.

So okay. I went up, and there was a little hallway there with two more doors. They were locked, but they had glass in them. I looked into both shops, and I could see inside pretty good. Later I found out that was because there were skylights. I will say more about those in a minute. The first shop I looked into made me think of the one that had taken Rosalee in. There were hats on fake heads and beautiful silk dresses on dummies. Bras and lacy underpants, too. All that stuff.

The second one had the darnedest jumble of junk I ever saw. There were boxes and books and about a hundred dried roots on a string and something that looked sort of like a man's head. It had a mustache and a scrawny beard, but it was not much bigger than my fist. My brain started itching when I saw all that, but I was way too tired to be even a little bit smart.

Well, I went back down the steps and the door at the bottom had locked. In the States a door like that would probably have had some way you could open it from inside. This one did not. There was a sort of brass box on it, and the bolt came out of there and into a smaller brass box on the frame, and that was it.

So I sat down on the steps and rubbed my feet, and cussed it, and tried to think. I could have kicked that door down, but it would have made a racket and drawn a crowd, and by the time I got it open there would be a cop out there. Maybe two or three.

I could sit on those steps all night. In the morning somebody might unlock the door, and I might be able to get away from him without getting busted, but maybe not.

So how about the shops upstairs? If I could get into one, there might be a back door. And if there was, it was probably just bolted from inside. What was more, I could probably break the glass in those doors without anybody outside hearing. I would be doing it up on the second floor, and the windows were closed.

So up I went. Hats or head? I felt like flipping a coin, but I did not have one. After a minute, what I really did was flip an imaginary coin and call, heads! Naturally that settled it. The glass broke as soon as I kicked it, and in I went.

That head felt like leather and I was tempted to boost it, but it reminded me of the hand way too much. What if it came alive, too? I let it be.

There was no back door, no back stairs, nothing like that. On the other hand, there were windows at the front and back of the building, and one on one side. They were locked, sure. But anybody could turn the catch from inside and open the window. I opened one myself just to prove it. It was a back window with a dirty patch of bare ground down below. Maybe I could have let myself down and dropped, and walked away from it. But maybe I would have broken my ankle, too. Basically, looking out of the back and side windows showed you big trees. Out the front windows, you saw a few little trees, then the street, then the trees on the other side.

I had already noticed the skylights, and it seemed like they might be better. I cleared some stuff off the top of a table and climbed up on it. Opening the skylight was a piece of cake. It took me a couple of minutes, no more than that, to get it open and pull myself up onto the roof. It was flat, gravel over tar. I went to the edge, and sure enough, one of the big trees on the side of the building had reached a limb over the roof. I grabbed it and climbed into the tree, going from limb to limb until I was only about six feet above the ground.

That was better than okay, but once I was down I had a thought. It was a crazy idea and I was tired, but getting out the way I did had perked me up. What I did was climb up again, which was pretty easy, get up on the roof, and close the skylight.

I was not just trying to be nice. That skylight was closed now, but not locked. Whoever ran the shop was going to see his glass door had been busted, and he was going to check his stock and find out nothing was missing. (Really I had taken one thing, but it was not from the stock.) So he would figure somebody had broken in but had not found anything he wanted and had gone out the same way. It could be weeks or a month before he noticed his skylight was not locked. Meanwhile I could get in anytime I wanted to by climbing the tree and pulling up the skylight. Want to know why I thought that might be handy? It was just because the head had reminded me of the hand.

So after that I went back to Naala's. I did not have a key, but when I

knocked on the door she let me in right away. "You I was expecting earlier. I had begun to think some hurt had befall to you."

I shook my head. "Nothing. I've been walking my feet off, that's all."

"You are not hungry?"

I just about said I was starved, but I thought about it for half a second
or so and realized I was not. I was too tired to be hungry. "No," I told her,
"or not very. If you were to offer me a bowl of corn flakes I'd probably eat
it, but I wouldn't walk outside the building to get one."

She gave me the grin. "You fear I will wish you to walk a hundred kilometers to some café."

I shook my head. "I fear you'll wish me to walk fifty meters. Okay if I
take off my shoes?"

"You are my guest, how can I refuse? A glass of wine? Some I have that
is not so bad."

I only had one shoe off, but I stood up anyhow. "I'll get it. You must be
tired, too."

It worked. Naala jumped up and said, "No, I. I know where is it, and
you do not. Besides, you would drink the bottle in the kitchen."

I sat down again. . . .

Something touched my hand. Naala's voice. "It is here."

I had leaned back and closed my eyes. Now I opened them again and
took the wine.

"Taste. If you do not like, I will drink."

I tasted. "You think I'll think you're trying to poison me, right? You
won't, because it wouldn't make sense."

"Also I like you. More also I have the uses for you. So no. Do you like it?"

It was too sweet for me and not cold enough, but I said I did.

"A gift from someone who desires many favors. I will complain of it."
She giggled, something that always caught me off guard. "If I complain
well, he may give me better. You have walked from shop to shop, yes?"

"Yes. One hell of a lot."

"You did not find Rathaus?"

"I didn't even get a smell of him." I was taking off the other shoe. "Let
me tell you something. Either he doesn't know Rosalee's out of jail, or he
knows she doesn't need clothes."

"Or he is unable. Or too much frightened. Or a hundred other things."

"You're wrong. It's one of those two things. You'll see when we find him."

For a while Naala did not say anything. She sat down and studied me, sipped from the glass she had poured for herself, and studied me some more. Finally she said, "You do not speak."

"I'm tired, like I told you. I'm tired and my feet hurt."

"You have found something or learned something. You have that to say which is of interest, but you wait the moment."

I shrugged.

"The moment has arrived, Grafton. What have you learn?"

"Well, for one thing there's nobody looking for Rosalee except the JAKA. I saw one, a middle-aged lady. Nice dress, gray hair. Do you know who that is?"

Naala nodded. "Proceed."

"Here's the bad one, and it may be the biggest I've got. I know why Rosalee escaped."

"It was not as I said?"

"No. Or anyhow, not exactly. You know, you could have some food for us delivered here."

"Ah-ha! You must be bribed."

I grinned. "A pizza or something. That's pretty cheap for what I've got."

"That word I do not know, only that it is food you want. I am to walk to the café. There I am to pay and walk empty home. In time someone will bring our food. All so you may remain in my chair and be lazy."

"It was just a suggestion."

"If I do this you will tell me?"

I nodded. "Absolutely. Word of honor."

"All right. I go. All day I am here. Now for me the breath of evening."

She went out, but she was back before I could fall asleep. Say, five minutes tops.

"Now I have done as you say. Tell me."

I said, "I didn't know there was a café as close as that."

"Tell me!"

"Not til the food comes. I'll tell you something else instead. Rathaus sent Martya to Papa Iason with the hand."

That opened her eyes.

"We thought that the hand was sent so it would kill Papa. That was wrong. It was sent so he could kill it. That's the only way the stuff I found out makes sense."

"Tell me." Naala was leaning way forward, and her eyes caught the light. I thought of a German shorthaired bitch I had seen one time. In a second or so she would get the signal to range, then she would run from side to side, farther and farther out, sniffing and listening and looking for birds. If they were there, she would find them and point them for the guns.

"Let's start here. Martya isn't hurting. She had on good clothes when she came to see Papa Iason. New shoes and so forth. The hand was wrapped in a shawl—you know that already. I saw it and it's a good one, not cheap and just about new."

"Go on."

"As soon as she got there she wanted to know if Papa owned a crucifix. Naturally he did, and his housekeeper said so. When she saw him, she told him he must hold his crucifix in his right hand and throw the hand in the fire with his left."

"There was no fire," Naala said. "This he is tell us."

"Huh-uh. He was lying, I think because he was afraid we'd blame him for not burning the hand."

"He tells this woman he will do this?"

"He didn't say that, but I think he did. Then he got interested in the tattoos and decided he ought to take it to the bishop instead. Either she told him how dangerous it was—he didn't say she did—or he just sensed it from the way she acted. So he locked it up. She'd had it wrapped in the shawl and the shawl sealed with wax, then both of them put in a basket with a latch. There were crosses on the seals."

"You will tell nothing of importance until our food come."

"Right."

"So I ask no more questions. Instead I tell you. Do you not wonder what I have done?"

I nodded. "Sure. What were you up to?"

"I am look for the hand. I tell myself it must be here, in my apartment. It cannot have gotten out. It is too big to crawl through the drains. Can it climb the flue? That is too small for a man, but once I have a squirrel come down, very dirty. He try to climb back up, but he cannot. Always he soon fall back. Can the hand climb where a squirrel cannot? I do not think so."

"So you shot him."

Naala shook her head. "I open the window for him, but he does not see. Always he tries to climb up and scratches down more soot. At last I try to hit him with the poker, but I cannot. He tries and tries until he falls dead."

"So you don't think the hand could do it."

"I do not. There is nothing to grasp but soot, and always the soot give way. Also, if the hand try to climb it must knock down soot. I look, but there is none. It is here, I tell myself. It must be here."

I said, "You're probably right."

"It is not. I look everyplace it might be and in many places where it could not be, places too small. I look also in places that are locked. It is in none of them. Have you eaten today?"

I remembered the crispy bread and plum jam. "Yeah, a little."

"I have not. Not since you go."

"Okay, I get the picture. Ask me a question. I'll give you a straight answer if I can."

"Where is Rathaus?"

"I don't know. I've really got no idea. Outside the city, if I had to guess. Is there a big park outside the city? Or a swamp? Anyplace with lots of trees and animals?"

"The Frost Forest, perhaps."

I had some trouble translating that name for myself. Later I talked to a few other people about what it meant, because I had come up with "Forest of the Small Ice" and a couple of others along that line. "Little-Ice Forest" made sense until you thought about it. Anyway, I asked Naala why they called it that.

"Because the ice there does not melt until midsummer. In the old time, people went there and cut ice in June. This they brought into the city and sold. It is no longer needed, but perhaps you understand."

"I think so." I had been letting my eyes wander around the room looking for places where the hand might hide. "Did you look in that closet?"

"Everywhere I look. This closet? Pah! I take out everything. I search each as I put back in."

"How hard would it be to search the Frost Forest for Rathaus?"

"Hard, yes. Impossible, no. We would call upon the army, which we do not like to do. For it we must go to the Ministry of War without hats and bow very low. It would take three weeks, a month, and if Rathaus is warn . . ." Her shoulders rose and fell.

"I got it. We'll try to smoke him out on our own."

"With which you must help. You say you do not find him, but it seem you find much. Soon our food come. Tell me more."

"Okay. There's two things. I'm pretty sure they're going to come together eventually, but they haven't done it yet. One's Rosalee. The other's the hand. Which do you want to hear about?"

"The hand. It is for the hand I search."

There was a little tap at the door. Naala motioned to me, so I walked over in my stocking feet and opened it. The kid outside was so small I thought at first there was nobody there.

"He won't send nothin'," the kid said. "Tell the lady. The man at Horváth's. Tell her."

Naala was behind me by then. "For this he suffer."

"He say he got nobody to carry. I got your money." The kid fumbled in his pocket.

"That is for you. You did as I said and so earned it. You may keep it." Naala turned to me. "Put on your shoes. We go out."

If arguing would have done me any good, I would have argued. The sound of her voice told me it would only get me shot.

"First to Horváth's. You are a good fighter."

"No, I'm not!"

"You must be, so you are. After, we eat."

I could only hope the other guy was worse than I was.

Horváth's was smaller than most of the cafés I had seen, and maybe a little cleaner. It might have held eight or ten, but there were only three or four customers inside, plus a big man and a girl, both wearing aprons. She was sweeping out, and he was behind the counter packing coffee mugs back into a cabinet. The mugs were in a tin tray and had probably just been washed in the kitchen. I tried to size him up while I hung my sports coat on the back of a chair. A good wool sports coat is something you do not want to fight in.

Naala got his attention by grabbing the edge of the tray and dumping the cups on the floor. A couple of them broke. "So," she hissed, "it is impossible for you to send someone with my suppers." He was a lot bigger than Kleon but maybe twenty years older.

There was a glass case half full of pastries on the counter. Naala had better luck with that than the cups. The glass broke when it fell and the pastries scattered all over. He had turned around to look at her by then, his eyes popping.

"You wish to summon the police? Do so! Many I know. Them I shall be glad to see. Hit him, Grafton!"

I feinted with my right and busted his mouth with my left, figuring he was not expecting it. Most likely he was not expecting anything. He took a step back and threw his hands up to his face the way you do. There was a metal carafe on the work counter behind him, so I picked that up and banged him over the head with it, putting everything I had into the bang. It must have been at least half full, because it felt heavy and he went down and stayed down.

I was putting my jacket back on when the girl with the broom ran up and whispered, "Thank you! Oh, thank you!" I knew then that I had seen her before, but for half an hour or so I could not remember who she was.

Outside, Naala said, "His mouth bleeds. You have cut the lips. This I see."

"Probably his teeth did it. He had good, strong teeth." I was rubbing my knuckles. I had turned them horizontal and nailed him with everything I had, and they still hurt.

"When you knock at my door, you are a most tired young man. No longer. You will be strong and straight in my bed tonight, and this too I see."

Hearing Naala say that I felt like whistling, so I whistled. She would think I was an idiot, and I knew it. Only if I had not whistled, for the rest of my life I would remember that moment and how I had wanted to whistle but had not had the guts.

I was still whistling when we sat down at an outside table at a café sort of down the street. (I mean as much as you could talk about down the street in that crazy city. In Puraustays the blocks with buildings had been square or else rectangular, but mostly square. Here some were round or kidney-shaped.)

It was pretty cold for outside tables by that time. There was another couple two tables over, and maybe half a dozen empty tables. There were a lot more people inside. "Here is more private," Naala explained. "For you and I, private is good. Also I hear better the things you say. Why it is the Rathaus woman do not need clothes?"

"Because she's hiding out in one of those dress shops. She's scared of you, and I promised her I wouldn't tell you which one. So I won't. But you could find her easy enough anytime you really wanted to, and I'll produce her if we need her."

"The shopkeeper hides her?"

"Right. And gave her some nice clothes. The thing is, we mustn't send her back. You thought at first that somebody must have gotten her out."

Naala nodded.

"Well, in a way somebody did. There was a girl named Yelena in there who looked a lot like Rosalee. She slept in the same building, and had a bed not very far from where Rosalee slept on the floor. Rosalee was lying there nearly asleep when she saw a man come in and go from bed to bed looking at the women. When he came to Yelena's bed, he stabbed her. Or anyway that was what Rosalee thought she saw."

Naala raised an eyebrow. "But he did not?"

"I don't think so." I was getting close to things I really did not want to talk about. "I think it must have been a hypodermic needle. Something like that. Only Rosalee thought it was a knife, and as soon as he was gone she got out fast. I never asked her exactly how she got out, but we both know security's pretty lax. They're counting on the women not wanting to get out all that much."

A waiter showed up about then, and we ordered *kabanos*.

When he had gone, I said, "I told you about Yelena. Nobody saw anything wrong until she collapsed. They took her to the infirmary, and I went to see her there."

"Yes. What did you learn from her?"

"More respect for death, I guess. She couldn't talk much, but I was sitting beside her when she died, thinking about the man Rosalee'd seen."

"It was Rathaus? Like him?"

"It was everybody. She couldn't see him that well, just a man. I asked her how she knew it was a man, but she couldn't tell me. She just knew. Men move differently, I guess."

"This Yelena, she does not cry out?"

"When he stabbed her? I doubt it. Rosalee didn't say anything about it." I thought back. "Yelena gave me a name, a guy who kept hanging around her. Ferenc Narkatsos. She said he wouldn't try to kill her, but I don't think anybody really wanted to kill her. I think they were after Rosalee."

"I, also," Naala said. "We will remember this name when we have nothing else, perhaps. You have more for me, you say. The woman who brings the hand to Papa? You say Rathaus sends her. This is because you wish to find her. You will say Rathaus and I will look for her for you."

I shook my head. "I said it because it's true. I'd like to find Martya, sure. But she's mixed up in this, and if I'm going to get her out I need to understand what's going on. For one thing I've got to find out how Rathaus got the hand. Another one is I have to find out how he got Martya."

"If he have her, of which you are too confident. You speak again with Papa."

I nodded. "You were the one who said Martya might have mentioned me to Papa Iason, and that might be the reason Papa Zenon was sure she was here."

"I am guilty. I do not know this, or anything. Only that Papa Zenon believe she have come here. He is not like you—for say it he must have some reason. Papa Iason does not tell you she says this?"

"No. I was hoping he would, but he told me everything she said while she was with him. Or anyway he said he did. And that wasn't in it."

Naala looked thoughtful. "Too many are elbowing, one pushing another."

"What does that mean?"

"What it say. Those who send the gray-hair lady and three more hope to find Rathaus first. I hope to find Rathaus first. Papa Zenon hope to find those who free him before us."

I said, "You still haven't asked me how I know it was Rathaus who sent Martya with the hand."

"I do not ask this because it is too easy. She is go to Rathaus's son, of all priests. Rathaus think, 'My son will do this and will not bungle.' Others would not think this."

"Nope. I've got more. There are two shops, right side-by-side. One handles ladies' clothes, good stuff. The other one magic supplies. Not for tricks with boxes like that guy we saw, but roots and dried flowers, funny stones all polished and packed in cotton in little boxes. Powders. Bones. Stuff in bottles with labels I couldn't read. Like that. It was one of the places that bought dolls from Russ."

"The Rathaus woman tells this?" I could see Naala was interested.

"No. She can't remember the names. I know about it because I broke into the shop and saw some of Russ's dolls. That shop next door, with women's clothes? It's where the shawl came from."

After that, Naala was quiet until our sausages came. There was bread and butter and mustard, and lots of other stuff with them. So while she was thinking hard, I built a sandwich, *kabanos* and grilled garlic on nice soft white bread.

Finally she said, "It may be that Rathaus is hiding in that shop."

I shook my head. "He isn't there. I looked."

"They let you search?"

Head shake again. "I broke in. I told you that."

"You perhaps break into prison."

"I've been in prison already," I explained. "I was put in for nothing and locked up in there until you got me out. I figure I might as well do whatever's handy. Then if I have to go back I won't waste a lot of time thinking how innocent I am. Hey, if the American embassy knew about me, would they try to get me out?"

"You are rich and famous?"

"Okay," I said. "I've got it. Don't laugh at me."

"I am not laughing. You find much in one day. I am try to think of one in JAKA who sometime find out so much so fast, but I cannot. We send a letter to Papa."

"Papa Iason?"

"Of course no. Papa Zenon."

She clapped her hands, and when the waiter came she got paper and an envelope from him. I watched her write for a while, and that was when I remembered the girl with the red pen. The guy I had punched out in the coffee shop was not the one who had been sitting with her in the other café. I was pretty sure of that. When Naala had finished, I asked her what she had said.

"I say that we are not his enemies, and he is not ours. Friends is better. We are search for Rathaus, Papa for those who work magic by the help of devils. These are not the same, but we believe Rathaus know who they are, also that they know where Rathaus hide. They are key to him, and the hand is key to them. We are given the hand by His Excellency, as he know. Let us work as one."

"That sounds good," I told her, "only you said you couldn't find the hand."

Naala smiled. "I do not say we have it still. Also, it may be we find it tonight, you and I. Too soon it is to say it is forever gone."

"Okay."

"At end I say let us meet for breakfast in the Great Square Café. It is where we see him this morning."

She had been folding the paper while she talked. She waved to our waiter, and when he came over she showed her badge and gave him the letter and some money. He nodded a lot, listening to her instructions, and when he left he was almost running.

"Will he read it?" I asked her.

"This I do not think, but perhaps I am wrong. If he read, he will not learn much. What is he to do? Say to Rathaus the JAKA look for him? Rathaus already know, I think. Tell to the magic workers, 'The arch-bishop does not like you?'"

I ate and thought. Pretty soon my sandwich was gone, and I had hardly tasted it. Finally I said, "You're after something Papa Zenon knows. Or anyway, something you think he might know. Something you want to find out."

Naala laughed. "To you I am glass. Two things."

"Will you tell me?"

"If you wish. First I desire to know what it is Papa Iason tells by which Papa Zenon know the woman who brings the hand is your Martya."

I said, "I see what you mean. Yeah, we'd sure like to have that."

"Also does Papa Iason know where is Rathaus? He will not tell Papa Zenon this, I think. But Papa Zenon is more clever than him. He may know Papa Iason knows, or know he does not. This will be most useful for us."

"You ought to have somebody follow Papa Iason. That's how they would do it back in America."

"Amerika have more operatives than we, perhaps. We cannot waste three on this priest. If he knows, it is not waste and so is good. But we must know he knows this."

"You could assign one."

"To which hours? Shall he begin at nine and go home at five? If Papa Iason go, night is most probable, but night is most hard, too. Two operatives by night, then. Or three. Five should be enough, perhaps. Now this. A man come to see Papa. Our operative do not see his face. He go away. Should two operatives follow? Or it is better they stay to watch the house?"

So more thinking for me. Finally I said, "Could you put a bug on his bike?"

"I have ask for this already. Tomorrow it is done, perhaps. We will find out."

"Got it."

"Let us go back. What is the name of the shop you find that have the dolls?"

"I couldn't read it. I've been trying to catch onto the sounds of your letters, but I'm not very good at them yet. You get fancy, like English."

"Then is easy for you."

"I wish it was." I was fishing in my shirt pocket. "I didn't steal anything from that shop, but I took a business card. There was a little stack of those on the counter." I handed the card to her.

"This is good." She pointed to a corner. "Here is name of owner."

"That's what I figured it was."

"It is a name I already hear. Do you know this?"

I shook my head. "I couldn't read it. I told you."

"Then I read for you. 'Abderos Narkatsos.'"

It sounded familiar. I scratched my head.

"You say Ferenc Narkatsos."

"That's what Yelena said. That was the guy who always hung around her."

"It is the same family? That would be good to know. Tomorrow I will find out."

I said, "I don't see where that's a clue at all." I had finished my sandwich by then and was sipping wine.

"Nor I. But when you investigate and here is the same thing twice, you look more. This I will do."

That was the gist of what we said that evening, and pretty soon we got up to go. There were cops at Horváth's, one talking to some man I had never seen before, and one eating some kind of sweet roll. The girl who had been sweeping, the girl with the red pen, was out of sight if she was still around. Naala did not stop, so neither did I. I stuck my right hand in the side pocket of my jacket, I guess because I was trying to look cool.

Only there was a hand in there already. It took hold of mine and gave it a little squeeze, like it wanted to be friends.

17

FROM THEIR DARK PLACES

We were both tired. I had drunk a couple of glasses of zip-code wine at the café, and more wine back in Naala's apartment. Not a whole lot—it might have been three glasses. About like that, and Naala had killed the bottle, so we were fuzzy when we got into bed. One of us would go to sleep and the other one would wake that one up doing stuff. It went on for quite a while.

Of course we both went to sleep eventually. When I woke up the first time and looked at the clock, it was five a.m. Or that is the way I remember it. I had a headache, but I found some aspirin and took two before I went back to bed. I knew it was aspirin from the smell, and the taste when I bit one.

You will probably think I was worrying about the hand the whole time. Well, you are right, but you are wrong, too. I had jerked my own hand out of that pocket as quick as I could get it loose. Boy, did I! After that I kept trying to believe it had not really happened. Most of the time I did, but sometimes I knew it had been real.

When we finally got up that morning it was almost time to meet Papa Zenon. We got dressed as fast as we could, no shaving or anything, and off we went. I had on the wool sports jacket. I never put my hands in the pockets, but I could tell from the way the jacket hung that pocket was empty. About the time we got to the café, I patted the outside and it was empty all right.

Papa Zenon was there already, with coffee and a plate of Eggs Minsk in front of him. He put down the one he had been eating, stood up, wiped his hand with his napkin, and shook hands with us, Naala first. A real gentleman.

We sat down and he offered us his eggs. Naala shook her head but I took one.

Papa Zenon sat, too. "The anchovies, I suppose. Many people object to those."

"I like them," Naala told him, "but I have not been up long. For me, coffee first. After it, pastries."

I bit into mine. They are sort of like eating a deviled egg, only hot from the oven.

"You have just left your beds? If so, it was I who made you leave them. I apologize."

"I set the time," Naala said. "You did not reply to my letter."

Papa Zenon smiled. "It seemed unnecessary. I am here."

"So are we. Now we fence, you and I. The foils clash. They separate to clash again. Tell me, for what prize do we contend?"

"For command, perhaps, if we join forces." He was still smiling.

"That cannot be. I cannot put myself under your orders, nor could you, a priest, put yourself under mine."

The waitress was at Naala's elbow. She and I ordered, and the waitress left.

"I watched His Excellency this morning." Papa Zenon sounded like he was talking to himself.

"You rise early, in this case. Grafton and I were up late, and so slept late also."

"May I inquire what kept you up?"

"You may, and later I may tell you."

Papa Zenon chuckled. "Let me guess. A young woman died at the Harktay yesterday. You spoke to members of her family."

"We did not, but I wish very much to know why you think it might be so. I find this interesting."

Papa Zenon spread his hands. "From you, I withhold nothing. Can you say the same?"

"I will say this. If we join forces as I proposed, I will withhold nothing."

"Then I am the more generous. Yesterday evening, I spoke with His Excellency. Another priest was present. His Excellency mentioned the hand, which the other priest wished to see. His Excellency explained that he had given it to an operator of the agency we know, and happened to say also that you had turned it over to a young foreigner who was assisting you. At this the other priest looked a trifle surprised."

"Yes?"

"When we were alone I asked why, and he told me he had been asked to say the funeral mass of a prisoner. When he inquired as to the circumstances of her demise . . ." Papa Zenon paused. "It is always prudent to do this. There is a danger of unseemly speech in the homily. One seeks to minimize it."

Naala's coffee had arrived. She spooned sugar into it, but her eyes never left Papa Zenon's face.

"He learned that the unfortunate woman had not died unattended. A foreigner associated with the agency we have had reason to speak of had been at her bedside, or so he was told. A young man."

"Her name was Yelena," I said. "I don't know her last name."

"You were there to extort information from her."

I shook my head. "Just to ask her a few questions. She was awfully weak, though. She couldn't tell me much." Maybe I should have shut up after that, but the look on Papa Zenon's face forced it out of me. "I held her hand while she died."

Everybody was quiet for a minute or two after that. I guess I could have been looking around the Great Square Café then, so I could give you a big description of it now, the army officer and the girl he had probably paid to spend the night with him and all the rest of that shit. But the truth is that I was just staring down at the tablecloth and thinking about Yelena and sugar bowls. In the States we have sugar bowls at home because we trust the people there. In restaurants you get your sugar in little paper packages, because the government knows better than to trust you. Yelena had probably died because somebody made a crazy mistake. America is full of crazy people who might put anything into a restaurant sugar bowl if they got the chance, and maybe you are one of them. Cocaine or sand or powdered bleach. Rat poison. Anything. It had always seemed to me that life in America was a whole lot better than life where I was then, but in some ways it has to be a lot worse because it drives so many people crazy with hate. I have gone on a lot about a crazy country, and while we were quiet and the café was emptying out and quieting down I wondered if my own country was not crazier.

Naala touched my arm. "Papa is speak to you. You do not hear him, I think."

I apologized like you do.

"I do not ask what she tells you," Papa Zenon said, "but I would much like to know what questions you asked her."

I asked Naala if we were partners.

"Already partners I do not think. You may tell him if you think it wise. Or not. You must decide."

I nodded. "I'll tell you, Papa, if you'll tell me how you knew Martya was here."

"This I must tell before, I think, because you do not trust me. I must speak first?"

"That's all right. I'll trust you."

"Ah! I win the bargain." He grinned. "We priests are bad bargainers, all of us. Rarely do I win. Tell me and I tell you what you wish to know. Also I show you. That is better."

Two things happened at once then, neither one of them in words. Naala stiffened up, and I felt the hand come out of my left jacket pocket. At first I thought it was hers, but it was not. I sipped coffee, choked a little, coughed, and sipped some more.

"You are disturbed, my son." Papa Zenon sounded really sympathetic. "I have spoil your breakfast. I apologize."

"Not me, Papa. I was just trying to remember all the questions. I think I've got them now. I asked how she was feeling, and didn't people get her mixed up with Rosalee. You probably know who Rosalee is."

"You will tell me?"

"Sure. She's Russ Rathaus's wife. She and Yelena looked quite a bit alike, which was why I was talking to Yelena."

Papa Zenon nodded. "I see. If one cannot question a witness one questions another who resembles her. Science progresses."

Naala said, "We explain this later, it may be."

"After that, I asked Yelena if there was anybody who might want to kill her."

Papa smiled. "I see."

"She said no. Then I asked if there was anybody who hung around her a lot when she didn't want him to. We call those guys stalkers in America, but I don't think I told Yelena that."

"Your next question?"

"There wasn't any. She wanted a nurse, and I tried to get one for her but nobody came. Then she wanted to sit up, so I cranked up her bed. After that all I did was hold her hand, but she jerked it away just before she died. She was shaking and everything by then."

Naala put her arm around me, and the hand squeezed my left thigh. There was some talk I missed after that. I did not really start paying attention again until my food came. I know how that sounds, but that is how it was.

Naala was saying, "It is like this. We believe those who say the Unholy way free Rathaus. We seek him, yes. But it is not him we desire, or not so much. It is they. You also, for His Excellency. But what is His Excellency to do but summon us? He commands no police."

"He will investigate," Papa Zenon said. "He wishes to drag them from their dark places, not just a few but every one of them. If so many cannot be imprisoned, they can at least be made known. Let their neighbors understand what it is they do."

I said, "One of the things they did was kill Yelena."

Nobody said anything for a minute, so I said, "She was some sort of criminal, I guess. I don't know what kind, and I don't even know her last name. But I mean to get them for it. Only right now, here and now, I mean to straighten you out. Your Unholy Way didn't free Russ. He freed himself, and they're trying to kill him for it. When we find him—which we will—maybe we'll find out enough about them to keep him safe, and that's what I want. He was my friend, and he'd do the same for me."

"Already I know what you believe," Naala said. Her voice was gentler than I had ever heard it. "Also what the JAKA believe."

I felt the hand stir.

Papa Zenon said, "It may be good for us to differ on certain points. It is when one side corrects the other that both progress."

I said, "Thanks, Papa. After that, you don't have to tell me how you knew Martya was here if you don't want to. But if you do, I'll sure listen."

"Photographs." Papa Zenon was smiling the way you do when something hurts. "His Excellency was able to provide me with photographs of three persons I may be sure are among the black magicians. He asked me to look at them, and to identify them if I could."

Naala glanced around the café, which was starting to fill up. "You will show them to us?"

"Yes. We are partners already, though we have not yet agreed. So much information already has been shared. In a moment I will ask you to show me the hand."

"Ah. What if I refuse? Does our partnership remain?"

I put my left hand on the hand then. This was under the table where they could not see me doing it, but the hand was there. It seemed like something dead to me, cold and flaccid, until it started to tremble.

"It does." Papa Zenon was answering Naala's question. His eyes shone, and I had the feeling that the mouse would run but circle around behind us. He would be friendly and understanding if Naala cooked up some bullshit to explain why we did not want him to see it, and pretty soon he would come up with a way to put pressure on us.

Naala said, "Let us see these pictures."

"I will. You understand, I hope, that I am not the only investigator His Excellency has looking into this matter. There are several of us, but he fears that one may be a spy. Which one he does not yet know. For that reason and others, none of us knows the identity of the rest."

"It is a poor system," Naala told him, "but it is one we, too, are often forced to employ."

Papa Zenon had reached down and pulled up a scuffed black leather case with a zipper. He unzipped it and got out three photos maybe three by five, all old-fashioned black-and-whites. He offered them to Naala first.

She shook her head, but when I spread them out to look at, she leaned over so she could look, too. The first one was Russ and the second one was Rosalee.

The third one was Martya.

I gave them back to Papa Zenon and said, "Okay, that answers a question Naala and I have had for quite a while."

That got me the elbow. "Her he knows in Puraustays?"

"He met her there, yeah. He caught up with Martya and me in some café, and the three of us talked about a lady we wanted underground. He did it after I was gone."

I turned to him. "You still say that? The suitcase and everything?"

Papa Zenon nodded. "I told you the truth."

"I know you must have said some prayers. Maybe you sprinkled holy water on the suitcase or in the grave. Something like that. Martya must have been there, since I wasn't. Did she have fits or anything?"

"Ah!" Papa Zenon grinned. "You think she may be a vampire. Or you think I think this."

"Did she?"

He shook his head. "Vampires and certain others are said to react so. Mere witches do not. Do you know how a witch proceeds when she wishes a consecrated host?"

I said, "I guess she steals it." The hand had slipped into mine.

"Of course. But how?"

"Breaks into a church at night, maybe. Or maybe she could bribe a priest if she had money."

"It is easier than either. She attends mass, receives communion, and holds the host in her mouth until she can remove it without being ob-served. If she can hold a host in her mouth and escape unscathed, what is holy water to her? Ask whether I think your Martya a witch."

Naala said, "Do you?"

Slowly, Papa Zenon swung his head from side to side. "I do not. I have many reasons. Do you wish them?"

I said, "I don't. I knew her pretty well and lived in the same house. I'd have seen something. Besides, she was scared, really scared, one time when we were in the Willows after dark. A witch wouldn't have been, or I don't think so."

"Nor do I. She sins, as do we all. But witchcraft?" He looked as though he wanted to spit. "Not she."

Naala said, "The other two photographs. Them you know also, I think."

"I do not, but I believe you may. Identify them for me, and I will tell you anything you wish to know."

"For the man, I also can show a photograph. You will find his name on it."

It was a prison photo, of course. Naala took it out of her purse and handed it to Papa Zenon.

He looked at it, then at me. "This is your friend, you say."

I nodded. "Right. He is."

"He does not say the black mass?"

I made it firm. "Hell no!"

"And the other?" Papa Zenon held up the photo.

"That's Russ's wife, Rosalee."

"He has escaped. She also? It must be that they are together."

I said, "Maybe, but I don't think so."

"He will come to her, in that case. Or she will fly to him. You do not know where she is?"

"For sure? No."

"But you suspect."

I shrugged.

Naala said, "You tell us that if we identify those in your pictures you will tell us anything. We have done as you wished, and I have the question."

Papa Zenon nodded. "Ask."

"I ask a small question first. Where is Rathaus? Do you know this?"

Papa Zenon put down his cup. "I do not. If I did, I would tell you."

"The big question, in that case. Do you think Papa Iason knows this? I do not ask for proven fact, only for your opinion. Does he know?"

"I have no idea. I ask in return, why should he? Why is it you think he might?"

"Rathaus is his father."

I have seen some surprised people, but I do not think I have ever seen one who looked any more surprised than Papa Zenon did then. He froze. His mouth opened a little and stayed that way, and it looked like his eyes were going to pop right out of his head.

Naala said, "You must tell him, Grafton."

"How much?"

"All. We hide nothing."

"Okay." I scooted my chair closer to the table and sat up straighter. "Naala figured it out, not me. At first I didn't believe her, but pretty soon we found out Russ had come here three years ago to see Papa Iason ordained."

Papa Zenon got out his pictures again and stared at Russ's while Naala and I ate. After a while he nodded.

"Again I ask," Naala whispered. "Does he know?"

"This I have answered," Papa Zenon said. "For you I have a better question, but it is one neither of us can answer. If he knows, will he tell?"

I said, "Maybe you two can't answer that one, but I can. No. He won't."

"This you cannot know," Naala told me.

Papa Zenon said, "That may be true, but he believe he can." He spoke to me. "Why do you say this, Grafton?"

I sipped a little coffee while I pulled my thoughts together, glad that it was my left hand that the hand was holding. "Let's start here. Papa Iason isn't a good man. I told Naala that already, and it's true. He's a bad one trying to be good, like a lot of us. In English, we've got an expression, 'So good he's good for nothing.' Papa Iason isn't like that."

Papa Zenon said, "I agree."

"Russ is his father, and he knows it. I'm not going to take the time to explain how we know about them, but we do. If he knows where Russ is, he also knows Russ hasn't done a damn thing that ought to land him in prison. I've talked to Papa Iason enough to get to know him a little. Send his innocent dad off to rot in prison? No. He's not that kind. He'd die first."

"That is a big word, 'die.'"

Papa Zenon had spoken very softly, but we stared just the same. Or anyhow, I did.

Naala said, "Yes," almost as softly. Then, "How best to do it?"

They had lost me, and I guess my face showed it. Papa Zenon said, "If Papa Iason believes his father dying, he will hurry to him. A priest, a large man, all in black. It would not be difficult to follow him."

"He would take his bicycle, I think," Naala said. "We have a way to follow that bicycle."

I said, "He told us he hitched rides on wagons."

She nodded. "It may be so, but I do not think. He wishes to keep the bicycle to himself."

Papa Zenon got out his pictures and laid Martya's on the table. "Might she lie for us if you asked it?"

I said, "I don't know, but it doesn't make any difference. Martya knows where Russ is."

Naala set down her cup with a little bang. "You cannot know that."

"Sure I do. Russ sent her to Papa Iason with the hand."

Under the table, the hand squeezed mine. It meant *right on,* and I knew it.

"Just look at it. Here's Martya, a good-looking girl in Puraustays. She'd love to get to the big city, fame, the bright lights, the club scene, all that stuff. She and I went to some clubs in Puraustays. They're pretty awful, and she knows enough to know that. Here in the capital is where the action is."

Papa Zenon nodded. "Continue, please. I am most interested."

"I also," Naala said.

"All of a sudden, I'm gone and nobody knows where. Bang! and she's a widow because the cops shoot Kleon—Kleon was her husband when I knew her. Maybe she gets some money from his life insurance. For sure she can sell the house. So whatever, and off she goes. Next thing we know, she's bringing the hand to Papa Iason. How the heck does she get it?"

"You must ask yourself," Naala told me. "We do not know."

"I have and it's easy. The Unholy Way is trying to kill Russ. I told you that. They send the hand to do the job, give it to him or smuggle it into the place where he's staying or whatever. That doesn't work. Russ grabs the shawl from somewhere and wraps it up. He has sealing wax, or somebody there does, and there's this seal with the crosses he made for some other job, maybe sealing a letter. Whatever. He seals the shawl, stamps it with the cross, and gets Martya to take it to his son and tell him he's got to burn it. He's supposed to hold a crucifix while it burns, and pray, and so forth."

Naala said, "Rathaus is an Amerikan. She does not know him. Or how?"

"I don't know, but I can give one way it might happen easy. Remember the magic shop? I told you about it and gave you that card."

She nodded. "It I still have."

"Okay. Next door's a shop where you can buy women's stuff, clothes, accessories, underwear, all that. Good stuff. Martya has money now, so she goes there. Maybe she'll buy a silk dress or something. She notices the magic shop next door, she's curious and she goes in. But before she goes there she's heard me on the radio. The Legion of the Light has gotten its act together and is broadcasting some of my old recordings. Martya heard one somewhere and recognized my voice."

Papa Zenon said, "Continue, my son."

"She would look for me, or anyhow I think she would. While she was in the magic shop she asked somebody in there about me. Did they know me or know where I was, all that shit. They said, no, no, no. But Russ had told them about me, his cellmate. So the next time they saw Russ they told him. He wanted to talk to this girl Martya, so they found her and brought her to him. She was probably staying in a hotel, so it wouldn't be hard. He got her to work with him after that. That wouldn't be hard, either."

Papa Zenon nodded. "He might tell her he was trying to get you out of prison. He may not know that you are free."

"I'm not exactly free," I told him. "If Naala wanted to, she could pop me back in today."

"Then Martya may hope to free you from her."

Naala made a noise.

"Here's another idea, a good strong one. Russ has money, quite a bit of it, back in America. If he's found some way to tap it, he could have real money here. Martya likes money, and the money she got from Kleon's insurance won't be much. Russ may have hired her. It could be no more than that."

Naala said, "Money is always possible. Money or the promise of money. Other things there are also. How do we tell Papa Iason his father dies?"

"We must consider," Papa Zenon told her. He sounded thoughtful. "There are ways . . . many ways in which it might be done. I wish to consider all that I can call to mind before we act. Whatever we choose to do must convince."

"But you tell us, not act alone?"

Slowly, Papa Zenon nodded. "I will consult you. If I cannot persuade you, I must choose another. Or you must."

I said, "I've a question for you both that's a hell of a lot tougher than that one. How do we keep the Unholy Way from killing Russ after we find him? Suppose the JAKA sticks him back in prison, and in a day or two somebody cuts his throat?"

Papa Zenon said, "He was in prison before, in prison with you. No one tried to take his life, or you would have said this."

"Sure, because they thought he couldn't get out. Now they know he can."

"He will escape again?" Naala asked.

"Or try to. Absolutely."

"He will succeed?"

I shrugged. "How would I know?"

"I do not ask your knowledge, Grafton, only your opinion. What is it you think?"

"Yes, he will if he lives long enough."

Papa Zenon added, "Or he may be released."

"That is better," Naala said. "Better for us of the JAKA if he is die in the street. To die in prison would appear most bad."

"Then let him go," I told her. "Send him to Germany and wash your hands of him."

"I have not the authority. I can persuade, perhaps. I will try. But now we have say all we have to say, I think." She pointed a finger at Papa Zenon. "Do not tell Papa Iason of his father's illness without consulting me, and I will do nothing of that kind without consulting you. You agree?"

"I do, but I am not ready to adjourn. I have never seen the hand. Do you know that? You have seen it, you have held it. Not I, not even for a moment. It moves of itself?"

Naala nodded. "Like a rat it runs. It scuttle on the fingers."

"Most wonderful!"

I said, "Here's the way you have to think of it. It's a young woman's. She's dead, but her left hand is still alive. She's there, it's still on her arm, but she can't lift it or anything. She has to move it by moving the fingers."

"An earthbound spirit."

"Yeah, exactly."

"These I have encountered before, but not like this. Very much I desire to see the hand, to see it move, and to read what is inscribed upon it. You will show it to me?"

The hand squeezed mine. I thought I knew what that meant, but I was not sure. Then it let go and started to climb out of my pocket. I caught it.

"You are a priest," Naala was saying. "You will say it must be destroyed. Perhaps you yourself will try to destroy it."

"If you ask it, yes. Not otherwise. You have it here?"

"It is in a safe place. We can get it if it is needed."

Papa Zenon looked at me. "Do you know where it is, Grafton?"

I nodded, hoping my nod did not tell too much.

"You will not tell me? Tell me, and I will do all I can for you. I have many friends; some are people of great importance here in our little country."

I kept my mouth shut.

"Already I am friendly to you. I try to help you. You will concede this?"

"Sure."

"You have not forgotten the burial you wished me to perform. It was dangerous, and most dangerous for me. Yet I did it and received only empty thanks. I have dunned you for money?"

I shook my head.

"Tell me where is the hand, and I forgive the debt."

I was thinking then and thinking hard. Also I was holding the hand all the time. It would have crawled out onto the table if I had let it go. Finally I said, "Papa, I think you're a little bit of a crook, but you're our crook and an honest crook, meaning not a double-crosser. I want a bunch of things, and they're not the same things you or Naala want. I want Martya. I want to find Russ and get him back to the States in one piece. Let's make that Russ and Rosalee, and I want to get back there myself. Are you following this?"

"I am, my son."

"Will you promise, on your honor, to do all you can to help me if I tell you where the hand is?"

Naala was staring, but I paid no attention to her.

"Your answer will not be a trick?"

"Absolutely not. Honest as daylight, without one bit of bullshit."

"Then I agree. You have my word."

"Okay," I said. I was moving it as I spoke. "It's right here on this table." I was tempted to slap it down, but I did not. I laid it gently on the table-cloth, right in front of his eggs.

18

GETTING AHEAD

When the waiter came around with more coffee, Papa Zenon covered the hand with a napkin. That sticks in my memory, and I always want to laugh. Sometimes I do. It is the kind of nervous laugh that comes when I have a really close call but do not get hurt.

When the waiter had gone, Papa uncovered it and bent over the hand looking at the tattoos. "This is no curse." He pointed to the writing in the palm. "It is a spell to find treasure, first in Greek and after in Latin but the same. Here on the thumb, a prayer to Haaiah. It is very short."

Naala said, "He is a demon?"

Papa Zenon shook his head, hard. "Three times no. Haaiah is an angel, an angel most honored. The supplicant asks that the strangers become new friends. Nothing is in this prayer I myself would not say on my knees."

Naala looked like I felt.

"Here." He squinted at the fine writing on the index finger. "It begs Lamach for peace." He read the prayer to us in Greek, but I do not remember the words well enough to quote them.

"Another angel?" Naala asked.

"Indeed yes, the guardian of Mars." Papa Zenon turned the hand over. "You say this moves. It is a dead thing."

"It moves," Naala insisted.

I added, "I've been sitting pretty still myself."

He gave me a nice smile, a happy mouse. "All you ask me to do, my son, I will do it for you. You fulfilled your part of our bargain. I strive to fulfill mine."

I guess the hand ran across the table while Papa Zenon was looking up, but I did not see it. I did not know what had happened until I felt it climb back into my pocket.

He looked down and then stared at me, but I just shrugged.

When he had gone, Naala asked, "You have it, Grafton?"

"Right. In my side pocket. I didn't know it was in there until we were sitting down in here, and I wasn't sure I ought to bring it up."

"It likes you, I think. Even as I. You must keep it most safe for us."

I said I would.

"Papa is go. Where and to do what? Do you know?"

I shook my head.

"No more do I. What of us? What should we do? I ask the suggestion."

I said, "Go back to your apartment so I can shave."

She laughed. "Another."

"Not me. I gave you mine. What's yours?"

"The magic shop, of course. You say Rathaus is hide there."

"No, I didn't. I say he might have hidden there for a while, or somebody in that shop might know where he is. I think Martya tried to find out where I was, and somebody there recognized my name because Russ had talked about me. Only Russ wasn't in there when I broke in. I searched the whole place, and I would have found him."

"You found signs that someone had been hidden there, perhaps?"

"No. Nothing."

"They clean up most carefully, I think. Often I have find such signs. Bread crusts, perhaps. A blanket hidden it might be."

I shook my head.

"That I do not like, but we will go even so. The shawl bring you there. This you say."

"Right. It was from the other shop. There are two shops on that floor, the magic shop and a dress shop."

"I wish to see both, and they will be open now."

So off we went, walking pretty fast and not talking much. I was going over everything Papa Zenon had said. I do not know why I did it, except that I had a hunch he knew more than he was telling. He had kept saying that he was telling us all he knew. (I have not told you about a bunch of stuff that turned out not to matter.) When somebody does that, it is usually because they are not. So what could he be hiding? He had read more prayers from the hand to us. I have not told you about those, either, but I went over them in my mind as we walked along.

The only thing I came up with was pretty small. He told us he had watched the archbishop early that morning, and I figured it was probably when he climbed the tower where the bells were. That was all he had said, but he had looked worried. Maybe it was just because the archbishop was pretty old, or because he had been out of breath when he came down. But I wondered.

We got to the building and I showed Naala the sign I had seen, the one with the spotted cat pushing the lilies to one side.

She said, "This is the dress shop upstairs?"

"Right. Papa Iason read the label on the shawl for me. It said Lily and Civet. That's what he said, so when I saw this sign I got interested."

"I, too." Naala smiled. "More interesting even is what is not here. Did you see it?"

I did not know what she meant.

"We go to another magic shop once, it is Left-Hand Magic Supplies. We stop and go back because the Rathaus woman see the sign as we drive."

"Right."

"Where is sign for this magic shop you search?"

There was not one, and I mulled that over as we went upstairs.

I had thought that Naala would start with the dress shop, but I was wrong. She went straight to the magic shop. The door I had broken was gone. It had been taken off the hinges and carried away, but you could still see little pieces of broken glass on the floor. We went right in.

A guy came out of the back fast. I suppose he had heard us. He was younger than I would have expected, a lot younger but stooped, and he looked worried.

"Yes. May I help you, madame?"

Naala laughed. "You may show us things if you wish. This I find most interesting."

"We are closed," he told her. "Our door would be locked, but . . ." He let it trail off.

"But you have none. This I see."

"Someone broke in last night. New glass must be fitted. Mounted also. Next week we are promised."

"By then you will have nothing left," Naala told him. "They come back every night and carry away big boxes until all is gone."

He shook his head. "Whoever broke in took nothing. We have examined and counted all the most valuable things. Nothing is gone."

"You have not have much time for this."

"We are two. It is sufficient."

"Ah! You open most early."

The young guy shook his head. "In morning we do not open at all." He cleared his throat. "We are closed. I must ask you go out."

"I go most gladly," Naala told him, "when you have told me what you sell here and display for me your wares."

"You must tell your son to stop poking them."

I said, "I'm not poking."

Naala chuckled. "He is a bad boy. His poor mother he never obeys, but he will come with me when I go. This you will see."

"Soon, I hope." The young guy was about beaten, and he knew it. "You climb the stair to buy a dress?"

"I did not say, I know."

"I do not own this shop," the young guy told her. "To my father it belongs. He is in the dress shop. Go to him and ask to see as you desire. If he says yes, you will see everything."

"He buys a dress for your mother, I hope."

"No. Both shops are his."

I froze when I heard that. When Naala had said we would come here, I thought it was just because she could not think of anything better to do and wanted to keep busy. Now it seemed like a whole bunch of stuff was falling into place in my mind.

Naala was saying, "Then I will speak with your father also," when I came over and braced the young guy.

"You're Ferenc Narkatsos."

He said he was and held out his hand.

I ignored it. "I was a friend of Yelena's." I said that as I swung, and this time I did not go for the face. The heart is right in the middle of the chest, right under the breastbone, and that was where I hit him. Everything I had was behind it, and I followed up with my left so fast it caught the right side of his face before he fell.

Naala had her gun out when I looked around. "Stay down!" was what she told Ferenc. Only she did not have to. He was not getting up anytime soon.

"Much you are too rough, Grafton." She was pushing me back with her free hand, but not looking at me.

"He killed her," I told Naala. "He killed Yelena. You want a picture? I'll draw you one."

Nobody said anything after that, then Naala laughed. "He turn pale. You think you escape the law, Ferenc? It find you out most quick."

"I—I . . ." There were tears rolling down his face.

"You will enjoy hell. This I think. There you will find many like yourself. Do you wish to go and see? If no, you must tell us. Otherwise you try to escape and I shoot. You know about this? It is most easy. I am a senior operator of the JAKA. Here! Look!"

You could tell opening her purse with her left hand and getting out her gold badge was no new trick to Naala. She did it so fast and slick I could not believe it.

"I say, 'I arrest him. We will take him outside and wave to stop a police car, but he run.' They will say, 'Good. A trial cost more than bullets.'"

The young guy—Ferenc—did not speak, so I caught both wrists and twisted his arms behind him like Naala told me. He started gasping, and at first I thought it was because I was hurting his arms and backed off a little. As soon as I did, I saw it was not me at all. The hand was just getting a good grip on his throat. I let go of his arms then and clapped my right hand over his mouth. As quick as I could, I grabbed the hand with my left and jerked it away from his throat.

"You do not like," Naala told him. "Tell us, and you will not see that again."

After that he said, "She wouldn't sign. Everything I say to her, it is still no. She wants the police." There was a lot more after that. That was just the beginning.

Finally we took him downstairs and flagged a car with two cops in it. They put the cuffs on him and one cop got out to make more room.

So it was back to JAKA headquarters. The cop marched him inside, and Naala and I tagged along with me wondering when I would ever get out. And whether.

Next was Baldy's waiting room, only I did not know it was Baldy's until we went into his office. We had been parked outside for about an hour.

"Last night there is a death at the Harktay," Naala told Baldy. "Already it is report a natural death, saying in a young woman the heart fails. This report is what the warden believes."

"You do not," Baldy murmured. He had a desk as big as a boat, and a high-backed leather chair that looked like a throne.

"Better we know. It is murder. She is murdered by a youth of the Unholy Way."

Baldy sat up straighter. "You have identified him?"

Naala nodded. "He is Ferenc Narkatsos."

"You have proof?"

"He has confessed. To Grafton," a wave of her hand showed who she meant, "and to me. Intelligence have him now. He will confess to them, also."

Baldy put his fingertips together. "Tell me of the murder."

"I have learned from Grafton. I will let him speak."

I said, "We were interested in a young woman named Rosalee. Blond and quite attractive. She had been a prisoner in the Harktay but had escaped. Naala sent me there to investigate. I was told that a man had entered the building where they sleep in the middle of the night. Everybody else had been asleep, but the woman I spoke to was awake and saw him. He went from bed to bed looking at faces. When he came to a young woman named Yelena, he looked like he was stabbing her in the chest. Naturally, I went to the warden to ask why we had not been informed of the stabbing."

Baldy nodded.

"She told me there had been no stabbing, but Yelena had collapsed about noon and been taken to the infirmary. I went there to question her. She was weak and couldn't tell me much, but when I asked whether anybody had it in for her she named Ferenc Narkatsos. He'd had the hots for her and she had turned him down. That was all she was able to tell me before she died."

Naala started to say something, but Baldy motioned for her to keep quiet and said, "Had she been stabbed? Did you look at her for a stab wound?"

I nodded. "Yes, sir, after she was dead. There was no knife wound in her chest, but there was a little speck of dried blood between her breasts. It looked to me like somebody had stuck a needle in there."

Naala said, "This concerns the Unholy Way, sir. In them Grafton and I are most interested. Grafton found a shop where many suspicious things are sold. He searched this shop and to me reported much I found of interest. The owner's name is Abderos Narkatsos."

"Ah! I see."

"This morning we go there. Abderos Narkatsos is not present, but his son Ferenc watch the shop. We identify ourselves, and I say you think you kill and escape the law? We have found you most quick. Soon he breaks down, weeps, and confesses, as I have said. In the shop are many poisons. He showed us the one he used and told us how he made a paste of this poison and smeared it on a hat pin. In my purse I have a sample."

She opened it and got out the little glass vial I had found for her back at the shop. "Here is it, sir. What need have I to tell you be most careful?"

That one made Baldy smile. "I will not open before I turn over to Chem. What about the Unholy Way? Might this man's father be their Undead Dragon?"

Naala shook her head. "He is not so high, I am sure. We must watch him. He will know his son is of a sudden gone. Perhaps even he learns his son is arrested. He will be most careful or perhaps run. If he runs, where? To whom does he speak? To these the answers will be of much interest."

Baldy nodded, I think mostly to himself. "You will receive cooperation, operator. I will see to it. This foreigner is useful to you?"

"As you have heard." Naala smiled. "That, and much more besides. He is of talent."

Baldy spoke to me. "Already you are working for our JAKA. This you must know."

I nodded and said I did.

"Now you join us formally. You will be paid, which is always important. More important, you will know we trust you." He got up and went into a little storeroom or walk-in closet that opened off his office, and came back with a badge in a black leather flip-case and a gun in a black cardboard box. Of course I had to swear and so on, and my fingerprints were taken again, just like they had been at the prison, and there was another mug shot. But I am going to skip all that. It was not very interesting.

There was something else first that was interesting to me. It still is, but I can only tell you about it. If you can explain it, I would like to hear from you.

About the time Baldy handed me the badge case and the box, the door of his office opened and somebody else came in. I wanted to look around at him, but I did not. Only when we left to go get me fingerprinted, I saw him. It was the man who looked a little like my father, I mean the third border guard, who was the man I had seen sometimes riding next to the driver in police cars. He was not in uniform this time, and he looked more than ever like the man on the posters. He was sort of short, and had a round face like my father's and a stiff black mustache with a little gray in it like his. After that, I saw him pretty often. I will not always mention him, because it would get boring. Once or twice I asked Naala about him, but she did not know what I was talking about.

So anyway, when we got back to Naala's apartment I opened the badge case first. I wanted to open the black box and have a look at the gun, but I had the feeling it would piss her off, so I did not. My badge was silver instead of gold, and she explained it meant I was a plain operator and not a senior operator. She also showed me the little slot where my ID card would go when it came. It would come by messenger, she said. I put my badge case in the side pocket of my jacket, along with the hand.

After that I got to open the box. My new gun was in there, and it was brand new and very cool. It looked a lot like Naala's, but not exactly, and I ought to say that. With it was a small box of ammo. I counted them, and it was twenty rounds. There were two holsters, too: a belt holster and an ankle holster that I never did use. I loaded the gun, put it in the belt holster, and put it on.

After that, Naala wanted to know if I was hungry. I said I was not; what I wanted to do was go someplace where I could shoot my new gun enough to get used to it.

"You are thrill." She grinned at me.

"Yeah, I guess I am. I've fired guns before, but I've never owned one til now."

"You do not own that one. It belongs to JAKA, which will take it back when you return to Amerika."

I nodded. "Sure. They'll have to, because they're not allowed on the plane. That's okay, because it's mine for as long as I'm here."

"You wish to shoot."

"Yeah. A lot."

"Then I say this. We will go to a range. There I will buy more ammunition, also teach you to shoot. When we are finish, we eat. It will be for us lunch. Dinner also. You agree?"

"Sure," I said. "Absolutely!"

"After this, you must find Rosalee, if she is still where you say you know. You must bring her to me."

I said okay, so that is what we did. The range would have been a really stiff hike, but we got lucky and a car stopped for us. It belonged to a guy who was pretty high up in JAKA, according to Naala, although I do not think he was as high as Baldy who was probably the top man. The neat thing about it was that I got to flash my badge, the first time I had ever done it.

The sportsman's club we were going to was out on the edge of town and about the classiest thing I saw in the whole country. The JAKA had an organizational membership according to Naala. That must have been right, because all we had to do was flash our badges and they let us right in. I got the feeling that most of the members were high up in the government, and the ones who were not, were. You know what I mean. Officially they were not, but they did a lot of favors, and got a lot of favors, too. There was a golf course, a big swimming pool, a casting pool for fishermen, a rifle range, a shotgun range, and a pistol range. All that and more besides, including a bar, a restaurant, a ballroom, and a library. Everything very posh.

Also there was a shop where you could buy various kinds of ammunition, cleaning supplies, and things like that. We rented eye protection and earmuffs, electronic ones that were unbelievably cool.

My gun was a lot simpler than I expected. There was the trigger, the magazine release, and a disassembly lever. That was it. No safety, no grip safety, no little lever in the trigger, nothing like that. Just a long pretty hard trigger pull like you were shooting a revolver double action. The semi-auto I had shot back in the States had a three-position safety lever. Up for safe, down for fire, and down farther for decock. My new JAKA gun did without all that.

That one had a staggered magazine, too, to hold more rounds. This one did not. Just a single column magazine, eight rounds. Like my dad used to say, KISS. It means Keep It Simple, Stupid.

So eight in the magazine, shove the magazine into the grip, shuck a round into the chamber, and off we go. At first I spent way too much time trying to get perfect sight alignment. And to keep it while I pulled that trigger, which was a lot harder. Naala showed me that you did not need it at practical distances. You taught yourself to hold the gun right, got your front sight on the target, and fired. You could not nail the king of hearts that way, but there was not a real good chance the king was going to pull a knife on you. What you could do was score on the chest of somebody with a knife before he got close enough to cut you. Was he going to go down? Probably not, so shoot him again.

So she shot some and I shot some and we had a lot of fun doing it. She was a lot better shot than I was when we started, and when we got finished she was still a better shot. Only just a little, not a lot. Between us we burned up four boxes of ammo, but she said that was good because you wanted to shoot at least a hundred rounds from your new gun to get it running right. Sometimes a new gun would have some problems, like maybe the slide would not close tight now and then for the first forty or fifty rounds, and then the problems would disappear because the parts had smoothed out. That did not happen with my gun, but it got easier to load and the trigger stopped feeling gritty. It still took a pretty hard pull, but the sand was out of the works.

When we got through shooting we went into the dining room and ate. Naala said there was a lot of pricey stuff on the menu, but if we stayed away from it and did not order wine it would not be too stiff. So she had tea and I had coffee and we both had spanakopita with a big salad on the side. When we were about finished, Naala showed me what she had bought for me while I was looking at gun stuff in the shop. It was a watch, not a really nice one but a hell of a lot better than no watch. So I thanked her and we kissed. You know.

After that Naala looked around for a ride home, but she could not find anyone. So we hiked. It had cooled off quite a bit by then and before long the moon rose, so it was not as bad as it sounds. We split up when we got back to the city, me going after Rosalee and Naala home to her apartment.

When I got there empty-handed, she naturally wanted to know what happened. I said, "She wasn't there, that's all. The shop was closed, but the lady that ran it was still inside. She let me in when I showed her my badge. I told her I knew all about Rosalee's hiding there, I was a friend of Rosalee's, and I wouldn't bust her if she'd open up with me. But if she wouldn't, she was going to headquarters. I'd have no other choice but to run her in."

Naala nodded.

"She opened up. When she had come in that morning, Rosalee had been gone. She had left a note, but the lady couldn't read it—some foreign language. I said probably I could read it, and she showed it to me. I read it to her, but I kept it. She didn't mind."

"You must read it to me also, I think," Naala said.

So I did: "My husband is ill and needs me. I must go to him. Thank you! Thank you! Thank you! If we ever get home I will repay you." It was signed: "Rosalee Borden Rathaus."

"This could be the best that could happen for us." Naala was heading for the phone. A minute later I heard her telling somebody to get on the tracking device they had put on Papa Iason's bike.

"It does not yet move," she told me when she hung up. "Soon, I think. Someone know where is Rosalee. About Papa Iason he know, too, I think. Now I go to Papa's house to watch. You must go to the house near the archbishop's palace where priests stay. Find Papa Zenon. Tell him what happen and after you do this—"

The door of her apartment opened. It had been locked but not bolted, and maybe I ought to say that. It stayed open for just a second or so while somebody threw something into the room, then it shut quietly. Its quiet click has stayed with me. I still hear it about once a week, when I am almost asleep.

I went to see what had been thrown in, but Naala beat me to it, rolling it over until the face showed. It was somebody's cut-off head. Thinking back, it seems like it was a long time between the time I realized that and the time I recognized the face. It was Butch Bobokis.

19

OLD FRIENDS AND NEW

The tracer guys had been right: Papa Iason was still at home. This was even after we had spent almost an hour with five JAKA men who rushed over when Naala phoned to report that Butch's head was on her living-room floor.

Did I know who he was? Yes, I did and I told them about him, which was a big mistake. I got about a hundred more questions after that, none of them questions that went anywhere. Naala would not even try to tell them everybody who knew where she lived. About the tenth or twentieth she told them they were wasting our time and ought to get on with the real investigation—who had been seen coming into the building, who had been seen carrying something heavy down the street, and all that—they gave up on us and we scooted. I guess it must have been about midnight by then.

Like I said, Papa Iason was at home, but he was talking to somebody else in the parlor. His housekeeper was up, too, in a moth-eaten old robe and curl papers. She got us to promise to wait in the hall. Which we did, for maybe five minutes. Then I heard a woman's voice say, "Hurry! Oh, please hurry!" I recognized that voice and forgot about my promise.

She was standing in the middle of the floor having a cow, and Papa Iason was pulling on his boots. I yelled, "Martya!" and hugged her. Her eyes just about popped out of her head.

Then she said, "He will want you! He will want you, too!"

We left as soon as Papa Iason got his boots on, all four of us packed into the one police car, both women in back with me and Papa Iason up front with the driver. It was dumb, but I kept wanting to remind Naala that I had never gone to tell Papa Zenon about Rosalee. Only I could not, because I was listening to Martya. Also to Naala's questions. And I was asking Martya quite a few of my own.

You can split all women into two groups. There are the ones who will give you a straight, simple answer, and the ones who tell you a dozen things you don't need to know before they get around to what you need to know, if they ever do. My guess is there are maybe a hundred in Group 1 and all the rest are in Group 2.

So here's Martya, definitely a Group 2 girl, with a whole bunch of editing by me. "When you disappear my husband—you remember my husband? Remember Kleon?"

"Sure."

"He knows they shoot him as soon as they know you are gone. He tells me he will leave in the morning but I think he fears I tell them because when I wake up he is already gone. I wait for him to come home, but he never comes so—"

"Where is Rathaus hide?" Naala asked across me.

"There will be much walking. I will show. I search the whole house for money, because I know Kleon hides money somewhere, but he takes it. In cellar, even, is no money. So I take the money I find and shut up the house. I think where does Kleon not go? It is to the capital! There are the police everywhere I am tell so he does not go there. So I go. Only I have the little money."

I said, "Maybe you've got relatives here?"

"With no money it is no travel. I must find food, find work so I am paid. Once I find a picnic. Three boys they have, also two girls. Their names . . ."

And so on. Naturally I wanted to know whether Martya had sold it and how often, only there was no point asking about that because I would never get the truth that way. What was also natural was that Naala wanted to know where Rathaus was, because that was the main thing for her. Only after a while I could see that Martya did not know the name of the place, only how to get there.

Papa Iason up in the front seat wanted to know what was wrong with him. I got the feeling that Papa knew a good deal of medicine even if he was not a doctor, and I could see how he would, working with poor people all the time and going to sick beds the way he did.

It boiled down to just about everything. Russ could not keep anything on his stomach. He could not move his arms (or not much) and his hands shook when he tried to feed himself. Plus a bunch of other stuff, and it all sounded bad.

"So they make me sign the paper or I will go to jail," Martya was saying. "On this paper are many terrible things I never do. If they give to the police I will hang, but I must sign or they go to the police. I sign and after this I am a slave."

"You were shoplifting," I told her.

"No! I never steal. I take nothing ever!"

"Oh, yes you did! You were shoplifting and they caught you. Listen, it's okay with me, only we've got to have the truth. You went to that shop and boosted some stuff, including the shawl you wrapped the hand in."

I was talking to Martya but watching Naala when I said that, and her eyes went wide for just a second. It made me feel really, really good.

"Some of it you probably sold, but there was some of it you kept," I told Martya. "Only you made the dumb mistake of going back there again because it had been easy the first time. The second time they grabbed you as you went out the door and found their stuff on you. So they had you dead to rights and made you sign. Was the hand supposed to kill Russ?"

"I would not kill him, the hand does it."

"Got it. Did they tell you where he was?"

"He is in Frost Forest. This they know. I find out where."

Naala wanted to know how, and I said, "Two drinks. Remember?" That turned out to be about right. He had a guy in one of the little villages bringing him food, and Martya had found the guy—seen him sneaking off at night with a package—and gotten him to talk.

After that she had gone to see Russ with the hand in a shopping basket the Unholy Way had given her. He was well then, and he had caught the hand and tried to throw it into the fire, only something had happened then that scared him. So he ran down Martya, who had just left, and talked her over onto his side. There would be money, and he would give her a lot of it, enough to buy pardons for her and Kleon with plenty left over after it. Besides they would knock the props out from under the Unholy Way, and she would get her confession back. He was a magician, too, only a good magician and his magic was stronger than theirs. Eventually, she went over. Then he sent her to Papa Iason with the hand.

I knew damn well that sooner or later we would have to get out of the car and hike, and it was sooner rather than later. The Frost Forest was big and empty and quiet. Also cold and as dark as black paint because it was on the north side of the mountain. The cop had a flashlight and Martya had a lantern, but the darkness and the cold seemed to press in on us just the same.

The trees were big and far apart. Their foliage must have been green, but it looked black that night. Most of them did not have limbs until you got three or four stories up. Sometimes it seemed to me like they were just trees, but sometimes it seemed like we were walking over a broken stone floor inside a big, big building with columns all around us, rows and rows of columns that stretched off into the night one hell of a lot farther than I could see.

Somehow I had always thought forests were more or less level. This one was steep, a mountainside like I said, and there were big rocks and little cliffs between the trees. As far as I could see there were no animals, which figured because there was nothing there for them to eat. I asked Martya if Russ was in a cave, and she looked at me funny and said he had a tent. Before I get into this further, I ought to say that the cop who had driven our car did not like being there with us. Naala had made him come.

So was another cop. If I have to tell you who that was, you have not been paying attention.

Let me level with you here. I was expecting to find the man in black with Russ and the prospect scared the crap out of me. He was not there. Nobody else was, either, until we came.

Papa Iason gave him a special blessing for the sick, and that seemed to help him some. Then we went back to the car, with me holding up one side of him and Papa Iason holding up the other. Russ could walk a little, but it seemed to me he was pretty heavy anyway. Naala had put him under arrest, and promised Papa Iason and me that he would get medical treatment and there would be no rough stuff until he was well.

Do I have to say that it was a lot slower, and a lot harder, going back than it had been coming? Sure, we were going downhill. But it was steep and we had to be careful not to fall or drop Russ, and by that time I was so tired I could have laid down right where I was and gone to sleep. I had new blisters, too, and the old ones that had burst or I had lanced hurt like hell.

We were maybe halfway back when it started to get light, not the sun coming up, but a sort of gray light in the sky. That was when it hit me and I knew what was wrong. I said, "He's a doll!" It came out louder than I had wanted it to.

Naala wanted to know what I meant and I said I would tell her if we could take a break, set Russ down, and sit down ourselves. So we did.

"The dolls are magic," I told her. "You've got one, so you know what they're like. You bought yours from that old man with the pencils."

She nodded.

"They're magic, and it stands to reason that the bigger they are the more magic there is, right? Yours is little. Those were the kind Russ sold. Only he made a really big one, a doll as big as he is. I don't know how he got the stuff, but he got it." Of course I thought I could make a real good guess, but I did not say a word about the man in black. Not then and not ever. On my list of people I did not want to piss off, he was Number One.

"That doll was to fool anybody who looked into our cell. Also me, even though I was right in there with it. And it worked like a charm because it *was* a charm, a real one. When I looked over at Russ's bunk I did not see the doll. I saw Russ. Russ, and no doubt about it."

"You are fool," Naala told me.

"Sure, and that may have helped, too. So what happened to the doll when Russ was gone? Well, the last time I saw it two JAKA guys had it. One was Butch Bobokis. You know what happened to him."

"So. We must find the doll and take it from them."

I was standing up and did not answer, and after half a minute or so Naala called, "Where it is you go, Grafton?"

I said, "Come here, and I'll show you." After that I held up both hands and said, "Papa, you come, too."

He came, and Martya after him, and after them the two cops, although you could see the one who had driven hated to leave Russ behind.

About then I heard Naala gasp, and I said, "Yeah," in English.

Because the thing all of us had left behind was not Russ Rathaus. It was sort of like a scarecrow, only a lot better. It lay limp on the moss and rocks, and maybe, even from that distance, you might have thought it was a dead man. Only if you looked closer you would have noticed how boneless it was. Later I found out that it had been in the trunk of his car.

Here I am going to skip a lot more, because what we said and did then does not matter much. Going back to the city, we picked up Rosalee, who had found out from Martya more or less where Russ was supposed to be and was trying to get there. We did not tell her what had happened, just that Russ had gone. I did not want to send her back to prison, so Naala arranged for another female JAKA op to take care of her and Martya. After that, Naala and me finally went to bed. Not the same bed, and no playing around or showers or anything. Naala bolted the door first and disconnected her phone.

When I woke up it was getting dark again. Naala was sound asleep, but I got dressed and went out. Here is the way I figured it, and since it turned out to be pretty much right I am going to fill you in. Russ had been hiding in the Frost Forest in that tent we found. He had gotten sick—really truly sick—and that was when he had sent Martya into the city to tell his wife and his son. He thought he was going to die, and he wanted to see them before he went.

While she was away, he remembered the big doll he had made and got wise that it was being used against him. The bigger the doll the stronger it is, just like I figured. But the closer it is the stronger it is, too. So somebody had the doll and knew about where he was. Or else they were taking it all through the forest and happened to get close. Either way, the thing was to get away from it.

So he had tried, but he had stumbled over it instead, which was even better. The guy who had been using it against him was not there, so Russ had pulled the pins out and taken it back to his tent where he figured it was safe.

Only nobody came. That was because Rosalee had been really hard to find, and after Martya finally found her, she had probably gone back to the place where she had been staying to get some sleep and a bite to eat before she went off looking for Papa Iason. Back in the forest, Russ had gotten worried.

Also scared. The Unholy Way had found out where he was, or pretty close. It was a good bet that when they found out the big doll was missing they would do something else. So Russ took off. If he found Martya, fine. He would call her off. If he did not, he could at least make sure the Unholy Way had a tough time finding him.

That was the way I had figured it, and like I said that was pretty much the way it had been. So where had Russ gone now?

My first guess was the U.S. embassy and I did not know where it was, but I happened to think of a story of my father's. This young lieutenant had to get a pole up to hold wires. It was raining, the ground was mud, and he did not know how to do it. So he grabbed a sergeant and said, "Sergeant! Put up this pole!" Then he walked away.

Should work for me, right?

I flagged down a police car, flashed my badge, and said, "Take me to the American embassy." It worked like a charm. The cop took me to the U.S. embassy, which was maybe a five-minute drive. I said thanks and told him to go back on patrol.

The problem there was that the embassy was closed, and ringing the bell did not work. Neither did pounding on the door. I snooped around for ten minutes or so, but that got me nowhere. I thought things over, and it seemed to me that the next place to try was Papa Iason's. I started walking, figuring I would see a cop in a car eventually. My sense of direction is pretty good, and in spite of the odd-sized blocks and the wiggles the streets had to make to accommodate them I knew about where Saint Isidore's was and kept walking toward it.

What stopped me was a window with a left hand and a white rabbit painted on it. The old guy was still inside moving things from a high shelf to a lower one, and there was a question I had been wanting to ask him.

So I went in, gave him a nice smile, and said, "Remember me?"

He nodded and smiled back. "You will wish to know of the Amerikan magician. He has not been here."

"That's too bad," I said, "but I've got something else to ask you. You know that trick you sold the lady who was with me before? The doll with no face? You put a picture in front of it and it copies the picture. Can you tell me if anybody else in town sells those?"

He shook his head. "I cannot. Where there has been a crime you find one? I am afraid it comes from my shop. I have sold seven now." He paused. "Eight it might be. No more than that. I can give the names of some who have bought them, I think. . . . But not all."

Sometimes you can see when somebody gets a new idea. Their face lights up, and they stand a little straighter.

I said, still very friendly, "You just thought of something. What is it?"

(Right here I am going to change the rules a little. In this book I have called people by their right names, even though I stuck to first names, mostly, and may not have spelled all of them right.)

"Magos X," the old man told me. "He does not sell his dolls, but he has several. Once he tells me he orders from a man in Amerika."

I said, "I ought to talk to him. Can you tell me where he lives?"

He did. So many streets that way and so many streets this way, a big old house that had caught fire once. "His trees are a foreign kind I do not know." Under his breath he added, "They bear strange fruit."

All that sounded interesting. I told him I would pay a call on Magos X but I would not say who sent me.

"Oh, you may tell. I feel sure he has done nothing wrong, but he may know things of value to you."

I tried to follow the old man's directions and went a little wrong. Those streets will do that to you. But pretty soon I spotted an old house a good bit bigger than the others in the neighborhood, and there were enough streetlights for me to see that part of it had burned.

I knocked and listened, and knocked again, and finally heard footsteps. They sounded to me like a big man walking quickly, careful not to make a lot of noise.

The door opened, and I saw a big man with no belly and a big black beard.

I showed him my badge. "Nothing serious, sir, but I'd like to talk to you for a few minutes. All right if I come in?"

"Oh, most naturally!" He stepped to one side, smiling a little. "I warn that I may keep you. Few come here, nor are they intelligent. I have, um . . . the hundred-year brandy. Wine, naturally, some not very bad. Milk and coffee."

The coffee sounded good, and I said so as I stepped inside.

"Already is late. Perhaps you do not sleep."

"Fine with me. I'm going to work all night, if I can find enough work to do."

He chuckled. "Come, then."

We went toward the back of the house and down a few steps into the kitchen. Once in a while I heard a board creak under his weight, but his feet made no noise at all.

"My kitchen you do not mind, I hope, operator? There is also a parlor wherein I speak with those I do not like."

"I'm glad you like me, sir."

"I and the ghost. Of you we two are fond. You are not unaware you possess this ghost?"

I said, "Sure."

"You do not object?"

"Nope."

"You have seen her, it may be?"

"Can you show her to me, sir? I'd like that."

"Very much you know about me."

"You know a lot about me, too, sir. That's how it seems, anyway. Did you know I was coming?"

"Not I." He had gone to the sink. He opened a tap while he spoke, filling an old percolator with water. "I knew someone was coming, because I know such things. I did not know it was to be so young a man with a badge, a gun, and a ghost. A young man who fights."

He turned to look at me, his mustache twitching. "Do not feel surprise. I see your knuckles. A bad fight?"

I thought back. "Depends on which one you mean, I guess."

"I see."

"Yeah, you're good at that, sir. Can you see my ghost?"

He nodded.

"Will you show her to me?" The hand was climbing out of my pocket. I could feel it, and I was tempted to catch it and stop it.

"Now not. Later it may be." He set the percolator on the stove and spooned in coffee. "A dish of fruit? I do not have much."

I waved it off. "Not now, thanks. Later maybe. If I get to eating, I'll forget what I came here for."

He sat down at the table with me, and I started to say something about not wanting to make trouble for him. I stopped when I saw the hand run across the table and roll over on its back.

He stared. Whatever he might have been expecting, it was not that. Then the mustache twitched. He picked up the hand, very delicately. He had big, strong hands and long fingers. He held the hand as if it were porcelain and might break, raised it to his lips, and laid it gently back down on the table.

That was when I saw her, just for half a second maybe. A tall girl with long hair and a good face. She did not look dead, but her dress did. As soon as I saw her, she knew I was seeing her and smiled.

It kind of paralyzed me. All I could do was stare. Then she was gone, and the hand was back in my pocket.

Magos X said, "She likes you, operator. That is most fortunate."

I just sat there. After a while the percolator began to bubble, and that kind of brought me out of it.

He got up and got mugs for us, and poured cream into a little pot-bellied pitcher.

I said, "You're the real thing, sir."

"Do not ask me to tell your fortune."

"Okay, sir. I won't. Thanks for letting me see the lady."

"I did not do it. You did it."

"Really? You're not kidding me?"

"I do not play such games. You speak with our tongue most supplely."

"Thank you, sir."

"For what do you come here?"

"You've got a guest, sir. His name's Russell Rathaus. He's a friend of mine, and I need to talk to him."

"Let us imagine that I tell you I have no guest. What then?"

"It would be a lie, sir, and you don't like to lie."

"You are correct. I do not."

"Suppose I were to ask you a question you didn't want to answer. Would you lie to me, sir?"

I was looking for the twitching mustache that meant a smile, but the big shoulders went up and down instead. "I might, operator."

"Who is the Undead Dragon?"

That got me the twitch. "I do not have to lie, or even remain silent, which I prefer. I do not know."

"Do I?"

"You think I am he, operator? I am not."

I shook my head. "I never thought that, sir. You would've killed Russ, not hidden him. I'm just asking because I think I know, and I thought you might know if I really do."

"You will tell me?"

I shook my head again. "I don't think I'd say even if I was sure, and I'm not. It's just what I think."

"Someone you would not willingly slander, then."

"I wouldn't willingly slander anybody, sir."

"You may slander me, if you wish. Many have. What I ask is that you do not arrest me." Magos X looked dead serious when he said that. *Serious* may not be the right word, but it is as close as I can come. He looked like he was not going to be arrested without a fight, and he had ways of fighting most people had never even heard of.

I said, "Arrest you for hiding Russ? Hell no!"

"You would like coffee. I will get it." He stood up, took the percolator off his old cast-iron stove, and poured us each a cup. "You do not fear I may poison you?"

I shook my head. "You wouldn't do that, sir. You're not the type."

"Many think I am."

"They're wrong." I had heard a noise somewhere in the house just before I said that. Russ was coming to listen, or that was how I figured it.

"You seek Russell Rathaus? This you say."

"That's right. Russ was in prison. You probably know that. He escaped. You—"

"How he does this you know?" Magos X was staring at me like he wanted to hypnotize me.

I was not about to let him do it. "If I do, I'm not telling."

"Proceed, operator."

"Russ is a friend of mine, like I said. We were cellmates for a pretty long time. I'm American, too."

"This I knew. Also JAKA. They know you were in their prison?"

I nodded. "They know, too, that I didn't really do anything. I made some broadcasts for the Legion of the Light—"

That was as far as I got. Magos X started laughing, and it was like a lion laughing, roaring and rocking in his chair. It about knocked out the windows.

When he finally stopped he said, "You are that one! I know I hear sometime the voice. It is you on the radio."

"Yeah, they were holding me prisoner, and they made me do it. I don't believe any of that shit."

"A pity!" He chuckled. "A terrible pity, because some of it is quite true." He raised his voice, which was pretty loud already. "Come in, my friend! You must join us for coffee."

20

THAT CRUEL LOOK

"Hello, Grafton," Russ said. "How did you get out?"

"You got me out," I told him. "I told them I didn't know how you'd done it, but I knew you pretty well and I could help them find you. You want to hear the rest of it?"

"Sure." Russ took one of the old wooden chairs. "They bought it?"

"Right. Especially a senior operator named Naala. I'll introduce you to her by and by. She sort of adopted me. I helped her with this and that, and they made me an operator myself."

"I hope you're not going to snap the cuffs on me."

Magos X said, "He will not."

"Right," I said. "What I'm going to try to do is show them that you're worth a lot more to us loose than locked in a cell. We'll offer a deal. You work for us, and when the job's wrapped up we let you go back to America with our blessings."

He looked skeptical, so I added, "That's not just you, that's you and Rosalee. I've sprung her already, by the way."

Magos X said, "Well, well, well!"

"She's a dish," I told him. "Wait til you see her."

"You are going to have to do a lot more explaining," Russ said, "before I buy into any of this."

"Then I'll do it. This is your big chance to get home safe, and I wouldn't want to see you blow it."

Magos X was pouring coffee for Russ and everything got quiet for a minute. Then Russ said, "Yours, too, Grafton."

"No way! I quit worrying about me yesterday." That was stretching it a little, but it is what I said. "Just look at it. I'm a JAKA man with a badge and a gun. They send me out alone to snoop, because I'm good at it and

I've turned up some major stuff for them. Ever tried to get in touch with the American embassy?"

It took Russ a while, but in the end he nodded.

"I thought so. I know where it is, and I know I told you my dad was in the State Department. Okay, his old pals are still around."

Russ did not look completely convinced but he was coming over; so I said, "Listen up. This is no bullshit. I could go out on the street right now, stop a police car, and tell the cop to take me to the embassy. And he'd do it. If you were in my shoes, would you worry?"

"Probably not, if that's all true."

I pulled my gun. "Gun, okay? I'd shoot it for you but it would make holes in the ceiling." I showed him my badge. "Silver, okay? Naala's is gold. Maybe she'll let you touch it."

"Do you really know where the embassy is?"

I pointed. "Over that way, in a little park. Nice and private, and if you drive past, or walk, you don't think there's anything in there. Magos X here would know, too. Did you ask him?"

Slowly Russ nodded.

"Only you didn't go."

"I went, but after dark. I can't afford to be seen."

"And it was closed."

Russ nodded again.

"You must know the Unholy Way's trying to kill you. We found the big doll in your tent."

"You know about that." Russ looked tired.

"Sure we do. What do you know about the head? The one they threw into Naala's place?"

Russ's eyes went wide and Magos X said, "I must hear of this. Tell me, please."

"Sure. Naala's door was locked and she's supposed to have the only key, so they picked the lock. Or else they got another key somewhere. Whoever it was tossed the head in and beat it. The thing is, it was Butch Bobokis's. I doubt that you ever met him, but Russ knows who he was."

Russ said, "He was a JAKA man. He used to question us, question Grafton here and me, while we were in prison. What's this got to do with the doll, Grafton?"

"You left that doll in our cell, figuring it would fool anybody who saw it, which it did. Also figuring the JAKA wouldn't know how to use it, which was right, too. The last time I saw it was when Butch and Aegis pulled me out and questioned me about it. They had it then. I told them how you got the face on, but that was all I told them. I had already seen a note Rosalee wrote that said you were sick. When I saw Butch's head I knew why. They had made a cut in the face and let some of the pellets out, but Butch must have put them back in and sewed up the cut. Then the Unholy Way had gotten their hands on the doll, and they knew how to use it against you."

Russ muttered, "Right."

"We took it out of there and left it in the woods. I didn't know what to do with it. If we'd burned it . . ." I shrugged. "I don't think you would have liked that."

"Could the sunlight hit it?"

I didn't know what Russ was getting at, but I said it could, at least in the morning.

"Good. That's how you wipe the face."

"Super. But they could put yours back on, right? If they had a picture of you and the doll. Butch and Aegis had wiped it, so they must have one."

Russ shrugged. "Maybe."

"They probably know the spells. They're in the little book."

"Right. But they may not want to use them."

I thought about that and decided I might be getting out of my league. So I said, "You want to go back to the States. You and Rosalee."

He nodded.

"The JAKA, me included, wants to put a stop to the Unholy Way. If you'll agree to help us, I think we can get the brass at JAKA headquarters to put you on a plane to Germany when we've wrapped things up. You speak good German, so—"

"Wait up. How did you find out I spoke German?"

"There's a shop where they sell magic tricks. They bought some dolls from you. I talked to the old man who runs the place and he said no Americans had been in. I showed him your picture—"

"You've got my picture? Let me have it, please."

I got it out and handed it over, and watched Russ tear it up.

Magos X said, "He fears you will be captured."

"Sure, but I could get another copy where I got that one. Only I don't think I will. I've found him now."

"You've found me," Russ said. He had gone over to the stove. "Only it's not going to do you a hell of a lot of good." He dropped the torn pieces in the stove.

"You're saying you won't help us?"

"Be the worm on the JAKA's hook? No, I won't." Russ turned to face me. "I've fished a lot, Grafton, and I know what happens to the worm."

I drank some coffee. It was pretty good, and I knew I wouldn't be around there much longer.

Magos X said, "There must be another way you can find and arrest them. Yes?"

I nodded. "Sure. But there isn't any other way I can see to get Russ back home. Can he have free room and board here with you for another month?"

"He can."

"What about three years?"

"Yes, but he must be useful to me."

"Got it." I stood up. "When you gave me the coffee, I said I might work all night. Now I don't think I will. I feel like crashing."

"You must yawn when you say it," Magos X instructed me. "The yawn lends verisimilitude."

"Okay." I stretched and yawned. "Would you like to see the Unholy Way wiped out?"

"I would be most happy."

"Then maybe you can talk him into it."

Magos X showed me to the door and we chatted a little. With Russ still at the back of the house, both of us were a little more relaxed. "I wish you peace and good fortune," Magos X said before I left. "I do not know how effective my blessing may be. It goes and it returns. But you shall have it." Then he whispered in a language I thought was probably Latin.

I did not feel blessed while I walked back to Naala's apartment. It seemed to me that the only thing to do was to empty the bag for her and see if she had anything to suggest. The JAKA could pick Russ up, sure. And Baldy and Naala could use him for bait after that for as long as they wanted, casting him here and there and grabbing everybody who bit.

Only there was no guarantee they would let him go home when they were through, and in fact they most likely would not. So I tried to figure a way around that and came up empty.

Naala was wide awake and dressed, something I had more or less expected, sitting at her desk drumming her fingers. She said, "You have found out a thing important?"

"Maybe," I told her, "but I kind of doubt it. I'll open the bag for you if you've got the time."

"This ring." She pointed to her phone. "It ring most seldom. But it ring five minutes ago. I listen—"

It rang again. I stared, and I think she did, too. Then she picked it up.

When she put it down, she said, "I answered. This you hear. I say I am Naala and give my number."

I nodded. "Right."

"No one speaks. Not far off I hear music and glasses. People talk. No one speaks into the telephone. They hang up. Five minutes ago it is the same. What does this mean, do you think?"

I did not know, and I said so.

"Then I tell what I think. The one who telephones knows you live here with me. He wishes you to answer. That he wishes most fervently, because he calls twice. If this telephone rings again, you must answer."

I nodded. I would if she wanted me to. Then I began telling her about Volitain in Puraustays, because Magos X had said he knew him and I thought it might be a good way to lead into it. I had just gotten to our three-way deal on the Willows when the phone rang again. Naala motioned to me, and I picked it up.

"Grafton. Five, five—"

"This's Rosalee." It was in English and there was a lot of noise where she was, but she was good and loud. "Will you come here? Like please? You're a good friend, you're the only good friend I've got." She sounded a little drunk.

"Sure," I said. "Only you've got to tell me where you are. Tell me and I'll get there as fast as I can."

"Okay." She started talking to somebody with her. I could hear their voices, both women, but I could not make out what they were saying.

I looked at Naala and said, "It's Rosalee and some other woman, and

I'd bet money they're sitting in a bar. What I want to know is how come this woman's got a cell phone? Nobody here has them, and most people don't have any kind of phone."

"It is Aliz? We leave Rosalee with her."

Another girl on the phone: "Grafton? It is Martya! Kiss, kiss!"

I said, "Kissy, kiss, hug, hug, kiss! Where are you, Martya?"

"We are in Golden Eagle. Aliz is friends with the manager, so drinks on the house! You come, you get free drinks and we dance."

"Okay, Martya! I'll be there as soon as I can. Wait for me." I was looking at Naala when I said that, and she nodded. "Is this Aliz's phone you're using?"

"She lets Rosalee use it and tells the number where are you, Grafton."

"She's a nice girl. So are you, darling. Maybe she wants to talk to me, too?"

More voices off.

"Something's up," I whispered to Naala.

She nodded again. She had her gun out, checking it.

"Aliz is busy," Martya told me. "She is talk to some man, not so handsome like you."

I said, "Good! That'll give me more time for you. Be there as fast as I can." I hung up.

Naala was at the door. "Where they are? It is Golden Eagle?"

I joined her. "Yeah. How'd you know?"

"Aliz is take them there. JAKA own it. She is look for Rathaus, I think."

It took me a minute, then I nodded. "Show Rosalee and maybe he'll come. Martya, too. She was working with him. Only she gave Rosalee her phone and your number. Why would she do that?"

We were outside by then. It was about nine, with no moon or stars and only a few streetlights. They are never really big on streetlights in that country.

Naala had been thinking. "Two reasons. First reason, Aliz believe you are know where Rathaus hide and you will tell her."

I said, "The first part's right, but the second part's wrong. Unless you want me to. Do you?"

Naala shook her head. "Second reason. There will be trouble soon, she think. Already she ask more operators and they send two. Always they send no more. Two only." Naala looked like she wanted to spit.

"I get it! Rosalee phones your apartment. If she talks to either one of us both of us will probably come, which gives Aliz two more guns. Nobody can say she wasn't authorized to ask for us, because she didn't. Is it the Unholy Way?"

"This I think." Naala was walking fast and so was I. "I am their Undead Dragon perhaps, or another leader. I am tell that Rosalee is in the Eagle. You understand? We of the JAKA want Rathaus because he will bring us the Unholy Way. The Unholy Way want Rosalee because she will bring them Rathaus."

I was keeping an eye out for police cars, and I think Naala was, too. We did not get one, but we still got to the Golden Eagle pretty quickly, pushing our way through the crowds in a Mousukos street with a lot of bars and clubs and noise. Like I said, we walked fast and it was not far.

The Golden Eagle was bigger than I had expected, with a long bar all down one side of the big room, a bandstand and a dance floor, and gaming tables. Bright lights on the bandstand and gaming tables, dim on the bar and the dance floor. The band was taking a break, so I could not judge just then, but a lot of people looked like they had been dancing, which is usually a good sign. The whole place smelled of beer, something that was probably floor wax or furniture polish, and cigarette smoke.

Aliz was sweating and laughing at something the guy with her had said. He was mopping his face with a clean white handkerchief. It took me maybe three seconds before I felt sure he was JAKA, and maybe three more to make his piece. On his belt, left side in front, which would mean crossdraw for the right hand. To tell the truth I was thinking there were probably more JAKA there, but nobody else looked right.

Martya plastered herself all over me, saying she wanted to dance.

I said, "Sure, so do I. Only we've got to wait til the band comes back." I figured they were drinking at the bar.

"I will sing and we will dance."

Which is what we did for maybe five minutes. She had a good voice and was not too drunk to use it. I would give you the lyrics here if I remembered them well enough to translate them. Only my translation would have to scan and rhyme for it to mean much, even then you would not have the feel of the language. It was about telling mom and dad to suck socks, and doing whatever you wanted to like chugging booze and smoking grass, and not worrying about the future because there was not going to be any. It was a good song and some other customers joined in, clapping and singing along.

A dozen new people were coming into the bar while we danced and acting like they did not know each other. Only I figured they did. For one thing none of them looked like they belonged, and for another there was the same look on all their faces. When a cruel person is about to have some real fun, sticking it to somebody who cannot fight back and laughing about it, and doing it all over again only worse, he gets a certain look. It is not the same way a hungry person looks at food, but that is as close as I can come. You have probably seen it a few times. Think about it.

There were men and women—more women than men, which kind of surprised me—and they all had that look. One time I sat around with three whores in Vienna. They all looked hard, if you know what I mean. They did not like men, but they had to pretend they did. That was part of it. Another part was that they had taken it on the chin more than once, and cried, and gotten up and cried some more, and wiped their eyes, and kept going. They had done that a lot and they were going to do it a lot more and they knew it. I did not like that look, but it did not scare me. This did.

Most of the women were not good-looking, but three or four were okay and two were knockouts. A year ago those two would have scared me green, but now I figured I could talk to them without stammering although I sure did not want to.

A little man with buck teeth under a rusty mustache came over to Rosalee. "You are so beautiful," he told her. "I am a photographer and I wish to take your portrait."

He got out a card and gave it to her. "You will love it and I will give you copies without charge but you must permit me. . . ."

She turned away and started talking to the man who had been talking to Aliz, not saying anything particular, just chattering until the photographer went away. In back of him I could see an ugly raw-boned woman in a black-and-white polka-dot dress setting up a camera with a big flash. Off to the side a couple of others were setting up slave flashes. Just in case you do not know, a slave flash goes off when it sees another flash, which it does at the speed of light.

"Look there!" the photographer said. He grabbed Rosalee's shoulders and spun her around. "We make the beautiful portrait."

I slugged him just as he got the last word out and all three flashes flashed at once.

A lot of times you will see rockers on stage wearing sunglasses. It is not because of the spotlights on them; it is because of flashes from the audience. Usually there is a no-flash rule and security tries to throw out anybody who does it, but some people do not give a shit and they do it anyway. Somebody who steps off the stage by accident can get hurt really bad, and the flashes will blind you.

Which is what happened to us. They had been waiting for all of us to look, and naturally the photographer's grabbing Rosalee and twisting her around did it. We all looked at her and him and that was good enough. I could not see one damned thing, but I fumbled for my gun anyhow and heard a couple of shots, way, way too loud if you are only used to the shots on TV. Then I heard the boom of a shotgun (later I found out that was what it had been) and people started screaming.

Not just women. Some men were screaming, too.

Almost close enough to touch, a fat guy in a check suit who had been standing at the bar two or three people down from us was bleeding on the floor, gasping and saying, "Oh, God! Oh God, oh God, oh God, oh God!" There was a gun on the floor beside him, and I kept thinking somebody ought to pick it up only nobody did.

"Grafton!" That was Naala, turning her head just for an instant as she ran out of the club. She wanted me to follow her and I did, almost tripping over Rosalee, who was on the floor a little in front of me.

Out on the street it was darker than ever, which was bad, but there were a whole lot of people milling around, which was worse. Naala grabbed a guy who was pretty well dressed and shoved her badge in his face. "There was a car, yes? A truck? They force a woman in it?"

He nodded and said something I could not hear.

She asked a couple more questions, and I could see he was saying he did not know. She turned to me. "You saw them? Before the light? You watch them come in?"

I said sure.

"They have put her in a black truck for the dead. There is not room in such a thing for all. Some must be near here, but they scatter, I think. We separate and look. Bring him back to the Golden Eagle. I meet you there." She pointed. "You go that way."

I said, "Wait up! They didn't get her. Didn't get Rosalee. She was on the floor yelling when I went out. I didn't see any blood."

I think Naala stamped her foot. If she did not, she sure looked like she wanted to. "It is not the Rathaus woman they take. It is the other, the one who bring the hand."

Then she was gone, and all I could think about was that the Unholy Way had Martya.

The way I saw it, the big wheels would have gotten into the hearse. The rest had three choices. Go on foot, getting as far from the scene as they could, or get in a wagon, or go into one of the clubs and mix with the crowd. Three police cars were coming down the street, with people scattering to let them through. I figured they would take care of the people in the clubs, and it would be better for me to go off the way Naala had pointed, looking out for wagons and looking for anybody who had come into the Golden Eagle with the photographer.

Right about here I noticed there was somebody with me, and I might as well tell you about him. It was the third border guard, the guy I saw sometimes riding with cops. I had seen him in JAKA headquarters when they had made me an operator, and three or four times since then. Now he was tagging along. He had on a dark suit, a white shirt, and a dark solid-color tie that was probably navy. Conservative and classy.

As I have said before in this book, all the cops and border guards had never seemed like they noticed him much. Or if they did, it was the way you notice something you are not really interested in. The kids' books in the dentist's waiting room, maybe. Something like that. It seemed to me that I ought to speak to him just to let him know I knew he was there and did not mind. If he rode with cops and could get into the JAKA building, maybe he would give me a hand. So I said, "Good to have you along. If you see any of the people we're looking for, please tip me off. Only nothing obvious."

He smiled and nodded, looking more like my father than ever.

We went a ways and I heard a locomotive whistle, not like an American locomotive, but like one of the old steam trains you see in movies sometimes. Pretty soon after that, the third border guard turned a corner when I would have gone on straight. At first I thought he was just going off on his own, which was all right with me. But he stopped and looked back at me, and motioned for me to come along.

So I did, walking another eight or nine streets until I found something I had always known must be in the city somewhere, even though I had never been there. It was the railroad station, a red brick building, pretty big, with a little tower with a big clock in it. The clock struck as we started to go in: one, two, three . . . eleven o'clock. If you backed me into a corner and made me explain why I am telling you all this, I would make a really bad job of it. But it meant something to me. It felt like God was telling me something, but it took me a few minutes to figure out what it was.

The show was about over. We had been looking for Russ. Okay, I had found him. The JAKA (that included me now) had been looking for the Unholy Way. Fine, we had brought it out into the light. Maybe we had not seen all the members, but we had seen a bunch of them in the Golden Eagle and there were probably security cameras. Most of all, the JAKA had been looking for the Unholy Way's Undead Dragon.

And I was pretty sure I knew who that was. It left a bad taste in my mouth, but that did not change the facts.

God had used the tower and the clock striking eleven to remind me of all that stuff and maybe give me a clue about which way to go. He is good at that.

21

THE COVEN

We went into the station and I sat down on a bench. I had walked a heck of a lot by then, and I had danced some with Martya on top of it, so I would have sat down on the floor if that had been the only place. As it was, there were all these cozy hardwood benches with backs. At least a hundred empty seats, when I only needed one. The third border guard wandered off after I sat down. I looked around for him, but he had gone.

Pretty soon a big, raw-boned woman in a red-and-black-striped dress came in. Disguised, right? Okay, she had changed clothes somewhere and even changed the way she wore her hair, piling it on top of her head. But I would have known her anyhow, and there was a dead giveaway. She was carrying a long canvas case I knew damned well must have the camera and tripod in it, so the buck-toothed guy had stuck her with those. I watched while she rented a locker (there was a guy you gave money to who handed you the key) and put her canvas bag in it.

Of course I thought of busting her on the spot. There were two reasons I did not do it. One was that I did not have handcuffs. Give me a cop with cuffs and a patrol car, and I would have run her in right then.

The other was that the more I looked at it the dumber it looked. Suppose she ran. I would run after her and most likely catch up to her. (But I might lose her.) Or I could shoot, maybe. But I knew myself well enough to know I had no chance of hitting her where I wanted to unless I stopped to aim. That meant that she would get away unless I hit her solidly enough to bring her down. That meant a good hit in a leg, and her legs would be moving fast.

If I missed her, she would get away. If I killed her, she would not talk. Okay, we could probably find out where she lived and search the place. Maybe she had something that would tell us something, and maybe she kept it where she lived. And if she did, we might find it. About one chance in five, maybe.

On top of all that, the JAKA would not like a brand-new guy shooting in the railroad station. So no. Shooting if she ran was out, and I would have to catch her. I was fast but I was tired and she looked fast, too. It was dark outside, and there was a jungle of trees and shrubs around the building.

So I just watched, watching out hard for anybody who might be with her and not showing it. It seemed like she was alone, but after she had put the canvas case in her locker she went over to a door with a coffee cup painted on the glass and went in.

That gave me a problem, a good one. There would not be a whole lot of people in there at this time of night. Hell, there were not a lot of people in the whole station. If I went in there I would stand out like a pickle in the lemonade, and she would have seen me in the Golden Eagle just like I had seen her.

If I waited for her to come out, she probably would not. There almost had to be some other way out of that coffee shop, and ten to one she would take it. So I went outside and got around to where the coffee shop had to be. Right, there was an outside door. I backed into the trees.

And waited.

First thing. If she went back into the big room where people waited for trains, I had no way of knowing about it. From there, she could go out the front of the building and I would not see her. Or she could walk the tracks out back. I would not see her there, either. Or she could even take a train, and it was a dead certainty that I would not see her. I was just about ready to stroll into the coffee shop and ask for a glass of water when she came out.

Not through the regular door I had been watching, but through a big overhead door that opened onto a loading dock. For half a minute I wondered whether she was really strong enough to lift that thing, but it was probably counterbalanced some way. It could even have been powered.

Whatever the answer was, here she was, walking fast and leaving the freight door open behind her.

I did not dare to get too close and I almost lost her twice. If I were to go into all that here, it would take half the book. It got later and later, and we got into a really crummy part of the city. There was almost nobody on the streets there, but you saw guys—it was always guys—waiting in the weeds between the trees. I was one building behind her when she opened a door with a key and went in.

I walked past it and had a look. There was black lettering on the window, but I could not read it and there were no lights inside. After that I walked past again on the other side of the street. Sure enough, there was a guy standing in the shadows under a tree.

If I had money, I would have slipped him a little for information. I had nothing, and all of a sudden it hit me that if he was selling something, like peddling crack or maybe pimping, he would have money already. Maybe quite a bit.

So I went up to him and said, "I've got a question."

He looked right past me as though I was not there, and I tried a couple more lines before he slugged me. It was a pretty good one. I staggered backward, but I did not fall until I tripped over something. Then I went down for two or three seconds before I got up and went for him.

He stumbled into some bushes and I should have given him half a dozen more, but I grabbed him instead. He tore loose, leaving most of his shirt behind, and drew. His piece had been stuck in his waistband under the shirt. I kicked him and it fired, the bullet hitting a rock or something and singing away. I know I kicked him then and tagged him some more, but I cannot remember which came first. He went down still holding his gun until I kicked it out of his hand. I will not tell you the rest, but the fight went out of him pretty quick.

There was a wad of bills in his front pants pocket. I got it and got off him, checked to make sure the hand was still in the side pocket of my jacket, and tried to clean myself up a little. That was when I noticed that my new watch was broken.

I was still swearing when a black and silver skidded to a stop and a cop jumped out. You can probably guess what the first thing I did was—I looked for the third border guard in the front seat. He was not there.

The second thing was to flash my badge.

The cop touched his cap. "Need help, operator?"

I nodded and found the gun the guy I had just robbed had dropped. It was an old Walther, the kind the German Army used to use. "You better take this," I told the cop. "I don't want it weighing down my pants."

"Yes, operator." He took it. "This I will see to. You will file charges?"

"No. He wouldn't talk to me, but I've got a feeling he'll talk now."

The cop chuckled.

"What do you know about that place across the street?" I pointed.

"The mortuary, operator?" The cop scratched his head. "They must close soon. A funeral every few weeks, it might be. They have the fine dead wagon, however. It I see now and again. It is behind if it is not out. Good blacks to draw it, operator."

"Did it go out tonight?"

He pursed his lips. "You know, operator, it did as I think. I passed it."

"I think it did, too," I said. The guy Naala talked to had called it a hearse, probably, and when Naala said *truck* I had thought of the kind of hearse they use here in the States. Over here, quite a few bands buy old hearses for transportation. I asked the cop, "You know where the Golden Eagle is?"

"I do, operator." He sort of hesitated, which told me he knew it was JAKA.

"Go there and ask around for Naala. She'll be there. Tell her you talked to five five eight, and tell her where I was."

"At once, operator."

"Nice looking, about forty, white blouse, gray jacket, gray skirt. She's a senior operator. Do you know her?"

He shook his head.

"She'll be there. Find her and tell her what I said."

"Yes, operator. I fly."

I watched him drive away, then told the guy I had tangled with to stand up.

He did, moving pretty slowly, but moving.

I said, "I could take you to JAKA headquarters, and they'd hold you for a year or so just to practice on. Maybe once a week they'd knock you around or burn you a little. I'm not going to do that this time, but I don't ever want to see you again. You got that?"

He turned his head and spit blood. "Cross the street and you will not."

I took a step closer and said, "Maybe you'd better tell me about that."

He ran instead, and he was fast. I watched him duck into the deep shadows, and made a mental note to corner the next guy I wanted to question.

There had been a fight and a shot fired, so I figured there was a pretty fair chance the woman I had followed was looking out a window somewhere, and it would not do to just stroll across the street and try the front door. It had been locked when she got there anyway, so there was a real good chance she had locked it again once she was inside. So I walked a couple of streets down before I turned a corner and circled around to get at the back.

You may have noticed that every once in a while I put something in this book that I cannot explain but think I ought to tell you about anyway. Okay, this is another of those. I passed a store that had a big picture of the third border guard in the window. He was younger in the picture and maybe a little bit better looking than he really was, but it was him.

Here is another thing, but I do not believe it is much of a mystery. Most of the stores I passed had a few lights on. Even some of those that had burglar bars did. But I think that was just like it is here. You leave some lights on so the cops can see in, and like I said, that was a seedy neighborhood. If the lights are on, the cops can see there is somebody in there when there should not be. If they are off in a store that usually has them on, maybe they will check that out, too.

The cop had told me there was a coach for bodies out back, and a couple of horses. What was really there was a barn. It was stone up to about four feet, with wood above that, and I got the feeling it might have been there back when there were farms where I was instead of city streets. Doors front and back, both of them padlocked. I figured I could probably get in pretty easily, but it was not worth doing. The woman I had been following had gone into the building, not the barn.

The thing that threw me was that there were no lights in the windows of the building. None. If she had gone in there she had not turned on a single light, or that was how it looked. The cop would have given me his flashlight if I had asked for it, but I had never thought of it. So live and learn.

I tried the back door. Locked, which was what I had expected. Then the windows. The first three I tried were closed and locked good. I pushed up hard, but nothing doing. The fourth one (I have always thought since then that four was my lucky number) was open at the bottom about three inches. It would not go up any farther no matter how hard I pushed. At first that made no sense, but it was summer and the people inside would want some ventilation. Nobody here seemed to have air conditioning, and it would have been miserable in there with all the windows closed.

So leave one or two open a little, but locked or blocked so they could not be opened any farther. And I remembered the hand.

I took it out and whispered, "I hope you can hear me, and I hope you really like me like Magos X said. I'm going to put you halfway in, through this little opening, see? I want you to unlock the window for me so I can raise it and get inside. Will you do that for me? Please?"

Most likely you think I have too much imagination, and maybe you are right. But a breeze sprang up just then, not a strong wind but plenty strong enough to ruffle my hair. Up until I talked to the hand the air had been still that night, like it mostly is in the summer.

I laid the hand on windowsill and waited, and as soon as I looked away it was gone. Pretty soon I heard a rattle inside. I waited a few seconds more before I lifted, and the window went right up just as slick as you please.

The hand came out then, so I picked it up and said thank you and put it back into my pocket. Sometimes I have wondered how the ghost felt, walking along beside me all the time with her hand in my pocket. But I did not think of that then.

Jumping up, pushing aside some velvet curtains, and crawling through the window were all pretty easy. Doing those things without making much noise was a whole lot harder. I did the best I could, because as soon as I was inside I had heard voices. Not loud, and a long way from being loud and clear enough for me to understand what the people were saying, but voices for sure. When I stood still and listened hard I thought I could tell the men's voices from the women's. It sounded to me like there had to be at least four people talking, and it could have been more. Later I found out there were thirteen, but I did not know that then.

The worst thing, and it was really pretty bad, was that I did not have any kind of a light and it was blind dark in there. I walked as slowly as I could and as carefully as I could, too. The floor creaked anyway, little slow creaks every time I took a step. I knew there was a really good chance that I would trip over something even if I was careful. Knocking something over might be just as bad.

Only I was tempted to do it. For one thing I was tired and I had taken some good solid punches. I wanted everything to be over so I could maybe take a shower and for sure go to bed. For another, when the people I could hear talking heard me, they would turn on the lights.

And I cannot tell you how bad I wanted those lights. If they got rough or even looked like they wanted to, I was going to shoot. And if I ran out of bullets they were in for one hell of a fight.

Only hell was on their side, or at least they thought it was. I had never thought that heaven was on my side, but I told God I could sure use an angel with a flaming sword right about then.

What I got instead was tables with stone tops, or at least tops that felt like stone. I found a couple of those and had just figured out that there was a row of them side by side when my fingers found one that had somebody lying on it. I felt him, and he was not exactly cold, but you probably know what I mean. A kid, I thought, not moving and no clothes on. There should have been a stink, but there was a heavy smell pretty much like roses only not as good as a real rose. Not as good as the rose perfume a girl I used to know wore, either. You could tell it was chemicals formulated to smell like that.

So it was an undertaker's for real, and I was just wishing that I had found a row of empty caskets instead when I saw a little gleam of light. Not much. Very, very small. Only light just the same. You know I went toward it.

The tough thing was going quietly. I wanted to walk faster, and I had to make myself go slow and step down easy and keep feeling my way with my hands.

It was a door, an old wooden one from the feel of it. It was closed and latched, but it was not tightly fitted enough to keep a little light from getting through here and there. Just a few gleams.

I laid my ear to one that was about the right height, and that was where the voices were coming from. A woman in there was saying, ". . . and the news would get out."

The latch squeaked even when I turned the knob slowly. In fact, it squeaked so much I felt certain they had heard it, but when I pulled the door open they were still talking among themselves. The hinges squeaked, too. So, do I go in or stay out?

That one took maybe half a second. It would be dumb to go down there. I had sent the cop to Naala, and she would be here in another ten minutes or so. Probably she would bring the cop with her, and maybe a couple of other operators. So stay upstairs.

By then I had gone down the first couple of steps, and I kept going.

Call it pride. I did not want Martya to know that I had been there but had waited for backup. I knew I was being stupid, and cussed myself, and went down anyway.

Every old wooden step creaked. I was being as quiet as I could and keeping to the edge of each step, but they still creaked under my weight and I could not do one damned thing about it.

They saw my feet before I could see them, and by the time I could they were ready. A man I had not noticed in the Golden Eagle and the woman I had followed had guns and had them out and aimed at me. The little guy who had said he was a photographer had a knife. He was holding it to Martya's throat. I ought to have been watching the whole bunch of them. I know that, but I was not. I was looking at her. Only at her, really, and not paying much attention to the two with guns.

She was naked and tied to a cross, with ropes around her wrists and ankles. Here and there they had stuck skewers into her, long steel pins with metal ornaments at the ends. There was one in each arm, and one through her right leg about halfway between the ankle and the knee. They had gagged her, too, but when she saw me her eyes got big.

"Don't worry," I told her. "Help is on the way." She could not nod or anything. She just stared.

The photographer said, "You struck me." He made it sound meaner than I could make anything sound.

I said, "Yeah. I think I'm going to do it again."

He held up his big knife. "This is good for both. If you come nearer, I cut her throat. Nearer still, and I cut yours. You think I cannot? Make the test."

I gave him my best smile. "Later, maybe. Nice place you got here."

"It will be the last place for you. This I think."

"Maybe I'll come back in fifty, sixty years." I relaxed and had a look around. There were pictures on the walls, pictures that had been blown way up by an expert. They showed men raping women who looked dead, and naked women giving a little oral sex to dead men. One I remember a lot better than I want to showed this really good-looking brunette. She had stabbed a man's corpse in the chest, or that was what it looked like, and still had her hand on the hilt of the knife.

"You have a gun." That was the man who was holding one on me.

I shook my head. "Not me." I had been trying to keep things casual, and I felt like I had been pulling it off pretty well. There was something about that place that was getting to me just the same. There were a lot of candles, which I do not think I have mentioned yet. Most of them were black, something you do not see often. One of them, burning in front of Martya, was as thick through as a young tree and had four or five wicks. Seeing them, I wondered if they were putting something into the air besides smoke. I was getting depressed, angry, and sad at the same time. Tonight I was going to be tortured to death and it did not seem right. Naala was not going to come, or if she did she would just look at this place from outside and go away.

All that stuff was crowding into my mind, but there was something else, too. It was the feeling that something really, really huge was studying me the way I might study a bug, something I could not see even though it could see me fine. The whole world had cancer, and the thing watching me now was the cancer. It did not make a lot of sense, but that was how I felt.

"You have a gun. Take off your jacket."

I ignored him and talked to the photographer. "You think you're going to get away with this and be somebody big and important. You'll rule the world."

The woman I had followed said, "We have the secret knowledge. He, I, all of us. You trust in God. Poor fool! The battlefields of all the world are manured with the bodies of those who trusted him."

"I don't trust in him," I told her. "I don't even trust in myself. But what if he trusts in me?" I was moving toward her as I said it.

"Stop!" That was the photographer. "Stop, or she dies!" He held his knife as he said it like he was about to stick it in Martya's chest.

The woman's shot came then, and for a minute I thought she must have shot me and wondered why it did not hurt. It had been so loud I felt deaf, but I heard the boom after it. I did not know what that was, but I dropped to the floor, and I must have drawn my own gun without thinking about it because it was in my hand. There was a little rattle that sounded faint, then another boom and another.

After that, people started screaming. They were trying to run out of that basement, but the stairs were the only way out. I had my gun up to shoot the photographer, but it seemed like he was gone. I ran toward

Martya and slipped in blood and fell, but I kept my hold on my gun and did not shoot. That was because my father had taught me to keep my finger off the trigger until I was ready to shoot. It had sunk in, and I might have shot her if it had not. All this happened in a lot less time that it is taking me to tell you about it.

The guy on the stairs, the guy with the shotgun, was yelling at the Unholy Way people. I think he was trying to get them to shut up, but he was not having a lot of luck with that. For maybe ten seconds I felt absolutely certain the photographer was going to stab me; then I saw his knife lying on the floor and grabbed it with my left hand before I straightened up.

When things had quieted down a little, I pulled the skewers out of Martya's leg and both arms. Then I cut off her gag and cut the ropes. She gasped for breath and just about fell.

"Oh, oh, oh!" and then, "I love you. Oh God, I love you so much!" I was not sure whether she meant God or me, but I figured either way was good. She was hugging me, only not hard because of the holes in her arms.

The guy with the shotgun was Russ Rathaus. Maybe you had figured that one out already, but I had not. I did not know until I saw him. You will want to know why he showed up, and I mean to tell you. But quite a few other things happened before I found out myself.

One was that I took off my shirt and cut strips from it to bandage Martya. Those skewers had been driven all the way through and into the wood of the cross. They were just puncture wounds, but they were bleeding from both ends so I had blood all over my shirt and jacket anyway.

I was about finished when Naala showed up with Aliz and the guy who had been dancing with her and three cops. She sent the one I had talked to back to the station house, and after what seemed like a pretty long time we had a paddy wagon for the prisoners and an ambulance for Martya. I think it was really about an hour and a half, but it seemed like forever. American cops would have latched onto Russ's shotgun, but Naala told these cops to let him keep it and they did. She told them he was working for the JAKA, which surprised both of us.

22

THE UNDEAD DRAGON

From this point on, there is not a lot of interesting stuff for me to tell you. After quite a bit of waiting around in JAKA headquarters and Naala, Russ, and I shaking hands and fielding tough questions, sometimes together and sometimes separately, we went back to the Golden Eagle. There are no closing laws in that country, so the Eagle (which was what people mostly called it) stayed open just about twenty-four hours a day. Naala said that in the morning they put the empty chairs up on the tables and swept the floor, but there were always at least a few people working there. If you wanted eggs and coffee there would be somebody there to make them for you, or you could go into the kitchen and make them yourself. We were all hungry, so Russ and Naala cooked, with me trying to help out and getting in the way.

Finally we sat down, and that is a meal I will always remember. Hot coffee made just before it was poured, three kinds of sweet rolls that had been warmed in the oven, lots of bacon, and Naala's eggs poached in wine. I was tired and looked like I had been working all night in a butcher shop, so I should not have been hungry. But I was not only hungry I was practically starved. While I tell you what Russ said, you have to picture me nodding and nodding and chewing and swallowing and spreading butter on rolls, particularly a big fat kind that had nuts on top and jam inside.

"When you found me," Russ said, "you told me you had gotten Rosalee out."

I said sure.

"I don't think I ought to use the name of the person I was staying with. What do you think?"

I looked at Naala and she looked at me. Finally she said, "He will not be arrested, I will see to it. But if he become known . . . there is the Unholy Way. We are fools if we think we catch all tonight."

I chimed in. "We don't have the Undead Dragon. As long as he's around they're going to be dangerous. How dangerous I don't know." The hand came to life in my pocket when I said that. I had almost forgotten about it.

"So after you had gone," Russ said, "I asked the friend who had been sitting with us where he thought Rosalee might be. He has hunches. Maybe you know."

I nodded and kept nodding.

"He said for me to try this place and told me where it was."

"She is here when the hour is not so late," Naala told Russ. "She is elsewhere now. Asleep I hope."

"Right." Russ used his handkerchief for a napkin. "I found her here and talked to her a little. She told me—"

"This is before I go? You are here and I do not see you?"

I wanted to say, "Magos X," but my mouth was full, so I just nodded. It would have been a bad idea anyway.

"She told me the Satanists had taken Martya. I went back to my friend and asked where he thought they might have taken her. He had several suggestions, so—"

Naala said, "I wish to hear them."

He told her. One was an old mansion on the lake shore. One of the others was the undertaker's.

"I went to the closest first," Russ said. "It was all dark, but I snooped around. I found a window that was wide open and climbed in." He waited for us to say something but neither of us did.

"You'll say it was a damned fool thing to do, but when I did it I didn't know there was anybody in there. One part of me was thinking there was nobody in there, so it would be pretty safe, and the other was thinking maybe they had Martya in there tied up and gagged. Which they did, except that I pictured her lying on the floor in the dark."

Naala was watching him and not talking, and my mouth was full.

"Once I was inside, I saw light from a doorway and heard voices. I was pretty sure one of them was Grafton's, so I went to have a look. I was still going down the steps when one of them took a shot at me. That stopped me, and I started shooting back."

I said, "You had that shotgun."

Russ shrugged. "They're legal here. Only the army and the police can have pistols, but anybody can have a rifle or a shotgun. Even foreigners. I had mine wrapped in a throw rug so I could carry it through the streets, but I took the rug off before I climbed in the window. Now you're going to ask what it was loaded with, and I don't know. Some kind of bird shot, probably, but we were close enough that even quail shot would do a hell of a lot of damage." He hesitated for a moment, then he said, "It only holds five shells."

To keep him talking, Naala said, "They have shoot first. Grafton says this."

"That's right. There was a woman in there with a gun, and she fired before I had gone down the steps far enough to size up the situation. She was on the other side of the basement, and she missed. I shot back. You must have seen her body."

Naala nodded.

"There was a man who had a gun. I killed him, too." Russ paused and swallowed. "Probably you've killed people. I'm over sixty and I spent some time in the U.S. Army, but I never shot anybody until tonight. I killed three people tonight, and I haven't worked my way through it yet."

I was buttering another roll. "They were going to kill you, Russ."

He said, "Uh-huh." And then, "One was going to kill Martya. I don't love Martya, but I like her. I owe her. He pulled his knife back to stab her and I shot him."

Naala said they were killers and would have killed both of us if they had gotten the chance.

He said, "Is the U.S. government going to find out about this?"

She shrugged. "They do not care. It is our law here, their law there."

"I suppose."

Everybody got quiet and ate after that, which I had been doing already. After a while I went to the door and looked at the sky. It was getting gray, so I knew then why I was getting sleepy. Night was nearly over. Besides, I had eaten my eggs and six or eight buttered rolls. My jaw ached, reminding me of the aspirin I had found in Naala's medicine cabinet.

While Naala and I were walking back to her apartment I asked her if she knew who had killed Butch. She said she did not, but we had ten prisoners and they would be quizzed all day. "Also others search there for papers. It may be they find something. If so, I will be told. Also who throws the head in. I must have the lock changed."

There is not a lot left to tell about that night. I had a shower and Naala had a bath and got me to come in and scrub her back. "So you are useful after all," she said, and grinned at me.

We had a drink before that, and we had a couple more before we went to bed and talked some. It was mostly private stuff so I am not going to give it here. Then we went to sleep.

When I woke up I was in my room and Naala was gone. So were all the clothes I had worn the night before. My gun and my badge case were lying on top of a stack of new clothes. I thought of the hand and was worried sick. It was not in the box or anyplace else I looked in. When I dropped my badge case I saw there was an identity card in there now. It had my picture on it, and it probably said I was JAKA. I put on the new clothes, threading the new belt through the holster, and so on. I got a paring knife from the kitchen to cut off the tags. The wad I had taken from the guy I fought was at the bottom of the stack.

The clock on the mantel said it was almost three, and for a minute I thought it had stopped. I watched it until the minute hand moved. So I had slept all day and most of the night. I went into Naala's room, being very quiet, and she was in there sound asleep and snoring.

After I had shaved I knew what I had to do. God knows I did not want to, but I had to. I found a new jacket in the closet. This new one was wool, too. When I went out I made sure the door had locked behind me.

The walk to the cathedral was long and dark, cold and lonely. I kept hoping to catch sight of the tower, which did not really happen until I was just about there. Then I saw it, dead black against the stars, and it seemed to go up forever.

The big door in front was locked, but there was a little path around to the side, and a little door there that was not. I went in and up a narrow, pitch-black stair, and found I was right underneath the tower in an alcove full of hanging ropes. It had no ceiling but just went up and up. It was still dark as hell in there, even though a little starlight sifted down. One side was open to the main part of the cathedral. It was dark in there, too, although a candle was burning on each side of the altar. I did not see the ropes until one bumped my face.

There was another stair off to the side. It was wider than the one I had just come up, but steeper, too, with nothing to hang on to. A cold stone wall on one side and a really good drop on the other. The steps were narrow, like they had been made for feet that were smaller than mine. I kept telling myself that if I fell I would grab one of the bell ropes, but I do not believe I could really have done it. Pretty soon I learned not to try to take those steps fast. You went slow or you stopped every so often and sat down on a step. Your choice. I went slow, feeling the wall with my left hand.

When I finally got to the top, it was maybe twice as big as I had expected. I have had hotel rooms that were a lot smaller than that. My bedroom in Kleon's house had been smaller, too. There was a big hole for the ropes in the middle, and a walk all the way around it with a low wall around that. No rail on the bell-rope side. For a while I tried to figure out why it was the way it was. Then I realized that eventually the ropes must wear out, and when they did somebody would come up here with a plank and lay it across the hole so he could get to the broken rope, cut the knot and let the rope fall, and tie on a new rope. I would not want the job, but somebody must have done it. Of course you could reach some of the ropes just standing on the walkway.

So now I was up here, and there was nothing for me to do but wait. My broken watch had disappeared with my old clothes, but I figured it must be about four a.m. Or it could be five. I went to the front and stood there a while, looking out over the city. There were only two buildings taller than that tower in it, and you could see the roofs of all the rest. Later on, when the sky started to get light, you could see down a lot of the streets, too.

That was when I moved to the back to wait. At first I tried sitting on the flat coping back there, but it was too high for my feet to reach the walkway. So I just leaned against it and checked my gun, and put it back, and waited.

It seemed like a long time but it cannot have been, because the sun was not showing yet when I heard his feet on the steps down below. I knew that if he looked around, he would see me. That was when I looked around good myself and saw there was somebody else up there with me already. It was the third border guard, just standing in a corner. He did not say anything to me, and I did not say anything to him, either. The two of us just waited.

The first thing I saw was the archbishop's little black cap and his white hair under it. He was facing away from me when he came up the steps so

I could not see his face. He went to the front and leaned against the low wall with his arms stiff and his hands on the top, and he looked out at the city pretty much like I had. He was saying something, but I could not quite hear what it was. Just whispering to himself.

So I edged closer until I could see his profile, and then I knew I had been right. Maybe I should have cleared my throat or something to let him know I was there, but I did not. I knew what I was going to have to do, and I was not looking forward to it.

Finally he saw me and turned to look at me, and began to say something. Only he thought better of it and shut his mouth instead.

I said, "Good morning, Your Excellency. Do I have to show you my badge?"

He did not speak, so I pulled it out of my pocket and opened it for him to see, and stuck it back in. That was when I would have noticed the hand was in there, if it was. But I did not.

I said, "You know why I'm here. You knew it as soon as you saw me. I could see it in your eyes. We caught a bunch of your people last night at the undertaker's. Did anybody tell you?"

He shook his head, moving it just a little.

"It was pretty late. Probably they didn't want to wake you up. Three are dead, but we got ten alive."

I waited, but he did not say a word.

"Here I could tell you they ratted you out. Maybe I ought to. The truth is I don't know, but if they haven't, they will. Ten of them? Most of them women? We'll keep after them day and night until they pass out, and go after them again as soon as we can wake them up. One will talk. Probably they all will."

He said something too soft for me to hear, and he kept on saying it, his lips moving and moving. Pretty soon I realized there was somebody else there besides the third border guard, the archbishop, and me. Just having it there made me angry and sad and terribly down, but I kept going.

"I said I could tell you they had, but I won't. There have been too many lies in your life already, or at least that's how I think it must have been. Shall I tell you how I knew?"

He said, "Please do, my son. I wish you would."

"Two things. The first was the hand. You told Naala and me that the tattoos were curses. I got someone I trust to translate a couple of them, and they were prayers."

He did not speak.

"I guess they looked like curses to you, so that was what you told us they were."

The archbishop said, "What was the other?"

"It was something I picked up from a priest I know. I won't tell you his name, but he had been in a hurry to talk to you."

I paused for a few seconds before going on.

"He knew you climbed this tower every morning, so he got up early and waited for you to come down. He told me about it, and I could see something was bothering him quite a bit. He never said what it was, so it bothered me, too. The first thing I thought of was that he was worried about your health, afraid you had a bad heart or something."

He said, "I do."

"Yeah, I know what you mean. Only if this priest had been worried about a heart attack, he would have said so."

"Papa Zenon."

"Right. So what else could it have been? For a while I thought it was something you told him that he couldn't tell other people. Then I thought about the tattoos that were really prayers, and it hit me. It was the way you had looked when you came down from—"

I stopped talking because he was not paying attention. He was staring at something beside me, so I shut up and looked, too. It was my gun on the coping, stood up straight and pointed right at him. The hand had it.

Maybe I should have grabbed it. I did not. I froze, and I saw him throw his leg over the coping, moving a lot faster than I would have thought a man his age could. The rest of him followed his leg. I tried to grab him. My fingers brushed his sleeve, and he was gone. People in movies scream all the way down. He did not make a sound until he hit.

He just fell. When I looked over, I saw him way down on the pavement below, a little splash of black and a tiny dot of red beside it.

When I had gone down the first three steps I turned around and looked back, thinking I ought to remember how it had been up there, and that I would probably never go there again. The third border guard was standing at the top of the steps like he had known I would do that. He touched his forehead as if he were saluting, and it looked to me like he was smiling under his mustache.

Then he was gone.

The bad feeling I had when I was up there came down the first twenty or thirty steps with me, then I tripped on something I could not see and almost fell. After that I started saying certain things under my breath. I am not going to tell you what they were because they probably would not work for you. A lot of it was from my mother, who passed away when I was six. I still remember her, though. How pretty she was and the songs she used to sing, and some of the stories she used to tell me.

I thought by the time I got down to the ground there would be a big crowd around the archbishop, but there was nobody. I guess it was too early. I did not want to look at him and just walked away.

By the time I got back to Naala's apartment she was up and moving around. I could hear her in there, so I tapped on the door and she let me in. She was not dressed yet, but she was wearing an old robe. She looked at me for a minute and then she said, "This is most bad, I think."

I shrugged and went over to the chair I usually sat in and sat down.

"You are going to tell me."

"Not now," I said. "Later. Only yes, I've got to. Maybe you won't want to report it. Maybe you will. I don't know."

"I must dress." She bustled away.

After a minute or two she called from the bedroom, "We go out and get something. My green dress or the black one? Which is it you think?"

I told her to please wear the green one.

"I agree. Green is better."

We went out, and when we had gone past several cafés, one closed and two or three already open, she said, "We walk and walk until you are ready to stop, Grafton. You must tell me then."

I saw a café on the other side of the street that had tables outside, and pointed. "There. All right?"

She said it was.

Once we had a table she glanced at the menu, we ordered, and I had a good look around. There was nobody close enough to overhear us if I kept my voice down, so I said, "The Undead Dragon? It was the archbishop, Naala. It really was, and he's dead."

She drummed her fingers on the table and looked away, and looked back. Then she looked away again. Finally she said, "Tell me."

"There isn't much to tell," I said. Really there was a lot, but I had decided not to tell all that. "I figured it out last night, and this morning . . ." I did not know how to say it. "He climbed the tower of the cathedral every morning. Remember how he told us that?"

She nodded.

"I decided to go up there and wait for him, and hit him with it when he came up. So I did. He came up, and after he had looked out at the city for a minute I came over and showed him my badge. He hadn't seen me til then. I told him we'd picked up a bunch of prisoners last night, and they were talking."

Her eyebrows went up. "Are they, Grafton?"

"Not as far as I know, but I said they were. Then I told him that if he came along quietly there'd be no rough stuff, but I wanted to pat him down first. When I reached out to take hold of him, he jumped."

"From the top of the tower?"

"Right. That drop would kill anybody."

She stared at me. I think she was seeing if I could look her in the eye. I could and did. Finally she said, "You shoot him and throw his body off the tower."

I shook my head.

"I must see your gun. Take it out and give it to me."

I said, "Sure," and handed it over.

She sniffed the muzzle, then pulled the magazine out. You could see the cartridges through holes in the sides, and it was full. She put it in again and gave the gun back to me. "You throw him off the tower. That will be better for us. There will be no bullet—"

"The hell I did!" I made it as strong as I could. "I swear I never laid a finger on him. Not one single finger! There's a stone railing up there and he went over it before I could grab him."

She was quiet after that until our breakfasts came. Then she said, "Who sees you there?"

"Nobody."

"You are sure of this?"

I said, "Yes. It was about five. Nobody saw me except him."

"We do not speak. Not now and never it may be. I must find a telephone."

"Who are you going to tell?"

She grinned. It had hit her hard, but she was over it. "Nobody. Did not I say this? We tell nobody, but when we have eaten I must find a telephone."

So we did, walking quite a way before we found a police phone on a light pole. She opened it up, pushed buttons, and asked for the man I have been calling Baldy. There was a wait and some hassling back and forth. When she had him she said, "Grafton and I go out for breakfast this morning, sir, and in the café in which we eat there is a rumor concerning the archbishop. You have hear of this?"

. . .

"This rumor say he has taken his own life. Perhaps it is untrue, but I feel you should know of the rumor, sir."

. . .

"That is most well, sir. Grafton and I will go if you wish it."

. . .

"Yes, sir. We will continue, as you say." She hung up, smiling.

I asked what Baldy had said.

"He say he will send operators to see if it is true. Should it be true, they will keep safe the records of the archdiocese. These must be secure. It is what I wish."

"Will they have a look at them?"

"But of course! Here is a most wonderful chance for us to look at everything when there is no one to object. Tomorrow, I think, the oldest bishop comes. He will say this must stop. They will continue. He will complain to the Leader. The Leader will wait a day, two days, three it might be. Then he will order them to stop and they will stop. By this time we know much and perhaps we know everything." Naala started walking. She always walked fast.

Almost trotting to keep up, I asked, "Where are we going?"

"You will see!" I got the mean grin. "You will not like, I think."

I believe she started to tell me then, but maybe not. What is for sure is that I was not paying much attention. Up ahead I had seen somebody. He saw me, too, and when he saw me he ducked into the trees around a building full of shops he was passing.

He got out of sight fast, but not fast enough. I knew I had seen Kleon.

23

THE DEAD DRAGON

I should have guessed where we were going, but I did not. It was one hell of a long way, but we flagged down a black-and-silver and got a ride to a low gray building on the far side of the river in the oldest part of the city.

He had beaten us there and was already stretched out, face up on a slab. All the other dead people were face up, too, and I felt like I was back at the undertaker's, only with bright lights and more bodies. I told Naala that in America we covered them up with sheets and put each of them in its own compartment on a metal slab with rollers. She said, "Here we do not," and she was right. It was really cold in there, but not freezing.

The attendant, I do not know what you call those, was a big ugly guy about fifty who had not shaved that morning. He came over like he wanted to help, and after a minute or so he asked us, "They cannot be buried in holy ground, yes? What will they do?"

"He falls by accident," Naala said. She was still looking at the arch-bishop. I think looking for bulletholes or stab wounds. Anything like that.

The big ugly guy was quiet for a minute. Then he said, "I will remember."

After that we went to Papa Iason's, which was maybe half a mile from there. He was still eating breakfast and invited us to sit down. We told him we had already eaten, but we got coffee anyway.

"For you we have good news," Naala began, "also bad. Which is it you desire to hear first, Papa?"

"The bad, of course."

"As you wish. His Excellency is climb the cathedral tower each morning for exercise. You know of this, I am sure."

Papa Iason nodded.

"This morning he falls, Papa." Naala's tone made what she had not said pretty clear.

Papa Iason crossed himself, bowed his head, and began to pray. It was loud enough for me to catch a few words, but too fast for me to follow what he was saying. Naala and I sat and watched and sipped weak coffee. I wanted to whisper a little prayer for the archbishop, but I could not do it.

Finally Papa Iason looked up and said, "He will be remembered a long, long time."

We nodded.

"I will dedicate my mass tomorrow to him. I have already said my mass for today, you understand."

Naala said, "He was a man of many years. A man older than most men will ever be."

Papa Iason sighed. "He should have had a rail on the steps. It could have been done easily, and many suggested it."

Naala nodded.

I said, "He certainly should have!" I was remembering whatever it had been that had tripped me on those steps in the dark. I got scared every time I thought about it.

"There will be a mass in the cathedral with every priest in the country in attendance." Papa Iason smiled. "We will fill all the seats and stand in the aisles. Every priest and every nun. Monks from the monasteries."

He looked at me. "You come from the West and know nothing of this, I suppose, but our monasteries nearly failed when the communists were in charge. Things are better now, but it is a hard life. A most hard life. Few men will live as they do. I thought long about it, but in the end— well, you see what I chose."

Naala said, "What of my good news, Papa? Would you not wish to hear also?"

Papa Iason smiled and ate a piece of bacon. "Yes, indeed! And I must eat, otherwise Mrs. Vagaros will think I am ill and make me soak my feet in the water that steams. What is your good news?"

"Your father is no longer a fugitive. He assists the JAKA against the Unholy Way."

Papa Iason just stared at her. You do not see the color go out of some-body's face very often, but I saw it then. Finally he said, "You know."

"I am of the JAKA, Papa. I have not concealed this from you."

Papa Iason nodded, really slowly. "Surely he was in great danger."

I said, "He was. Maybe he still is. They took a shot at him last night."

"God grant they missed."

"Yeah. They did. He didn't."

Naala said, "Three he kill. Three of the evil one's worshippers. It was brave work, but we prefer prisoners. We got ten. This, too, was the good work of your father. Of Grafton, also."

I shook my head. "They just about had me."

Naala said, "First you send the policeman to bring me. If you had not, we would have taken none. This I know."

Papa Iason said, "Three he killed. It was my father who did this?"

I said, "Right. He had a shotgun."

"I see." Papa Iason looked troubled.

"He's been staying with a friend in the city. Maybe we could take you to see him, if you want to go. It's up to Naala."

"I ask a favor instead. A great favor. You owe me no favors, I know. I ask it even so. Will you take me to the cathedral?"

So we did. There was no blood at all, just a clean spot on the pavement in front. I pointed it out to Naala after Papa Iason had gone inside. After that she wanted to see the steps to the top of the tower. I was afraid she was going to want to climb up, but she did not. We were leaving the tower when another JAKA operator ran up to us. It took me a minute to place her, but that was only because I am really pretty stupid. It was the gray-haired lady who had tried on so many hats. She told Naala, "I see a car through window. I think it may be you." She was a little breathless.

"You have news?"

"Yes! Yes!" Then she wanted to know if I was me, so I got out my badge case and showed my badge and ID card.

"I am Omphala. You are to go to Central at once, both must go. First you find three people, then go. The man is Russell Rathaus. His wife, also, and the woman with her. You bring them all. At once go!"

I said, "Martya?"

"Yes, I think. She is with the man Rathaus? Her you must bring, too."

When Naala and I were in the car on the way to pick up Russ, I asked her what was up.

She laughed, but it did not sound like she was having fun. "Everything I know. That you think. I know nothing. We must go and find the answer."

Getting Russ was easy. As it turned out, that was the only easy part. He was at Magos X's, and came right away, looking happier than I had ever seen him. "I'm going back to America," he told me. It was in English, and it was the first thing he said after he got into the car.

I said, "That's great!" and shook his hand.

Naala said, "What is it he say, Grafton?"

I told her, then I asked him how he knew. After that I told Naala his host told fortunes, but he had told me he would not tell mine when we first met.

She laughed, and this time it was for real. "You are a bad, bad young man, I think. He does not wish to spoil you. He will tell you of all the women, beautiful women. Famous women. Rich women. You hear all this and you are unbearable."

I said I would settle just for beautiful, like her.

"Now you say this, later it is not so. Then you say rich."

Russ laughed, and so did the cop. I did not think it was all that funny, but I grinned anyway. "Beautiful *and* rich." I should have said already that I was sitting in the middle with Naala on one side and Russ on the other.

He leaned close and whispered in English, "He says the Undead Dragon's dead."

I nodded and said out loud, "Yeah, we know."

Naala wanted to know what we were talking about. She did not say so, but I could see it. I just said, "He's heard the rumor, you know?" and sort of nodded at the cop in the front seat.

When we got to Aliz's building Naala told Russ to wait in the car. She and I went inside and up a flight to knock on Aliz's door. Nobody came.

"They are somewhere gone."

I said maybe they had gone to lunch, and we ought to look in the cafés.

"It is too early. We must look elsewhere."

So instead of looking anywhere, we had the cop drive us to a police phone so Naala could call headquarters. She talked for a minute or two before she hung up and got back in the car. "They are not there. Not the Rathaus woman, not the other woman, not even Aliz."

I said, "What do we do now?"

"The Golden Eagle. It may be they are there. It may also be they go elsewhere, but someone there may know. No one in JAKA building know."

We went quite a ways farther, then I yelled for the cop to stop.

Naala grabbed my arm. "Them you see?"

"I saw Kleon again," I told her, "and this time Kleon didn't see me." The car had stopped, and Russ was getting out so I could.

He was out of sight among the trees and bushes before I got out. I ran and looked and ran and looked, but no Kleon. Finally Naala and Russ caught up to me in the car and I gave it up. Naala was mad, and I do not blame her.

"All right," I said, "I shouldn't have done it. I should've known I could never catch a guy as scared as he is when he had a little lead."

Russ was polite enough not to use English this time. "What did you want him for?"

"First off," I told him, "I wanted to beat the crap out of him. He beat me awhile back and someday I'm going to get even. Second, I wanted to fix it so the cops back in his hometown won't kill him. I was supposed to sleep at his place every night, only I got kidnapped by the Legion of the Light. You know about all that."

Russ nodded.

"So the cops are going to shoot him for it, and that's why he's on the run. Only I think maybe I can fix it, and I'm going to try."

"If you can't, he gets shot," Russ told me.

Naala called me five kinds of fool, which is one of the worst things you can say in her language, especially if you make the gestures. Which she did. Maybe it should have bothered me, but I was thinking about what Russ had said, and it did not.

So we went to the Golden Eagle and Aliz was not there. Neither were Rosalee or Martya. I told Naala I needed to talk to her in private. To tell you the truth, I expected her to tell me to go to hell, but she did not. She just stared.

Then she nodded and we went over to a booth in the bar and sat down. "I know where they are," I said. "If you want I'll go there alone. I'll collect them and bring them to the JAKA building for you, or we can all go there. Your choice."

"Where is it you think?"

"Papa Iason's. You want me to explain?"

Naala shook her head. "If they are there, then you explain. Not now. We will go."

We did, and they were there waiting for him. Naala sent the cop to find us another car, and gave me a look that made me feel ten feet tall. Then she touched her finger to her lips.

"Now you tell," Naala whispered. "Most quiet you tell me how you knew."

"Well, seeing Kleon like that made me think of Martya. Martya's his wife."

"This I knew."

"And I remembered that somebody had sent operators to a bunch of dress shops to look for Rosalee that time. It seems like sometimes they like to help out with other people's cases now and then. Lend a hand."

Naala nodded. "This is so."

"Women like to talk, and I don't remember Russ ever saying that he had sworn Martya to secrecy when he sent her to give the hand to Papa Iason. She never said anything about that either, not that I heard."

Naala snapped her fingers. "The hand! It is in your pocket?"

"Sure." I took it out and held it up. "Only Aliz doesn't know that, and Martya didn't know it, either. They probably patched her up at the hospital, gave her a tetanus shot, and sent her back to Aliz. There would have been a lot of talk about witchcraft and black magic. She would have told Aliz about the hand, and Aliz would go to Papa's looking for it. When we told Papa about the archbishop, his housekeeper was back in the kitchen. You remember how it was? She brought us coffee. Then she went back there, probably to have some breakfast herself. He went off with us and we took him to the cathedral, but his housekeeper didn't know where he had gone."

"Here Aliz waits for his return." Naala looked like she wanted to laugh. "We have made the most large arrest. She will make the great discovery, perhaps. She does not know she is most far behind us."

"Right, and she has to keep Martya and Rosalee with her until somebody else takes them."

So there were six of us going to headquarters: Naala and me, Russ and Rosalee, Aliz, and Martya. The driver of our car had found another police car for us, but Russ wanted to ride with Rosalee, so that was a complication. We tried to keep the seat beside the driver open when we could. Naala said there was a regulation about that. This time it meant Martya sandwiched between Naala and me. Naala had wanted me to sit there, but I would not do it. Martya was smaller than I am, curves or no curves.

I won and I was not sorry, but Martya started in on Kleon. No, she did not like him, but it was not right to kill him. Besides, he wanted her to help him but she would not even if he was her husband because she had not wanted to marry him anyway. And they were going to shoot him if they found him and they would shoot her, too, if they knew she had brought him that ham when he had been hiding in the empty building but had only brought it because he made her. He would have beaten her and he needed to find work here in the capital and she had found one he could do because he could weld, but . . .

And so on and so forth all the way to headquarters. When we got out there Naala told her to shut up, she would fix things for Kleon if I could ever catch him. And of course that started Martya off again, only trying to be really careful so Russ, Rosalee, and Aliz would not hear anything, particularly Aliz.

I guess it gave us something to do. We must have waited about two hours, and I kept thinking that I had a lot of money now, and why was it I did not have a watch? The answer, of course, was that I had busted the one Naala had bought for me and had not had time to shop for another one. I wanted a good one, not flashy, that would stand up to a lot of knocking around. And I knew that even in the capital that was going to take some real looking.

Baldy came in person to fetch us, saying nothing, just motioning for us to follow him. We went through a corridor and down a flight of stairs, then along another corridor, and came out into trees and shrubs that looked like they were not getting a whole lot of care. I suppose that was the back of the building, although nobody said so. A stretch limo that would have reached from the pitcher's mound to home plate was parked and waiting for us. It had a bunch of doors, and they were all open.

All of us got in including Baldy, who sat up front with the driver regulation or no regulation. I was on one of the side benches, facing Rosalee on the other side. Russ was on one side of her, naturally, and Aliz on the

other. Martya was on my left and Naala on my right. Martya and Aliz
had the backseat, so they faced forward. None of this stuff is important, it
is just that I remember the ride so well.

Our driver took it slow and seemed to be trying to avoid the main
streets. I asked Naala about that, but she just shook her head. I decided
the limo was bugged, and the JAKA knew it. Very likely JAKA had put
in the bugs.

Pretty soon we were out of the city and on a road that could not have
been much smoother if it had been a black silk ribbon. After a while I
caught onto the fact that it was always climbing. Not steeply, but we kept
getting a little bit higher. We were taking it slow, considering how good
that road was and that there was hardly any traffic on it. By and by Naala
whispered, "Soon we stop for ices?" She was grinning.

I was looking out the windows and seeing mountains off in the distance, big ones with white peaks. Closer to the city there had been farm-
houses at first, with barns and fields and trees. We kept going and there
were more and more trees and fewer houses, barns, and fields.

Then there were none, just trees, big ones, oaks at first, later some kind
of spruce. Trees that always had dark green needles, summer or winter.

After quite a bit of those, sunlight and a log cabin on steroids. I could
not see it well until I got out of the limo, but it was really worth seeing,
four stories in places, with wings sticking out in every direction. I do not
think there was a log in it that was less than four feet thick.

Nobody told me who lived there, but nobody had to. I could guess
pretty easily, and I was right.

There were guards in uniforms I had never seen before, all bottle green
and black, with caps that must have been designed about eighteen ten.
They had bigger pistols than mine. Some had assault rifles, too.

Baldy led the way into one of the wings, and walking through the doorway cut through those big logs was almost like walking through a tunnel.
The room we went into was a sort of lounge, wide and roomy and bright.
The brightness came from three skylights in the roof and from the floor
lamps and table lamps that were scattered all over. Every one of them was
turned on. Also from the furniture and rugs, pretty much all earth tones,
yellow and brown and red. There were wolf pelts scattered around, and the
skin of a white bear in front of the fireplace.

Baldy told everybody to sit down and relax, so we did. We also used the restrooms. Eventually, I think everybody there used them. There was some talk (I remember that Aliz and Naala talked about soccer) but not a lot. Russ and Rosalee whispered and necked like newlyweds. I tried not to look at them and pretended not to know that Martya was trying to get me to sit next to her on one of the couches. Also I got up and wandered around quite a bit. Peeking through doorways and looking out windows at the forest.

Two maids came in pushing carts, one with food and one with glasses and bottles. I ate (it was far and away the best food I ever got in that country), and drank club soda over ice. Baldy had vodka and tonic, I noticed, and everybody else drank wine. Russ's eyes opened wide when he tasted the wine, and after that he just took tiny little sips, rolling them around in his mouth.

I am not sure what I should call the person who came in about an hour after we had finished eating. They call him "the Leader." Mostly I have been calling him the third border guard. You could not pronounce his name at all. I could pronounce it, but it would not be exactly right. He looks like my father. That was the first thing I noticed about him when I saw him on the train, and it is the thing that still sticks with me. He is about the same height, which is maybe four inches shorter than I am. His features are about like my dad's, especially the eyes and the nose. Also the black mustache. He looks older than his pictures on the posters, and his hair is getting gray and thin.

He was wearing a blue suit, pretty dark, that most people would not realize had cost at least a thousand bucks. White shirt open at the collar. No tie. He came striding in with a couple of generals in uniform trailing him. When he saw me his face lit up. "My young friend!" He has a great smile. "How wonderful that I should see you here!"

First thing I knew, I was getting hugged. I hugged him back, and I have always been glad I did. Okay, I have hugged a dictator. How could I not have hugged him back, when he looked so much like my dad?

"Something I have that you will most like," he told me, "a little gift, also."

Then he was shaking hands with Baldy, still smiling only not so wide. He said something I could not hear and Baldy said something back, then turned around and started introductions. Naala was first, and you could see she was proud enough to bust, standing very, very straight and looking very, very serious. The Leader shook her hand and put his arm around her for a moment. Then he turned to one of the generals who was carrying a flat black-leather box. The general opened his box, and the Leader got out a medal. It was on a long ribbon. (They all were.) After he had put it on her neck he said something to her and she said something to him and stepped back.

Aliz was next. She shook hands with the Leader, too, and they talked a little, but she did not get a medal. Russ was after Aliz, and he got one. It was not the same as Naala's, but it was silver like hers.

Then Rosalee, and she was crying. The Leader put his arm around her and stood there telling her everything was all right and she should calm down, there was nothing to cry about. Still crying, she told him she had to cry. She was so happy she could not help it. I thought sure he was going to turn her over to Aliz, but he did not. He stood there with her and motioned for Russ to come over. The two of them stayed with her, sort of petting her and talking to her until she finally stopped. I could not believe what I was seeing, but that was how it was.

Martya was next. She went down on her knees to beg for a pardon for Kleon, which surprised the hell out of me. The Leader called Baldy over and they talked, the Leader wanting to know what was going on and Baldy telling him he did not know. I would have gone over, too, if I had not known they would get to me in a minute or two, which they did. I explained to the Leader and told them Naala had already promised to fix it. He smiled and told her she had his authority to do it.

Then it was Baldy's turn. He got a medal, too. He saluted the Leader, and the Leader returned his salute. Later I found out that was a big deal.

I thought I was finished, and the gift was something somebody would deliver later. That turned out to be wrong. (And I had them turned around anyway.) I was called up, the general opened his box, and the Leader got out a gold medal. Somebody behind me gasped, but I do not know who that was. When the Leader hung it on me I stepped back and saluted the way Baldy had.

The Leader returned my salute and raised his voice enough for everybody to hear. "You do not understand why he should receive this." That was what he said, only I knew that Naala knew. Then he said, "It is a confidential matter."

I had sense enough to nod, but then I started to go back to where I had been standing before he had motioned for me to come forward again.

"This is yours." The Leader (maybe I ought to call him the third border guard here) reached into his suit coat and pulled out a dark blue booklet. He handed it to me, and for a minute or two I could not believe it. Generally I do not stammer much, but I stammered then.

It was my passport.

24

BACK TO PURAUSTAYS

Russ and Rosalee came around in a couple of days to ask what flight I was on. When I told them I had not booked, they wanted me to go to Germany with them. Russ had gotten his car back, a big blue Mercedes. I had to explain in all the different ways I could come up with that there were things I had to take care of before I could leave. Then Russ wanted me to tell him, and when I would not, Rosalee said I had a girl on the string. As it turned out, that was a little truer than I thought at the time.

After I found a watch that satisfied me and paid for it, I did not have a whole lot of money left. I went down to the docks and looked around, and when I found a guy who had a neat little boat I was able to talk him into taking me to Puraustays at the far end of the lake. We went to the market then and he bought enough food for four days and four bottles of wine. I helped him carry it back to his boat and felt guilty as all hell, because he had spent just about all the money I had given him on food for the two of us. Only I knew I was going to need what I had. Need that much and more, most likely.

Our sail on the lake was a lot nicer than the one I took as a prisoner of the Legion of the Light. I was not tied up, I had a bunk to sleep in, and the food was better. The big thing, though, was that this was pretty much your average summer sailing. The weather was warm and friendly. That first time we had gotten hit by a couple of storms. Wind gusts of sixty or seventy miles an hour are no joke when you are out on the water.

We got to Puraustays in good shape and I paid the guy who had brought me what I had promised, with a little extra for not bitching about how much I ate and just being nice in general. He usually took out fisher-men, so much for a morning, so much for an afternoon. His boat only slept two, but he said he had as many as six onboard sometimes.

I went to the Willows first, figuring I knew the place well enough to get in without a key, which was right. I stashed my sports jacket there, with the hand still in the pocket. I stashed my gun there, too, and my badge, not just leaving them but hiding them.

Then I walked to Kleon's.

When I knocked on the door I remembered how the boss border guard had knocked with the barrel of his pistol. That's when I decided for sure that I would not write the travel book yet. That I would write this book you are holding instead, and get started just as soon as I got back to the States.

Martya opened the door. I was not sure she would be back, even though I had waited a few days so she would have a head start. But there she was, and she opened the door wide so I could come in. She motioned to me, and we went back into the kitchen. "You are hungry. I will make you something."

I said, "Sure," and sat down. "How did you know I was hungry?"

"Always you are hungry. Something else, too." She made a gesture I know my editor will not let me describe. "We cannot. It is late and Kleon will be home soon."

That gave me the opening I had wanted. I said, "I wouldn't do it anyway, Martya. You're Kleon's wife."

"You no longer think me beautiful!" She looked ready to spit. "I feed you, yes! But poison!" She got out a couple of big sausages, threw them into a dirty pan, and put them on the stove.

I did not say anything.

"This you see?" It was a big black thing shaped like a mug that I knew darned well was her pepper shaker. "It is poison!" She shook pepper over our sausages.

I said, "You're beautiful and I could go for you in a big way. But it would be wrong and I knew it would be wrong when you got down on your knees and begged the Leader to save Kleon. What we did before—"

"You would not sit with me! You humiliate me before all the rest! I pat the seat beside me, over and over I pat, but you will not sit!"

"With Naala right there watching? She'd have cut my throat." I decided not to say anything about Martya's begging Naala to help Kleon in the car going up.

"You are strong." She came over and felt the muscle in my arm.

"Not as strong as Kleon."

"Stronger!" She sat on my lap. "Is harmless, you see? He come home soon. When I hear door open I jump up." She gave me a big kiss and went off to apply more lipstick.

Cut to the chase. Kleon came home and you can imagine how he felt about me being there. I told him I did not want a fight, which was probably a mistake. I tried to explain why I had come back, and he swung at me.

He did not even try to hide it, just took a short step toward me and swung a roundhouse right. I ducked a little and rolled a little, and moved in.

I will not even try to give you the whole thing. I do not remember it well enough for that, just to start with. My guess is it lasted less than two minutes, although I do not really know. He landed a couple of punches while I worked over his belly and chest. Pretty soon he went down and I stepped back to give him a chance to stand up. He did and he wanted more, which I had not really expected. That was one tough little man.

I put him down again with one to the side of the neck, and he stayed down while I explained that I was not going to touch Martya and it was over between us. He was still down when I left, only Martya was trying to help him up.

Volitain would have been next if I had the hand, but I had to go back to the Willows and get it. My face was a little beat up and my lip was bleeding. Sure, everybody I passed stared at me, but before I get into that I ought to say that nobody who is not wearing gloves should head-punch the way Kleon had. If you cannot land a solid one, it does not do much good. And if you can, you will bust up the bones in your hands. Kids do that and get away with it because they are not strong enough to do any real damage to themselves. Grown men learn pretty soon to punch the soft parts.

Anyhow I was getting stared at, so when I got to the Willows, I decided to wait until sundown before I went to Volitain's. There would be a better chance of catching him at home then, or that's what I thought, and I was not going to have to worry so much about a cop seeing me. It was getting to be late afternoon by then, so that is what I did. Just to pass the time I got the hand out and to make sure I still had it and it was all right, and when I saw it was fine I tried to explain to the young witch I had seen one time what I had planned.

Nothing doing, as far as I could tell. She did not appear, and the hand did not move at all. The rest of the time I sat around telling myself that I had been crazy to come back to Puraustays and by this time I ought to be in New York writing this.

Only sometimes I told myself I really should have gone to Germany with Russ and Rosalee. But it was bullshit, all of it. This was something I had to try.

The shadows got long and I heard a wolf howl, or maybe it was a dog, and off I went. I remembered Volitain's house pretty well and his cherry trees really well, so I found his place without much trouble. I rang his bell and pounded his front door with the knocker, only nobody came. After that I went around the house looking for an unlocked door or an open window. Nothing. So I was just starting to sit down on his stoop when I heard somebody on the path. I stood up and it was him, only he knew me about half a second before I knew him.

We shook hands and he asked if I had been back to America. I said no, just in the capital and out on the lake. I was going to tell him my face was beat up, but I figured he had seen that already. We went into the house, and I told him I did not have a lot of money but I would pay him what I could afford if he would doctor my face a little.

He said he would, and the price would depend on how bad I was hurt. When he had gotten me under a light and looked me over, he said there was nothing there that would not heal of itself in a few days so there would be no charge. I got some ointment and a couple of bandages. My idea was to wait until he was through to talk about the Willows, but he asked about it while he was putting on the second bandage.

"You say you have but little money. Thus you did not find the treasure after all."

I said, "No, but I'm going to try again tonight, if you'll help me."

"Ahhhh!"

"You didn't know what happened to me?"

"To the contrary," he said, "I did know. You were taken away by the Legion of the Light."

"You're right, I was. How did you know?"

"I listen to my radio now and then."

"Sure. You heard me and recognized my voice, and that was all there was to it. Got it."

He laughed. "Not quite as you say."

"Want to tell me the rest?"

"No. I wish that you tell me how you propose to find our treasure."

I said, "Do you laugh at magic?"

"When to laugh is appropriate, yes."

I took out the hand. "Would you laugh at this?"

He shook his head.

"Good. Can you read Greek?"

"So many questions. Why do you wish to know what you ask me?"

I bent the fingers straight and pointed to the palm. "This blur is a spell for finding treasure. If you'll translate it for me, I mean to use it tonight."

He bent over to look, then pulled out a drawer I remembered and got out his big magnifying glass. After moving the hand into a better light, and lighting up the spell with a little flashlight, he said, "Yes. There is Greek, and Latin, too. There must be candles for the ends of the fingers. Did you know that?"

I shook my head.

"Five small candles. I will provide them. Also I will go with you. The spell must be pronounced correctly and by one having authority. That is always true. I am such a one, so I shall recite it. Afterward we search for the treasure together." He gave me back the hand.

I said, "You're afraid I'll cheat you. I wouldn't do that."

"I know you would not. More also. I know you will not find it by this method without me."

"I'll be glad to have your help."

He stared at me. Volitain had a stare that went right through you. You not only felt like he was trying to read your mind, you felt like he was doing it and it was pretty easy. With Magos X, you felt like he already knew.

Finally Volitain said, "This means you must give me my share. I will be there when the treasure is found. Do you realize this?"

"Sure," I said. "You get a third and Martya gets a third. That was the deal."

"Shall we have Martya with us?"

I had not thought of that and I said so, adding that it seemed like a good idea if we could get her.

"Her husband has beaten you. Will not he beat you again if we attempt this?"

I shook my head. "He didn't beat me, I beat him. I'll fight him again if he wants to fight, only he won't."

Volitain said, "Then let us try." He went out for a minute and came back with a dark lantern, and off we went.

While we were walking back to Kleon's, I got to thinking about the wolves and how they killed people at night.

Also the man in black. I do not like being scared and generally am not, but I wished I had not left my gun behind in the Willows.

Martya answered the door, saying Kleon was asleep. "He have drink much. He know you have won me."

I shook my head. "I beat him, that's all. You belong to him, not to me."

She kind of studied me before she said, "In time your thoughts will change. Tell me when this happens."

I wanted to say I would write her a letter, but I did not.

Volitain told her, "We go to find the treasure of Eion Demarates. You need not come with us if you are afraid. We will divide it honestly and present your share to you."

"You know where this is?"

I said, "No, but we think we know how to find it."

"I come. Wait here. I must get his key from Kleon's pocket."

It should not have been cold, and I guess really it was not. But the wind was off the lake, and the sun had been down for quite a while. I was glad I had on my wool sports jacket, and maybe I should have let Martya have it. But the hand was in the pocket, and I could see all kinds of trouble if she found it. She wanted to link arms. I did not. If she was cold she never showed it.

I could see she was listening for something as soon as we got into the Willows, so after a minute or two I asked her, "Hear anything?"

She shook her head. "No . . ." She swallowed. "No footsteps upstairs."

"Sure. He's right here with us."

She blinked. Her mouth opened and closed, but she did not say anything.

Volitain said, "You heard me, eh?"

I nodded. "We both did. Okay, it could have been a spook, but I didn't think so and if it was just some guy, which was what it sounded like, it had to be you. Nobody else knew that Martya and I had come here to look for the treasure. You slammed a door once, too."

"Did I? Yes, I suppose I did. I was disgusted, not with you but with myself. I had been spying on my friends, a thing I would have supposed beneath me."

Martya said, "It is not haunted, this house? That is what we must believe?"

I got out the hand. "It probably is. If it wasn't before we got here it is now, come to think of it."

Volitain nodded and chuckled.

"You wish to terrify me! Volitain, too! You make a pact before you come!"

"Not us." I pointed. "That looks like a table under the dust cloth. How about if you pull it off?"

"Serve yourself!" Martya wanted to spit.

I put the hand back in my pocket and pulled off the cloth. Under it was a little egg-shaped table, just right for one man eating alone. I laid the hand on it, on its back, and watched the fingers straighten themselves out. They moved slowly but they moved, all five at the same time.

Volitain got out his candles and a box of matches, sticking a candle on each fingertip with hot wax. The candles were about twice as big as the ones you might put on a birthday cake, but there was nothing fancy about them. They were black or maybe dark brown.

I wanted to know if they were corpse fat.

"The fat of a human corpse? No. If an animal's corpse will do, yes." He was bending over the hand with his magnifying glass, reading the fading tattoo by the candlelight. Pretty soon he started reading the Greek spell, or prayer or whatever it was, doing it loud and slow.

Before he started, I had been hearing all sorts of little noises, none of them loud and none noises I paid a lot of attention to, the moan of the night wind in the chimneys, crickets, and small quiet things that were most likely mice. Another noise that may have been the lapping of the lake water. The lake is not very far from where we were. When it started everything got very quiet, not so much like the wind had stopped blowing or the crickets had stopped chirping, but like I had become deaf to all that.

It only lasted a few seconds. Then it started to get noisy. Things were waking up all around, or maybe coming to life. They were stirring, pushing off whatever it was that had been covering them. They were making all sorts of other noises, too. Moaning and grunting. Maybe some were talking to others, or just talking to themselves. Claws were scratching at the broken floors, going up the walls and across the ceilings.

Then something was looking over my shoulder, and I knew it would be a really, really bad idea for me to turn around to see what it was. Martya had grabbed me and was sticking to me like paint.

The hand turned and pointed.

25

HOMEWARD BOUND!

I was scared, but for some reason I had thought Volitain would not be. I was wrong. His face was as white as the dirty sheets that covered the furniture when he got out something I thought at first was a pocket watch and opened it up. Later I found out it was a fancy compass. His hands shook when he took the compass bearing, but he took it just the same. He wrote it down, too, scribbling in a little black notebook before he shut his compass and put it back in his pocket.

Then he blew out the candles.

The other noises stopped and the moan of the wind came back. The crickets started chirping again. Probably the mice came back, too, but I was not paying much attention.

"Over there," I said. I pointed.

"Indeed." Volitain had started off.

Martya said, "That wall. We must tear it down. Are your tools here still?"

I said I did not think so.

Volitain waved to us. "We must go into the next room and take a second bearing."

Martya caught up with him, insisting that the treasure was in the wall.

"Which it would take us all night to tear down even if we had brought tools."

This time I put the hand on top of an instrument of some kind. I suppose it was a harpsichord, but I do not know a lot about the old stuff. I will not tell you again about putting on the candles or reading the spell, because it was pretty much the same as last time except that all those things we woke up the first time were already awake.

Only what happened next was different. There were lights, faint lights, mostly white, some blue. Some stood still, some circled around us. I had the feeling that if one were to touch me I would die, and that I would want to die, too. I know that does not make a lot of sense, but it is how I felt. Martya started screaming, and that made everything worse. The room rocked. We talk about that at clubs sometimes because it feels like that, but here there was nobody dancing, and no music until the instrument we had put the hand on began to play.

That was when Volitain blew out the candles.

I said, "I wanted to hear it." I was bullshitting because I wanted him to think I was tough, and I think he knew it. He did not say anything.

Martya stopped yelling and whispered, "The hand pointed the wrong way." I was surprised she had even noticed.

Volitain shut his notebook. "It pointed the right way, although it was in almost precisely the same bearing as previously. It may be that the treasure of Demarates is buried outside. Had you thought of that?"

He did not wait for her answer, and neither did I. I followed him into the next room. It was one I recognized, the big downstairs bedroom with the painted ceiling. I had lain on my back taking pictures of that ceiling for quite a time, getting up to tinker with my lights and so forth. There was some furniture in that room, the bed and some other stuff, but we crossed the room and laid the hand on the floor, not far from the wall. Then I got a really big surprise. Volitain said, "You must place the candles this time," and he was talking to me.

It was like getting slugged. I wanted to ask why, but I was afraid I knew. Or at least I had good guesses. The first one was that he had been scared—hell, I had been scared, and I had not done it—and did not think he could do it a third time.

The second was that he knew it was dangerous and felt like he should not have to take all the risk.

What I said was, "I'll try, but you have to tell me if I'm not doing it right."

He nodded. "I shall." That is one word where they live: "*doekei*."

I got another surprise a minute later. He helped. He squatted down behind the hand and lit the candles one by one and passed them to me. I thought he would have to read the spell, but I suppose he had memorized it by then. He whispered each line to me, and I repeated it loud and firm without knowing what the words meant.

To me, that was the worst one because it was the only one that made me feel like something was happening to me, not just to the room or the house. I cannot describe it any better than by saying I felt like I was turning into my own shadow. I was getting thinner and darker somehow, and I felt light enough to float away.

Other stuff was happening, too.

The one that got my attention first was that the white witch was there. Her hand was on the floor where I had put it, with the candles I had put there burning at the tips of her fingers. But it was back on her arm, with her kneeling down to keep her hand where it was, pointing slantwise into the wall. I backed away. I did not think about it, I just did it. I smelled woodsmoke from the fireplace and the sour reek of the candles on the fingers of the hand.

Another thing was that more furniture was coming back. A table and some chairs and two more chests of drawers. A wardrobe as big as the cabin on our boat had been, and a lot taller. There was a carpet under my feet, and the dustcover had been pulled off the bed. I think the man sitting up in it was screaming, but I could not hear him. He had a beard and a mustache, and I want to say that only his eyes showed how scared he was but that would not be strictly true. Something inside me kept saying, "Blow out the candles!"

Martya was on her knees blowing them out before I understood that she and Volitain were inside me somehow, and it was Volitain who had told me to blow them out.

Here is what I think. I think that he and Martya were really there, but I could not see them. The only Volitain and Martya I could see (the Volitain and Martya I thought I saw) were my idea of Volitain and Martya. Does that make any sense? Either that, or I was spread out all over the room somehow.

I wanted to sit down but the chairs I had seen were gone, and I did not want to sit on that bed. So I stood.

Martya said, "It's in the wall!"

Volitain shook his head. "The chimney, I think."

He turned to me. "The hand is yours. Do you still desire it?"

I said, "Sure," keeping my voice as steady as I could.

"Then take it. Cast the candles into the fireplace, please. That I think will be the best."

Martya said, "I will not touch it. You cannot make me." She was trying to sound brave.

"I am not trying to make you touch it. But you are to share equally when we find the treasure of Demarates. Even now you wish that?"

"Yes!"

"Grafton brought the hand. It is his. He has placed the candles also, and recited the spell. That is much. I say it, and you need not agree with me. I do not care. I have placed the candles twice and extinguished them twice. I have lit them three times and recited the spell twice. It was I, too, who recorded the information we gleaned. That is much also. You have blown the candles out once. Nothing more than that. Now we have another task for you if you are to share with us."

He waited, and after a second or two she said, "What do you want me to do?"

"Get into the fireplace." Volitain pointed. "The chimney will be large enough for you when you stand. I will lend you—"

"I'll get filthy!"

"Yes. You will. Rich, also, if you share in the treasure. Not otherwise."

For a minute or two, I could watch the wheels in her head spinning. Then she went to the fireplace, dropped to her knees, and crawled in. Soot fell when she stood up.

Volitain went to her. "Do you want my lantern?"

Her answer was muffled by the chimney. A little more soot fell. Then she crouched again and laid a small black box on the hearth. "This is most heavy. Almost I dropped it."

Volitain was already bending over it. He did not speak.

Martya crawled out and stood up. She was smeared with soot, but did not look as bad that way as I had expected. "You loved me once."

She was talking to me, and it was not a question.

"Yeah. I guess I still do, but you belong to Kleon. Like I said."

"I have asked few favors. One more, then no more ever. You must see that I get my share."

I had been planning to already.

The box was iron and looked tough, but the key was in the lock. Volitain tried to turn it but got nowhere. "It is rusted," he said. "If I twist harder it may break."

That was when I remembered the oil can Martya and I had bought more than a year ago. It seemed to me that it might still be here. I had gotten it so I could oil the lock of the front door. I had done that and gotten it working smoothly. . . .

It seemed to me that I had not taken it back and left it with the other tools. I said, "Wait here," and went looking.

There were two fireplaces in the front hall, the reception room or whatever you call it. My oil can was waiting on the mantel of one of them, pushed away from the edge where it was not easy to see.

I got it and carried it back, feeling like a hero.

Even with a lot of oil it must have taken us fifteen or twenty minutes to get that strongbox open. I still remember how the gold glowed in the light from Volitain's lantern, and how Martya got down on her knees beside the box (Volitain was already in front of it) and picked up coins and let them trickle through her fingers. I wished then I had brought my cameras. That was before I found out Kleon had sold them.

Here I am going to cut to the chase. Volitain divided the gold into piles, getting them as even as he could. He said I would choose first, then Martya. He would take the pile that was left. That sounded good, but I traded turns with Martya, letting her go first and taking second choice.

Maybe that was a bad idea, because it took her a long time to make up her mind, and Volitain would not let her touch any of the piles before she picked one. Finally she asked me to pick one for her, so I did and she took it.

I took one that was left, and Volitain took the third one and put his coins back in the iron box. I had been thinking about taking that too, because I was planning to bury the hand if I could get Papa Zenon to pray over it. Only Volitain wanted the box, so I let him have it. Later, after I had sold two of my coins, I bought a regular brass jewelry box for the hand. It had a red silk lining and everything. Martya and I closed it and wrapped it in a couple of plastic bags we sealed with red wax and the cross to keep the water out. I will not tell you where we buried it, but Papa Zenon and Papa Iason prayed over it.

That is almost it.

I sold five more coins, very carefully. They went for enough for a plane ticket with a lot left over. I hid four more in my luggage.

And I buried the rest. If you are smart, you can probably figure out where. Only I am not about to tell you. I counted those coins before I buried them, and I studied every one of them. Gold coins are heavier than regular American nickels and quarters, and there is a serious feel to them that regular coins do not have.

Here is almost the last thing. Martya came up to me at the airport. She had new clothes and quite a bit of jewelry. I knew how she had gotten that stuff, but we did not talk about it. The thing was that she wanted to go to America. Her idea was that we would get married first. Then the U.S. embassy would issue her a passport (and maybe Naala would kill her before we got out of the country). We could fly to America and get divorced there.

Or stay married if I wanted to. Martya was easy with that, she said. We would do just like I wanted.

I told her to go back to Kleon before she got into trouble.

Right here I need to explain that I have not quit the JAKA. I left my gun with Naala because I could not take it on the plane, but I talked to Baldy about my going back to America and everything is cool. No, I am not a spy. I am just an American employee of a foreign government, which is not at all against the law. I get paid through the embassy in Washington and run errands every once in a while. The JAKA is as worried about terrorism as the FBI is, and there is a good deal of cooperation on that.

Maybe I should tell you here that I have taken a short course at FBI headquarters, too. Like I said, cooperation.

That is just about it. Except that I switched seats on the plane. You are not supposed to, but I did. I was giving up an aisle seat for a middle seat anyway.

Thing was, the girl with the red pen was on the plane, just sitting there with her red pen and writing away on her tray table. I sat down next to her.

She looked up. "Oh! Oooh! It's you!"

I said, "I know how you feel. It's exactly the same way I felt when I saw you. Is it all right if I ask why you're going to Germany?"

Pretty soon I got the feeling it was very all right since it meant we would not have to talk about her being her and me being me. I will let my lady boil it down for you. She answers me in English.

"I have win a poetry competition, Grafton. Nationwide, and I win! For the prize I go to Harvard Amerika where I may stay all year and study poetry. Do I speak English good? My teacher says good but not perfect."

"Your teacher's right. You speak it much better than a whole lot of people from other countries do, but it could be better yet. At Harvard they'll have you reading a lot of English and American poetry. You'll need really good English to appreciate everything."

"Not many there speak as we do in my country." My lady was looking thoughtful. "Very few, I am sure."

I nod.

"You—you speak as my country."

"Not perfectly," I say. "It could be a lot better."

"You will perhaps stay with me?" We were holding hands by then.

"I'd like that very, very much. We ought to stick together."

So I have sublet my old apartment in New York again, and we have leased this one in Massachusetts. She goes to class most of the day, and I mostly stay right here in our apartment and write this book. At night we go to clubs and do other things. You can probably guess.

Now this is finished except for polishing up, which should be a snap. My lady does not have to go back home right away when her year is over. There is no law that says that. It is just that her prize money stops coming. We have been thinking about South America, maybe Argentina or Chile. I could do another travel book, taking another year or so, and after that I would take her home to see her family. There is her mother and father, a brother, and two sisters. Plus some uncles and aunts. We could tour her country, dropping in on the relatives while I collect facts and pix for the travel book I planned originally.

(When I explained to my editor that this would be a travel book written by an American member of their secret police and showed her my badge and ID, she just about went nuts.)

After that my lady likes Italy or Greece, and I like the Greek islands plus maybe Sicily and Corsica. I do not know nearly as much about women as I would like to, but I have not sprung that one on her yet. I am going to wait for the right moment.

APPENDIX

This is a lecture and you do not have to read it. I just want to say something about dictators and dictatorships.

Dictators get in when democracy sucks. The elected governments do a bad job, one after another. Or they are so crooked the elections no longer matter and nobody cares. Are dictators bad? Sure. But some are worse than others. Hitler, Stalin, and Pol Pot were about as bad as they come, but there have been a whole bunch of others. They were bad, too, but look at the governments they replaced and the governments that replaced them.

If you do not want a dictatorship here, vote. But be careful who you vote for, and be careful about who gets on that ballot. Democracy means rule by the people, and if the people will not do the job—well, somebody is going to step in and do it for them.

Spreading democracy is a really good idea and I am all for it. Just keep in mind that ruling is work. It means staying informed and making the tough choices. And if the people do not want to do the work of ruling, democracy will not work. It is a lot easier to shoot a dictator than it is to replace one with something better.